About the Author

Christian Winship was born on the 12th of August 1986 in Aylesbury, UK. He grew up in a small village called Long Marston. He had an instant love for all things space and comedy, having grown up watching *Blackadder*, *Red Dwarf*, *Father Ted* and *Monty Python* religiously. He has a background in graphic design and art but found writing to be his strong point. Chris worked for a construction company for many years, which allowed him to progress with writing. *The Discount Multiverse* is his second publication, and he hopes to expand this into an ongoing series. All artwork he does alongside writing *The Discount Multiverse* can be found on Instagram #thediscountmultiverse.

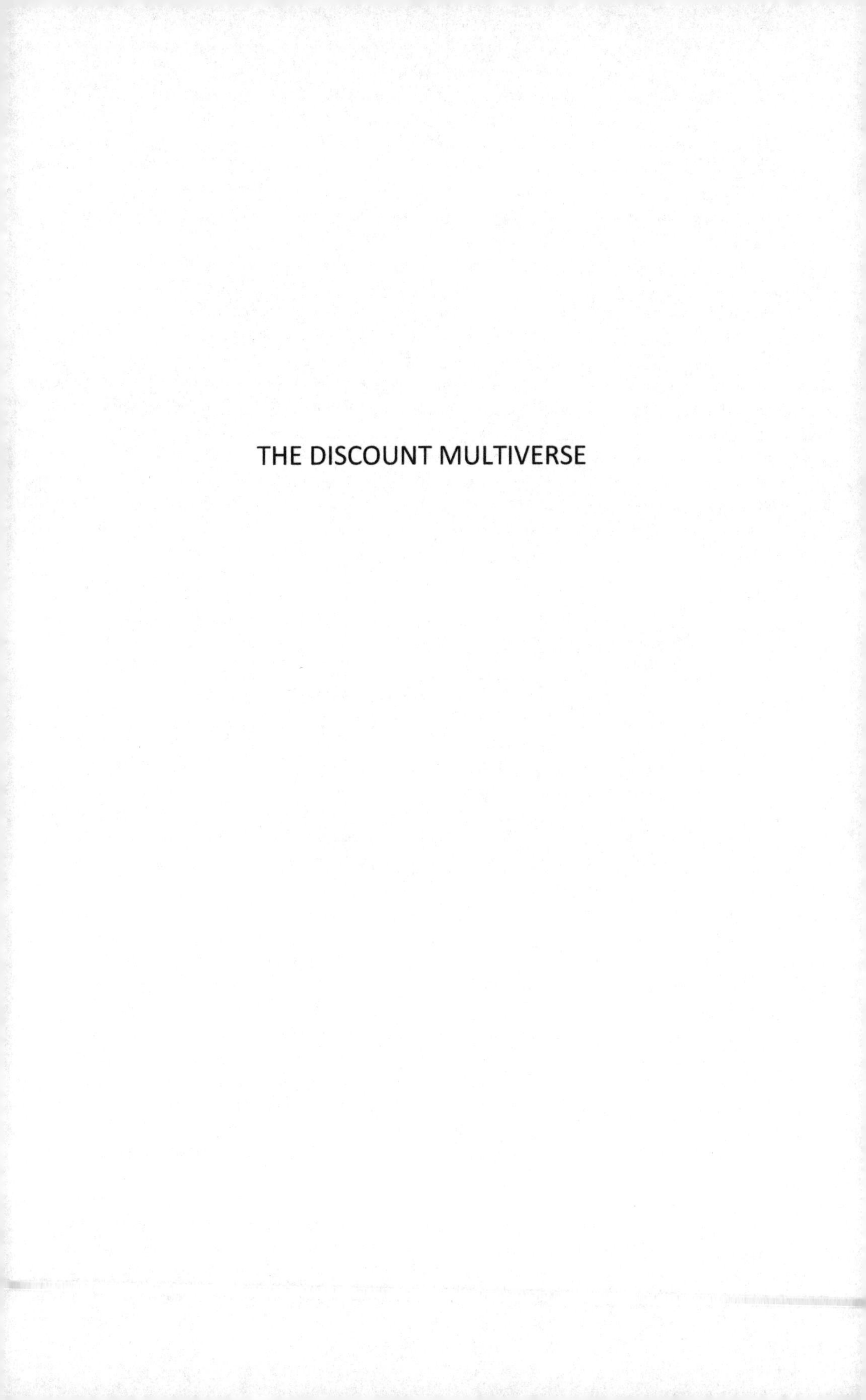

THE DISCOUNT MULTIVERSE

CHRISTIAN WINSHIP

THE DISCOUNT MULTIVERSE

Vanguard Press

VANGUARD PAPERBACK

A CIP catalogue record for this title is available from the British Library.

ISBN 978-1-80016-425-3

Vanguard Press is an imprint of
Pegasus Elliot Mackenzie Publishers Ltd.
www.pegasuspublishers.com

First Published in 2022

Vanguard Press
Sheraton House Castle Park
Cambridge England
Printed & Bound in Great Britain

Dedication

For Lana and Ralph. Never forget to remain happy and optimistic. Life is complex. It is an ever-expanding experience full of infinite moments that we exist within…
When life comes knocking, grab your coat.

Acknowledgements

I would like to thank all the team at Pegasus House for their support and help with bringing the book to life. Also, to my wife, Monika, for her support and solid confidence in me. And a massive thank you to William Craig who helped in editing and crafting the book in its first moments.

Prologue

Before there was the complexity of the countless universes; before life had rooted and set foot within the chaotic twist of the multiverse and prior to any known star system, galaxy cluster or spatial vibration, there existed only a single dimensional level. This was the highest plane of reality where time and space simultaneously prevailed. Within this Continuum of matter and antimatter lived a race of omnipotent beings, free to create what they wished, living without even the concept of age, nor death.

The space-time Continuum saw their existence filled with wonders and mysteries that mortal men would never fully understand or consider, constructing everything they could ever need from thought alone. In this highest of infinite realities, eternally existing before our own reality, their omnipotent civilisation ruled untested, championed by none.

One being, however, saw this mindless construction as basic. He sought to undo the conditioning of his people by building with his hands, crafting life from sweat and graft alone. Alas, his peers saw little value in his deeds.

The years of failure wore down on God heavily, pushing him to near breaking point, kick-starting a drinking problem that would last billions of years. Though unsure he would one day taste success, his wife Sheila, never once gave up on him. She saw his future and knew that he would come to fame.

All that was needed was time…

And space.

And alcohol… but mostly time and space.

Genesis

The glowing distortion of the Continuum never relented, never subsided; it was day every moment that passed. Yet this perpetual day was never wasted nor taken for granted. God threw his latest project to one side, cursing his own failure within his small shed at the end of his garden. His shed, sanctum to a black sheep, regularly saw discarded items that had not met creative standards regularly getting tossed to the bin's gaping mouth.

He stormed from his wooden cave, tired of missing his goal for what seemed like the tenth time in so many fleeting moments. He paced up his pathway to his back door knowing that a stiff drink would be the key to calming his celestial tremors born from an ever-increasing frustration.

Omnipotent mice scurried here and there taking shelter behind the various plant pots littering his small vegetable patch; half his home-grown carrots and lettuces thriving, the other half eaten readily by his pet sheep, Bernard. Bernard lived form a thought that came to God many years ago, his being an effect from yet another failed goal; it had seemed that grazing cattle to keep lawns cut at a precise height didn't catch on; why have a garden sheep if you could simply wave a hand lazily and cut the grass from your bedroom window? Regardless, Bernard lived, and God hadn't the heart to take his life away from him.

God grabbed his coat by the front door after having a small heart-to-heart with Sheila, deciding that a nice walk might clear all his fifty-nine senses. Perhaps when he returned, he may have had the eureka moment that so many others he knew had already achieved. An old class friend of his that he'd kept in contact with had found fame with a new line of thought: David Smith, who later changed his name to Buddha by deed poll had invented something called Enlightenment. Apparently, it was the new hot thing, but God was sure that like most new hot things, it would soon die out. All he needed was one moment of genius.

Outside, light from the Continuum waved and morphed high above him; the distortion of power, time and space led an unrelenting battle that raged silently yet formed amazing colours and patterns at random. There was nothing better than a healthy long walk to clear a quaking mind, to reset, readjust and revaluate the direction that was needed.

A few hours went by, and God came from the local pub feeling no better off. He'd forgotten exactly how strong he'd made God's Own beer; it'd been a while since he'd had any and was now, to put bluntly, a little wobbly in the knees. He made his way to the nearest pizzeria searching his pockets for any spare change he may have misplaced. Even in the Continuum, which was free of scrutiny, free of bias or even religion, there were plenty of people that always said when something unexpectedly lucky happened, 'Finality is King'. God had walked the route from The Continuum Arms to Pizza Life several billion times, yet not once had he ever noticed the little shop next door.

Inside, dust had settled everywhere, except from where the countless spiderwebs hung. Shelves lined up from one side to the other stacked with equally dusty boxes. At the rear, a small till sat, with an elderly man whistling tunelessly while reading *The Continuum Times*.

"All right?" God said louder than he meant to.

The small man looked over his glasses at God, folded the newspaper, and nodded.

"Yes. And you?"

"A little shaky…"

"I can see… was there something that I could help you with?"

God felt the slosh of alcohol in his stomach, and thought he'd better materialise some food into his hands; a large slice of peperoni pizza would do the trick; plus, it saved him walking next door.

"What do you sell here?"

"Ah," The Shop Keeper said lifting a finger. "Interested already. Have you ever wished to be better than you are? More hands-on? Less mind manipulation and more crafting with tools? This shop is the place for you. I was once called crazy by my old teacher for thinking such things, ridiculed for putting forward the idea that we should create with graft, not simply think up what we desired. In this shop you'll find everything from, Planets for Beginners, to Galaxy Clusters for Experts

— ages one to nine trillion. Please," The Shop Keeper continued, raising a hand, "please, be my guest, take a look around."

"What's that there?" God said gesturing to a damaged box on the floor behind the till.

"No, no. You wouldn't be interested in that… how about a Nebula? You seem the colourful sort."

"It says 'Multiverse' on the side…"

"How about an Asteroid to get you started?"

God swallowed the last bit of pizza and pointed at the box. "Can I have a look?"

The Shop Keeper huffed, and reluctantly brought the frail box to the counter side, while a mousetrap snapped in the storeroom somewhere out of sight.

"In this box is what I can only call a headache. My business partners and I have tried to make the thing work on multiple occasions, yet the thing seems to be broken for good. It was meant to have a stand, some ghastly gold troll looking thing. I think it was meant to keep the multiverse from spasming out and falling into total chaos. Anyway, it's definitely got missing parts, must've fallen in the many universes by accident when we shipped it over."

"That's all right, mate, I can use a dinner plate to keep it on."

"That's not going to look very nice on your window ledge though, is it?"

"A multiverse" God whispered to himself. A feeling of purpose filled his celestial bones. "I'll take it."

"Sir, please. I do not think that—"

"I'll give you half the asking price."

"Sir. It's not for sale. I cannot legally sell you a damaged product."

"I'll give you double the asking price."

"Done!"

Later in the eternal day time of the Continuum, God was busy again, only this time he had true direction, cause, and more importantly, a physical goal he was working towards. Sweat lined his brow, the heat in the small garden shed became fierce, a relentless rhythmical beating filled the air in between spaces. Within his hands, unknown designs formed formless shapes, a million specs of light wove like illuminating webbing, curving, rising and breaking like a swelling wave of fission, bringing forward the tiniest singularity. On his single palm, an infinity grew from nothingness, a spiralling beauty twirled from darkness, and as the discounted seeds of a crumbling box found in a dusty old shop began to take root, the first galaxy came to be. It spun like a pin wheel, glowing in the centre, with arms of equal wonder curving outwards. Not a moment later, it ripped violently down the middle becoming two of the same, then four, eight, sixteen… its multiplication quickened till the celestial eye could no longer make out single galaxies. Galaxy clusters became galaxy strands; strands became netting.

God brought a plate from one shelf next to him to the workbench and sat the expanding existence carefully down. He sat at eye level with his creation, watching as the netting of countless galaxy strands wove tighter, becoming firmer. A ball, much like a crystal that soothsayers use to con others out of saving sat momentarily alone, wobbling slightly from the raging conflict within. Soon it split again, this universe resting upon an old dinner plate fell in two halves, then four quarters. The multiverse began to bubble; under the immeasurable weight of this small multiverse, the dinner plate cracked, splitting into pieces. Though Sheila had been looking for her favourite plate a good few months, God was sure she would be forgiving.

Within his deep retinas, the shimmering glow of the multiverse flowed and sparkled; every second it sat simply being, more realities forked off, other parallels divided, an infinite number of possibilities ignited, giving chance and reason a billion-trillion paths to go down.

The old crumbling box sat next to him by the workbench. He reached in and took out a few small bottles, each having faded labels stuck to their curved sides: Time, Causality and Finite. The instruction manual seemed easy enough, and as a man willing to put his masculinity first over any logical thinking, he read a few lines getting a general gist of what was needed, then placed them in his pocket to study later. God took his time to drip exactly three to four drops of each onto the surface of the multiverse. The Shop Keeper would later explain how gathering liquid causality was more difficult than collecting the others; simply crushing a pocket watch and boiling it for an hour and a half gave you concentrated liquid time, and finite, ironically, rained every few days in the Continuum.

Was this it? God stood and wondered what possibilities would open for him, if any? If The Shop Keeper had been ridiculed by all, much like a famous rapper claiming that the Earth was flat, would he too become a punchline for a bad joke? His intent was just, though he had not simply made something work that had been apparently broken for good, he'd taken it upon himself to go out and prove that the Earth was flat, or in this case, building by hand in the Continuum was realistically possible… Perhaps he would've strung this idea out more and arrived at a reasonable conclusion, if it wasn't for noticing two leftover parts resting at the bottom of the box.

What possible use could a lump of clay have in the multiverse? God held its unshapen lumpiness in his hands, pressing with his thumbs, creating indents, pondering what else was possible. If a multiverse could be achieved, then surely having another crack at an action figure wouldn't be too hard; Christmas was just around the corner, and action figures usually sold like hotcakes. He'd stepped over a line into forbidden territory, physical labour was a concept too far ahead for most to even be deemed worthy. Yet here he was, his hands browning from the damp clay, his thoughts wild and full of pull strings and automated voice boxes. His gaze set straight, he peered through the small shed window out towards the eternal fields, beyond the Continuum limits, far away towards either ends of the time stream, and daydreamed of success and fame. Plus, Bernard had chewed through the string holding the garden latch and escaped…

"Balls!"

A man moulded of clay rested in his palm, not in any way a healthy-looking man, of course, neither verging on obesity. Simply one that you may class as having a dad bod; a bit chubby, nothing special, though comfortable in his own skin. Your average male specimen, I suppose. He seemed more real than the last; the last having unrealistic features, such as chiselled abs, a chin that set squares could be measured to. No, his new figure looked just how he imagined.

From the box God dug in again and pulled out a small jet-black marble between his finger and thumb, its reflectiveness at a state of complete zero. It was neither matt, nor glossy. He held it up to the hanging lamp above his head, yet still it did not brighten, simply soaking up the light as if it fed on it.

"Blimey," God said feeling the excitement build inside him as he came to realise just what exactly he was holding. Only once had he seen a black hole before, it was years ago at a rock concert. He recalled meeting the lead singer backstage, the pair experimented with a black hole and an Overture; they were days that God knew he'd never see again. Unlike stars, galaxies, nebulas and other spacey types of things, black holes have been around forever. When God was just a nipper, his uncle — or at least one of his dad's closest friends, worked in a Black Hole Mine, the things were everywhere. You couldn't walk through the nearby shopping centre without seeing black hole cake in the bakery window, or black-hole-encrusted earrings down at the local market.

The power of a black hole was unmatched, and soon the mines ran dry, only a few remained in the Continuum, and those who had them new all too well to hold on to them and protect them as best they could. Except rock singers, of course, who always decided smoking one seemed a much better choice.

God brought the small clay man up to the light above him, opened his back with his thumbs and placed the small black hole inside. A few sparks came off its deep abyssal surface as micro forces of nature electrified the clay around it. Another spark came, then another. The clay man arched and creased over upon God's palm as power surged his body, bringing forth consciousness and desire, life… he was alive.

He fell to his clay knees, looking up at God, stretching out a hand.

"Who am I?" he croaked.

"You," God said in disbelief, "are Adam… no, hold on, Norman. Yeah, sorry, Norman's much better…"

Norman coughed and stood upright. His skin hardening, his mind resting, "I am alive?"

God nodded… "Yes. You are alive… oh balls!" he exclaimed as he dropped Norman from his palm straight into the glowing multiverse beneath him. Norman disappeared through its shimmering surface, without even the smallest of splashes.

God bit his bottom lip.

"Balls!"

The Traveller rubbed his eyes as he sat at the bar of the Sleeping Nun, his local free house he always came to after a long shift at work in the Continuum. He'd worked at the Warehouse for longer than he could remember, it wasn't the job he intended to have growing up in the Continuum, but it was stable, nevertheless. The Warehouse was, well, a huge warehouse — you'd never have guessed it — that stored all the creations that had, was, will have, and soon would have been created by thought alone.

From start to finish, he spent his work hours shifting boxes, stacking boxes, and unstacking boxes. Making boxes, and on the odd occasion, hosting poker nights for successful business owners he was well in with; this was a lie, but he thought that Anne, the receptionist, would be more interested in him after telling her.

"She'll never go out with you," The Fixer said as he sat down next to The Traveller.

"And why not?"

"You're too old," The Fixer replied gesturing at his entirety.

"We live in a time-free time zone, where everything that was is still is, and everything that can, has always been has. I'm as old as my father and as young as my great-grandchild that hasn't been born yet, because he has been, due to the nature of things."

"You're talking out of your rear..."

"I'm not! He's sitting over there by the fruit machine."

"Excuses," The Fixer scoffed, "if you're not too old, then you've had a rough life."

The Traveller laughed, picked up a small glass half-full of rum and toasted another work shift with his friend. The two joked and reminisced about their old times at the Continuum University till The Finder came through the front door, spotted them by the bar and sat down to join them.

"Took your time," The Traveller said.

"Yeah," The Finder replied. "I got a bit lost."

The Fixer shook his head in disbelief. "We come here every Wednesday. Literally. For about twelve years now. How is it that you can still get lost?"

"You know my directional sense isn't great."

"You're 'The Finder', though…" The Traveller pointed out.

"And you're 'The Traveller'" he replied bluntly, "tell me, exactly how much travelling have you done?"

"Touché…"

"I can feel the burn from here," The Fixer joked.

"Regardless… what are we doing here?"

"Every Wednesday, for twelve years," The Fixer said.

The Finder rolled his eyes and ignored the statement.

"Yes. Obviously. But if you didn't notice from the strange message we all received earlier, we've been asked here today."

The air dropped to a cold wobble as the feeling of curiosity and thrill settled on the bar around them. "Close the bloody cellar door!" the bar tender shouted to the bar staff. "You're letting the beer get warm."

"Mystery solved," The Traveller said.

"Even so, who in their right mind has the audacity to call themselves God?"

"I think it was his mother," The Fixer mused. "Think his father wanted to call him Malcolm, or was it Dave?"

"No," The Finder said, "Dave's his middle name, after his great-grandfather."

"…Who's sitting over there by the pool table." The Traveller pointed.

"So?" The Finder said waving a hand in the air, "where is he?"

"Over by the pool table!"

"Not Dave… Hi Dave!"

"All right?" Dave said as he waved from the pool table.

"Where's God?" The Finder said flustered. "He asked us here, and he's late!"

"No, he isn't," The Fixer said taking a swig from his Cucumber Water.

"All the drinks you could've had, and you choose water?" said The Traveller.

"Watching my weight, aren't I."

"Vodka's okay, if you're trying to be healthy?"

"Is it all spirits?" asked The Fixer, "or just vodka?"

"You know, I'm not really too sure."

"Guys!" The Finder said impatiently. "Please! Can you focus?"

"Sorry…"

"Someone! Tell me please. If he's not late, where is he?"

"He's already been and gone. You're the one who's late, think you got your times mixed up."

"Are you sure?"

"Pretty sure."

The Fixer laughed, "So, it's time and direction you have trouble with. Anything else?"

After a few more rounds of beer and drinking games, it was a short walk back to God's house…

God smiled as his three best friends crammed into the small shed at the end of his garden, jostling for space around the workbench. A minute or two passed before God said anything, before he did, he simply giggled manically gesturing to a small box in the middle of a broken dinner plate.

The Fixer leaned towards The Traveller.

"Think God's finally lost his marbles," he whispered.

"Either that, or he's planning the old stink bomb routine."

"Are you okay?" The Fixer asked.

God's eyes widened as a smile took the space between his ears, "Oh yes. Yes, indeedy."

Another moment passed; this one was a little more awkward than the last.

"What's in the box?" The Traveller said.

"Do you three like working in the Warehouse?" God asked.

"Oh yeah!" The Fixer said sarcastically. "Love it. The long hours shifting other people's mess around, fixing broken air-conditioning units and office chairs really pumps me up each day."

"At least you fix stuff" The Finder said, "and at least I find stuff… stock take, that is. Feel sorry for him," he said pointing at The Traveller.

"Hey!" The Traveller said coldly, "you know I lost my delivery job unfairly."

"You didn't lose it," The Fixer laughed, "you quit, due to your inflated ego."

God brought a fist to his mouth and coughed politely, "Do you want a job where you can travel?"

The Traveller looked at him blankly, "Of course. But unless you've got a miniature universe in that box, and you happen to need someone to travel around logging all the hotels and hotspots for you, I'm not interested."

"Ah," God said, "then unfortunately, I haven't."

"Stink bomb?"

"No," God replied scratching his head, "multiverse."

"I'm sorry?" The Finder asked. "A multiverse?"

God nodded, smiled, and lifted the box from the workbench revealing the bubbling shimmering multiverse underneath. The three looked in disbelief watching the countless universes collide, divide, expand and bounce within the distorted tangle of existence. God explained how he'd found the small shop, where in turn he found the discount multiverse, thrown it together, and unfortunately, losing the instruction manual, and his favourite sheep in the process.

"Lost?"

"Well," God said shrugging, "I put them in the recycling bin with some other bits..."

"Well, that was silly!" The Fixer said.

"Yep."

"So" The Traveller asked, sounding as upbeat as he could, using only a single word, "you mentioned a job?"

"Indeed! A job for you all!"

"And here I was counting down the hours till my next shift" joked The Fixer.

"I need each one of you on this one," God continued, "and, well, I kinda need it to remain a little secretive."

"A bit hush-hush? Why's that?"

"It's not strictly looked at as ethical, what I've done here, you see."

"Ah," The Fixer said rubbing his hands together; if there was one thing that The Fixer enjoyed, it was being a little unethical. "Well, count me in."

"You don't even know what you'll be doing yet," The Finder said, "for all you know, he might want you to wipe out an entire race of beings so he can build a swimming pool?"

"What's wrong with that?"

"Heartless…"

"It's not that," God smiled. One by one he went through the tasks he needed from his friends. To start, The Fixer would go around the multiverse, and fix everything that wasn't right, broken, or low-spec. The Traveller would, of course, travel the multiverse, rating all the hotspots and hotels he could; this was strictly an informal job needed only really when God needed somewhere to holiday. The Finder, now his job was perhaps a little more important; wormholes, singularities, individual universes and anything else he considered vital data would fall under his job title, except planets, solar systems, nebulas and galaxy clusters, these were given to The Explorer.

"Not The Explorer!" The Fixer said outwardly. "He's such a knob. A party killer! A buzzkill!"

"I know," God said.

"You haven't brought him into this, have you?" The Traveller quizzed worriedly.

"I have, yes…"

The Finder had his opinions about The Explorer but thought twice about voicing them. The history between God and The Explorer was, at most, turbulent. Turbulent being the very best description without venturing into mature content. Growing up they were inseparable, though it all changed on that fateful day, at a festival in Continuum Park.

"I mean really," The Traveller said flatly, "there's plenty of other people you could've asked. Plenty of nicer people. My nephew, Stan, for example, he's on his gap year and would love to go travelling. I could ask him if you'd like?"

"Maybe Stan would like to fill your new job role instead?" God quizzed.

"Maybe I'll mind my own business," The Traveller replied.

"Look," God said, "I know he's not your first choice. Lord knows, he's not mine. But I'm trying to patch things up with him, and this, well, it seemed like the perfect way to apologise."

“Apologise for what?” asked The Fixer. “You didn’t do anything? I tell you, that guy took it far too personally.”

“Even so. I’ve asked him. He’s already in there now.”

The Fixer picked up the multiverse in his hand and smiled. “Who’ll give me a bottle of vodka to throw it in the bin?”

“Very funny,” God said flatly.

It took no more than two seconds for The Fixer to call his supervisor to say he probably wouldn’t be in for work in the morning, and consequently jump into the multiverse just behind The Finder, who had also handed his notice in, though not with so many colourful and censored words as The Fixer.

“I hope you realise that if any problems come from this, it’ll be down to your new best friend,” The Traveller said wisely.

God nodded and patted him on the back, “And if anything does happen, I know I can count on you.”

“…as you always do.”

“Very true.”

“Where are you going to be when we’re finished?”

It was a good question. One that God hadn’t really thought about. Plus, the safety of the multiverse hadn’t occurred to him either. He was sure that once all five were in the multiverse, sorting things out to a good enough standard, no one would be silly enough to damage it, even so, the idea did not sit well in his celestial gut. Putting it in a ‘safe place’ simply meant that it’d be lost for years until it definitely had no use at all, such as car keys and winning lottery tickets. No, what he needed was a safe, secure room, that not only was away from prying eyes, but also, God thought, inside the multiverse itself, perhaps?

“Yes,” God said to himself while questioning his own sanity. A storage room inside the multiverse, which held the multiverse inside it. Did that make sense? Or had he been spending too much time inhaling glue when putting together his Air Fix models. Even then, with a storage room inside the multiverse that held the multiverse inside it, the thought of someone accidentally finding it worried him. God made his way back inside the house, ventured over to Mr Squibbles’ cage — Sheila’s hamster — and pondered whether turning Mr Squibbles into the keeper of the multiverse was ethical. Mr Squibbles had had a very lovely and long life. He'd fathered over six thousand children, slept most days within fresh bedding, drank clean water and had his little belly rubbed when he was feeling a bit down. It was time for him to give a little back, God thought.

"What are you doing with Mr Squibbles?" Sheila asked, flipping between *Lemon is the New Black* and *Love Planet.*

"Nothing," God replied, "just want to test something out…"

"Okay," Sheila said, one eye on the TV. "Just make sure he doesn't get scared… you know he doesn't like flashing lights."

God gulped and took Mr Squibbles from his cage, "I'll have him back safely…" then whispered, "or a hamster that looks just like him…

Though technically not his direct fault, the story of Norman after he fell into the multiverse led to quite a lot of trouble; trouble being an understatement, a lot being even more so.

You see, Norman had the unfortunate luck of drifting through the multiverse for at least fourteen billion years. This was plenty of time for things, such as life, civilisation, multiple-planetary kingdoms and interstellar space travel to spring up.

In the time Norman twirled through space like a dropped lollipop in a puddle outside a children's birthday party, he came to understand his own being. Not in any way his reason for being, just simply that he was alive, and that, for Norman, was enough; that, and the fact that God had incredibly long nostril hairs.

He ruptured the filament bursting into universe one heading straight for a pinwheel galaxy locally known as The Milky Way (FYI, The Milky Way name is derived from Hellenistic Greek, galaxias kyklos, translated it literally means 'milky circle'; you see, who said this wasn't an educational book?). His entry through Earth's atmosphere was rough, very hot, and made his mouth extremely dry. Out of all the places he could've landed at the end of his journey, Earth would've been at the bottom of his list; that is, if Norman had any idea of what wonders the multiverse had elsewhere. The Planet of a Thousand Circus Mirrors for example would've kept him quite happy for years.

Norman fell through the oil-stained sky above the city of Chumpton, in a fashion that could not in any way be classed as graceful. His arms flailed, his legs kicked, and for a moment he truly missed the loneliness that he'd befriended over the past fourteen billion years journeying through space with only himself for company.

His clay entirety hardened slightly as the rushing air around him heated. He covered his face trying to keep his vision clear, yet his hand simply slapped his forehead repeatedly as his speed increased. For the life of him he couldn't see; the building side came out of nowhere, so too the opposing building on the other side of the street as he bounced off it like a giant pinball.

Spectators gathered on the streets below; great gatherings of Chumpton-folk flocked together hearing the news that a strange, disfigured meteorite had entered Earth's atmosphere and had shot into Chumpton airspace. Chumpton was the kind of town that enjoyed things like this; things falling from the sky and hitting other things. Chumpton-folk never missed an opportunity to hit something, they enjoyed hitting things. Stealing things too, they definitely enjoyed stealing. And vandalising. It went without saying that any good upstanding citizen of Chumpton knew how to vandalise things to a high standard. You needed key skills if you were to survive in Chumpton.

"It's a man!" one woman shouted, pointing up towards Norman as he sped overhead down Main Street.

"Quick!" a man replied from the crowd, "after him! He might have a wallet on him!"

"Not before me you don't!"

Norman ricocheted off a cathedral's spire, chiming the bell inside that boomed its clang throughout the street signalling his arrival to Earth in a very anticlimactic way.

"Quick!" the man said again, "there's a bell in that strange building!"

"It's a cathedral" the woman shouted as the pair headed a small mob down Main Street.

"I don't care what it's called; how much do you think a bell goes for these days?"

At the end of Main Street lay Chumpton Station; a huge building that dwarfed everything around it. Inside a spaghetti of rails criss-crossed from a multitude of platforms, heading off towards other colourful and less crime infested cities. Trains and carriages littered the tracks, the few that were still sitting had not been used in many years; this was either due to tourism going downhill, or the fact that each train now sat upon piles of bricks; people would steal anything.

Norman cleared pieces of debris from his view and saw the huge clock on the side of Chumpton Station's outer wall racing towards him. He hit it with such force the metal struts that kept it hanging securely gave up letting the large clock fall to the ground.

"Quick!" the man said hastily.

"I'm not carrying that as well!" the woman said flatly.

"Fair enough..."

Norman collided with the outer wall of the station with a crash, carried on through to the inside and impacted the floor with enough force to create a small smouldering crater. He lay there for a moment; the feeling of touching something solid was quite the shock. Floating through space for fourteen billion years with only yourself to touch can have a strange effect on any man.

A single hand came through the weaving smoke around Norman where he lay, a helping hand that immediately helped itself to the black hole shimmering in Norman's back.

"Hey!" Norman shouted jumping to his feet.

"Ah c'mon!" a man said disappointingly. "It's so nice and shiny."

"No!" Norman shouted and took off running in any direction that seemed the safest. By now a small crowd had gathered where Norman had crash landed, it didn't take long for crowds to gather in Chumpton, especially when there might be something shiny and expensive to steal.

He zigzagged through the masses and out the back door, finding himself crossing abandoned platforms, passing small oil drums upended with fires lit inside and a few seasoned hobos lurching closely to get warm, and made it through a wire fence that someone before him had managed to shake lose. On the other side lay a car park where Norman found another crowd standing, though this time totally oblivious to Norman and his alien origins.

"I'd like to thank all of you," a man with a microphone said looking fairly happy with himself. "Thank you, all of you for coming here today, to see me, Thomas Moore, unveil my new road sweeper. With its onboard sweep assist, super-suck eco drive and extra cup holders, this monster will make easy work of… hey!"

"Sorry!" Norman shouted pulling the driver to the floor and climbing inside. He'd heard enough. Extra cup holders were indeed a great selling point for Norman, plus the angry mob had followed him from Chumpton Station, across the train tracks and past the fiery oil drums and was now squeezing itself through the fence.

"Stop that meteorite alien man!" the woman said firmly still heading the mob. "He might have a wallet on him!"

That was all the encouragement Norman needed to start up the road sweeper and head off into the city. The key turned, the engine bellowed, and the power of the black hole enveloped the road sweeper, took leave from Norman's back, sinking its gravity heisting teeth into the brand-new vehicle. It shook fiercely, rocked from one side to the other, its wheels spun where it sat kicking up smoke and debris and become nothing less than something that would've been more at home in a robot fighting pit.

"Blimey," Thomas Moore said, "the guys at Development really went above and beyond."

And with that…

Norman shot off into the concrete madness of Chumpton.

Elsewhere in the multiverse, The Fixer, The Finder and The Explorer were busy at work, cataloguing and recording, and fixing, of course, everything they could since their arrival. God was hard at work too dealing with a built-up frustration that came from constructing the perfect office space inside the multiverse for his workforce that was rarely used. The only person who enjoyed the 'out of order' coffee machine and the lack of pencils was Anne, who'd secured the job of receptionist after The Traveller had told God, "The job's hers, or I find work elsewhere!"

It took The Traveller a few thousand years, but eventually he wore her down like a slow flowing stream running softly over durable granite. Apparently, according to Anne, they weren't officially together, though that never dampened The Traveller's spirits.

The Traveller had just finished reviewing a small hotel called The A Void Inn in universe 9 thousand and 13. If you ever find it on a travel website, please be sure to give it a miss, as it's so far from the nearest star or planet, when you set off towards it, it'll be your great-great-great-great grandchildren that will eventually enjoy the four TV channels and reheated continental breakfast.

He placed his pen back inside his inner pocket after giving The A Void Inn one of the lowest scores he'd ever given, when his phone began to ring from the ether, and with a hand's shake, it appeared in his palm. "Hello?"

"Hello? It's God."

"This usually means something bad… what's up?"

"Look, I've a job for you. Leave the ratings for now. I need you to find something for me. I've misplaced something rather important. I asked The Explorer, but he said he was busy."

"Misplaced?" The Traveller quizzed.

"Okay fair enough, I dropped it into the multiverse."

"When did you last see it?"

"Mm," God huffed, "about fourteen billion years ago."

"Jesus!"

"No, Norman's his name. He's got a black hole and I need it back. Turns out it was quite bloody important. Just shows what not reading instructions can do…"

"Mm," The Traveller murmured recalling a very distressful coffee table construction. "Okay. Leave it with me. But I'm not contracted for this you know! I want a travel expense account, and a Christmas bonus. Not just a hug like last year."

God laughed. "Yeah, that was funny."

"Do we have a deal?" The Traveller asked sternly.

"Yeah, fine. We have a deal. Contact me when you've found him."

"Of course," The Traveller replied and went off on his way.

Later that day, after travelling around ninety billion light years and through countless universes, The Traveller reached a small hill, behind it lay a dark and smoky city, which, if he were being honest, didn't look appealing in the slightest. Taking his notepad and pen from his inner pocket, he took a note of the signpost in front of him knowing that he had definitely not been here before. The sign read, *'Chumpton Welcomes You. Crime free — Punishment Chargeable.'*

As The Traveller furthered his way through the streets of the city, he became more aware of how wrong his previous idea of Chumpton was. It was not, as first thought, unappealing, but in fact extremely unappealing. He could even go as far as to say revoltingly unappealing; Chumpton was not a place to book a family friendly weekend away.

Fearing the worst, he girded his loins and made his way towards the town, with the idea that perhaps looks could be deceiving.

"Give me everything from your pockets!" a thug ordered as he drew a gun from his belt moments after The Traveller had passed the towns first few houses. The Traveller, unamused, simply waved a hand in the air and walked on. The thug warped through space-time and reality and now sat on the street side as a very large flowery garden design. Surprisingly, this was a step up the career ladder for the thug, as he went on to win 'Best Outdoor Flower Arrangement' three years running.

This strange town was unlike any other place he'd ever gone to before. For example, while he was visiting the Crystal City of Gliese 34b, the multi-breasted women he'd entertained and rated very highly on his 'Best Massage Extras' list were shaven and clean, unlike the women who lived in Chumpton — they seemed to be moonlighting as coal miners — one asked The Traveller if he liked to party whilst combing her bird nest beard. The Traveller could only assume that this was due to the universal overpricing of razor blades; a problem that reached each corner of the infinite cosmos.

As he walked, the apparent sound of gunfire could be heard a few streets away with the faint noise of police sirens approaching from the distance. It's never been determined if curiosity did eventually kill the cat, but The Traveller was curious, and knowing full well that he was in no way, shape or form related to a cat, he was curious enough to take a look for himself. In front of him, two converging gangs were trading shots at one another from either side of the street. There must've been at least fifty or so gang members involved in the fire fight. The Traveller sat down to watch the conflict continue when from behind him came a small wobbling sucking machine with what looked like idiot at the wheel.

"Ah," he said, "Norman."

And it was.

Norman put his left indicator on and mounted the curb, switching the sucker on full blast. Usually, it may have been the odd drinks can, or an unlucky sleeping cat that would've been sucked up inside (curious about a new sleeping spot, no doubt), but as this was a black hole powered street sweeper, it was so much more. The Traveller sat watching as gang members, cars, and even lamp posts were swept up inside the road sweeper, never to be seen again. The Traveller thought for a moment and decided that undoing everything that Norman had done was definitely not in his contract.

Norman drove on. He swept up mobsters, he swept up cars. He swept up elderly ladies coming from bingo nights and thieves stealing bingo winnings under the cover of tights. Anything on the roadside, regardless of size disappeared into the swirling vortex of the black hole.

The Traveller had had enough, in an instant he teleported from where he sat to the passenger seat next to Norman and sighed heavily feeling job satisfaction lowering to new levels.

"Is your name Norman?" The Traveller asked.

"It is," Norman replied happily.

"Can you stop?"

"Of course. Are you here to report back to Mr Moore?"

The Traveller simply shook his head, stepped out and opened the back door to the sweeper and poked his head inside. Amongst the odd shocked-looking cat and swirling car, the occasional gang member appeared still shooting and shouting, which The Traveller had to give credit for.

"Okay, Norman. You're coming with me."

God stretched out on his sofa at home in the Continuum, feeling quite cosy in his fuzzy bear onesie, TV remote in hand, flicking through the channels as he usually would do on a Sunday afternoon. It was quite amusing that even with more than a million channels to choose from, he always found himself stopping on some documentary about the lifespan of ladybirds.

"Sheila!" God shouted towards the kitchen, "fetch me another beer, would ya?"

"I've put your dinner in the oven," Sheila said walking back in with a beer, "don't forget, I'm meeting Doris later for some interstellar bingo, then the girls are coming over tonight to catch up on The Real Housewives of Betelgeuse"

"You and that bloody show! I told you I'd take you there next month."

"I know" Sheila replied.

The buzz of the house phone went off somewhere underneath the growing pile of empty cans on the side table next to God.

"You need to clean up a bit," Sheila said in a completely nag-free tone, "and maybe get some breath mints too."

"I've only had a few drinks."

"A few too many…" Sheila said digging the phone out from under the empties. "Hello?"

God cracked open the can and took a huge gulp; the taste of Jovian 9% Ale was all he needed to unwind after a hard week or so of creating.

"Okay, thank you," Sheila said placing the phone back to the wall where it belonged, "that was Anne, she says your friend is here with Norman?"

"Norman. Good lad, didn't take long."

Sheila walked back into the kitchen fixing some large hoop earrings and checked her lipstick in the mirror. "You going to give Anne the week off? She's due a holiday."

God chugged the rest of the Jovian Ale and stood fitting his feet into two very warm and fluffy pink rabbit slippers.

"Do me a favour love. I might be out all night with the lads, so make sure when you're back, hide the vodka somewhere. Bloody Grace, I don't want her making a mess of the bathroom like last time."

"She won't."

"And no Arogian Blast shots."

"Of course."

"And definitely no Neptuniun male strippers. Took me two weeks to get them to leave last time."

"Should've stopped tipping them, then love."

Norman sat in the reception area of what he assumed was Heaven; although his idea of Heaven was somewhat different to his surroundings; the stacks of paperwork everywhere and a coffee machine with a note stuck on it saying, *'Out of order, use next door's'* seemed out of place. The Traveller took his seat next to Norman, pulled his phone out from the ether and began to play scrabble on it.

"She doesn't look happy," Norman said pointing over towards Anne behind the reception desk.

"Nope," The Traveller said, "she definitely is anything but. Why can't women understand? It's my job. I had to rate the Crystal City night life. It's not like I went there strictly for fun."

"You gave it five stars and a 'Watch This Space' rating though?"

"Beside the point."

God materialised behind the desk next to Anne holding a fresh ale in his hands, and immediately began to search through the desk drawers in front of him.

"Looking for anything in particular?" Anne asked as she blew another bubble with her gum.

"Just being nosey," God replied.

The Traveller and Norman stood and walked over to the desk; Norman had a smile on his face as he seemed to always have, while The Traveller hung his head low like a well-travelled dirty dog, who knew he was heading for the doghouse.

"Wotcha lads," God said. "Why don't we take a seat and have a little chat."

"Okay," Norman said smiling.

"You been drinking?" God chuckled. He led both over to a large sweeping window on the far wall, with a beautiful view of stars and general spacey stuff outside. In front of it there was a nice comfortable sofa waiting to be sat on. God clicked his fingers and a Lazy Boy with fridge attachment fizzed into existence. "Please," he said gesturing for them both to sit.

"She hasn't forgiven me," The Traveller said softly.

"I'm not surprised. You had a bit too much fun. I told you to rate them, not date them."

"...I didn't think you knew about that."

Norman grinned…

In a twist of fate so unfortunate it would've made Jeanne Rogers feel lucky, the boundless depth of the spheroidal black hole held the key to the multiverse's continuing survival; God would've known this if he'd ever shown more interest in reading the instructions. Once, he'd taken Sheila to a Continuum furniture shop, purchased a large flat pack bedside table, and ended up building a radio satellite dish. So, we can be a little forgiving here, as following rules had never really been in his nature.

For argument's sake, let us pretend that God had read the instructions fully and realised that without the immense power of the black hole, the multiverse was unable to recycle its countless universes, therefore inevitably leading to a multiversal clogging. Like all things sentient, all that life needs to grow a personality is time. Time to gather its thoughts, gain an opinion regarding things that have nothing to do with itself, and voice those opinions like an over-sun bedded desperate housewife. Mould, it turned out, was not the exception.

After Norman was sent hurtling through space for fourteen billion years, it wasn't long after that the Fungal Empire came to power, spreading across the outer regions claiming solar systems, galaxies and entire universes in the name of the fungus king, Stinkhorn the Great. At first, Stinkhorn the Great was known as Stinkhorn the Puny, then the Small. After a time, he had successfully shot up the fungal ranks claiming the title Stinkhorn the Mildly Inconvenient. God made a vital misjudgement when he ignored Stinkhorn the Mildly Inconvenient, about twelve billion years ago, when he saw him only as an inconvenience that of course was slightly mild. As you'd expect, this upset Stinkhorn the Mildly Inconvenient terribly, and thus, the spreading of his rotten ways became top priority. His home world of Portobello 9 would be the epicentre of it all.

Thankfully now, however, The Traveller has brought Norman back to God so that he may reset the black hole…

"I'm sorry," God said quizzically sitting upright in his chair, "you left it where, exactly?"

Norman sank his head low; he hadn't a clue what difference this made, he simply saw The Traveller doing it and guessed it was the right thing to do. Maybe a kind of apology, perhaps?

"I thought he had it on him," The Traveller said.

"He did!" God pointed out, "I put it in his back. So, come on Norman, what you do with it?"

Norman, realising that the low-hanging head neither made God any happier nor himself invisible, lurched forwards on his chair.

"It's in the road sweeper," Norman began to tell him, explaining how he started to clean up a crime-laced town when The Traveller stopped him and brought him in. Leaving the black hole inside a badly parked road sweeper.

"So, you're telling me, that possibly the most priceless and rare object is now sitting somewhere on a small dirt planet, inside an even smaller road sweeper?"

The Traveller felt like curling into a small ball and going sub-atomic; embarrassing was too small a description.

"Yep," Norman said.

"Right," God replied, getting up. "Let's go and get it then."

In a space of time, just slower than instantaneous, God had taken hold of Norman and The Traveller and simultaneously visited every planet with a town called Chumpton on, in the universe Norman had ended up in. Strangely, there were only three; Earth, Flatulancia, which of course suffered greatly from high winds, and Diaretica, which we won't go into. In the fizz of matter exchange from one place to another, The Traveller knew that their journey couldn't be counted in seconds, however, he could feel God's disappointment in him, making the entire trip longer than it needed to be.

With a puff of photons, all three landed nicely in the dead centre of Chumpton. It was early in the evening, so the nightclubs were still active, with many punters staggering around holding kebabs and empty plastic glasses. The air was thick with the smell of alcohol and fast food; the former being more of an interest to God. Norman, knowing roughly where they were, set off towards the sweeper's last known whereabouts.

"How much trouble am I in?" The Traveller asked.

God took off behind Norman as both followed his lead. "None whatsoever; it's my fault really. That's quite nice" he pointed noticing a small outdoor flower arrangement with a 'First Prize' banner hung over it.

"Honestly, I should've realised it wasn't with him."

"Don't beat yerself up," God replied happily, sucking a strange liquid through a curly straw.

"What's that?"

"Screaming Orgasm, apparently. Just nipped into that club there, Heaven. Nice place, nothing like the real thing, obviously."

"No?" said The Traveller.

"No. Our strobes are brighter, and our toilets are more modern."

After a second or two The Traveller had taken God's advice, whooshed off to club Heaven, danced like a mad man, drunk a barrel of cocktails, obtained numbers to women that he would go on to argue he'd never met before in his life, whooshed back again and now walked by God's side holding a multicoloured glass of his own.

"What's that then?"

"Sex on the Beach," The Traveller replied.

"And?"

"Nothing like the real thing."

"And you would know," God laughed. "Christ, you'll be in the doghouse for years! Have you no control? Take me and Sheila. How long have we been together, two? Maybe three trillion years now. Look at us, still happy!"

"The Continuum is timeless… what are you basing that on exactly?"

"The multiverse," God said. "Time moves nicely here, don't you think?"

"Anne's a nice girl, but she's young," The Traveller said, "and look at me, I could be her great-great-great-great granddad."

"Maybe she's looking for a really great father figure?"

Norman came running around the street corner in front of them heading their way, with a look that could only be described as a child that knew they had done something bad.

"It's gone!" Norman shouted worriedly. "It's gone!"

"What's gone?" The Traveller asked.

"The road sweeper," he huffed looking appropriately worried. He then handed God a small yellow piece of paper, looking fittingly more worried. On it was a lengthy and altogether unwarranted description of how the road sweeper had been parked illegally in front of the Chumpton Dairy Mill for several hours, and due to this had been rightly towed away by the city council and was now ready to be picked up from the impound centre, along with an equally unwarranted parking fine.

"Christ!" God said, "how much?"

"I'm sorry" Norman shook.

"Can't you just tell them that you're with me, and I'll pay it later? If I knew the multiverse was going to be such a problem, I'd never have haggled for the damned thing."

"Probably not a wise move," The Traveller said. "Most places here are very open to the idea of an all-powerful higher being, and how you are all-knowing and wise. But Chumpton is more of a 'why did you dump it all on us, you selfish bastard, give me everything you have in your pockets' type of place."

"Jesus!" God said. "Fine. Look, you two go and sort this out. I'm getting a bit frustrated with all this running around. Pay whatever, do whatever. I don't care. But I need that black hole back. I'm off."

"Where to?" asked The Traveller.

"Nowhere in particular. Just fancy a look around. Never been to this planet before."

With that, and a howl of photons and dust, God vanished into the ether.

Steve the security guard made his last round of the impound centre, his loyal dog Bud pacing by his side as usual. It had been a relatively quiet shift. A few taxis had been brought in with no insurance, a rental car that someone had been sleeping in for a few days; a husband on the wrong side of his wife's rage; it seemed that being in the doghouse was a fairly standard thing throughout the cosmos. And of course, the road sweeper.

Steve swept his torch across the dark compound a few times, then retreated to his hut. Bud took to his bed circling it a few times before deciding on the most comfortable spot. Steve patted his head kindly and looked at his watch, only another ten minutes till the end of his shift.

He'd been tactical with his lunch today. His wife usually packed a few sandwiches for him, a sausage roll or maybe a boiled egg, and it wasn't uncommon for Steve to eat through the lot in the first hour of his shift. As he began to unpack his lunch that he'd somehow saved, thinking now that he'd been very smart about it, the security feed on the monitor in front of him fizzed a touch, then blacked out altogether.

"Mm," Steve grumbled.

"Woof!" Bud said. Of course, what he really said was something much more complex than that, but Bud had come to realise that the human ear is not the best for picking up the warnings that many other dogs have tried to tell their owners before it was all too late. So, as always, Bud simply said 'woof' again.

"What's up, boy?" Steve asked standing to his feet. "Something got you spooked?"

And sure enough, something had. Bud had come up against The Fungal Empire before when he was stationed on Walkees Prime, a planet some five hundred light years away from Earth. After he'd defeated the invading armies of Stinkhorn the Great two thousand years ago, he'd been ordered to Earth by the head of the Rex Elite to ensure the safety of mankind. Unfortunately, it had been a while since he'd made his long journey, and as it was, Bud wasn't feeling that enthusiastic about going head-to-head with the enemy. So instead, he chose to woof once more and hide under the desk.

Steve took his torch in hand and made his rounds one last time.

The Traveller and Norman walked quietly in the direction of the compound; a stillness hung between them. Not awkward, but close enough. Norman understood the importance in regaining the black hole; its role in the cosmos was neither here nor there; God wanted it back, and that's all he needed to know. He'd overheard two little old ladies nattering outside a bingo hall as he was doing his sweeping rounds, that God moved in mysterious ways. Norman thought about that intensely. What was mysterious, exactly? Since Norman had met God, he had never once noticed him moving mysteriously; maybe a little zigzaggy, but that was because of the Jäger Bombs. Perhaps the little ladies were talking about his ether-photon-corridor-creating ability, but that was standard, wasn't it? Most celestial life from the Continuum could do that.

“Does God ever move mysteriously?” asked Norman after a while of silence.

“Only after a heavy session,” replied The Traveller.

“Ah, that’s what I thought.”

Both rounded a building’s edge and saw the compound in front of them. Its spotlights lit up the darkened streets all around. Its high wire electric fence kept out unwanted visitors. And Steve the security guard, who night after night had fought off countless muggers and drug-taking thieves, now hung upside down held by his ankles by a very large and very tall humanoid oyster mushroom; Oxyn the Big was his name. The Traveller knew this quite well; he’d made a point of trading a few lower-priced Fungal Empire Playing Cards for a single one that said ‘Oxyn the Big’. It wasn’t really an especially amazing name, not one that struck fear into the hearts of his enemies, but it got the point across rather well. That being that Oxyn the Big, was in fact quite big.

Behind Oxyn the Big two smaller characters could be seen hustling a road sweeper-shaped silhouette into the rear of a Type 4 Boletes Speeder; The Traveller never managed to find the playing card with this craft on, and as such, had no idea that even he, with all his omnipotence would be unable to keep pace with it. Fast was too small a word; instantaneous, that too was too small a word. Godly, now that was getting to the point. Most crafts in the Fungal Empire fleet had speed capabilities that made others look like they were standing still. This was the reason for their success. It was a trait that had been kept throughout the evolution of the Empire. Even back when fungus and mould hadn’t gained full mobility, it managed to get around a tiled bathroom quicker than a hormonal teenager.

“Someone, help!” Steve shouted. “Bud!”

Bud was smart. Bud was hiding under the table. “Woof!” barked Bud.

“I know that dog!” The Traveller exclaimed. “I know that oyster mushroom!” he continued.

Norman had already run off towards the commotion to help Steve the security guard in any way he could.

“I know that man,” The Traveller huffed holding a hand to his head. With a flick of his wrist, he sped forwards flying a few inches off the ground, lifting Norman under his arm and tackling Steve the security guard from the grasp of Oxyn the Big. In a blink of an eye, all three stood on the other side of the compound safely. Oxyn the Big looked puzzled for a moment staring blanking into his open palm, then realised what had happened; realisation is a tricky emotion for any evolved fungus to depict, as most only grow up feeling either angry, really angry, or impossibly angry. It was only Stinkhorn the Great who ever took on the emotion of physically shaking angry; one reason he obtained so much praise in *Who's Who Mould Monthly*.

Oxyn the Big now looked really angry. "Mrarmahah!" he shouted.

"What did he say?" Norman asked. Both he and Steve the security guard turned to The Traveller.

"Mm. Well, apparently, he wants to dice us up, marinade us in a duck sauce, cook us in a pot with a few vegetables and stock, and serve us to his grandchildren for a Sunday afternoon snack. But not before he steals the black hole, hands it over to Stinkhorn the Great and claims his rightful place by his side. Receive the prize, that, if rumours are to be believed on Portobello 9, are three extremely good-looking mushroom virgins from the house of Gla."

"Mrarmahah!" Oxyn the Big shouted again.

"Oh sorry, I mean the house of Gli."

"Is this some sort of game show?" asked Steve the security guard, "I only ask cos it all seems, well, a bit silly, don't it?"

"It does, doesn't it?" Norman smiled. "But you see, after God made me, the Fungal Empire appeared, taking over a lot of the other universes and so on. And the black hole that was in my back is now in that road sweeper, and God has asked my friend here to help me retrieve it for reasons I'm not too sure of."

"Right," Steve the security guard said, "gotcha. Well, God does move in mysterious ways, don't he?"

"That's what I said!" Norman replied.

Meanwhile, Oxyn the Big had climbed into the speeder and was now in the middle of engaging take-off procedures; ready to take off, funnily enough. The ship's boosters spewed thick smoke to the ground as it began to take flight, lifting higher and higher into the air. The Traveller turned to Steve the security guard and flicked his hand accordingly. A puff of protons later, and he was a sunflower.

"I liked him," Norman said.

"Too bad," said The Traveller. He pulled his phone from the ether and rang God. "God?"

"Yep," he replied drunkenly.

"Where are you?"

"At a bar, what's up?"

"Do you have to be constantly drinking?"

"It's five o'clock somewhere."

"Yes, you've probably altered time and space just to make it that way. Look, the sweeper's gone, and the black hole with it."

"Christ, man. It's only a few forms you've to fill out. Sign a few bits, get the keys and..."

"It was Oxyn the Big!" The Traveller shouted. "The empire has it."

God appeared in the compound next to Norman in a blazing flash of light, wearing a toga and holding a fancy lime-green cocktail with a small rocket in its syrupy contents. A thorn crown upon his head.

"You look ridiculous."

"I like it," Norman said.

"What happened?" God asked sipping his lime-green drink.

"Oxyn the Big happened. That vast oyster stole the black hole and is heading for Portobello 9 as we speak. You know I can't go there!"

God squeezed his eyes closed in frustration, "Ya gonna have to, mate."

"But you know I can't!"

"Look!" God said raising his voice. "If it comes to it, I'll just take the multiverse back to the bloody shop and get a refund, I've still got the receipt somewhere. I really don't want to, but that's my last resort. I'm leaving it all up to you two to sort this mess out. Or, if you like, I can ask my new best friend The Explorer to take over your job roles too."

"You wouldn't."

"I would! This is a serious matter and I need it fixing, but if you mess it up, it's back to unemployment for you. Understand?"

"Yes," The Traveller said soberly.

"Good."

"Woof!" Bud barked as he ran up to God.

"All right Bud!" God said happily, "Long time no see! How's the family?"

"Woof!"

"Crikey. Sounds intense. Come with we, I know a pretty little pug that you'd get along with."

Another blinding bright light flashed and God along with Bud, vanished leaving Norman and The Traveller standing quietly in the corner of a dark and empty compound.

"Bollocks," muttered The Traveller.

In the far-left corner of space, not anywhere near anywhere else, a small ship raced through a backdrop of stars with a small road sweeper in its cargo bay. Its destination, also light years away from everything, also in another universe completely.

As Oxyn the Big tore through the void of space like a mushroom possessed, his two associates did what they could to break into the road sweeper. Unfortunately, mushrooms never had the patience to evolve fingers, and so their fists were simply squishy lumps of matter on the end of each arm. This, as you would imagine, did little to their moods other than anger them. Fortunately, getting angry was second nature to a mushroom.

Oxyn the Big had plans of his own and getting inside the road sweeper was vital to this plan. He'd been ordered by Stinkhorn the Great to gain the black hole at any cost, bring it to him with no stops straight to Portobello 9; however, like most mushrooms, Oxyn the Big was very happy to double-cross his boss and take the road sweeper for himself now knowing its value and wealth.

"Blaggaly!" one of his mushroom footmen said. Roughly translated into English: "Oxyn the Big, for the life of me I can't open the doors. I am truly sorry. But my mushy lumps can't grip the door handle, I am literally stumped. But fear not, for I have a plan. In the time that it takes to travel to Portobello 9, I will have grown some vestiges, and gain access to the goods that we seek!"

Oxyn the Big smiled and replied "Gluk." Which in turn translated to, "Don't bother." And opened the back door of the speedster, hurling both of his footmen out the back into the void of space, never to be seen again. As the door closed, Oxyn the Big squished a few of the squishy buttons in front of him bringing up a small picture on a screen. An even smaller angry man appeared within its frame.

"Oxyn the Big," said The Explorer. "I gather you have it?"

"Blah!"

"I didn't ask for your life story. Good. Bring it to me as planned, and together we will readjust the order of things. See you in say, a day?"

"Blah!"

Norman held onto The Traveller's hips tightly; he'd spun through space before, twirling around unstoppably like a crazed spinning top, yet he was not used to this straight-line flight path. They'd set off from the lonely vehicle compound directly upwards towards the night sky at light-speed, flying in the direction of the speedster carrying the road sweeper. Norman gulped, felt a little sick, and asked The Traveller to tell the story again.

"Really?"

"Please!" Norman shouted closing his eyes; his head a turntable of stars. At one point he saw what looked to be a vast turtle swimming through the void carrying four goliath elephants who in turn held up a flat disk like world; he had heard of such a thing during his quick visit to earth written by a fellow called Pratchett.

"Can we just not talk for a bit?"

"We can," Norman replied, "but I may throw up."

The Traveller huffed. "It was simply a case of unsatisfactory, misplaced job roles. I never liked delivering things any way."

Norman croaked, lurched a bit and sighed relief as the moment passed.

"You, okay?"

"Travel sickness," Norman replied.

The Traveller huffed. "Anyway. We began to build the multiverse that you see around us. Well, God did. After he was finished, it was The Explorer's job to go in and create an all-knowing map of everything. After he'd finished, The Finder would go in and begin an even more detailed map of everything. Finding everything from wormhole gateways to civilisations that had come to be. After he had done his job, The Fixer would enter reality, and well, fix things. Whatever was broken. Come to think of it, I haven't heard from him in a while."

"And then it was your job next?"

"Yes," The Traveller replied looking suddenly glum.

"What's wrong?"

"You know, I had always been a kind of third wheel in our group of four. Anyway, my job was simple: I just had to travel around the entire multiverse, and find good spots to holiday at."

"And?"

"And what?"

"And what else?"

"There's no 'else'. That was it."

"Oh."

"Yep."

"Okay."

"God insisted that it was a very, if not the most important job there was. But I'm not sure."

"Of course it is!" Norman said happily. "The others only have to look at things and log stuff down, but you get to experience the multiverse first-hand. I'd say you haven't just got the most important job, but the most fun too! After all, you need to enjoy your work, otherwise, what's the point?"

The Traveller smiled and squeezed Norman's shoulder, "For such a young man of fourteen billion years you sure are wise and worldly."

"Well," Norman said, looked ahead, closed his eyes and threw up again.

The Traveller just patted his head like a dog, or a downed drinking partner not lasting the evening. "That's it. Get it all out."

The Finder sat in his small house on a tiny rock floating in the middle of a million more rocks; it was to him the best-looking asteroid field he had found in all his years. To the untrained eye, an asteroid may look like every other asteroid, but really that is simply not true. Though confusing at first, The Finder found, as The Finder usually does, that if he searched enough, he could find anything. And it just so happened that after jumping from one universe to another, he came across this asteroid field of his, where every single rock that floated by his window had the fortunate shape of a large pair of breasts. Here, The Finder knew he could draw up his maps of existence in peace and happiness.

Norman asked again, though he struggled with his words that were mixing with whatever was in his stomach. “Where are we going?”

The Traveller slowed his flying, backing away from the distorted and weirdly addictive pace of light-speed and came to rest on a planet’s ring.

“We’re never going to catch up with Oxyn the Big, he’s too fast. And I can’t simply fly, or appear at Portobello 9, we’d both get stuck in the stickiness of everything.”

“You can just call him Oxyn from now on, if you like,” Norman said.

“I’d love to,” replied The Traveller, “but I can’t. You see, my aunt is called Oxyn, and if I say something like ‘I’m going to vaporise you, Oxyn’ when referring to Oxyn the Big, whenever that time comes that is, I may hesitate, thinking of old Aunt Oxyn, and Oxyn the Big will get the better of me. So really, I can’t afford to simply say, ‘Oxyn’.”

“I see,” Norman said emptily. “Have you ever thought about changing your name? Maybe something with ‘The’ in the middle?”

“Like… The ‘The’ Traveller?”

“Mm… maybe not that. More like, I don’t know, The Traveller of Existence. That sounds pretty cool.”

“What?” The Traveller said sharply, “the name The Traveller doesn’t really do it for you?”

“No, no,” Norman said innocently. “It’s fine. It’s fine. I mean, all I’m saying is that maybe when the time comes, and we’ve got to do some sort of fighting or something, shouting out loud ‘The Traveller has arrived’ isn’t really that scary.”

“So, what then?”

“I don’t know.” Norman shrugged.

“So, I guess you think Norman sounds like a sharp intimidating name?”

"Ah," Norman said raising one finger, "I've thought of that. When the time comes when we face whoever to get this black hole back, I'm not going to introduce myself as Norman."

"Introduce yourself?"

"No. At that moment I will be The Readjuster!"

The Traveller looked stone clad for a moment then shook his head disapprovingly, "Please don't."

"Okay. I'll have another stab at it."

"Good."

Behind them the crescent glow of an alien world cast its gigantic shadow down upon the rings where they sat. The planet's oddly satisfying whirls of storm systems and layers moved like multicoloured ink within fast-moving water. Outwards a few moons twirled elegantly against the black and green blur of a distant nebula. New forming stars within the dust cloud twinkling and popping as the fusion heat reactions began to give life to another space within space. The Traveller looked outwards at it all, marvelling at its beauty.

"I guess all this will disappear at some point," Norman said.

"Only if we fail," replied The Traveller.

For a spell, the two sat, taking all the colours and un-colours of space in; all the spiral and elliptical galaxies, all the beautiful shapes and wonders that had been crafted by a half-drunk God with mould issues. They soaked up the basic vastness of it all, and both began to see past the gun crime and oddly enjoyable multi-breasted women of the Crystal City and understood what God had been attracted to when he first bought everything. Granted, it was only a picture on the side of the box, plus it came with half the stuff needed to actually finish the thing, but all in all it was quite pretty.

"We can't let him take it back for a refund," Norman said. "It's too nice."

"Too nice?" asked The Traveller curiously.

"Yes," said Norman smiling from ear to ear chasing the tail of a fiery rock as it flew past disappearing behind a star. "Too nice."

"So, you think that this universe, which is also part of the bigger and far more complex multiverse, which contains all life and matter, antimatter and opposite antimatter… you think that everything that has been, is and everything that will be, is nice?"

"Yes," Norman said happily.

The Traveller nodded in agreement. "Yes, I guess it is too nice to be returned." He rubbed his nose. "Plus, if God returns it, you'll have to be taken apart and returned also."

"Mm." Norman grimaced. "There is that. So…" he said with an urgency, "what's the overall plan then?"

"Yes," The Traveller said, "there's that too. As much as I don't want to, we may need to gather a bit of help for this one."

"Help?"

"Yes."

"But you're impotent, right?"

"Mm?" The Traveller said.

"Important, then."

"Nearly."

"Incompetent?"

"Please stop."

Norman stood up and stretched to crack his back. Though in his limited time since his aliveness had begun, he found that there was not much in the multiverse that could rival a good long stretch.

"Well, I'm ready."

The Traveller sighed with reluctance, "Okay. First things first, we need to find The Finder."

"And is he easy to find? Being the type that finds things?"

"It all depends really."

"On what?"

"On if he wants to be found."

"Oh."

"Let's just start and think less about things."

The Traveller stood with Norman and took a large ring of keys out from the ether with a flick of his fingers. He had come to know a few truths, the first being that if you could help to not do anything inside the multiverse, it was to not bother thinking about things. As it would simply confuse and irritate matters. The second, that totally contradicted the first, was to always keep an open mind about things and try to stay three and a half steps ahead of yourself; obviously, this would involve a small amount of thinking leading to possible irritation.

In front of him The Traveller moved his hand mysteriously, which caused Norman to giggle. Amazingly, a door appeared in space time and slowly opened.

"It's not mysterious!"

"I didn't say anything."

Norman stood and looked through the door, on the other side he saw a completely different yet much the same kind of universe. There were stars, dust clouds, planets and so on. "Is he in there, then?"

"Maybe."

"So, you don't really know?"

"No," The Traveller said, "but we do actually need to find him, jokes aside."

"Okay," Norman replied, "we have to find one man, who I take it is a normal-man-sized man, in the multiverse, which is quite big."

"Yes. Like trying to find a needle in an infinitely large field full of infinite haystacks."

"Cool."

Both stepped through the door to the new universe; looking rather blasé about the whole thing.

"It's okay," The Traveller said while locking the door behind him. "I have a plan."

Norman took a few steps towards the new universe, he couldn't tell what it was, but something was definitely different. Maybe the smell; something like strawberry milkshake crossed with the colour green; nice, satisfying, yet a little confusing. On the endless horizon, both horizontally and vertically, a wide spread of galaxies of all sizes speckled everywhere the eye could see. Like strands of spiderwebs, all the spirals and ellipticals lined up one after another creating a flawless cosmic web some billion-trillion light years away from where they stood. Wherever they had found themselves it was so distant from the new universe that Norman could see all of it, from one end to another. The entirety of this infinite universe laid out in front of him. Every single star, galaxy, cosmic strand and mega structure could be seen within this glowing webbing that to Norman was a mere foot wide. Besides this small hazy universe, everything else around them was black. Not just plain black that is, but space black.

"Beautiful, ain't it?"

"Yes," Norman said.

"Absolutely," The Traveller agreed.

"Just don't touch it as I've just finished sweeping it all up," the small imp-like being said.

Norman fell silent, then realised that the two weren't standing alone, a third was with them. He looked over The Traveller's shoulders to where the small imp sat on a floating rock holding onto a broom. He smiled back at Norman who in return waved like an idiot.

"Who are you then?"

The imp picked up his broom, looked down its handle as if checking for any flaws or imperfections in its build, then placed it down again and started to chew on a length of hay.

"Don't tell me he never mentioned the Amazing Five?"

"No," Norman said floating over to where he sat, "Just the four: God, The Traveller, The Finder and The Fixer. But never once a single mention of you."

The Traveller closed his eyes knowing what was to come. He'd hoped to avoid any sort of awkward talk between the imp and him, especially after the last time they'd met. Unfortunately, this time Norman was with them, and any such 'normal' chit-chat could be forgotten about immediately.

"Really?" the imp said slowly staring over at The Traveller. "Well, that doesn't shock me in the slightest. He's always been jealous of my role in things."

"You have no role," The Traveller said. "Unless it's some kind of sausage roll."

"So, you think that taking care of the multiverse is a less important job than say, I don't know, sploshing about in a hot tub with multi-breasted women of the Crystal City?"

"I was working!"

Norman smiled and took a seat next to the imp and began to look at his broom.

"So, I guess you know each other?"

“Yes, we do!” the imp said. “We used to be good friends.”

“He used to be God’s pet hamster,” The Traveller said coldly. “Until—”

“—till God gave everyone a job to do after creating the multiverse then realised that he needed another hand to keep everything organised and together. That’s when he waved his hand in my direction, morphed me into what you see before you and gave me charge of everything.”

“You’re not in charge!” The Traveller said loudly.

“Don’t mind him,” the imp said dismissively waving his way. “He’s just upset because my job is more important than his. And I didn’t even need to try.”

“Actually,” Norman said, “we’ve talked about this and have concluded that The Traveller’s job is in fact the most important.”

To that The Traveller smiled and felt proud to call Norman a friend; it didn’t last.

“I’m The Keeper,” the imp said. “Keeper of everything.”

“I’m The Readjuster,” Norman said strongly. “Readjuster of… well, nothing yet.”

“Nice,” The Keeper replied.

“His name’s Norman,” cut in The Traveller. “And he’s an idiot.”

“Still bitter after all these years.”

Norman let all insults and negativity roll off him like a cheese wheel down a hillside. It wasn’t that he didn’t understand things, it was just that he enjoyed being involved in it all.

“May I ask,” Norman said looking towards the distant universe, “where exactly are we? Has each universe got its own name?”

The Keeper lifted a finger to the air and winked, “Ah! A fine question. Though actually, we’re looking at the multiverse, not a single universe. You see all the strands and things that look like glowing string?” Norman nodded. “Well, they’re in fact single universes, not galaxies. You see, we are in the multiverse now, in a kind of storage cupboard-”

“More like a kitchen drawer,” The Traveller said bluntly.

“Have you got your own kitchen drawer?” The Keeper asked sourly. The Traveller fell quiet and turned his back to them both. “That’s what I thought. Every now and again the entire thing starts to come apart, as if reworking itself, adjusting and making changes, that's when I must sweep it all back into one heap. Like a pile of leaves. Anyway, there's something wrong with it," he said loudly towards The Traveller.

"Can't work out how to use a broom?" The Traveller said in a tone that was nowhere close to sulking.

"Ha, good one."

The Traveller closed his eyes; if only he were allowed to morph him back to a hamster, The Keeper would be belly deep in straw by now. "I mean the multiverse. You'll have to tell the big guy that it's broken."

"Have you tried kicking it?" Norman asked helpfully.

"Kicking the multiverse?"

"Yeah."

"You mean physically kicking the multiverse?" The Keeper repeated.

"Yes!"

"You mean standing up, walking over to the multiverse, and kicking it?"

"Yes," said Norman happily. "Kicking it!"

The Keeper nodded. "Yes, I've tried it. Just hurt my foot on a neutron star."

"Oh."

"I know what's wrong with it," The Keeper said pointing his broom's handle in its general direction.

"Mould?" asked The Traveller.

"Yes!" The Keeper stated, "mould. It's everywhere. Seems to be clogging things up and making a mess of everything."

"We know. That's why we've come here." The Traveller, becoming quite deliberate, started to pick his nails, staring off into the distance. "It's just that God has asked for my personal help on this matter. It's more of a trust thing than anything else. You know how it is."

The Keeper choked on the lump in his throat that grew exponentially with the passing of each word, a small amount of real envy took place in his chest. Though he'd never admit it to his face, The Keeper had missed seeing The Traveller after all that time; it had been fourteen billion years after all, who wouldn't start to miss someone after that time? The Traveller stood tall inspecting more of his nails. Deep down he hoped that what he'd said made The Keeper jealous and upset, though even deeper down he felt a little guilty about bringing an ex-hamster close to tears.

"Well," The Keeper said sadly. "I guess I'll be off then… you know, off to do something else, something, I don't know, unimportant."

Norman looked at him equally sad, then looked at The Traveller, then back at The Keeper as he began to walk away. He beamed a stare towards The Traveller like a mother might to a father who'd needed to tell their son they were proud of him. In the end The Traveller gave in.

"Hold on."

"Yes?" the Keeper said emptily.

"There is something that you can do for me."

"Really?"

"Yes. You are The Keeper, and besides keeping the multiverse in order, you also keep the whereabouts of the five of us too."

"Yes," The Keeper said happily, "that's true. I knew you were on your way anyway."

"Well, you can start by telling us where The Finder is."

"That I can do." The Keeper walked over, sat back down on his rock and began to riffle through the multiverse at an insane speed. Flashes of light peppered Norman's face as he watched in delight. Universe after universe came and went as The Keeper searched each one for The Finder in a fraction of a nanosecond.

"There we are!" The Keeper said, pleased with himself. "The Finder. He's at home drinking tea and making maps. If you arrive through that door," he pointed to his side where a door handle appeared from nowhere, "you'll arrive right next to this nebula. Carry on till you see a star that's kind of blueish-octerine, he's between the large red gas giant and the small rocky world. Can't miss him."

"Thank you!" Norman said.

"Yes," The Traveller said then added, "thank you. I mean it."

"You might be interested in the whereabouts of the others?"

The Traveller thought about this for a second; he'd always known where God was, but the others he hadn't seen in aeons. "Go on then."

"Well," The Keeper started. "God seems to be on this world called Earth, in universe 1."

"Yep!" Norman shouted, "been there! Very nice place. Great street theatre."

"It's really not."

"The Explorer," The Keeper continued, "is somewhere in this universe." The Keeper searched through till he found the correct one and brought the whole thing up in front of the three of them. This universe glowed differently from the others; it had a kind of brownish funk that slowed everything down. "Does that look right to you?"

"No," replied The Traveller. "That looks like mould's bigger brother."

"I wouldn't worry too much about that for now though," The Keeper said, "it's The Fixer that concerns me."

"Oh?"

"Yes."

"Where is he?"

"Portobello 2."

"Mm," the Traveller grunted worriedly. "That's no good."

"No."

"They're probably going to get him to fix the black hole next to their empire's capital so that they can spread themselves to every part of the multiverse," Norman said casually. "You know, cos mould spreads."

The Keeper and The Traveller both turned slowly to Norman who was closely inspecting the zoomed-in picture of the giant fungal planetoid where The Fixer currently was.

"Have I missed something?" asked the Keeper.

"Lots," replied The Traveller.

The wormhole opened in front of Oxyn the Big; a smile on his face symbolised his distance from his usual anger, this angered him as he always liked a bit of rage to make him happy, and so his smile faded feeling his hatred for happiness enlarge, and due to this he felt a lot better. The speedster rushed inwards, past the closing wormhole entrance behind him. All around the cockpit, colours of unknown origins spat and bubbled as if alive and a whirring sound fizzed within the air. Oxyn the Big didn't like colours, nor did he enjoy the ongoing whir. Fortunately, the exit of the wormhole was just up ahead.

The speedster exited the psychedelics, popping out into a region of space that shouldn't have existed; God himself didn't even know of its being. The Explorer had crafted this region from his own mind, and the reasons for doing so were totally immoral.

Besides the occasional fiery rock hurtling through space, or the odd twinkling star a google plex light years away, this area was completely empty, save for a large square metal platform that floated in the middle of nothing. On it, The Explorer sat behind a large wooden desk.

The speedster flew overhead as Oxyn the Big went through the usual fly-by that all heroic pilots were obliged to do. A quick barrel roll and twist, and he was ready for landing. Underneath the belly of the speedster, wheels protruded out; not actual wheels though, more like rounded squishy things designed to bounce a little. The engine's hum softened as the power lowered; the boosters and wing jets fizzled, and everything turned off. A few seconds later, the back end of the rig came apart as a thick plume of fog rolled outwards — more standard heroics and unwarranted mystery that pilots were shown to do — The Explorer rolled his eyes and wished for all this showmanship to come to an end.

The road sweeper was finally dumped right in front of the desk with a thump.

"Brunnli bugger!" Oxyn the Big said sternly.

"Language!" The Explorer replied, "I'll open the door."

"Glop!"

"Please don't go on."

The Explorer stood and made his way round Oxyn the Big's larger than life fungal frame and stopped at the rear of the road sweeper. Using his divine ability that all Fungaloids lacked — of which I mean fingers, The Explorer unclipped the latch and opened the door to the inside. And there it was! The black hole.

"Ah..." The Explorer said exhaling slowly. "My word it's a pretty thing. Trust that drunken fool to miss out the most important thing in the entire multiverse. You know he never once really trusted me with things. I was always his least favourite."

"Slahh!" Oxyn the Big pointed out.

"Yes. You are right, I am quite evil. But it's for good reasons. Why should a half-hearted fool create something so complex and wonderful but do it at half measure. You know who really should be in charge?"

"Mobz?"

"No!" The Explorer said firmly, "me!"

Oxyn the Big scratched his oyster shaped squishy head and thought that he would make an excellent supreme overlord. He would of course be fair, but firm, like a busty blonde bosom.

"Try not to think out loud," said The Explorer, "you'd make a terrifying pair of double Ds."

"Klukl," Oxyn the Big said defiantly and crossed his arms.

The Explorer looked into the depth of the black hole and saw complexity itself, also cats and armed thugs. The spiral rift that churned inside the road sweeper was so much more than just nothingness circling an endless sinkhole. It was power, infinite and unmeasurable. Godly, perhaps, though The Explorer didn't like that phrase, something being 'Godly'. After all he knew God quite well and thought little of the man.

Oxyn the Big grunted and became impatient.

"Very well," The Explorer said at last. "But I need a few things done before I can re-centre the black hole where we want it."

He turned and scooped up three armed thugs from the depths of the vortex and stood them up next to Oxyn the Big. As you'd expect, they were a little shocked.

"Who d'ell are you'den?" one of the thugs said to The Explorer.

"I'm your new boss, of sorts. Tell me, how would you like to search the multiverse, looking for my so-called equal counterparts?"

All three thugs stared blankly at The Explorer as if he'd just spoken Chinese in a Welsh accent.

"Wow," one thug said, "I ain't gots no clue what you just said. But if you's is talking about us gettin' pay, then yer, what we gots to do?"

The Explorer smiled and flicked his hand towards them; all the thugs started to get cramps in their stomachs, wobble from their bones and then they began to change. They grew swollen like Olympic weightlifters, butch and strong, yet somehow hoglike and foul. From their backs, metal formed, cylinders and fuel tanks sprouted, and fire blazed bringing their feet from the floor. Oxyn the Big looked on in dismay, wondering why in all the time he'd worked for The Explorer he'd never been given a jetpack or even fingers? Needless to say, he sulked for a few weeks.

"Hear me now!" The Explorer said loudly. "We're looking for three people. They are The Traveller, The Finder and The Fixer. You are to locate these men and bring them back to me. In one piece!"

The Explorer manifested three life-size mannequins in front of the hellish thugs for them to study, though none was really paying attention. "You are to bring these three to me, and then you will, 'get pay'."

"And how much you goin' pay us boss?"

The Explorer's grasp on money, or even standard economics was poor to say the least. When he used to play poker with the others, any time one would lose it wasn't how much money you could cough up, but how much alcohol you could chug down. It was a wonder that anything got done at all.

"Mm…" The Explorer said, as he thought about it. "How about, say, five pounds each?"

"What?" the thugs shouted in shock.

"You can stuff dat!"

"Yer! We ain't no fools!"

"How about we give you a pounding now, huh?"

The Explorer laughed, flicked his hand at the thug closest to him and a fizz of blue light shot from his fingers, hit the screaming thug and transformed him into a bouquet of tiger lilies. Silence fell as expected.

"Any more questions?" asked The Explorer.

A pause followed. Then, "No, no!"

"No, five pounds works for me boss!"

"Just three guys, right boss, you need shopping or anything picking up?"

"No," The Explorer said.

"Maagly!" Oxyn the big shouted.

"You want fries or wedges with that?"

"Fries!" Oxyn the Big shouted.

Though it is not commonly known, there are a few constants that run through the entirety of the multiverse. Such things as we've covered already like the overpricing of razor blades, the complexity of it all, God's drinking problem. Yet the strangest of all constants, was the word ‘fries’. This meant the same thing in every language, in every universe. It made it a lot easier at government trade deals when talking to the Spitting Globual Pods of Decortis 4, as no one had ever managed to lock down a deal with their kind until a man from Milton Keynes asked them kindly, “Fries?”

“Now go,” The Explorer said mystically, “go and bring back the people I need, and I shall make all your dreams of wealth come true… with five pounds each.”

One after another the warty hogs flew off towards the multicoloured wormhole. Oxyn the Big turned to The Explorer. “Hujik!”

The Explorer frowned. “You don’t need a jetpack!”

The nebula glowed in the distance of the new universe, though huge and vast, the nebula was still rather far away. And although it was only dust and gas swirling around in coincidental patterns, it looked so magnificently delicate.

The Traveller realised that flying at super-over-the-top-ultra-light-speed was a little too much for Norman to handle, and as such, crept along at a snail’s pace of a few thousand miles per hour. Norman enjoyed this much more than he thought he would; much like a dog hanging its large tongue out a car window, Norman dribbled profusely.

The Keeper had agreed to keep in contact with them both if he came across anything else that seemed out of place, though this would be difficult, as The Traveller and the others all knew that the deeper you went into the multiverse the more out of place things you found. “The weirder the better” God used to say. Take for instance the Space Slug of universe 6 trillion and 1, it lives its entire life inside out and eats only radiation that comes from antimatter it finds in quasars. Or even stranger, the Cutlerians, a race of spoon and fork people inhabiting the Sink System of universe 97 million. They believe that when a baby spork was born it was a sign from the great messiah Plate (correctly pronounced Plar-tay) that the silver war would end, and everyone should be responsible for the washing up, not just the bread knives.

Up ahead The Traveller could see a distant blurry brown stain against the blackness; it had to be the asteroid field.

"Not long now," he said to Norman who had begun to feel that same sickness as before. "Do you need to stop for anything?"

Norman closed his eyes and tried to breathe as slowly and relaxing as possible, "I think I'll be okay."

"It's not a problem," The Traveller said kindly.

Norman pondered aloud. "Why are you being so nice to me?"

The Traveller felt a little embarrassed, as he replied, "You stood up for me back there with The Keeper, and you didn't have to."

"But we're friends."

"Are we?"

"Yes!" Norman croaked, then swallowed whatever had visited his mouth. "Yes. I like you a lot."

"Well thank you, I somewhat like you too." The Traveller found this statement a little hard to get out, like regurgitating a brick. "Are you sure you don't want to stop?"

"What for?" Norman asked. "Maybe for some chocolates, or a bottle?"

"Excuse me?"

"Maybe a bottle?" Norman said again. "Wine is quite nice."

"Wine?" The Traveller said feeling his fondness for Norman fade a little. Regrettably, he made the foolish choice of asking what Norman was on about.

"Well," Norman began, "it's customary, isn't it? You go and see someone you haven't seen in ages, so you take a bottle."

"Ah, I see."

"Maybe you could just whip up a pyramid of chocolates like on the adverts," Norman suggested. "Everyone always seems to like those."

"Mm," The Traveller mused.

"Or not? What's the time? Is it after eight yet? cos if it is…"

"No chocolates!" The Traveller said sounding tired. "And no bottle."

"I thought you were friends with The Finder?"

"We are friends," The Traveller said, "but it's not like we haven't seen each other in decades; it's only been around ten billion years. You don't have to get all correct and polite."

God waved at Bud as he took off from Whisker 4b; a world populated entirely by highly intelligent cats. A world that always had problems with Walkies Prime and had been at war with Dog-kind for many, many years — though Bud was just there to cause mischief, not at all for a secret mission as he had told God. Bud was an old dog, experienced and worldly, and as such had over sixty-seven thousand puppies all across the cosmos. Unbeknown to Bud, after telling Princess the Pug that he was there when they took back the capital city of Good Boy from the evil dictator, Bull the Bulldog, and though history is written differently, Bud was the one who singly stopped the Blutterbores of Bactorian Brown from blowing up the Bafter Bank of Burleez (whatever that means), Bud would soon be father to another puppy cross.

"Take care, mate!" God shouted down from the clouds, "if you need a lift just bark, I'll come around when I can."

"Woof!" Bud barked from the ground as a small battalion of Litter-Tray Tanks surrounded him.

"Good plan! See you soon."

With that, God shot off into deep space leaving a whirling vapour trail behind him. His toga flapping madly in the spatial breeze. He'd thought about changing, but the costume he was in had become so comfortable and light that he began to wonder where the Romans went wrong.

Whisker 4b went from a shining ball to a distant spot in the vast blackness within a fraction of point zero, and for a time God simply floated through the stars considering everything that he'd ever done. He lay on his back like a man dazed in a swimming pool after a heavy night in the clubs of Ibiza. His heavenly digestive system, though powerful in its own right, felt the aftermath of a long and heavy drinking session with an old friend. Bud had been right, female dogs led everyone astray.

God blinked, and swore he heard a voice in the back of his mind. And for a moment he began to worry that Sheila had stumbled across his whereabouts; a sobering thought for even an omnipotent being. God sat up, shook off the blur of drunkenness, and whisked a double espresso into his palm, drank the lot and thought that it would've tasted better with a little brandy in it.

"God?"

“Yes?” God said.

“All right?”

God hiccupped and smiled, “Pretty good. You?”

“Yes, thanks…” the voice said, “you know who this is. Right?”

“Mm…” God wondered. The espresso in his hand had morphed into a can of Jovian Ale — 16% — the strong stuff. He bought the curly straw to his mouth and pulled the Ale round his eyes where the straw curved to simulate a pair of extremely hilarious drinking glasses and wondered some more.

“Sheila?”

“Not quite,” the voice said flatly.

“Is it Anne?”

“No,” the voice said, “God, listen, it is I, The Explorer. I—”

“Hey man!” God interrupted happily, “how are you?”

“Yeah, great. Listen, I—”

“Where are you?” God shouted, looking around him blurrily. “Haven’t seen you in bloody ages!”

The Explorer’s voice huffed, “Yes. It’s been a while. Look—”

“Here!” God said smiling, holding out another can in his hand and opening a fresh one for himself. “Come. Sit!”

“God” The Explorer said bluntly, “I need you to listen to me, I have—”

“Aw come on, we’ve got all the bloody time in the world!” God replied slurring his words. “Come and sit with the big guy and we’ll talk history.”

The Explorer appeared from thin air like a frustrated ghost unable to establish a decent haunting, pulled a shovel from his pocket like a murderous magician and stood next to God, arms high above him, grip firm and stable.

“God?”

“Yes matey?” God chuckled drunkenly.

“I have the black hole you’re looking for. I have it and I will use it to become the boss of things. You are no longer in charge!”

The shovel came down on God’s head with a thud, and The Explorer was unsure as to what he was happier about, the fact that his plan was starting to form, or that God was finally quiet, and his drunken ramblings had finally stopped.

Norman held out another bottle for The Traveller, "No!" The Traveller said emptily. "Absinth?"

"What's wrong with that?"

"It doesn't really say, 'I've missed you', does it?"

"Oh," Norman said, puzzled, "what does it say?"

The Traveller plopped it back on the shelf and grunted, "Not that."

"How about brandy?"

"No."

"Gin?"

"Definitely not."

"Maybe some kind of tequila?" Norman asked.

"No! Look, I think I'd be safer going with this."

"Apple Sours?"

The Traveller thought it was silly, but it was the obvious default drink you took when going to visit friends. Were you heading for a nice little drink, or a hardcore, drinks-till-the-morning session? Either way, Apple Sours covered the lot.

"Does it really though?" Norman asked slowly. "I mean, it's bright green. Is it safe?"

"Oh yes indeed," the till attendant of this small alien shop said. "Please, have a look around. I have fireworks in the back."

"No, no," The Traveller said, "we're just looking for a bottle."

"Maybe I could interest you in some discount tobacco?"

"No."

Norman stood by the counter looking over the man towards a half-open door, "What kind of fireworks?"

"The very big kind!"

"No fireworks!" The Traveller said flatly.

"You look like the sparkler type of man to me," the till attendant said observantly.

"Yes!" Norman said, "I do love sparklers. How did you know?"

"Just a feeling. How about a pack of twenty?"

"Yes!"

"And 500g of Old Musky?"

"No," The Traveller said angrily. He walked over holding the bottle of Apple Sours and a packet of biscuits, feeling quite drained. "We'll take these."

"Biscuits?" Norman asked.

"Biscuits."

"Biscuits," the attendant added, "Apple Sours, twenty sparklers and the Old Musky."

"No!"

"Just ten sparklers will do," Norman said.

"No sparklers!" The Traveller shouted. "No Old Musky! I want this bottle, and I want these biscuits!"

"Okay," the attendant said packing the items in a bag, "just five sparklers."

At that, The Traveller took a step back, flicked his hand and turned the man into a plant pot with a small Monkey Puzzle sprouting from the soil. Feeling the strain of it all, he apologised, threw some loose change on the counter, and headed outside.

Norman rubbed his nose and followed. Outside the glow of an alien Aurora Borealis lit up the night sky, and though beautiful and amazing, it was tainted by The Traveller's need to turn innocent beings into plants and flora. Norman thought it was very kind of the man to open his shop even when the sign outside said he'd been closed for half an hour.

"That wasn't very nice."

The Traveller stood looking down at a bottle of Apple Sours and a packet of biscuits and felt that no being with unlimited power should ever have to go through such stress as to what kind of biscuit he should take when seeing a friend after a few million years.

"Are you upset?" Norman asked.

"No," The Traveller replied, "but actually yes. Let's go."

After an hour of flying — very quiet flying — both stood within the swirling mass of the X-rated asteroid field in front of The Finder's front door, and rightly so, Norman was finding it difficult to look anywhere else but at the rock-firm breasts idly floating by. The Traveller managed to hold the bottle and biscuits in one hand, brought the other up to the door, waited a second for the feeling of anger and impatience to leave his lungs, and knocked once.

Norman waited by his side; after a few minutes had passed, he ventured, "Do you want to knock again?"

"I will do, yes," The Traveller replied. "I know he's in there, we have a secret knock to let each other know it's us."

"Okay," said Norman. And went back to staring at the passing busts. A few minutes came and went and nothing much happened, apart from a very flat-chested rock showing up and Norman lost interest. "What's the secret knock?"

The Traveller closed his eyes, thought about turning Norman into a daisy, or maybe a few amaryllis, and considered God's foul mood regarding said choices.

"First, I knock."

"Okay."

"Then we wait for a bit, and then I knock twice."

"Right," Norman said nodding, then a moment later asked, "how long do we wait between the knocks?"

"Three weeks."

"Oh."

"Yes."

"Question…"

The Traveller shook a little. "Yes!"

"Say one day, The Finder orders some stuff from somewhere. I don't know, like a new window. Or maybe a new door? Though saying that, his door seems to be well kept, and his windows are really nice and clean. Modern too! Plus—"

"Norman!"

"Sorry. I mean, how does he know that it's you, or not you? I mean, if it's not you, he wouldn't know, right? cos of the knocks?"

The Traveller thought for a bit, and as puzzling as Norman may have been at times, The Traveller was getting good at translating the verbal garbage that he came out with. He rubbed his head, looked down at the bottom of the door where a pile of unopened boxes and letters were — one of which had a date of a few hundred years back on it — threw the Apple Sours and biscuits to the ground and went inside.

“Are you sure you don’t want to wait a bit longer?” Norman asked.

“No!”

The small cottage that The Finder had built for himself using nothing but limitless powers of the mind was shockingly normal. Quaint and loving, it was a home that echoed sensibility and a long-lasting romance with the acquiring and collecting of many small yet curious things.

After God had all but finished with The Finder, The Finder had considered changing his name to The Retired, but knew that that name had already been taken, plus with the long-winded and maze-like system that one would have to navigate, The Finder found that in the end, he was quite fond of his name.

Norman eyed the walls that were covered with strangely drawn star-maps, planetary systems and family pictures. Each ledge and every shelf had items from every part of the multiverse stacked and squeezed into every space available. On the barely visible floor, wooden furniture sat everywhere like a hoarder’s front room, with every table and chair also covered with small trinkets. Nothing but the ticking of a tall standing clock with twenty-four hours, thirty-seven minutes and twenty-two seconds on its face filled the living room with noise. The crackle of wood on a fire in some other room vaguely jostled the eardrum.

“Nice place,” Norman said.

“Come over here. I think I’ve found something.”

Norman laughed, “If you were to find something it would be in The Finder’s house, of course.”

Just then The Finder appeared from another room holding a steaming mug of hot chocolate, topped with cream and marshmallows.

“In fact,” he said, “everything in my house has already been found. So, you can’t really find anything in here, only re-find it. And even then, it’s not really re-finding it, as I’ve shined and polished everything three times till it’s all been properly refined, so indeed, you could be right, by finding it all for the first time again.”

Norman smiled; The Traveller frowned, “You two will get on nicely.”

‘Like a house on fire’ he wanted to say fighting the urge like the lexicographer trying to kick a three-hundred-word a-day habit.

"Where was the second knock?" The Finder asked coming to The Traveller's side. "I thought we agreed on that years ago. You know you can't just go and change things without my knowing about it! It's rude."

"We haven't got time to stand around while you count the weeks between the knocks. You know you've got unopened letters and stuff out the front. Some of it could be important you know."

"Like what?" The Finder chuckled. "A late water bill, perhaps? Or maybe there's an SA100 that I've not filled out and now the taxman is after me."

Norman smiled; he liked The Finder. He seemed a bit more upbeat and chirpier about things than The Traveller.

"You know what I mean. There could be a postcard that I sent you that you never got."

"And did you ever send me a postcard?" The Finder asked.

"I could've done!"

"The only thing I've ever received from any of you lot was a birthday card from The Keeper wishing me a happy forty-five septillionth birthday, and yes," he said holding up a hand, "though I may at sometimes lie about my age to make myself younger and more appealing, it's the thought that counts."

"I'm sorry," The Traveller said innocently, "there's a bottle outside that I got for you."

"Of?"

"Apple Sours."

"Mm, any biscuits? You can't have sours without biscuits, see. It's kinda the rule."

Norman, in a moment of precognitive thought, marched outside and grabbed the bottle and biscuits and was happily handing them over just as The Finder turned to see him shutting the door.

"Here you go!"

The Finder looked at the packaging. "Plain biscuits?"

"Yes."

"They didn't have any chocolate ones?"

"No," Norman said sadly.

"Well, I guess they'll do. Please," he said gesturing randomly about his living room. "Take a seat. Me-Costa-Soo-Costa!"

"It's *'mi casa es su casa'*."

"Whatever."

"You never were any good with languages," The Traveller said with a smile. "Even when we were at school you kept failing language."

Norman toppled a few boxes and stacks of paper off a chair and took a seat holding a small alien creature he'd found in the fridge on his lap.

"I didn't think you went to school."

"Everyone goes to school," The Traveller said.

"I didn't," Norman said glumly.

"The best ones don't," said The Finder.

"So, what language did you struggle with?" Norman asked stroking the scaly critter.

"Just language. You know, like in general."

"I was tongue tied!" The Finder exclaimed.

"Your tongue was four sizes too big."

"The ladies loved it…"

"…So I've heard."

"I like it here," Norman said. "You guys are funny. You seem to get along more than you did with The Keeper."

"You saw The Keeper?"

"Yes," The Traveller said. "I needed to see him to find out where you were hiding."

"Well," The Finder said with a puff, "if in the future there's a get-together, please let me know."

"Of course. If you open your mail every now and again."

"Ha!" The Finder laughed. "No promises."

Thomas Moore sat at his desk feeling pretty good about himself after relieving a few road sweeper drivers from their permanent duties, though he was a little concerned that he'd not seen that crazy nut ball who flew in and took the brand-new sweeper away for quite some time now, after going through all outcomes and situations, he came to realise that whatever happened, it was definitely not his fault.

"Poppy, how's my day looking?"

Poppy, who was not his secretary, shouted through to his office, “I’m not your secretary!”

Thomas never liked her attitude, though her attitude wasn’t the reason why he had invited her to have some good old-fashioned slap ‘n tickle on his small wobbly desk.

“Fantasy roleplay is extra,” Poppy said slipping on one of her shoes she’d found sitting on top of a filing cabinet, “so’s bondage and fetish. Would you like to see a menu?”

“No, no,” Thomas said standing, “maybe next time.” He took a money clip from his pocket that looked as healthy as a prison bar of soap, pulled a few notes from it and helped Poppy with her coat. “Perhaps next time when I call you, you can dress like a construction worker?”

“Yeah” Poppy said counting her pay, “sure. Whatever.”

Poppy left the small metal container, which somehow had been classed as a Main Site Office and walked straight for the bus stop to catch the 408 to her next client. The door swung back as Thomas took his seat again, master of his own universe. Shunting a few P45s together within his hands and feeling quite light-headed after Poppy’s forty-five-minute special, he’d completely missed the two great lumps of meat that were now standing at his desk side. One of which was holding onto the door, having failed to open it properly and decided to simply rip it from its fastenings.

“Oi!” one of the hogs said with a grunt.

Thomas jumped, then screamed a little, then picked up a plastic ruler from the desk and attempted to simulate a stationary samurai. For a moment he felt gutsy, then after another moment he felt flatulence — maybe a bit too gutsy.

“Sit down!” the other hog said throwing the door to one side. “Know who this is?” he shouted thrusting a mannequin’s head on the desk. Though this false head had no hat, no hair or any other details on it, it did somehow resemble The Traveller quite a bit. Unfortunately, Thomas Moore had never seen The Traveller before, plus, due to the lightness of his head and the pumping of his blood — both due to Poppy and the hogs — Thomas slowly folded like a failed paper swan in the corner of his office and curled up on the floor.

“Idiot!”

"What I do?"

"Not you!" the hog said to the other. "The guy."

"So now what?"

"First," the hog said confidently, "we trash the joint. Then we keep looking."

Norman pulled back the top drawer of a filing cabinet that stood in one of the many corners of the vast study. All around him there were artefacts from everywhere. He thought that this room looked more like the great Cleminetinium Library, though he realised that in all the minutes on Earth he'd spent he'd never once visited Prague, and in fact had no idea what the great Cleminetinium Library was.

A through to Z, folders lined up that he flicked through, casually stopping at the letter T when one particular piece of paper stood out. He slid it out and inspected it slowly.

"What's this then?" he asked cheerfully.

The Finder left what he was doing with The Traveller at another desk and came to his side.

"Ah" he said, "that's a very important map indeed. Please be very careful and don't get any crumbs on it."

Norman smiled swallowing that last bit of his biscuit and brushed some crumbs from his mouth.

"I won't."

"It's a map," The Finder went on, "that shows all the time holes in a universe. Completely pointless, of course."

Norman liked the look of it. It seemed very pretty and complex, so as The Finder went back to his desk, Norman rolled it up and slid it down his trousers. "Return the map before I turn you into an avocado."

"Sorry," Norman replied.

"Stop messing around," The Traveller said bluntly holding up a few scrolls against the small lamp in front of him. "Seriously, why in all creation you still carry scrolls is beyond me. You've heard of a desktop, right?"

"Yes," The Finder replied happily, taking each scroll back with intended care and checking for greasy fingerprints. "I have heard of it. Have you ever heard of sentimental value?"

"What's so special about a piece of paper that says, 'Secret Entrance to the Universe of a Thousand Circus Mirrors'?"

"I'll have you know that's a one of a kind!" Hearing this Norman became very aware of which drawer The Finder placed it in, and then tried to memorise the lock combination to the drawer itself.

"Anyway," The Finder said turning to another desk, "I think what you're after is over here." The Finder stood in front of another desk, though, to everyone else in the room — Norman, The Traveller and a small pack of freshly hatched aliens ganging up on the house cat — it was completely bare and free of clutter. In fact, it had been the only space bigger than a chair that was not packed with things that The Traveller had come to call 'useless junk'.

"Don't tell me!" Norman said excitedly. "It's some sort of invisibility cloak?"

"Well—"

"Yes. That must be it" Norman went on. "It's obvious."

"What's obvious?" The Traveller said as he came to The Finder's side. Norman, like some sort of invisibility cloak inspector, drew his eye closer to the desk's top as if he could really see something there.

"Don't tell me," Norman repeated. "We take the cloak, travel to the Fungal Empire home world of Potato 9—"

"Portobello 9…"

"Right! Sneak in undercover, unseen, infiltrate the home world, knock out all the guards, rescue The Fixer, take back the black hole and make everything right again."

"Weeell," the Traveller said sarcastically.

"Blimey."

"Do you even need our help?" The Traveller said.

"Don't be so silly," The Finder added. "Invisibility cloak, well, I've never heard so much silliness."

"Oh," Norman said feeling a bit deflated. Just when he thought he had a grasp on the unexpected and strange, things became dull and boring again.

"Oh indeed," The Traveller said. He looked at The Finder and both shared a rolling of the whites as if Norman was a simple inexperienced teenager. "Invisibility…"

"Sneaking in..."

"And rescuing people," The Traveller said, then added, "actually, there will be some rescue-type stuff involved."

"Yes," said The Finder, "and the sneaking-in part too."

"Yeah. Definitely some sneaking in."

"Mm," replied The Finder. "Maybe even a bit of rendering guards unconscious?"

"Perhaps..."

"But definitely no invisibility cloaks of any type."

"Definitely not," agreed The Traveller.

A moment passed, it was a silence that felt like a long wait for a punchline, then Norman said, "So what is it?"

"Well," The Traveller began.

The Finder took a deep breath. "It's an infinite compressive multiversal storage desk. In each drawer there's a different multiverse."

The Traveller nodded as if this were common knowledge.

The Finder continued, "In each drawer there's an infinite number of places that are stored simultaneously in one spot from an infinite number of universes, each separated into their individual relevance marked on each drawer."

"Exactly," The Traveller added, "simple."

"Simple," agreed The Finder. "If you want to go anywhere, all you have to do is climb into one of the drawers and you'll be where you want to go."

"Simple," said The Traveller.

"Simple," agreed The Finder.

Norman nodded and looked down at the desk drawer next to his leg and thought very long and hard as to what would be the best way to fit in a drawer no bigger than his left foot. Perhaps some kind of calzone style would be the best? He wasn't sure, but smiled anyway. "How do I get in it?"

The Finder huffed and laughed like he'd just asked how to breathe, "It's a distortion field set at the speed of light to warp all matter and antimatter into whatever shape is needed."

"Simple," The Traveller said feeling like he'd been designated to one word. "Anyway," he went on, kneeling down and sweeping a palm over its wooden top, “where d’you find it? I thought you threw it out years ago.”

“I did,” The Finder said, “but I found it again.” Norman smiled to himself. “And it was actually the big fella that threw it out. No sense of humour sometimes.”

“I can’t blame him. You did keep hiding his car keys in the top drawer.”

“It was only a laugh!”

“Mm.”

“You know I can find anything.”

“I know. Right then,” The Traveller said turning to Norman, “you ready?”

“Ready?” Norman asked rhetorically. “Have we finished here?”

The Traveller smiled, shook The Finder’s hand passing him a large pouch of Old Musky, and jumped into the top drawer, dragging Norman in by his sleeve, both nearly hitting God’s car keys on the way in. Their bodies contorted and pulled, warped and twisted in all ways. Each cell of their beings tore apart, fizzed and whizzed turning into pure light and energy, spiralled and bounced off nothingness. In front of the group of molecules that happened to be Norman’s eye a light began to shine up ahead within the distorted blackness. Behind them The Finder shut the drawer; he stood for a moment in the quietness of his house wondering how long it would be till he saw any of his friends again, then spotted his cat chasing a group of small aliens across the study floor.

“Jerry! Get back here!”

God awoke to the stinging feeling of chains around his wrists and ankles, though he was more unhappy with the feeling of aches and distortion that wobbled in his head; even God can overdo it at times. In front of him The Explorer sat at his desk occasionally looking his way and drawing something down on a piece of paper.

“Christ!” God said loudly; it hurt his head. “You don’t want me to strip down, do you?”

The Explorer paused, placed his pen down on the desk and expressed no jovial reaction whatsoever. “You think that this is all a joke, don’t you, ‘Big Man’?”

"Hey, steady on now." God burped. "I've lost a few pounds at least in the last century." His vision steadied slightly, though not all the way, but enough to realise that the whirling colours and dots of light were not in fact his eyes but the wormhole above him. He took a curious look around him and noticed that he'd never been to wherever he was. "I don't recognise this place, where are we?"

The Explorer stood and came to God, marvelling at the chains he'd crafted to hold a God.

"We are in the space between spaces, in the none-space of none-space."

"Right." God smiled. He wanted to burp again but the bile taste in his mouth was a bit off-putting. "So, where's that then exactly?"

The Explorer walked slowly around God as he sat on the floor, helpless, tied up and unable to move.

"You will not escape. So, don't even try."

"Escape? Bloody hell, mate, I'd have a problem trying to stand at the moment."

"Then you should begin to understand that you are beaten."

"Please," God said worriedly, "don't bloody beat anything, my head is pounding as it is. Any chance of a bit of water?"

"Water?" The Explorer exclaimed. "Don't you understand? I've trumped you!"

God tried to look up at the top of his head to check his hair; what he didn't need was a flailing uncontrollable blondish-grey wig taped onto his head. "You will soon be nothing but a thought, floating aimlessly around without direction."

"Hey!" God said angrily, "how do you know what I did last night? Whatever Bud told you, it's all lies."

The Explorer became quite obviously impatient and understandably irritated.

"I've won, you fool!"

"...The lottery?"

"The multiverse!"

"Come again?"

"The multiverse! The entire multiverse!"

"This multiverse?"

"Of course, this one!"

"Right. Obviously."

"So?" The Explorer asked, "have anything to say?"

God focused for a minute with a concentrated look, staring outwards into the endless speckled horizon of The Explorer's none-space of none-space. Finally, he looked up meeting The Explorer's gaze with rival steadiness, opened his mouth, and "Brrrpppp." Then he rolled backwards in a drunken heap, coming to think that trying to keep up with a ten-thousand-year-old battle-hardened dog at a bar that only served Boggle-Rotter Chugdowns was a bad idea.

The Explorer shook his head.

"Idiot."

Norman opened his eyes and thought that if he could compare what just happened to anything it would have to be a roller coaster and came to think that if he had half the chance in the future, he would definitely not at any stage in his life make the free choice to get on one. His stomach had taken a beating, and although after all the things he'd been through recently his stomach should've got used to high speeds, in fact it hadn't in the slightest.

"Are you okay?"

"Who said that?"

"It was me."

"Who?" Norman asked standing up in the pitch blackness.

"Me!" The Traveller said stating the obvious.

"Oh. I can't see you."

"I know."

"Where are we?"

"I don't know."

The Traveller held his arms out in front of him; the darkness so painfully pitch-black it felt as though he were being swallowed by nothingness itself. The Traveller took a few steps forwards, shuffling with care. If the desk drawer had done its job, which of course it had, then all of his supreme omnipotent powers would be absolutely no use at all; even his floral-changing abilities.

In the distance of the surrounding nothingness the faint sound of thudding was apparent, and it was surely getting closer. Something then shouted a few words that were most definitely not English, and all the lights began to switch on. The blinding blur from one overhead caught Norman off guard, causing him to stumble a little, stepping straight into a small toilet in the corner of the room.

"My shoes!"

Outside the cell more lights began to flicker on in succession. The Traveller took hold of the prison bars in his hands and looked through towards the prison interior. It was called a prison, of course, but not in the sense that one might expect. There were cells, thousands in fact, but they weren't lined up in the norm; they were dotted and randomly placed. Everything seemed to jostle slightly, the walls breathing as if alive, and everything except the hardy prison bars themselves were made from a squelchy, slimy substance that The Traveller hoped he would never have to see again.

"So?" Norman said having a peek through the bars, "where are we?"

The Traveller sighed, and actually looked genuinely concerned, as he answered, "Portobello 2."

"Great!" Norman said. "So, we've made it. Where's The Fixer?"

The Traveller gestured outwards, his manner a tad defeatist.

"Well then. Let's get him. Open the door…"

"It's locked."

"Can you unlock it?"

"No."

"Can you break it?"

"I have no powers here."

"Can you turn the bars into vines, or something?"

"I have no powers!"

"Not even a bit of ivy?"

"No!"

"Grapes?"

"Norman!"

"Right. Sorry." Norman went back to standing quietly, he was good at that, though he hadn't really practised it much, if at all. Then, a spontaneous reaction happened in his mind: a bustle of chemicals collided with more chemicals, sending electrical signals through pathways and lobes, and thus Norman had had an idea.

"I could use my finger?"

"Pardon?"

"My finger. To unlock the barred door."

Okay, The Traveller thought, *it couldn't hurt to try.*

"It can't hurt to try." That sounded silly. "What good is your finger going to be?"

"Here," Norman said, "look, it's my finger." He held out his finger that surprisingly wasn't attached to his hand but was sitting in the palm of his other. "All this time and I'd forgotten that I was made out of clay."

"So, what do you suggest?" The Traveller said bitterly. "Maybe we could sculp some lovely teapots for the prison guards? Or maybe a vase or two."

Norman laughed, "No, nothing that fun." He knelt down to where the keyhole was and began to squash his clay finger inside. After a few turns and wiggles, the cell door made a clunky plant *bong!* and creaked open. Norman stood and smiled, placing his finger back onto his knuckle, holding his index out for The Traveller to look at. It was now the shape of a key.

"You see?"

The Traveller smiled. "Simple."

"Simple."

The prison was exactly how Norman had thought it would be, that being unimaginably big; it was a fungal planet, after all. He thought that ants and other colony living insects must've taken some pointers from its design. In every direction, seemingly endless tunnels ventured off everywhere, peppered with cell doors. The smell was much like a compost heap: damp, foul and littered with worms. Though the worms that lived inside Portobello 2 weren't your average sort. One was sitting curled up by a cell door as Norman and The Traveller ran by. It was holding up a sign that read *'Will Decompose Veg for Food'*.

"Poor thing," Norman said, "looked miserable."

The Traveller nodded, though his concerns weren't really focused on the well-being of a fungal worm. They carried downwards through the endless labyrinthian maze; every so often, a fresh gust of stale hot air rushed past them. Though entirely revolting and foul, the prison fungal planetoid of Portobello 2 had one feature that made it the envy of its planetary siblings. It'd formed itself in such a way that the tunnels and vast caverns under its crusty skin sucked in natural-forming atmosphere — a kind of global air conditioning — and thus, reducing the overheads for deodorant.

Norman huffed along, red in the face. He had to stop for a small rest. Even though he was in his billioneens — a very troublesome age God had observed — he wasn't the most athletic of sorts. The Traveller however was in much better shape, even in his infinite trillions.

"I pay ten pound a month for a full gym membership," The Traveller said, "I think that maybe you should too."

"How long…" Norman gasped, "how long have you been going?"

The Traveller cracked his fingers and began to do a few stretches and squats, as if showing that he could somehow prove that he was fit as a fiddle.

"Every day for the last million years," he said confidently, "today's leg day."

"What's your favourite machine?"

"Well," The Traveller said caught off guard, "well, it's the one you sit on. You know. You sit down, and kind of pull these cables…"

Norman looked at him expectantly with open eyes.

"You know, the arm one. Does your chest too."

"What's it called?"

The Traveller thought for a moment. "The arm 'n chest machine."

"And what days do you do that?"

Norman breathed deeply and was ready to go again.

"Monday."

"Today's Monday though. I thought today was leg day."

"Yeah!" The Traveller said reassuringly. "That's what I said. Arm and leg day."

Norman narrowed his gaze suspiciously.

"You don't go to the gym at all, do you?"

The Traveller stopped squatting and shook his head, "No…" he said quietly. "But! I do pay a membership fee."

"Why if you don't go? If you pay ten pound a month, that's one hundred and twenty pounds a year, so you've wasted a hundred and twenty million pounds so far. You could've bought a car or something."

Though The Traveller hadn't really the need for a car, or any kind of transport at all, he could see that Norman had a point.

"Fine. I went there once to check it out, it was Anne's idea for me to start getting fit. I didn't want to do it but there was this muscle-bound lump taking me round, showing me stuff, and well, I didn't want to look pathetic. So, I got a ten pound a month deal that included the use of both tennis courts and spa."

"Do you play tennis?"

"No."

"Oh."

"Yep." The Traveller stared at nothing and said, "I miss Anne."

"Me too!"

"Mm. Probably in different ways though."

"Probably."

"Come on, I'm sure The Fixer's here somewhere."

At the end of one rather slimy and misty tunnel, a cell was housed so far away from any other that a small fungal railway had been grown to escort the prison guards back and forth to save them from walking. Walking had actually been a fairly new trick that fungus did, and so most fungal empire employees hadn't managed to get the hang of it yet.

Inside the cell The Fixer sat; in one hand, he held a small tube of superglue while in the other he held an even smaller plastic wheel. With his tongue sticking out from the side of his mouth, and his lensed glasses over his eyes to zoom in on the intricate piece, he slowly moved the wheel closer to the plastic axle. Every movement was critical; every breath he took could mean the misplacement of another equally important part. Here it came, millimetres from the axle.

"Barbel, barbel, barble!" the prison guard shouted at The Fixer.

"Please!" The Fixer said frustrated, "can you not do that again. I'm trying to work!"

"Brickly!"

"I don't know what you're talking about," The Fixing said placing the plastic model on the bench in front of him. "I don't understand you!"

"Plonky!"

"I… don't… know… what… you're… saying!" he shouted loudly. The prison guard laughed menacingly from outside the cell.

"Gree!" the guard smiled.

"Whatever!" the Fixer said going back to his plastic model. He was running out of calm; not only did he have the only prison guard who wouldn't leave him alone, but to keep himself company, he'd been given the only thing that he couldn't fix. It had been a silly present that The Keeper had given him for a birthday, and for the life of him he couldn't finish building it. A plastic model tank that had about a gazillion little parts which had to be individually placed in the right order. The Fixer had done many things in his life; once he mended the fabric of space after a house party got out of hand, and another time he fixed a leaking blue giant star that got punctured after a game of darts, but this, this plastic model tank would be the death of him. "Wretched plastic abomination! Stick you piece of…"

A sound of falling glass echoed from the depth of the congealing tunnel, and just at the right time too. The guard, who had become very used to doing almost nothing, turned with the readiness of a startled deer. He held his giant club in one hand at the ready, took a few steps from the comfort of the cell door, and shouted, "Hraw!" which, although said loudly and aggressively, actually meant, "I, Bung the Quite Fearsome, have this huge weapon at hand, have gone through all the relevant training and have certificates to prove it. Not only this, but I am highly skilled in the art of negotiation, have a degree in cooking, and can speak all three known languages. So, if you feel like you are brave enough, please, step out and confront your enemy!"

"What did he say?"

The Traveller didn't know, because, as we have already covered, all omnipotence is lost when in close proximity to the Portobello System.

"I don't know."

You see.

"So, what's the plan now?"

This, The Traveller hadn't quite thought of; being so used to thinking at least four hundred years ahead, having to actually plan by the second was a skill that had not been sharpened.

"Do we have a plan?" Norman asked worriedly. "I mean, throwing the glass bowl we stole from the out-of-work fungal worm was a good idea to distract the guard, but now he's distracted, what do we do?"

"Mm," The Traveller said, "you have a point."

Both peered round the mushy side of the small curve on the wall where they had chosen to hide, and as they thought, Bung the Quite Fearsome was striding over their way, slowly.

"We haven't got much time. Probably ten minutes at his speed."

"He's quite good at the walking thing," Norman pointed out. "Nearly has the old 1-2 down." Norman looked again, "I mean 1-2-3."

A distant memory from school popped into The Traveller's head, a time back in school when they were being taught the problems that come with mould and other nasty things, and wondered…

"Can I reshape you?" he asked.

"Okay."

Bung the Quite Fearsome gripped his club tighter as he closed in on the sound, though, importantly it has to be noted how he gained his name. In the prison of Portobello 2 there had been no real breakouts for many, many years and because of that, it had been deemed totally valid to appoint Bung his new title, Bung the Quite Fearsome.

In all honesty though, he should've been called Bung the Runny Nose.

Norman abruptly stood out from the corner with his arms relocated on his hips and his head on his knee, stepping in the path of Bung the Quite Fearsome, who nearly dropped his club right there and then. And Norman, at a loss for words, and forgetting what The Traveller told him to say, said, "Raw" quite casually. The Traveller slapped his face with embarrassment.

"You're an oomycete," The Traveller whispered.

"You're an oo-me-feet!" Norman said loudly.

"Oomycete!"

"Right, sorry. An oomycete."

Bung the Quite Fearsome stopped and looked at Norman confused, flicking up one of his many eyebrows, "Uh?"

"Tell him you're a fungicide."

Norman looked at The Traveller who was hiding badly, nodded and repeated his line: "I'm a fungicide!" and added, "woo" sounding like a ghost as he waved his arms in the air. The sound of The Traveller's hand hitting his face echoed once again.

"Uh?" Bung the Quite Fearsome said.

The Traveller just about had enough and decided to stop hiding and come out instead.

"Look," he said angrily to Bung the Quite Fearsome, "he's meant to be an oomycete, which we all know, we who have been to school, occupy both saprophytic and pathogenic lifestyles, and include some of the most notorious pathogens to plants, such as late blight of potato and sudden oak death!"

Bung the Quite Fearsome cocked his head and scratched his cheek pondering what the little man was talking about.

"Okay," The Traveller said holding his hands up, "he's a fungicide, right." He spotted a root on the side of the tunnel that looked thin. He ripped it free, pulled Bung the Quite Fearsome over to one side and began to draw a rough picture in the slime on the floor.

"So. You, yes, are this…" he pointed, "and him there, the fungicide, is that…" he gestured. "So, he is able to kill fungus, right?" he said, pointing to the small picture on the floor and then scraping over it. "So, you have to run, yes?" The Traveller moved two of his fingers like a thrashing pair of legs. "You understand…? you run?"

Bung the Quite Fearsome didn't understand and was beginning to get a bit short with it all, especially when he saw Norman taking his arms and head off and placing them back in their rightful spots.

"Norman!" The Traveller shouted, "you've ruined it. Now it's obvious that you're not a fungicide."

"Sorry."

Bung the Quite Fearsome picked up the root and was drawing a picture on the floor. Everything had upset him about this situation, but mostly it was The Traveller scratching the drawing away. The Traveller, seeing the big Fungaloid's interest in the slime drawing and noticing his giant club sitting on the floor, picked it up with everything he had and smashed it over Bung the Quite Fearsome's head.

Norman smiled, “So that’s the guard knocked out. The plan is coming together nicely.”

The Traveller rolled his eyes and dropped the club, he was surprised to hold it and feel its weight; having power that stretches to untold distances, then having them clogged up by sentient damp can have an effect. Having once picked up a moon in a fierce game of marbles, it was a bit shocking to feel weight at all.

The Fixer had seen the entire scene play out and found it all rather boring.

“Still not finished that then?”

“I’m not rushing anything,” The Fixer said.

Norman placed his finger back on his hand and opened the cell door for The Traveller.

“Hello.”

The Fixer looked up, did nothing again, and went back to his wheel.

“I said, hello,” Norman repeated happily.

“You’ll get no answer from him,” The Traveller said. “He’s in a world of his own.”

Though it was true, The Fixer had no desire to break silence and talk to Norman, let alone register that he was there, he did shuffle a little when Norman stood over him ogling his plastic model.

“You haven’t done much?”

“I’m not rushing!” The Fixer said angrily.

Norman bit his lip. “Sorry.”

“He’s only been doing it for an aeon or two.”

“It hasn’t been that long.”

“Can I get you anything?” Norman asked kindly.

The Fixer huffed and turned to Norman, “Bog snakes!”

“Excuse me?”

“Bog snakes.”

The Traveller shook his head. “No idea.”

“Nervous looking,” The Fixer continued, “shaky rotten, up-the-back-trumpet, do-what-you-like, bog snakes!”

“I don’t follow…”

The Fixer held up the plastic model to Norman and frowned.

"I've stuck the wheel on backwards..." at which The Traveller laughed uncontrollably, at which The Fixer threw the plastic model on the ground over his shoulder, at which Norman picked it up placing it back on the table feeling like The Readjuster was a totally warranted name.

"Bloody bohemian belly diving draft excluding bog snakes."

"Are you finished?" The Traveller asked flatly.

"What are bog snakes?" questioned Norman.

"I'm finished."

"Good. Right, we both know there's no way we can get out of here without transport, so have you any ideas?"

"The radio," The Fixer said pointing to his workbench. "I can pick up the daily staff announcements on it. Seems pointless now you knocked out the only staff member on this planetoid."

The Fixer leant over his messy workbench and picked up a small radio that one Fungaloid guard must have acquired from Earth at some point in the distant past. It was rusted and beyond recognisable, yet still had a sticker on it saying, *'Made in Taiwan'*. He flicked it on, and a static fizzed the air; slowly, he rolled the dial through the frequencies; the obvious tone of folk music came through...

The folk music faded away into static once more, then a moment later the radio began to speak seemingly randomly, *"Die rote zone ist fur ankunfte! Die gelbe zone ist fur abfahrten!"*

"Is that German?" The Traveller asked.

"Just listen!" The Fixer said turning the volume up.

"...La zone jaune concerne les departs..."

"French."

"Shhh..."

"The red zone is for arrivals; the yellow zone is for departures."

"There you are!" The Fixer said with delight. "Told you."

It was well known that Fungle-kind knew of only three dialects, those being French, German and English. A complete shock in all honesty seeing how they invaded and took over many, many planets throughout the multiverse without a care for the local populous, yet it was only when one Fungal Admiral visited a beer festival years before hand in Munich and became very close with a French-speaking English exchange student whom he thoroughly enjoyed in a bacon sandwich.

Their own language was not classed as speech at all as most Fungaloids grunted, wheezed and snorted trying to make small talk. This can be said to be the main reason why there were no great novels or plays in Funglees, and why most meetings between fungal beings ended in one being deader than the other.

God weighed up his options, calculating his next twelve moves wisely. He had known for many years that The Explorer was indeed a worthy foe, a cunning being who had graduated from Cunning University with a master's degree in cunning, deceit and blackmail. A few reasons why God liked him so much. He exhaled, his eyes jostled from one side to another, huffed and pondered. He questioned his chances and pondered some more. He thought long and hard about…

"Can you just get on with it!" The Explorer shouted. "You take so long doing everything!"

"I'm bloody thinking mate," God pointed out. Then nodded and gestured with his nose, "That prawn, move it over there please."

"It's called a pawn, and you can't do that!"

"And why not?"

"Because! It can only move one space and one diagonal when taking a piece. You're trying to do an illegal move."

"Since when?"

"Since always…"

"Right then," God said again. He shuffled on the floor; though still in chains, he tried to make himself as comfortable as he could. "How's about the little horse fellow over there? Put it by that little guy."

"Just here?" The Explorer said moving God's knight.

"Please…"

"Aha! Then, you see, I have you!" The Explorer laughed. He moved a bishop over the board with two smug-looking fingers, smirking like an eight-year-old who'd taken a swig of his dad's beer without being caught.

God leant back, took a long look at the chessboard and said, "If you move my prawn here, I think that's check mate."

The Explorer narrowed his eyes, stared for a bit, then flung the board up in the air sending white and black pieces everywhere.

"You are the worst!"

"Hey, look, it was probably beginner's luck. Play again?"

"No," The Explorer said in a tone more bitter than citrus peel. "You ruin everything!"

"Aw come on mate. Just another game."

"No!"

"Please?"

"No!" The Explorer shouted. "You have been fooling around with this multiverse, and everything in it for too long! It is not right that you are in charge."

"Has this got something to do with Sheila by any chance?" God asked. The Explorer went quiet. "You took it far too personally, mate."

"She saw me first!"

"If you weren't going to talk to her…"

"I sent you over to talk to her for me! You were my wingman."

"It's not my fault. She just liked me more. I did say that you were interested but she wanted the big guy. What was I meant to do?"

"Say 'no, my friend likes you'. Whatever happened to 'bros before hoes?'"

"Careful now!" God said defensively. "Yes, at times she may slap on a bit too much makeup, and perhaps some of her clothes are a bit revealing. But my Sheila is not a hoe. So, say sorry at once."

The Explorer turned and faced God with the look of a man that knew victory was close.

"When I'm in charge, she will want nothing to do with a dropout like you. And I will have the girl, and all her 'revealing' clothes."

"C'mon" God said, "seriously, she'd eat you alive."

The Fixer grabbed what things he'd had on him at the time of his capture and turned to leave his cell discarding a half-finished plastic model on the bench behind him.

"You not bringing that?" asked The Traveller.

"Just don't start," The Fixer replied bluntly.

Outside the cell, Norman decided that he would help as many inmates of Portobello 2 to escape as he could. Of course, though The Traveller had told him in direct and colourful words that it was a bad idea, and their departure of the prison planet was vital, he couldn't stop Norman from doing as he wanted.

Norman sped down the squishy unstable corridor to the closest cell that he could find with a prisoner inside, readying his index finger for some professional keyhole fondling.

"Jesus Christ!" Skip said standing from a strange, disfigured bed in the corner of his cell while a young boy lay on the floor next to him admiring his badge collection.

"Hello," Norman said happily. "I'll have you out in a second."

"Thank you," Skip said. "I didn't know if the troop elders would send anyone to look for us… you know…" he gestured over his shoulder to where little Jonny was humming tunelessly. "You know how he his. Always getting us into all kinds of trouble. Last week, he insisted on seeing The Amazing Flute Boy take down his arch nemesis, The Conductor. It didn't end well."

Norman swung open the cell and smiled. "I'm afraid I've no idea what you mean. I've come here with The Traveller to breakout The Fixer so that we can put the black hole back in place."

"Right," Skip said, a little confused. "…We're Brown Bears. It's like scouts with less saluting. From the superhero planet, Super Alpha Prime."

"Right," Norman said equally confused.

"Anyway," Skip went on, "I guess it doesn't matter. We were on an outing when we were captured by these fungi, monster, creature things. Took me and little Jonny… and well, I guess that doesn't matter either… Jonny!"

"Will I be getting my Off-Planet Survival Badge?" little Jonny asked as he walked over flicking through his Brown Bears member booklet.

"Never mind that," Skip said.

Norman smiled again and pointed towards where he knew The Traveller and Fixer would be and sent them both on their way, then carried on searching for more inmates.

It would be fair to say that The Fungal Empire had put the legwork in when it came to capturing prisoners. The diversity of beings that had found themselves behind squelchy bars showed off the Empire's outward and devastating reach throughout the multiverse. One after another Norman freed creatures that had evolved on planets far beyond his own imagination.

The hive mind entity from Nabtoo 7 thanked Norman about twenty times as each individual being ran out from their holdings; the great Snaillix Worrier from Lettucia B bowed to him then slid unevenly out of sight. More complex life forms than Norman could shake a stick at thanked him as he went cell to cell offering freedom like an ex-convict selling toiletries at your front door.

"Oi!" a voice shouted from behind Norman, "C'mon! Over here. Let us out!"

"I'm coming," Norman replied and brought his finger to the keyhole.

"Well, lah-di-dah!" another voice responded sarcastically. "Look at him with his magic finger."

"He's only trying to help!"

"Oi," the second voice said coldly. "Stop 'trying', and just help."

Norman unlocked the cell easily and pulled the door free. From inside a tall being lurched forwards from the dark and loomed over him; two heads sprouting from one body eyed him up and down.

"Well?"

"Well… what?" Norman asked.

"Blimey," one head said rolling its eyes. "Is this a hero's rescue or are you knew to this?"

"Cut the guy some slack. He's doing his best."

"In my day, a rescue was a proper affair. Oh yes!" it said, raising a finger in the air. "I remember being rescued a few times. There were heroes, sword fights, maybe the odd rope swing from a chandelier."

"Yes darling," the other head said. "I was there too, don't forget. We both saw the same thing."

"It's your fault were here anyway! I wanted to go shopping with my girls… but oh no. You'd organised a fishing trip with your friends. Well…" the head said looking up to the ceiling, "what a great idea that was, wasn't it? Turned out just perfect, didn't it?"

"It's not my fault that the fishing lake was closed due to a Fungal invasion!"

"It's never your fault is it, Harry!"

"Oh! Remember my name do you! Well, Patricia, maybe I would've spent a bit more time doing my research prior to our trip if I hadn't been told to fix your wobbly spice rack… It's not always a man's job!"

Norman watched as the two-headed soul-bonded being from Nuptialla 7 wobbled from side to side away from him, listening intently to an argument that had possibly been a few years in the making.

The Traveller had to call time on Norman; he didn't want to risk their breakout attempt turning into a long over-welcome stay on Portobello 2. He assured Norman that if they succeeded then they'd return to free the rest of the inmates from whatever fate they were destined for; hoping that it would probably involve being eaten by a horde of Fungal troops. The Traveller thought that if they did return it'd be a lot less work the second time around.

"Where are they?" Norman asked meeting The Fixer and The Traveller once again.

"Don't ask," The Traveller replied.

"I sent them all this way. I thought we were going to help them escape. You know, we could have had a big group of all kinds of aliens working together, it'd be like a crazy sci-fi prison break movie."

"This isn't some silly far-fetched sci-fi film," The Fixer said coldly. "And I'm not a hero. I'm not babysitting lots of people that were daft enough to get themselves caught."

Norman hesitated. "But you got caught?"

"Beside the point!"

Norman's unbreakable smile seemed to sag a little "So, what happened?"

The Traveller sighed. "The Fixer shouted at them, and they left quickly. He's never been one for making friends."

"Oh," Norman said unhappily, feeling a little gutted that his idea of a mass breakout involving crazy abnormal creatures had slipped through his fingers. "I liked them."

"Come on," The Traveller said kindly. "Let's go…"

Roughly half an hour later they arrived at on open doorway, though doors were yet to be invented by Fungal-kind, so realistically they just arrived at the end of a tunnel that continued into a vast blob of emptiness which resembled a large squishy cave with a yellow zone and a red zone.

The Fixer huffed, "That run nearly killed me!"

"What run?" The Traveller asked rhetorically. "I carried you on my shoulders basically all the way."

"Yes, and your heavy running nearly killed me."

"I'm not your taxi!"

"Hey," Norman asked opening a plastic bag, "what do you think?" He flicked a small snow globe upside down sending small white flakes swirling around a beautiful mossy scene in which a statue of Stinkhorn the Great stood on a grassy hill, looking outwards to the future, heroically. "Do you like it?"

"No," The Traveller said bitterly.

"I like it," The Fixer said. "Did you get anything else?"

Norman smiled and dove back into the plastic bag, shuffled around a bit finally revealing a T-shirt that said, *'I Escaped Portobello 2'*.

"Why did we have to stop at the gift shop? For this?"

Norman saddened, "I got it for you."

"I told you, if you wanted to get me anything, I could've done with a key chain with my name on it."

"Yeah, I know" Norman said, "but they didn't have The Traveller. It was a choice between The Travel Guide, or The Transvestite."

"And I told you I know them both and want nothing to do with either."

The Fixer laughed, "We invited The Transvestite to his last house party. Swapped all his pants for panties, and his butter for foundation."

"It wasn't funny!"

"No," The Fixer said climbing down from his shoulder, "but spreading it on your morning toast was pretty comical."

"He didn't!" exclaimed Norman.

"He did!"

"No!"

"Seriously!"

"Bog snakes." Norman laughed.

"Don't use my line…"

"Okay," Norman said and thought quickly, "bucket worms?"

"Mm."

"Toilet tapes."

"We'll work on it." The Fixer pulled the T-shirt down over his head and over his existing clothes making him look like a body builder. He wasn't too sure what it was, maybe the understanding that Norman wasn't in fact The Traveller's new best friend but more of an unintentional annoyance, but he liked Norman. He seemed goofy but sweet.

"Fits like a glove."

"Yes," The Traveller said, "like a really small, badly fitting eight-fingered glove. You look great…"

"You weren't going to wear it were you?"

"Probably not."

"Were you not?" asked Norman. "But I got it for you."

The Traveller fell quiet, saw the disappointment on Norman's face and reluctantly gave in.

"Of course I was going to wear it. Pass it here…"

"No!" The Fixer said flatly. "You missed your chance now you bloody wobble bottom."

"C'mon, I'll wear it!"

"No!"

"It's okay," Norman said, "you don't have to wear it."

"I want too though."

"It's fine." Norman reached back into the bag and smiled while pulling out another T-shirt and passed it over to The Traveller. He rolled it over his head and straightened it out over his chest and belly. On it there was a picture of a mushroom with make-up on and the words *'My Wife's A Fun-gal.'*

"Swap?" The Traveller asked.

"Fat chance."

"Basin bugs," said Norman.

"Getting there."

The transport bay was less of a hive of activity, and more of a collection of mounds of decaying bio-matter. It was the sort of place you'd expect an old plant to go to die when he had lost all hope in life after finding his wife in bed with the cactus next door. Vines hung down from the uneven ceiling, heaps of compost piled up in every corner, and though there were no apparent insects in the thick air, the sound of flies seemed to be not too far away. Towards the end of the bay there was a large hole. A ship or two periodically zoomed by outside. It could've been easily mistaken for an abandoned transport bay; there didn't seem to be anyone in sight.

All three made their way down a flight of shifting stairs that seemed to grow in front of them and deflate behind them. They walked through all the towering compost heaps swatting the imaginary flies as they went.

"Halt!" a bodiless voice said. *"Hände hoch!"*

All three froze.

"You vill turn around, yar!"

All three did.

"Ver ist you going?"

Norman held his hands up in the air like a captured escapee and gazed at the huge fungal worm that snaked upwards. Norman, like all men, had a difficulty with measuring size, and as such he thought that it was at least a million miles long. Its mouth opened like a sinkhole circled with spikes and clawed digits, and eyes that blinked in their hundreds. From its head down, along the entirety of its wide body, a billion arms flexed and heaved itself back and forth. It was a sight that few visitors came to see, yet all Norman could think of was how unfair it was that the gift shop T-shirts didn't go up to its size.

The colossal fungal worm swooped its head down, flicking a tonne of slime from its jaw, bringing one of its car-sized eyeballs to Norman's level.

"Mm," it said in a voice like thunder, "you do not zeem to be mouldy, no?"

Norman opened his mouth to the response of The Traveller kicking his leg.

"Yes!" The Traveller said standing forward, "we definitely are, um, fungular."

"Vat sot of vungus are you' zen?"

"Why has it got a German accent?" The Fixer whispered to Norman.

"Are you a bog snake?" Norman said curiously.

"A vat?" said the fungal worm.

"A bog snake?"

The giant reared its head high up to the roof of the bay, bellowing an atomic cry of horror. "You dare to make laffs at me?"

"No!" The Traveller said hurriedly, "obviously you're not a bog snake."

"Then what is it?" The Fixer asked.

"I," shouted the giant worm, "am Baron Fluke, and I am zee leader and king of evrysing you see!"

"So, are you a baron, or are you a king?" The Fixer asked.

"Excuze me?"

"You said your name's Baron Fluke, yet you're also a king? So, what are you then?"

The giant worm hesitated for a moment considering this thought; if he were king then he could do what he wanted. Although there wasn't anyone else to order about, the idea of king was quite attractive.

"Well, obviously, I am zee king."

"Good," The Fixer said nodding and crossing his arms. "Glad we got that straightened out."

"You could be queen too if you wanted," Norman suggested.

"Shut up Norman," The Traveller barked.

"Sorry."

"Or prime minister?" The Fixer added. "Or even president?"

"What about emperor?" added Norman.

"Or commander."

"Yez," the worm said pondering the titles, "I like zem all actually."

"Well, you can't really have them all."

"No," Norman agreed. "I think it's just the one title people use."

"You can have them all!" The Traveller shouted trying to end this pointless chit-chat with a giant worm over formalities.

"Can I?" the worm asked leaning against the entire wall. "Is zat correct?"

"Of course," The Traveller said convincingly, "from now on you can be Baron King Queen Commanding Prime Minister Ruling Emperor and President Fluke."

The worm scratched its wobbling uneven chin, "Yez. Okay. Zis is now my name."

"May I just add though," said The Fixer, "that in the meantime while we're here we might just shorten it a little to save time?"

"Vat did you have in mind?"

The Fixer huffed and curled his bottom lip, "Baron Fluke?"

The Traveller shook his head and wondered if at any time soon things would get easier.

"I like that," Norman said, nodding, "nice ring to it."

"I agree," the worm added. "You may call me Baron Fluke."

"Much appreciated."

"Right," The Traveller said feeling deflated. "So, can we go?"

Baron Fluke shook his head and once again came down to their level.

"I vill let you go, but only if you proof to me zat you are really mouldy. Like zee other one. Bung somesing somesing."

"The Quite Fearsome," Norman said happily.

"Zat's 'im!"

"I liked him," Norman said to The Fixer.

"Okay," The Traveller said emptily. "How can we prove that we're like him?"

"You must tell me somesing that only a mouldy would know."

"Like what!?" The Fixer questioned.

"I don't know. Surprize me."

The Traveller exhaled and rubbed his face, "We get angry a lot."

"No. Too obvious," said Baron Fluke.

Norman thought hard, "We get, really, angry?"

"Mm, better. But still too eazy."

"We like Stinkhorn the Great."

"Who doezn't?"

"We spread everywhere!" Norman pointed out. "Like jam."

"I'm not too sure of zat one. Zow it is a nice analogy, no?"

"No."

The Fixer coughed and rolled his eyes, leant over to The Traveller's side and said with confidence, "We are mouldy, and we have to be, because if we weren't, we would know with confidence that you could very well be a bog snake. But as you've pointed out, you most definitely are not. And any mouldy that lived around here would know that you are not. And I can tell you that all three of us, even him," he said pointing at Norman, "know that you are not a bog snake. So really, we must be mouldy."

The Fixer looked at The Traveller who was shaking and winked.

Baron Fluke let the answer rotate through all seven of his brains, waited a minute for an answer to reappear in his mind and smiled, "Yez, zat is very true."

"So, we can go now," said The Traveller turning to walk away.

"Vell," Baron Fluke said, "he can go. And you too. I can quite clearly see zat you get more zan very angry, and zis iz a trait of a very high-ranking mouldy. But I am still not sure about zee funny little fellow."

"Who, me?" Norman said pointing at himself.

"Yez. You zeem to be too smiley. No mouldy vood ever be zat happy."

"Norman!" The Traveller shouted. "Stop being so happy."

"I can't!" Norman replied. It was true. Norman was at times a bit silly, moronic perhaps, but he'd been given the most pointless and universally agreed worst trait of them all: a sunny disposition. There had even been a vote for the emotion to leave and never come back, unfortunately Norman at that time was barrelling through space towards Earth.

The Fixer once again stepped forwards and patted Norman on the shoulder. "He's a magic mushroom."

"A vat?" Baron Fluke said with open eyes. "Magic! Vow, vell zen," he said curling up looking expectant, "pleaze, show me a little magic. Maybe you could make zee rabbit come out from zee hat, or chop a voman in hav?"

"Have you got a woman?" Norman asked.

"No."

"Have you got a hat?"

"No."

Norman thought for a moment, as did The Traveller — his idea of Norman doing a bit of magic was for him to simply disappear, although that was probably too much to ask for.

“Well,” Norman said cautiously, “I can do this.” He put one hand in the other and proceeded to pull off the old detachable thumb trick perfectly. He moved his digit away from his knuckle a few times, mystically.

Baron Fluke stared.

Norman repeated the act.

“Mm,” Baron Fluke said, “It’z good, yez. But it iz not really cutting somevon in zee havs, iz it?”

Norman placed his thumb back on his hand looking a bit upset; he’d never done magic for anyone, and this setback review made it clear to him that any future in children’s birthday parties was not an option for him.

Baron Fluke stretched all his tiny arms, cracked the billions of bones that lined his neck and said, “You may go. But zee little fellow I vill eat.” And abruptly he swooped his head to the floor, opened his cavernous mouth, flung Norman inside and swallowed him whole.

“Norman won’t like that,” The Fixer said.

“What have you done?” The Traveller shouted. “You’ve eaten Norman!”

“C’mon,” The Fixer added, “be honest. You weren’t really keen on him.”

“That’s beside the point!”

“We don’t even really need him, do we?”

“Well no. But you can’t just go around eating things without their say-so!” he shouted at Baron Fluke.

“I vill, and can do vot ever I vant, because I am Baron Flu—”

“Baron Flu?” The Fixer asked, one eyebrow cocked.

“Sorry… tickle in mine throat… I am Baron Flu… Baron…” the giant fungal worm coughed, “Baron Flu…”

He began to choke. The sound alone of a giant million-mile-long worm choking sent shivers down the spine of Portobello 2 itself — if it had a spine that was. Baron Fluke, like most panic-stricken people who choked on their food, began to lash and thrash out all over the place; he coughed up lumps of slime the size of houses, undigested matter and small ships that he’d eaten in the past.

“Should we help?” The Fixer said calmly.

The Traveller turned, looking mortified. "Help him? What do you expect me to do? Slap his back a few times? Maybe I could do the Heimlich…"

"I don't think they advise that any more."

"So just a slap on the back then, is it?"

The Fixer shrugged and went back to watching the scene. Baron Fluke coughed and choked a bit more, then his eyes rolled back in his head, and he flumped on the floor like a giant's draft excluder. The impact of his body on the squelchy ground sent the various heaps of compost a few feet up in the air.

"Well," The Fixer said, "he looks dead to me."

"Yes, thanks for pointing that out. Very observant."

"Not a problem."

Baron Fluke's head wobbled slightly, then a very slimy undigested Norman walked out from his mouth; still smiling, of course.

"All right?"

"…All right?" The Traveller said. "Are *you* all right?"

"Yeah. I guess. I feel terrible."

"I'm not surprised," The Fixer said, "being nearly eaten by a giant fungal worm can put a down spin on anyone's day."

"Yes, that's true. Poor thing," Norman said.

"What do you mean 'poor thing'?"

"Well," Norman continued. "Poor thing couldn't swallow me. Bless him, probably couldn't breathe with me stuck in his throat. To think if I was a bit smaller a harmless creature might still be alive."

"Makes you think, doesn't it?" The Fixer said. "One minute you're here, watching great magic tricks and so on, then suddenly you're choking on a snack. Don't feel too bad Norman, no one could've seen it coming."

"I guess."

The Traveller's head bubbled and ached, his bottom jaw wobbled, and his face went tomato red. All combining for a showmanship result of him throwing his arms in the air and kicking Baron Fluke with his boot.

"You will be the death of me Norman!"

The Keeper hummed tunelessly as he swept the multiverse back into a heap after another unplanned change — these were becoming more frequent — and as such had a lot less time to spend on his other hobbies such as keeping his broom tidy, and um… no, that's it actually, just keeping his broom tidy. One particular universe had always caused him a bit more trouble than the rest, number 41 million and 3. He'd watched it for eternity as the life forms evolved and grew into troublesome folk. One star-system had become aware of the multiverse and had tried for the last thousand years to break down the walls of the dimensional boundaries. The Keeper didn't like spatial tears at all, he could never get the thread through the needle for the patchwork and in the end decided that the best thing he could do was to take universe 41 million and 3 out of the multiverse and encase it in a glass ball to use as a paperweight on his desk. And by desk, I really mean rock.

He swept the last filaments and universal webbing back into place thinking that he'd done a good job, then went back to sit on his rock knowing that now, for the next thousand years he'd have to fill in the paperwork. Again, another time-wasting job that kept him from his life goals.

He set his broom down next to him and felt something on his hand, something that in all rights shouldn't have been there. It was a universe. However, this universe was one of the good ones, where all life was just starting to walk, and the wheel was still in the square stage of things. He inspected it closely like an old man might inspect his pocket ready hanky. He pulled one strand of the universe upwards, unreeling it like string. He narrowed his eyes so that he could focus on individual galaxies, stared a little closer so that stars and planets came to the right detail, and saw vast clouds of spores swirling over everything. Fungaloid children who had been sent pluming far and wide.

He tried everything, even wiping it on his clothes. That didn't work well at all and he was sure that a few billion galaxies now resided in his chest pocket. The broom too he noticed was covered in dark sludgy stuff. In fact, as he walked back over to the multiverse, he could quite clearly see that everything moved and wriggled slightly with a fungal colour.

He took his phone from the ether, speed dial one, "Big boy? It's The Keeper. If you have time, I need you to come down to my place, the multiverse is in a right state of affairs…"

There was a pause. Then another.

"Big boy?"

"Big boy," The Explorer replied down the phone, "is unavailable."

"Who's this?"

"It is I, you little rodent. The Explorer."

"Can you put him on please?" The Keeper said unhappily. The Explorer and he had never seen eye to eye. The Explorer had always nursed a special kind of hatred for him. He'd even said in the past that if a time ever came when he was in charge, he would not waste a minute to turn The Keeper back into a 'small smelly rat' and put poison down daily. The feeling of fruition came bounding over the nearest hilltop.

"The man you speak of is no longer in charge," The Explorer said casually. "However, I may point out that I am neither your new boss. Such a statement would indicate that you work for me, and clearly, for me anyway, I do not have any need for a rodent with OCD."

"You'll never find me!"

"Don't be so sure…"

"You never came to the storage room once; you have no idea where it is. Plus, I changed the locks. So there."

"I am more powerful than you think, and a simple lock change will not stop me from entering."

"Come and find out!" The Keeper said with certainty.

"Why?" The Explorer asked plainly, "when I can have someone do it for me?"

The doorway where The Traveller and Norman came through began to bounce on its non-space framework as hairy hog shoulders barged against it again and again and again. The Keeper rarely had visitors, and never had any of them been hostile. This, quite rightly so, brought panic into his mind.

"What do you want?"

The sound of The Explorer exhaling flatly was followed by a simple request: "Just try not to exist any more." And the line went dead.

"Open d'door!" a grainy voice shouted from the other side.

“Yeah!” another added. “It’s, um, room service.”

“Good one.”

“We’re ’ere to clean fings up!”

“Go away!” The Keeper shouted.

“C’mon, we only want to talk to ya!”

“I said go away! I have a broom!”

“What for?”

“Maybe,” the other voice pointed out, “maybe he don’t need room service. I mean, if he’s got himself a broom, he could just tidy fings up on his own.”

“We ain’t ‘ere to tidy his room really.”

“Are we not?”

“No! We’re ‘ere to change him from being able, to being completely, well, not able.”

“So why did you tell me we was room service?”

“Stop being a dog’s dinner and open d’door!”

The door began to crash and buckle again, it would seem that even a specially hardened door was no match for a couple of giant hairy hog thugs. After a few attempts, the door came crashing inwards.

“Check behind the rock.”

“Na. He ain’t there.”

“He must be somewhere else den.”

“Good finking.”

Upon the floorless floor by their feet the smarter of the pair noticed a slimy trail leading away from the rock towards the multiverse. It thinned out, as The Keeper had shrunk himself down and escaped into the vastness of it all. His broom left a snail’s footprint for the hogs to follow.

“Should we go after ‘im then?”

“Yeah,” the other said, “but first fings first.”

“We trash d’place?”

“We trash d’place up…”

God shook his head as he sat still chained up surrounded by scattered chess pieces. He’d always thought that The Explorer might one day betray him.

"I can't believe you're such a bad loser, mate."

The Explorer spun the phone round in his hand considering what he would do first when he was in charge and the others had all been replaced by new, more obedient life forms.

"I may not be able to get rid of you," he said leaning back in his chair lazily, "but I can, and will, rid my new multiverse of the others. The Traveller? Don't make me laugh; what kind of role is it to inspect hotels and hotspots. The Fixer? When the black hole's back in place I'll have little if any need for him. Then there's The Finder…"

"You'll never find him," God said confidently. "I can promise you that." This was true, and God knew it. It should be noted that The Finder, although obviously finding things was his main job, was also very good at hiding. He still to this day holds the record for the longest running game of hide-and-seek, even when everyone else had been found and lost interest in the initial game, The Finder stayed put and never once gave up his hiding stop for over seven billion years. Integrity was his middle name (it was really Simon but that's beside the point).

"I think that The Finder will eventually come out of hiding," The Explorer said. "His need to find everything that there is, it'll overcome this hiding obsession, and come to find this little place of mine. It will become such a niggle in his mind, an itch of curiosity that he must know of it."

God looked around him and pondered what that was meant to mean.

"Mate! Seriously. It's a bloody platform and some stars. Call me old-fashioned, but you haven't even hung any pictures. I mean a desk plant wouldn't be a stretch. Where's your coffee machine? Have some class, man."

Norman shuffled a bit, leant forwards and pulled a half-eaten jelly baby from the seat.

"It's a bit sticky in here."

"I like it," The Fixer said from the front seat. "You've really done it up nicely."

The Fungaloid driver nodded with appreciation and went back to the phone call he'd put on hold.

"Why did we need to take a taxi?" The Traveller asked angrily.

"Did you see any ships back there?" asked The Fixer rhetorically.

"I didn't!" Norman pointed out. "Well, except the ones inside Baron Fluke. You know, I'm surprised he didn't choke sooner."

"A dangerous game that. Eating willy-nilly."

The Traveller crossed his arms and looked out the window like an angry teenager on the way to a family BBQ. The window wasn't all that easy to look out of; the Fungal Empire hadn't invented glass, so the window was just a thick skin of slime that bubbled and distorted the view.

Behind them, Portobello 2 hung against a backdrop of blackness like an uneven half-eaten truffle; colossal vines and strands of moss and growth wove for thousands of miles grasping on to the various moon-like mushrooms that gave Portobello 2 the cool blasts of stale air that ran through its tunnels. In front of them far out in deep space, Portobello 9 sat like a tennis ball that a dog had had trouble digesting. It was huge. Actually, it was really huge. At points on its shifting crust, mists of spores blew through vents outwards, busting towards every region of space. A million billion baby fungi erupted each second; if it weren't for the obvious threat that they posed to the multiverse, it could've been seen as rather amazing.

"That looks amazing," Norman said, shoving his head out of the taxi window and sticking out his tongue.

"Norman!" The Traveller said firmly.

The taxi driver placed his phone on the wobbly dashboard and rolled down his window too.

"Ahhh, *Nojal*."

"What did he say?"

"He said," The Fixer smiled, "'Ahhh, can you smell it? What a beautiful sight it is, Portobello 9, our world of mould and damp. I hope it never dies.' Or something like that, anyway."

The Traveller shook his head. "I didn't know you spoke Fungalees."

"Mm, getting the hang of it."

The taxi driver took the roundish-disc that barely passed as the steering wheel with his five knees and took a wallet from his pocket. He opened it up and started showing The Fixer some photos of his family. He pointed. "Klopy."

"Yes, got your eyes. Very pretty."

“She’s a blob of green sludge,” The Traveller said.

“That’s his son.”

“Oh.”

“Tfirrrrr… buck!”

“Really? Well, I hope he makes it.”

“What did he say?” Norman asked moving in between the front seats for a better look. He took the photo of the driver’s son for a closer look. He didn’t want to be rude but wasn’t too sure if he was holding the thing upside down or back to front.

“He said,” The Fixer smiled, “that his son, David the Blob, works for the Palace of Stinkhorn the Great as his personal cook. Apparently, he’s a fine cook, and we’re all invited for dinner next time we’re in the system.”

“Ahh, that’s nice of him,” Norman said.

“Jesus…” The Traveller whispered.

“You could at least try to enjoy yourself.”

The Traveller uncrossed his arms, opened his palms and said, “How, exactly? We’re closing in on the home world of Fungal-kind; you’ve been eaten and spat out by a giant worm with personal problems, and I am no closer to finding the black hole.”

“You see!” said The Fixer, “where’s the bad in that?”

“Well, I’m having a good time,” Norman added.

“You are always having a good time,” The Traveller said coldly. “The multiverse could be falling down around you; the very fabric of creation could be in a final stage of destruction, and you would still be smiling. Honestly, Norman, do you ever feel bad about anything?”

Norman thought for a moment, recalled his lonely trip across space for fourteen billion years, his experience with the people of Chumpton, meeting God, Bud and Oxyn the Big. He thought about The Finder and The Keeper and how they’d been friendly and welcoming, and how nice and warm it was on Portobello 2, and said, “You know what, I love my life.”

“Me too.” The Fixer said. “Maybe you should take a page out of Norman’s book.”

“Which page, exactly? The blurb, or the index?”

"Seriously," The Fixer said shifting to turn. "I mean, you look at the boss man, do you ever see him stressed? Do you ever see him feeling a bit down or depressed? Of course not. And do you know why?"

"Because he's awesome?" Norman questioned.

"No."

"I don't know," The Traveller huffed, "because he's always pissed?"

"Funny, but no. You don't see him stressed out because what is there to be stressed about? We may be infinitely powerful, and we may be beings of pure energy and have intelligence of untold ends, but really, with everything that goes on in the multiverse, not even the big boy can control it all. And why would he want to? From leaving things be, and letting chaos and madness run wild, you end up with diversity and fun…"

"And bog snakes," Norman added.

The Traveller sat still, looked out the window and felt his mouth move in a way that it hadn't moved in a while, and although he tried to force the change away as much as he could, in the end he gave in and simply smiled.

"You pair are going to be the death of me." And he laughed. He laughed and felt the bad moods, the stressful knots and twists that had wound up in his chest and gut unravel and spring back to normal. He laughed and felt the tense and tenacious controlling persona run from his body like escaping the sun's heat under a well-positioned brolly on the beach. He realised that he had become the one thing that in all his years as a critic he had never wanted to become, and that was unhappy and tired. Tired of doing a job that he cared too much about. In fairness though, the multiverse was most definitely in peril, and if they didn't recover the black hole soon no amount of giddy laughing would save any of them, but that little fact could wait.

"Here," The Fixer said passing him a beer. "Drink this."

The Traveller took it and smiled, opened the can and took a swig. "Where did you get those from?"

"Prison gift shop," he said passing Norman one too. Together the three drank and laughed, relaxed and felt that they were somehow on the right path.

"So," The Traveller asked after a moment of reflection, "where exactly are we going? Have we got any kind of plan to find this black hole?"

"It hash to be here somewhere," Norman said; the beer hit his speech box like a wet fish to the throat.

The Fixer took another swig and nodded, "Yes. We're going to the Palace of Stinkhorn the Great."

"Are we?" The Traveller said in surprise. "How come?"

"The taxi fungus man is on his break and going to see his son. So, he'll just drop us off at the back gate and we can go in. The code is 1-2-3-4."

The Traveller laughed again and took another swig of the Moss Ale — quite tasty really. "How the hell did you arrange that then?"

"I just told him that Norman's a magic mushroom and we're going to put on a show for old Stinky himself. No problems." Norman sat upright and did the thumb trick again with a big cheesy smile on his face like a dog that had finally done his business outside.

The Traveller nodded, sat back, and looked out the window feeling a lot lighter and a lot more upbeat about things in general.

And it was about time.

The taxi driver, with one of his many uneven free hands, leant over and pulled out the last beer from The Fixer's bag, thinking that the celebration was due to his great driving; the fact that he'd been on a drinking ban and his picture had been passed around every fungal bar for the last three months had dodged the attention of Norman, The Traveller and The Fixer.

"Tipks," the driver said pointing out the window at a small cluster of stuff. *"Brizzle."*

"Mm," The Fixer said politely, "for shizzle."

"What was that?" Norman asked sitting facing the front seats once more.

"I think he wants to give us a small tour of the system as we go from one fungal planetoid to another. He said that that small field of debris was once a statue of Grim the Grim, the so-called 'taker of souls'."

"Like the Reaper?" The Traveller asked.

"Kind of," replied The Fixer, "I think he specialised in trainers though. Ever see a Fungaloid with shoes on? There all too scared."

"Myskl!" shouted the taxi driver.

The small transport buzzed through space heading for Portobello 9, which by now had become less a distant blob of gunk and offered a more close-up look at what the inside of a slug might look like. The traffic became heavier too. Within the vast clouds of small family ships, larger and more cumbersome vessels chugged along like giant rotting whales; one even had a sign in the window that said, *'Honk if you're horny, spikey, or even a little crusty'*.

"Jumg!" the taxi driver continued.

The Fixer, who was not at all interested in what the driver was saying, tried to make the translation as exciting as possible, though if you knew anything of the Fungal Empire history, you'd soon find out that it was all much the same: multiply, spread, consume, get angry. Multiply, spread, consume, get angry… and so on.

"That's a mushroom," The Fixer said pointing out the window. "There's another… that's one there…"

"Very interesting," Norman said happily.

"Look, an elephant!"

"Really?"

"No," said The Fixer, "sorry. I meant mushroom."

"Oh."

"And what about that?" said The Traveller directing their attention towards the planet's landscape. A single detail spat upwards from the otherwise flat horizon of Portobello 9. A huge free-standing shape, at least ten miles high dominated the surface, sucking the life from anything that tried to grow close by.

"Call me crazy, but that looks like a mushroom."

Norman jumped in his seat feeling the excitement a newborn would express when seeing their breakfast bosom heading their way. Indeed, it was a mushroom, though no normal boring kind that might be found in a field and later eaten for fun. This mushroom was monstrous; like some kind of fungal Valhalla, it echoed with mouldy beauty. Multiple heads shot off from its main root, the largest and uppermost head at least a mile from one side to the other. Vines and other types of scavenging plants had taken over its surface. It was so amazingly magnificent in fact, that The Traveller was feeling pretty gutted that he had no powers in this region of space and was unable to take his phone out from the ether for some incredible pictures and selfies. The Fixer, on the other hand, had thought ahead and had purchased a few disposables from the prison gift shop in advance.

"Smile, Norman!"

And he did. Somehow letting his grin go further than the sides of his face.

"You too."

The Traveller lurched forwards, smiled, then after the first flash, grabbed Norman and pulled him closer for a 'friends go wild' type shot. Soon the taxi driver was getting involved too, this was after he'd drunk his beer and had delved into his secret stash that none of the inspectors had managed to find during the so-called 'court case of the century'. Which left The Fixer to jump into the driver's seat and carry on the journey. The taxi driver had now finished off a few more bottles of vodka and was wobbling drunk. He would have got rolling drunk but unfortunately there was only so much room on the back seats and he didn't feel 100% natural around Norman. Norman, on the other hand, had felt comfortable around anyone since he was created, and so was now playing beer pong with a lump of God knows what he'd found rolling around by his feet using the taxi's cupholders. The taxi driver wanted to tell Norman that he didn't like him throwing his youngest cousin around like a ball, but after Norman had necked an entire bottle of vodka with him, he said, "Wow, you hate potatoes as much as I do… stuck-up good-for-nothing spuds!" Though what he really said was "brrup" and Norman took it as a burp and started to pat his back for support.

The Fixer gestured to The Traveller and soon the back door whooshed open, and the blithering taxi driver was pushed outside, closely followed by his wallet with its pictures streaming behind it.

"Take care!" shouted The Traveller with a wave.

"I liked him," Norman added disappointedly.

The vast tall mushroom was The Palace of Stinkhorn the Great (if you hadn't already guessed) and it was staggeringly big. The Fixer arced the taxi downwards taking a low fly over the planet's crust. What had looked like a grainy distorted surface from space could now be clearly seen as a never-ending fungal slum, rows and rows and blocks and blotches of small houses spread out far and wide.

Up ahead, the base of the mushroom palace stood. A thick fog rolled around its trunk, it looked like how a gone-off sauna might feel. Hundreds of doors lined up with a billion Fungaloids crowded like a mushroom party was soon to hit its squelchy peak. Further up the trunk, above the plumes of thick vapour, vessels of all sizes and ages lined up, each waiting for their turn to fly inside and perhaps get the chance to meet the great ancienter of a simple stinkhorn mushroom.

The Fixer spotted a small sign that had been etched into the skin that read *'deliveries round back'*.

"Are we delivering anything?" asked Norman.

"Of course we are!" The Traveller said drunkenly with the air of a pissed saint. "We are delivering a devastating blow to the Fungal Empire!"

The Fixer rolled his eyes. "Calm down. Sit down. And put the bottle down."

They flew in through a large set of hangar doors that seemed to have passed their sell-by-date by a good few hundred years, picked an empty parking stop and came in for a nice soft and squishy landing; the disabled sign obviously meant nothing to The Fixer.

"I have mental issues," he argued.

A well-dressed Fungaloid walked over and handed them a ticket in exchange for their keys. Which was altogether rather strange as no other Fungaloid they had met in the recent events had dressed in anything at all, so why parking attendants who worked in the great palace were the only ones to do so still remains a mystery to this day.

They strolled casually by as a large vessel opened its back hatch and tipped out some rotten food and scraps; it smelt worse than it looked.

"Royalty," The Fixer scoffed. "Only the best will do."

Rain, on the whole, goes downwards. Sometimes sideways, maybe even a little diagonal at times, but it most definitely should never go upwards. Which was why The Keeper had such a struggle seeing where he was running. The small clouds that rested on the ground of Fallacious 4, in the system of Wrong — a system where the star shined inwards instead of out — rained upwards forming small puddles about head height. It was a great planet for joggers in general as they never had to carry a water bottle, but the kind of jogging The Keeper was doing had nothing to do with numbered vests or charity work, only perhaps for the charity for his own well-being.

He hadn't chosen this universe specifically; it was just the closest one to his storage room at the time.

Behind him the two large hogs chased after him. Up ahead, a small building stood; it looked like a wooden barn but knowing the system it could very well be made out of strawberries. The Keeper swiped a few unwelcomed puddles from his face, sipping on one for hydration, and arrived at the front door with a thud. The rain lashed up at his chin, and unfortunately up under his clothes.

"Help!" he shouted banging on the door. "Help!"

There was a little knocking around from the other side, and then a faint little voice from an even fainter little old lady said, "We had our windows washed last week."

The Keeper looked back; the hogs were close. "Can you open the door please?"

"Alfred? Is that you?" the little lady said.

The Keeper shook his head, he needed help but knew he probably wouldn't get any from here. He took his big set of keys from his pocket, rolled through the few thousand he had and picked one out. He placed it in the keyhole and pulled open the door. On the other side an entire new universe looked back at him. He stepped through, slammed the door behind him and carried on running.

The little old lady peered through her window out into the rain and saw two huge dark figures standing by her front door.

"Open up!" one shouted.

"Yeah. It's da'police!"

The front door opened, and the little lady stood holding a small tray of biscuits and tea. "You look famished, my dear. Here," she said passing over a digestive, "take one for your troubles."

"Na," the hog said, "we ain't got no time for dat."

"No time for tea?"

"Na," he replied with a grunt. "We're looking for dis fella, he came dis way and—"

"What about a slice of cake, then? Victoria sponge."

"Na! This fella came dis way an—"

"How about a cucumber sandwich?"

The hog blew steam from his mouth and held his hands out. "We don't want no nofing, we're just looking for dis fella. He's about dis height and—"

"What about a little sherry? I have some glasses in my side table."

"I like sherry," the other hog pointed out.

"We ain't got no time for dat!"

"Maybe I'll just get the dominos out of the box."

"No!"

"Blackjack?"

"No!"

The little lady took hold of the hogs by their hands and pulled them in out from the rain and shut the door behind them. The last words heard by the upwards thrashing rain were, "Take your muddy boots off please."

The Keeper was still running, and though he didn't know it yet, the hogs were a trouble that he needed to fear no more. They never came out from that small little barn, and though big and menacing, being observant wasn't on their list of best traits; the piles of bones that lined her garden path probably would indicate to anyone with half a brain that the sweet little old lady enjoyed more than just cucumber in her sandwiches; that night she was having pork.

The Keeper had been through several universes at this point, each different and each more useless and ridiculous than the last. The first, universe 45, was a simple place; not much to see, a few wandering creatures that looked intent on growing out their foreheads and collecting larger clubs than their friends. The trouble was that The Keeper needed a physical door to open to enter the next universe, and as such he had to make do with a very large boulder that had been rolled in front of a cave entrance. Needless to say, it was rather heavy. Through that he found himself in universe 789 thousand, a place that was totally populated by train spotters, it was a tricky art opening the side door of the freight train as it whooshed by. Universe 8 hundred and 4 billion was where he struggled most. And for that matter, this was where most did too; it is the leading reason for the entire population of the universe to solely inhabit one single planet — the all-female nudist Beach'n'BBQ planet of Busty-Jelly-Wrestling Prime. It ranked a perfect score on The Traveller's guidebook and was mentioned twice in the annual newsletter published by *Trench Coat Weekly*.

But regrettably, The Keeper had to move on.

He pulled open the door of a small beach hut, and firstly, and forgivably, he forgot to place one of his keys in the hole and interrupted a group of women and one man who he assumed were acting out a deleted scene from an adults-only movie set.

"Sorry," he said with a giggle.

Once again, he opened the door, this time correctly, and in the distance, far away against the green-splattered backdrop of fungal spores, he saw Portobello 9.

Mrs Pinkletin took a napkin from the table and cleaned her mouth from any crumbs; the sweet little old innocent lady of Fallacious 4 had very much enjoyed her latest meal; albeit very large, she'd had no trouble slicing a few pieces of thick white bread to match. She burped abruptly and looked over to the dresser in the corner of the room where her late husband's skull sat smiling back at her; ironically, he had ended up as her dinner one fateful day because he'd been late getting back from work and forgot all about her bingo. That was the last time he would be late, Mrs Pinkletin had thought.

She apologised. "Sorry Alfred."

Then she burped again, and again, and felt a tingle of something new run through her ancient bones. Her age was something that she couldn't tell anyone, not that she was embarrassed, of course not, it was that she simply didn't know. Was she over a thousand years old, maybe a million? Who knew? All she was aware of was that the more she ate, the more energised she felt. And she was sure that she was about to feel more energised than ever before.

The hogs were made of power itself, and that power now streamed through her old bones giving her a hunger like never before; an uncontrollable hunger that took hold of her like the smell of a burger van precisely placed outside a 24-hour gym.

She nodded at Alfred's skull politely and excused herself from the table, took her raincoat from the hanger by the front door and proceeded outside.

The travel guide that The Traveller had spent a lifetime throwing together mentioned most places of interest. The majority took up an entire page in his travel guide, maybe two at a push, yet Fallacious 4, not technically a hotspot as such, only needed half.

It read as follows: *"To all visitors of the system of Wrong, please be sure to avoid Fallacious 4. There is a single inhabitant on the planet, and her name is Mrs Pinkletin. Although her Bed 'n Breakfast rates are cheap, stay at your own risk, which is a lot. Unless you are okay with being subject to the confines of a cucumber sandwich, you will take your money elsewhere. Quiet surroundings, nice landscape, free WIFI — Four out of five stars."*

The Godly power surged her body as the door shut behind her, lighting up her eyes like a set of headlamps. Whatever she had eaten before had not revitalised her spirit as much as this, and she hungered for more. Just like the hunting wolf in the whirling snowy blasts of some isolated mountainside, Mrs Pinkletin could smell her next victim; he was at this moment in time putting away a few more maps that Norman had rearranged, upsetting him and his cat.

Mrs Pinkletin licked her lips and set off with her brolly facing down in the upwards rain.

The Traveller had been in quite a few lifts in his time, most were your standard up-and-down affair. Even the lift in the Abyssal Hotel located in the Slightly-Damp star system of universe 5 hundred and 12 went up and down, albeit a little wobbly and compressed at times. Yet the lifts that were in the great palace weren't really lifts as such, they were simply the innards of the palace itself that shot nutrients from the ground up to all the different mushroom heads. He'd watched as The Fixer had thought nothing of it, as he usually did with most things. He had climbed into the open water vein happily, Norman, not really that bright, or perhaps too innocent to understand real danger, followed him without question.

Perhaps The Traveller was beginning to understand why people thought of him as uptight, a worry bag and at times a buzzkill. He wanted to know where this particular tube went, how they would get out at the right stop, and why the water that was being sucked up from underneath the crust of Portobello 9 was a distasteful purply-brown colour.

The Traveller shrugged, and thought if no one else cared, then why should he, and climbed in carelessly. Straight away he regretted it. The tube seemed to push and pull like a giant throat, having small ribs running the distance contracting everything in an upwards motion; not even the pleasant music helped alleviate his discomfort, nor the lift attendant who was there to aid in all the difficult button pushing.

"Hipt?" the lift attendant grunted.

"Bloj!" The Fixer replied. He was starting to get the hang of Fungalees, it was a simple case of understanding which bones you were willing to sacrifice in order to get the right tone needed — painful in every sentence. One entity, a former associate of God who went by the name The Talker, had learnt every dialect in existence, in every galaxy in every universe, and had said that Fungalees was most definitely the worst there was. Even harder to pick up than the indescribable language of the Mud-Bottom Tribe of Sector 4, and even tougher to say out loud than Welsh.

They proceeded upwards in the slime.

The only comfort from the onslaught of stench came from the randomly placed exits that sprung up every so often. It would be untrue to say that the great palace had floors, sure, there were levels, but the lift didn't follow the standard route. They had got in a minute's walk from where they'd parked the ship and headed sideways unexpectedly. The first exit that flashed past gave The Traveller and Norman the view of the Fungal Nursery, a damp floor where young royal spores could take root and become individuals with the right guidance. The second exit had showed them the second year's classroom, where all individual Fungaloids had now come to the conclusion that they should most definitely beat and pulverise their teachers with clubs.

"Aww," Norman said, "the one in the corner was smiling at me."

"I think she was trying to get her Maths teacher's arm unstuck from her teeth," The Fixer clarified.

The lift attendant said something and smiled. "Please don't show me any photos of your family," The Fixer replied, "I don't have the stomach for it."

Another exit zoomed past them, and another blast of cooler air gave a little refreshment; it wasn't much, still damp and gag-inducing. The lift attendant slapped his steak-like hand on the lift's stop button and began to rewind it backwards a few spaces. As if feeling the rib-like walls going past in one direction wasn't enough, backwards felt like a torturous massage. The exit slowly came into view and through it there was a room with a handful of Fungaloid creatures all sitting in front of what possibly were mirrors — reflective yes, good at reflecting, no. The lift attendant whistled and nudged The Traveller in his side winking with a few of his eyes. The Traveller was a bit confused, what he was looking at he couldn't be sure of; bipedal fungus had always been tricky to classify. The Fixer and Norman came down and looked through the hole as one of the concubines noticed them and began to wave.

Norman waved back. "Hello."

"Think she like you," The Fixer said.

"That's a she?" The Traveller asked disgustedly. "She looks like a half-formed play-dough foot."

"That one's giving you the eye," The Fixer said pointing to one who had her eye in her hand holding it out for The Traveller.

"I'm good thanks."

Norman had to hold onto the lift's door as one concubine grabbed at his sleeve and was trying to pull him through; word of the famous magic mushroom had spread like mould throughout the system. Coincidentally, news really was spread by mould throughout the system.

"Get back here," The Traveller said tugging him to safety.

The Fixer, who had begun to clear his throat, presumably prepping himself for some more choice fungal words, gestured for silence and said, *"Comhompomdox!"* and silence fell.

The concubines sat open-mouthed; the lift attendant stood shocked and embarrassed; The Traveller slapped his forehead, and Norman smiled. The Fixer coughed, and said, "Blah!" sticking his tongue out as far as it would go.

Abruptly everyone fell about laughing and the lift attendant patted him on the back, clearing a jovial tear from his own eye. What The Fixer had done, unbeknown to The Traveller and Norman, was to tell the funniest joke in the history of the Fungal Empire. Years from now, young Fungal descendants would mark this as a joculation of such greatness that it could never be rivalled nor surpassed.

"Would did you say?" asked Norman cheerfully.

The Fixer thought for a moment, then said, "I'm not really too sure. But it seemed to have worked."

They waved goodbye to the questionable concubines as one gave Norman a rolled-up bit of fabric and a kiss on the cheek. He looked at it and pondered whether it was a pair of knickers or an old dish cloth that had been soaking in a bucket of gruel. It didn't matter which was right, Norman appreciated the gesture as it was.

The lift carried on. This time there seemed to be no exits or stops for quite some time, and the feeling that they were getting higher as their speed increased was obvious. All three were thrown from an abrupt ending of the smiley tube and they went crashing to the floor, right in the middle of a large chamber with few Fungal guards standing next to Stinkhorn the Great, who was sitting on his throne.

He was big, though not tall, and not fat, just big. He did admittedly have a bit of a belly on him, but for a mushroom of his age it was quite common. He looked down at the three and rolled his giant hands around in the air like the Queen might do on one of her shopping runs. He inhaled slowly — it sounded like a tornado within his mouth, and said, "Entertain me," in a voice that could knock seafaring oil rigs of course.

"You speak English?" The Fixer asked in curiosity.

"I do," Stinkhorn the Great bellowed, "I ate a man who spoke a thousand words, in a thousand languages, from a thousand universes."

"Good" The Fixer said, "cos my throat was getting a bit painful trying to negotiate your tongue. Plus, I always thought The Talker never knew when to shut up… serves him right."

Stinkhorn the Great leant forwards on his throne, the weight of his body putting the chair to work as it held him upright with everything it had and gazed down at Norman who held a pair of knickers in his hand, "You!"

"Me?"

"Yes!"

"What?"

"Are you the magic mushroom?"

Norman hesitated, then replied, "I am."

Stinkhorn the Great sat upright and waved his hands in the air to his guards, "Leave us!" he commanded, and they did so without question. One by one they disappeared out of sight into a back chamber, until the room was silent and only the sound of the palace itself sludging about filled the air. Stinkhorn the Great moved slightly, looked over to the doors, turned to the back room to make sure all his guards were really out of sight, stepped down from his throne and stood over Norman like an elephant to an ant. Then, he opened his mouth and said, "Please, you've got to get me out of here!" in a squeaky voice.

"Excuse me?"

"Please, oh magicist of all mushrooms. Thy life, tis in anger."

"Tis?" The Traveller asked rhetorically.

"Yes," said Stinkhorn the Great.

"Thy life?"

"Yes. Look, I'm trying to convey the sense of danger that I'm in, in a style that one might pick up on. Is that not coming through?"

"I understood," The Fixer said smugly.

"Of course, you did…" replied The Traveller sarcastically.

"…I did!"

"Oh, you do not know the agony I've endured of the recent decades," Stinkhorn the Great said theatrically, "I've become a slave to thy own kingdom, and now, tis the time of reckoning, three kings hast cometh to save mine own life. Hast you cometh to save or quash my body, though mine own bread tis for eating, bless it to be poison, and I may eateth it, then die…" Stinkhorn the Great threw his hands in the air and fell to the floor in a lump of Shakespearian homage, and peeked an eye at the curious onlookers.

"Sorry," he said, "I was expecting an applause."

"Oh, okay," Norman said and began to clap.

"Stop, stop, stop," The Traveller said holding Norman's hands steady with his own. "Can we expect this sort of behaviour to carry on?"

Stinkhorn the Great nodded. He had eaten The Talker many years ago, and found that, much like Mrs Pinkletin had discovered, that after eating an omnipotent being you gained an unexpected thirst, or in Stinkhorn the Great's case, an unexpected flare for the dramatic. His vocabulary had gone from a few simple fungal grunts to a supercharged wordsmith's iron forge; his knowledge and understanding of things had become marvellous, "…And now I must sit and wait for the hands of death himself to relieve me from thy pain, for I am only a man, and—"

"Please stop," The Traveller said flatly.

"Sorry."

"So, you're in danger then?" asked The Fixer.

"Tis true…"

The Traveller covered his face with his hand feeling silliness surround him again.

"Thy stomach wast full of goodness, then my mind wast full of wisdometh, and knowledgeth."

"Just tell us what happened" The Traveller said flatly. "And no ths!"

Stinkhorn the Great looked taken aback, then huffed and sat on his throne like a bleeding Romeo. "Fine. When I ate that man, I could see that all that we were doing was infesting creation with our dirt and viral muck. I wanted no part in it any more. That's when that hound, Oxyn the Big, that fiend, took my kingdom, began to create his own spores and sentenced me to exile in this chamber that I now call thy refuge." He put a hand to his forehead and started up again uncontrollably, "Woe, how tis to be laden with pain, that I may never see the petal of mine own rosebud, and that sweetness of a baby's laugh, of innocence and joy. Tis darkness that keepeth my life now…"

The Fixer nodded and smiled. "He's pretty good actually. I've seen a few plays, and none were acted as well as this."

"Tis no act, my friend of valour."

"So, what are we going to do?" Norman asked. "Are we going to stop him, as it just seems that he's kind of stopped himself?"

The Traveller thought for a moment; drinking till he woke up in another universe seemed like the best option; even a gift shop would do. Stinkhorn the Great may have started it all, and his descendants may have spread throughout the cosmoses, but it was true, he had turned over a new leaf and seen his ways.

Norman looked around puzzled. "What leaves?"

"It's a figure of speech."

"Like a shape?"

"No, like a metaphor."

"What a'for?"

"Like if I were to say, 'Norman, you have come to a battle of wits unarmed', for instance."

"Who's instance?" Norman asked sincerely.

The Fixer laughed. The Traveller slapped his face. Stinkhorn the Great moaned again and started to reel off some more theatrical jargon.

"He's right though," The Fixer said, "we can't stop him as he's already stopped, and it would be wrong to just leave him here."

"You want to bring him with us!?"

"It'll be more like breaking him out. He's under house arrest after all."

"Mine rotten fruit from thy loins tis scattered like the love of mine heart… ohh how tis must be beauty to fly like the bird of freedom…"

"Jesus… fine. Okay. Whatever." The Traveller felt that same buzzkill vibe, take the driving seat again; while everyone around him fell about without a clue of any implications, or realisations of things to come, it landed again on him to seek out answers and sort out all the mess. He huffed heavily. "We'll get you out of here."

"Oh…! thy nights of shimmering beauty, I…"

"But!" The Traveller said abruptly. "You have to give us your word that you will help us to clean up all your mess. Deal?"

Stinkhorn the Great got to his feet from the throne then took to one knee on the floor, and nodded.

"Sir!" he said boldly, "thy word is a bond that neither sword or flame can break, nor will it be ignored by my arrogance. You have my allegiance, till death us do part."

The Bloodhound of Earth has the most scent receptors of any breed, yet unbeknown to Earthlings the bloodhound was more of a cosmic import. Throughout the many galaxies and many, many universes, there are creatures that make the bloodhound seem like a child with a bunged-up nose. The Armoured Chicken of the backwater world, Gringo Minor, for instance, has the capability of smelling things before they've even happened and is used mostly at large parties for when a senior member of the family has fallen asleep in front of the television and begins to show the side effects of a hot and spicy Mexican. Many nose hairs have been saved due to this little fellow. In other parts of the multiverse, other creatures have produced more ingenious solutions, such as the small and quite harmless Yaya Fish of the Abyssal System; it uses its sense of smell underwater in a kind of reverse motion. When it picks up the smell of a large predator, it will cleverly send a message through the scent line back to the incoming hungry critter letting it know that it is not in fact a small and quite harmless Yaya Fish but really a big scary animal with lots of teeth and an even worse table-side manner.

Although none of these compare or even come close to the smelling capabilities of the new and improved Mrs Pinkletin. Her nose, much like a highly powered camera, is able to pick up smells that aren't even on the usual scent spectrum. Now, thanks to her recent pork chop sandwiches, she can now smell the X-rated scents that float about in the highest of frequencies. Most creatures would reach for a sick bag at this point, but not Mrs Pinkletin. The kind of smells that are found in this untapped field belong to only a few entities in the multiverse, which only those same entities can pick up on. Mrs Pinkletin can now do the same.

She licked her lips as she walked up to the front door, the glowing scent particles leading out in front of her like a trail of breadcrumbs to her next snack. She could feel the surge of urgency run through her ancient bones. Behind her a few big asteroids shaped like breasts floated idly by.

She knocked on the door twice and rubbed her old, wrinkled hands together wondering what kind of sauce would go best with such a perfect slab of meat. Her eyes buzzed with hunger, rolling backwards, lighting up again like small torches, her stomach growled, and her taste buds quivered. Her impatience grew as time ticked away; she knocked again, then again, then again.

The door swung open as The Finder stood in the opening holding a newly drawn map he was inspecting. "I told you," he said, expecting to see The Traveller, "not so many knocks next time — oh, who are you?"

Mrs Pinkletin shook off any obvious savagery and smiled.

"Oh hello, dear. You look famished."

"Can I help you?"

"Oh, good gracious no, poppet. I'm just passing through. I got a little lost coming through the rocks back there, and was wondering if you could show me the right way to go?"

The Finder smiled, put his map under one arm and pointed towards a large belt of asteroids. "You see the large double Ds just there?"

"I do," Mrs Pinkletin said, gazing at The Finder's arm. She could hear the omnipotent blood pumping round his veins.

"You want to head straight for the nipples. Then at the last minute come about and head off towards the smaller sizes in that direction."

"Oh, thank you, dear."

"My pleasure," The Finder said turning to go back inside.

"Um," Mrs Pinkletin said searching quickly for something to say, "I don't suppose you have any biscuits do you dear? It's a long way for my old legs to go and I've got nothing to keep me going."

"I'm not too sure," The Finder replied, "why don't you come in and we can find you something."

"Oh, thank you pet. Or maybe a cucumber sandwich. Oh, there's nothing I like better than a freshly cut cucumber sandwich and a pot of tea."

The Finder, for reasons unknown to him, felt a small sense of danger at the mention of a cucumber sandwich, and though there was something most definitely off about this sweet little lady who'd found herself at his door, he pinned it down to something to do with God playing some kind of practical joke on him aeons ago.

Mrs Pinkletin closed the door behind her and shook herself as a chill ran down her spine. She placed her brolly by the front door in a large vase with many other brollies that The Finder had found and collected over the years.

The Finder placed his map down on the side of the coffee table and disappeared into the kitchen out of sight.

"I've got no biscuits" he shouted through, "but I could quickly throw a sandwich together for you."

Mrs Pinkletin took a few steps towards the kitchen door, taking off her raincoat and letting it drop to the floor.

"Oh, thank you, poppet, that's most kind."

"Crust or no crust?" The Finder asked loudly.

"Oh, crust please," she replied taking another step towards the kitchen like a starving cat stalking its next mouse.

"I didn't catch your name?"

"My name?"

"Yes," said The Finder, "you from round here then?"

"Oh yes dear. My name's Mrs Pinkletin..."

The sound of a knife dropping to the floor pinged and echoed around the otherwise quiet house, then a moment passed, and the heavy hungry breathing of Mrs Pinkletin dove into overdrive.

"Mrs Pinkletin, you say?"

"Yes pet, that's me..."

"...from Fallacious 4 in the Wrong star system?"

"The very same," Mrs Pinkletin said as her voice deepened, her teeth grew and extended another inch or so. "Have you heard of me?"

The Finder walked out from the kitchen holding a slice of bread in one hand and nothing in the other and having little practice with the art of transforming things into plants and flora he shot a fizz of energy from his free fingertips at Mrs Pinkletin who covered her wild face and closed her eyes. An instant later The Finder's front room began to fill with what can only be described as a very large and angry Picture Plant. Mrs Pinkletin's feet became roots that shot off across the floor and up the walls while her arms changed into thick vine-covered branches. The Finder was sure he'd gotten the power ratio right; he'd practised turning his cat Jerry into a cactus and back again a few times before, yet no one had bothered to tell him Mrs Pinkletin had eaten a supercharged pork sandwich, moments before. And as such, her vast and all-consuming Picture Plant head loomed over The Finder, who looked up and hoped that at the very least she wouldn't knock off his precious light fittings from the ceiling that he'd 'liberated' from a royal home in the English Midlands somewhere.

"Be good Jerry," he said lastly to his cat who sat casually licking himself, "and don't scrape the side of the chairs."

Mrs Pinkletin picked up The Finder, never bothered to chew, and swallowed him down whole. And hoping that this may be of some kind of resolution for The Finder, he did indeed taste amazing.

"…To the sky, thy must be but a leaf, tumbling in the wind, directionless and cold. But as ye can see, my beauty, well tis a thing of chance, and perhaps, just maybe, with the fortune of a second's breath, thy might be seen as a wonder, and not, as thou may think, a dried oaken greenery plucked…"

Stinkhorn the Great finished and took a bow. The Fixer clapped again, and The Traveller bit his tongue. He had made at least five attempts to get the escape underway only for Stinkhorn the Great to start reciting another play that he'd written and never had the chance to act out for an audience. This short piece, which was aptly called *'If I were a butterfly for a day'* had the lord of the Fungal Empire, a mushroom God to many, a creature whose savagery ran so deep that even the mention of his name struck terror into the hearts of the most vicious Fungaloids, prance about on a small stage with tiny little wings attached to his back.

Ridiculous was close to the word I'm looking for.

Norman felt pretty good about himself; he'd never seen a play before, except maybe the gun-crime street theatre on the streets of Chumpton, and now he not only had watched a play for the first time, but he'd also starred in one too. Being the fabled magic mushroom he was, Stinkhorn the Great had kindly asked Norman if he would be willing to join him on stage to become the only prop that he needed. So, Norman stood still for about an hour or so, grinning like an idiot with his hands and fingers extended in all directions, trying his best to look like an authentic tree; he even swayed a little and made windy whooshing sounds.

"Yeah," The Fixer said rubbing his chin, "it was good, though I preferred 'My little lamb', it seemed to be a bit more, I don't know, cuddly?"

"Oh," Stinkhorn the Great said gratefully. "Ye are far too giving, my shimmering knight. And what of 'Life as a fluffy bunny'? Tis my favourite piece, for it echoes within my chest with truth and warmth."

The Traveller believed it was simply written to echo a few times inside his skull, bounce off the temples and leave the next morning without even the courtesy of staying for breakfast.

"Are you finished?" he said coldly.

"I am!" Stinkhorn the Great said dramatically. "But fear not for I have been working on a romantic piece, *and!* before you ask, you may not peek a glimpse till tis ready for receiving…"

"Brilliant. Right, so what are we going to do?" The Traveller asked.

"I don't know," Norman replied, "we could always look it over once and give him some pointers?"

"I mean with the breakout!"

"The what?"

"The breakout the breakout, *the breakout!*"

"All right," The Fixer said with a chuckle, "calm down. What's wrong with you?"

"Me?" The Traveller said rhetorically, "oh nothing. Not a bean, oh except that Norman is dressed like a tree, the nightmare mushroom god is pretending to be a butterfly and you are just standing there enjoying every second of it like you're on holiday!"

"I *am* on holiday," The Fixer pointed out.

"You are?"

"Yes, well, technically I am. I booked it off a few thousand years ago. That's how I ended up in the fungal prison."

"It was?"

"Let's just say I tried to swindle a couple of fungal card players and they didn't take kindly to losing."

"Of course, you did…" The Traveller said nodding his head. It was just the sort of thing he usually tried to pull.

"Of course," The Fixer said happily. "I might be convinced to come up with some crazy scheme, some hare-brained idea to solve all this mess if you asked nicely."

Norman liked the sound of that.

"Fine," The Traveller replied. "Can you help please?"

“That wasn’t really asking nicely, was it?”

“I believed it not,” Stinkhorn the Great said, “very poor acting.”

The Traveller clenched his fingers, balling them up and trying as hard as could to not hit or lash out. He bit his lip, and spoke through his teeth, while a new vein popped up on the side of his neck. “Please! Can you be so kind? And help us, with some escaping?”

“Of course!” The Fixer said throwing his arms in the air. “You only needed to ask!”

Norman took the tree outfit off and placed it back in Stinkhorn the Great’s costume box; it was full of other costumes of trees. He had a talent for the written word, but no imagination for landscaping. The Fixer pulled a root from the floor to use as a pen and began to scrabble something into the sludgy wall. Norman went to sit with The Traveller as he rubbed his aching head. Stinkhorn the Great went back to his throne to wallow a bit more in some theatrical doom, resting the back of his hand on his forehead and groaning occasionally.

“It seems pretty easy,” The Fixer said. Norman nudged The Traveller in the side trying to lift his spirits a bit. The Fixer, much like The Finder who was also great at hiding, was equally great at breaking things. However, most of the things The Fixer broke were drinking records that had been held for years by Fermentius, the ethanol Deity; he didn’t stand a chance.

The Fixer continued. “The lift we used to get up here seems to use a combination of muscular shifting and back pressure, a sort of pushing from the ground up. We should be able to capitalise on this upwards thrust by simply occluding the pipette by hoarding a potpourri of fungal constructs into it via the open end, cumulating in an explosive burst of tension that will propel this topmost chamber to an altitude, and presuming that it is aerodynamic, it should glide us to a safe landing.”

The Traveller, who was sitting holding his head with one hand, huffed, and said, “So we stuff the lift till it explodes?”

The Fixer smiled, “That’s one way you could say it.”

“I preferred your way,” Stinkhorn the Great said, then moaned again in despair. “How it tis to be free as a sparrow or dove… I—”

“I like the idea,” The Traveller said cutting him off before he had the chance to start prancing around again in another play; God knows he hated them. The Traveller still hadn't got over the last one they went to watch before creation had started.

"Norman."

"Yes?"

"Grab that box of trees."

"No," Stinkhorn the Great said woefully, "please, I beg, not my hand-woven trees."

"I'm afraid so," The Traveller replied happily. "Start stuffing them into the lift."

Mrs Pinkletin found that after eating the two hogs she had gained an omnipotent hunger, of sorts, and was rather surprised that after eating her last meal, who happened to be the unfortunate Finder, her smell receptors had now gone into holy-smokes-I-can-smell-everything-that-has-ever-been-and-will-ever-be overdrive. On top of that, she found that she had an amazing ability to jump from one universe to another; this helped a lot, seeing how she kind of knew that her next amazing meal was in one direction, and on the way she would most definitely get hungry. She thought to herself with nostalgia, recalling the times her and her late husband, Alfred, had gone on long journeys and stopped off on the way at a roadside services for a bite to eat. *Yes,* she thought, *this was just like that.*

So, she had no remorse when, on the way to her next destination, she quickly jumped over to one universe, found a small planet that had been completely populated by a race of small fluffy mouse-type creatures, who had spent thousands of years and countless generations unlocking the secrets of the universe and conquering all diseases and so forth, and ate the lot. But this wasn't enough for her. Her hunger seemed to grow the more she ate. And now that she had eaten The Finder, finding things, especially things that didn't want to be found, was now a piece of cake.

The Sponge Nebula in the Lemon Cake Galaxy brought a tear to her eye; it was her second favourite type of cake and she used to love eating it with Alfred. Not even devouring the entire sentient plant life in the Thyme System helped her get over her homesickness, though as she was a giant plant it could've been classed as cannibalism. She took the small, prophesised Spork child from her waist that she had saved, this was after she'd eaten all the Cutlerians during their last civil war and used the poor Spork child to wrap up some spaghetti-like vines out of a swamp. Though she was heartbroken and alone and very much disgusting to look at, Mrs Pinkletin thought it tasted rather nice and cursed herself for not bringing a few plastic containers with her so that she could save it for later.

Maybe it was fate, or something else, as fate is a tricky topic when talking about omnipotent beings who basically created fate itself, but just at that exact moment she caught a whiff of something that sent tingles down her spine; she didn't have a spine any more, but for effect let's just say she does. When The Explorer sent the chessboard flying in the air after another soul-destroying defeat against God, he had unintentionally sent a few B.O. molecules hurtling through the wormhole that connected his none-space space to space. They travelled light years, thousands, maybe millions, maybe across countless galaxies and maybe into other universes too, all the way here, to where Mrs Pinkletin stood next to a swamp holding a Spork. And now, without a moment's thought, and with the hunger of a drunken teenager leaving a club at five in the morning heading straight to the nearest kebab shop, she uprooted herself from the ground, and flew upwards into the night sky, letting the young Spork fall to the ground leaving him to live out the rest of his days with the only surviving individual of the planet; a sentient raspberry, and his jokes were all the same.

Norman hid behind The Traveller, who hid behind The Fixer, who systematically hid behind Stinkhorn the Great who stupidly was trying to hide behind Norman, so really, they were just running in circles while the lift in the corner was bulging with fake trees. It had started off slowly, after the last costume had been squashed in; it took a while for things to heat up. Now, however, The Fixer was thinking that it may have been a mistake, and just jumping out of the window and using the signed fire escape that led to the ground would've been a lot easier in the whole.

"You could have told us about that earlier!"

"I thought you wanted a crazy idea to escape?"

"I did," said The Traveller, "just not one that might get us killed!"

"Can we die?"

"Yes," The Traveller angrily pointed out as he ran, "we can here."

"How long do we have to run for?" asked Norman. "It's just that I'm getting a bit dizzy."

"Thy too!" said Stinkhorn the Great.

So, with that, they stopped. The Traveller stood them all together and pointed out places around the room that would make better safe places than the open floor for when the entire mushroom head blew off in an explosion of purply-brown slime and fake trees. Norman would hide behind the throne, as the suggestion to sling himself out the window was one he'd not gone for. The Fixer could hold onto a large column that admittedly did wobble a little but looked sturdy enough. Stinkhorn the Great had chosen to try to hide in his costume box and realised that it would only fit one of his feet inside, which really didn't matter that much as just then the lift exploded, and the mushroom head tore off from the trunk in a fiery, slimy coloured ball of chaos sending them sky high.

Portobello 9 itself shook as the ground below heaved from side to side. The mushroom top rocketed upwards through the thin atmosphere, leaving the giant damaged stalk to topple downwards like a controlled demolition of an old chimney; there was little, if any, control about it. The countless millions of Fungaloids that'd been waiting outside the palace were either crushed or covered in horrid slime, though to them it would've been like being covered in chocolate cake.

The mushroom head sped on relentlessly, higher and higher it climbed. The crust of Portobello 9 receded as the planetoid's uneven roundness became apparent through the large gaping hole in the floor.

"I thought you said we'd go back down?" asked The Traveller as he stood next to the hole. The sudden excitement of the bang and the rushing of the wind had subsided and now the mushroom head was quiet again as it left the atmosphere behind and headed into space.

"Yes, well," The Fixer said scratching his head, "I may have miscalculated the thickness of the air. I mean was there any air? I didn't see any."

"So, what now? Do we just float about till when exactly? Hoping that by chance we just run into someone who can help? Great..."

The sound of heavy footsteps became apparent, not walking footsteps of course, more like marching quickly, and not footsteps, as that would suggest that Fungaloid's had feet with toes and stuff, when really, they just have randomly placed clumps of stuff that just so happened to help them move around. So really, the obvious sound of clump steps became apparent — it was the guards that had been hiding in the other room when everything had blown up.

They came out looking angry; nothing unusual there. They surrounded Stinkhorn the Great holding sharpened spears and mouldy disfigured swords chanting some strange Fungalees that sounded a bit witchcrafty mixed with reggae. Stinkhorn the Great cowered like Julius Caesar trying to defend himself from a brutal stabbing, which was very close to the truth. He looked into the eyes of his attacker and saw allies of Oxyn the Big, his sworn enemy and traitor to the throne.

"Ohhh…" Stinkhorn the Great began, "thrust thy blade deep into my heart, wretched beast and take mine life for I…"

The Traveller had come to the conclusion quite quickly that if he were to sit through another dreadful monologue from Stinkhorn the Great, he would throw himself out the airlock thinking it was probably a better fate, and as Stinkhorn the Great had just begun yet another dreadful monologue, it seemed like the perfect time to act on his impulse. And he wasn't going alone. Maybe bravery, or perhaps taking pity on the guards, The Traveller rugby tackled them both with open arms and thrust himself through the hole in the floor out into the vacuum of space. The bitter cold of it all froze him in seconds; behind him, the guards had gone the same way.

Norman ran to the hole and peered outside watching as his friend drifted off like a dropped lollipop.

"I liked him." He started to sob.

"Yeah," The Fixer said casually, "me too at times. To be honest he was a bit stiff… and now he definitely is."

"How can you be so cold?"

"It's he who's cold," The Fixer pointed out. "Frozen solid, in fact."

The Traveller was indeed frozen solid, like some kind of well-preserved portion of meat found only in the depths of a freezer during a tidy out. The cold spread through him unlike anything else. As the last thoughts ran through his iced mind, the distance from the Portobello System behind him and the great mushroom head in front of him let in his omnipotent powers once more, and immediately he felt worse for it.

He shook a little, cracking the ice from his skin like an extremely wet dog, held his forehead in his hand and drew the ache from within outwards. He breathed a sigh of unhappiness, as not only now he was alive, immortal and well, but he would definitely have to save Norman and The Fixer.

However, first things first.

The Traveller took his phone out from the ether, feeling the same as one might do if they hadn't checked their social media pages in about five minutes. He kissed its screen and decided to check his notifications later. For now, it was speed-dial God.

"Big man!"

"Who's this?" The Explorer said.

"It's The Traveller," The Traveller replied, "who's this?"

"It's The Explorer," The Explorer replied.

"What are you doing with his phone?"

"It's my phone now!"

"Since when?"

"Since now!" The Explorer stated. "Anyway, have you seen my hogs?"

"Steady on. I don't care what you call them, I never want to see them again after last time."

"Quite."

The Traveller paused for a moment and tried to recall what he was asking, "That's it. What's going on? Where's God?"

The Explorer huffed down the phone impatiently.

"I have taken over management of things. And all I need to do now is gather you, The Fixer and The Finder, and start my new multiverse in my image. So, if you could just come find me it would save the trip."

"Right," The Traveller said. "Is Oxyn the Big with you, by any chance?"

"He is," The Explorer said, "he's just playing chess at the moment, do you want a word with him?"

"No thanks. Can you give me your address there?"

"My address!? How dare you! I have created a space in none-space, a place that exists between existence, a location that has no location, a—"

"Do you want us to come or not?"

"...Fine. There's a wormhole just past the Crystal City; it's on the left just after the planet..."

"...shaped like a Neptunian Stripper's bottom, yes, I know the place well."

"Good. Come find us and we can end all this silliness and get things back to the way they should be."

"I couldn't agree more," The Traveller said making his phone vanish in his hand. He looked out into the vastness of it all; a billion miles away he could see the mushroom head making its way towards some random corner of the universe. On board, the only one who might be able to stop Oxyn the Big and The Explorer: Stinkhorn the Great. How The Traveller hated eating his own words; and he could actually do that now, as he was omnipotent again.

It would have been easier to transform the mushroom head, from a safe distance of course, into a ship, or a vessel of sorts, but not one for wasting decent materials, he spotted the Fungal guards' frozen bodies spinning in the blackness and thought what better use for them than to transform both into a couple of trans-matter engines. Then he could have them fixed to the huge mushroom head. The Traveller looked down at his hands; he felt alive. Though, could you feel alive if you were omnipotent? If you lived forever, did you live at all? Perhaps that's a question we'll leave for another time, for now at least let's just say that he had missed being able to do anything he wanted.

Being able to do anything he wanted wouldn't last though; at some stage a large amount of grovelling would have to be undertaken trying to convince Anne to take him back, and if she did, he knew that he most definitely couldn't do whatever he wanted from then on.

"It's a sacrifice I'm willing to take," he muttered.

He shot off in full attack mode, keeping his distance of course, and flicked with one hand the two great engines onto the sides of the mushroom head. Just like a racing game that he'd spent too much of his time playing — time that should've been spent 'snuggling' or 'cuddling', or shopping or listening, or, well, there's a big list of things that he hadn't really been doing much of, but it could wait — he leant back on a large chair he summoned from nowhere, took a swig of his drink that came from the same place, and grasped the steering wheel in front of him, taking full control of the great mushroom head as if he were racing at Silverstone for real. It handled surprisingly well.

He forced his foot to the floor. Stars that had been dots in the backdrop became lines as his speed increased, suddenly blinding shots enveloped him, again and again. Every time he passed through to another universe breaking through the cosmic filaments of space-time, another blinding light blew up around him. Through universe 6 thousand and 4, smashing past universe 12, breaking physics in universe 386 trillion, he stopped for nothing.

Coincidentally, in universe 37, a young boy was looking out of his window at the very moment The Traveller and the giant mushroom head raced across the clear night sky. This would've been completely meaningless, if moments ago the young boy's dad hadn't told him a very hard truth about Santa Claus. The boy was having a troubling time getting to grips with it all; fortunately, though, he looked up, saw the silhouette of a disfigured Rudolf followed by Santa himself, and smiled, understanding that his dad was a chronic liar.

Up ahead, the wall of a universe came closer. The Traveller nudged the speed a little more as the trans-matter engines bellowed and screamed. The wall came, punctured like a stone dropping into a smooth lake; ripples of spatial fabric wobbled for light years to come, and now in front of him, a trillion miles ahead, floating like a heavenly beacon, the planet shaped like a Neptunian Stripper's bottom stood waiting. Behind the beautiful sight, just over the left buttock, the Crystal City shimmered in all its glory. If The Traveller hadn't been so keen to visit this area of space so often, he may have got lost, but no, he came from the other way reading the universal roads like the back of his hand. He took a flying pass over the towering crystal buildings as countless onlookers watched a vast Fungal ship roar out of sight. Up ahead, a glowing shimmering multicoloured vortex span like a psychedelic sinkhole.

This had to be it.

A small idea to quickly stop off at the Secret Gardens Retreat fluttered in his mind. It would only be a quick visit.

"I've got a free dance," he said to himself taking his coupon out from his pocket and counting the five stickers he needed. No! If there was to be a happy ending it would come from saving the multiverse, and not from Miss Buttercup, though she *had* said pop in any time you're in the area again.

"No!" The Traveller repeated. He stayed strong. Though it would only be twenty minutes, half an hour, tops…

"No!" He argued with himself. "If I'm going to make things right, Miss Buttercup and her amazing assets will have to find some other punter to suck money out of."

The mushroom head disappeared first through the wormhole. The Traveller let his coupon drift from his hand as he closed his eyes, thought of Anne and how much he'd missed her and followed it inwards towards whatever state of affairs he'd find on the other side.

Colours that had yet to be discovered by most sentient life bubbled and popped in the vast tunnel of trippy lights and shapes rolling and spiralling around him as he raced towards a small white point at the end.

Oxyn the Big looked at God, and God, who had somehow wangled him to fetch a few beers, stared back casually. It had been a good few hours since God had made his last chess move, it had been a very cunning and smart move, and Oxyn the Big wasn't ready to commit to anything that might end up with him losing the entire game.

The Explorer huffed and felt frustrated, "He's moved one pawn!" he shouted at Oxyn the Big. "There's not much he can do after that! Just move a piece."

Oxyn the Big bit his bottom lip considering every outcome of his play, though he'd never played chess before, in all other games he had been deemed the same: a bad loser. And as such he didn't want to rush anything. Another few minutes passed, his clumpy hand jerking occasionally towards a piece, God shaking his head and inhaling as if it was somehow bad, then a moment of genius came. Oxyn the Big picked up a pawn in front of his king and moved it two spaces.

"Great," God said. Then gestured with his head. "Do me a favour mate and move that piece there."

It was his bishop; it swept diagonally across the board, stopped at the edge. Oxyn the Big smiled, and God said, "Checkmate, mate."

Oxyn the Big drew his head back, looked down at the board, and struggled to understand the concept of it all, then grasped the desk the board was resting on and hurled it up in the air with a deathly cry. Just then the great mushroom head came barrelling into sight from the depths of the wormhole. Flying at speed, it tore past just over God's head, clipped Oxyn the Big and came to rest in a large billowing mist of shredded plant skin and mould.

God looked down to where Oxyn the Big was half concealed and thought that it had been extremely unfair of whoever was driving this giant mushroom head to land on Oxyn the Big. Now who was going to tip beer into his mouth for him?

"That's just bloody brilliant..."

The Explorer jumped up from his desk and felt all his power drain away from him like a god that had just lost all his powers; it's the only analogy that really works, as there's nothing quite like a godly being losing all his powers, except maybe the feeling you get when you've been hungry for ages, finally ordering a Chinese takeaway and they've missed out all the chicken balls: soul-crushing I guess would work quite nicely.

"My powers!"

"My beer!"

The Explorer wanted to shout, then stopped. "Your beer?"

"Yeah. I can't bloody drink it now, can I?"

The Explorer walked over to where God sat amongst the scattered chess pieces, picked up his beer can from the floor, and proceeded to drink the entire contents of it in front of him. Then, when he'd finished the can, he hurled it over his shoulder and opened the next. Downing it all in one hit.

"It took me ages to get them!"

"I don't care!"

The great mushroom head wobbled a bit as it came to a standstill on the small platform, most of its bulge dangling over one side. God heard a noise and looked up the vast thing towards the peak and spotted The Fixer climbing out from a small window. Norman followed close behind and both clambered down the large mushroom head towards God. Most of the thing had survived the crash landing, save for a few of the stronger internal columns and fungal structural beams that protruded through to the outside. Behind God, The Traveller appeared from the wormhole, and immediately lost all his power too. His chair disappeared, his drink vanished, and the steering wheel turned to nothingness within his hands as he too came downwards towards the small platform. He hit the thing with a bounce, and another for effect, then collided with the side of the mushroom head right in front of God.

"All right?" God asked casually.

"All right?" The Traveller said standing, rubbing his backside feeling an instant bruise rise up on one cheek. "Where's Oxyn the Big?"

God nodded to the floor behind The Traveller who turned and saw the big Fungaloid's legs just sticking out from underneath the mushroom. "Can't see him surviving that. On the plus side, your Fungal Playing Cards will increase in value now."

"True," The Traveller said happily.

The Fixer and Norman slid down the last few hundred metres of the mushroom head, coming down on the platform next to The Traveller. The Fixer smiled, and with his remarkable breaking skills, tore the chains straight off God's wrists.

"Cheers," God said stretching down to pick up the last beer he had. "How are you? It's been a while, hasn't it?"

"It has," The Fixer said merrily. "Been in jail for a few thousand years. Out now though."

"That's great."

"Surprised you didn't break these yourself," he said shaking the chains in his palm. "They're nothing but cheap thin locks and rusted bolts."

"I know, I know," God nodded. "But it would've been too easy if I'd done it myself."

The Explorer stood facing them all clenching his fists into tight balls, ready to explode. "What do you mean, 'too easy'!" he snarled.

God took a sip of his beer; it wasn't his usual brand but Oxyn the Big had done well.

"I've some bad news for you," he said to The Explorer. "It's come to the end of you probational period, I've had a think about things, and well, you're not really what we're looking for."

“What do you mean, probational period? It’s been fourteen billion years.”

“I’m sorry,” God said raising his hand, “I wanted to give you a fair try, but I think we’ll be going another way. Don’t take it personally. But if you could collect your things and be out by the end of the day.”

“Very mysterious…” Norman said quietly. “…Mysterious ways, and things like that…”

“Codswallop!” The Explorer said loudly. “You gave me my job, and that was that. This isn’t a job interview.”

“Of course it’s not,” God said, “but here in the multiverse we need speedy and organised workers. Take The Traveller here, I gave him something to do, and he did it. With you however… I saw you write down on a piece of paper about seven billion years ago, ‘must overthrow God’, and thank God, you’ve finally done it; that’s the kind of slow pace we don’t need.”

“How dare you!” The Explorer said in a mad rage.

“How dare I? Look, I need fast workers. Take The Traveller, not only did he manage to find the black hole for me and break The Fixer out of jail, but he also managed to sort out Stinkhorn the Great.”

“You killed Stinkhorn the Great?”

“Course not! He’s just over there.”

The Explorer turned round and saw the massive Fungal lord trying his hardest to squeeze through a window in the distance; again, his word play and dramatic skills were on point, yet his size-analysing and measuring ability was not at all that good. He’d met Baron Fluke only once and thought of him being only a few feet long. ‘Men and their difficulty with judging size’ Sheila was wont to say.

A strange noise came from the wormhole. All turned and watched as a giant snapping plant came diving into sight from the swirling mass. Mrs Pinkletin had arrived. Her roots flailed behind her as she sped towards the platform with an intent much like a fox whose target was a coop of crippled chickens. Her nose could smell that ever so sweet smell of godly bodies, three of them lined up like kebab sticks ready to be scoffed, and one that smelt like an old clay blob that had seen to many kilns.

Her arms spiralled through the air and took hold of the platform as she came into land with a thud. Her large thorny body rose up from the ground, her picturesque picture plant head opened up. Her entirety was covered in small flowers, shrubs and other plant life; small insects that had been caught up inside her flight path buzzed around her. Mrs Pinkletin had become so powerful and grotesque that her old self was lost forever, her memory of Alfred a thing of the past; his taste, however, was something she wouldn't forget in a hurry.

She wove a vine arm towards God, picked him up and drew him closer to her mouth, knocking his beer from his hand.

"Steady on… was my last one!"

"Swallow him!" The Explorer yelled victoriously.

"You look famished pet," Mrs Pinkletin said in a deep gargling voice, "why not come inside and have some cucumber sandwiches?"

"Are we going to do anything?" Norman asked helplessly.

"We could order some food?" The Fixer said picking up the dropped beer.

"He means about God!" The Traveller said angrily.

"Oh right." The Fixer swigged the beer; most had spilt out. "Could do… some crazy nut ball plan, something like that, I guess?"

"Exactly!"

"Maybe not nut ball crazy, just a good plan would sort things out" The Traveller replied.

Mrs Pinkletin licked her full and ghastly lips with a tongue that belonged nowhere near an old lady and opened wide for her most precious and tasty meal. When abruptly — and just in the nick of time I might add — Stinkhorn the Great came down with a thunderous boom by her side, took her in his revolting Fungal arms and swept her off her roots.

"Oh …" he began, "Thy beauty, tis blinding."

God dove to the floor, instinctively took his beer back from The Fixer with a jealous snatch and stood back to watch.

"Thy hast a heart of love and kindness, though tis lonesome and cold. In all my years of Kingship and cracked ways, I hast never seen a rose, a lily nor a dandelion as sweet and fragrant as you…"

"What's going on?" God asked curiously.

"It's his romantic piece I think," Norman replied.

"Looks like more silliness," The Traveller added.

"'Kittens and raindrops were much better," The Fixer said.

"...If you were to be mine own, I would surely waken each morning's dawn to the sight of your lustiest figure, and my temptation to have you, why, tis but the tip of an iceberg that 'tis full of care and emotion. A touch... a single breath on my skin... a glance in my direction would be enough to satisfy my need for companionship. Tell me, my cutest little bunnykins... would thou be mine forever?"

Mrs Pinkletin gasped and felt weak at the knees — well, her roots, sort of halfway up, and became limp within the Fungal king's arms. She gazed into his eyes — ignoring the tiny growths and small amounts of slimy stuff that had collected at the sides — and saw her counterpart that she had been missing all her life.

"Alfred," she said in a disbelieving tone.

"If Alfred meaneth love, then I am your Alfred..." Stinkhorn the Great took her head with one hand, planted her lips on his own and felt love course through his veins for the very first time.

"Jesus!" God said disgustedly, "that's enough to put anyone off their beer." He then swigged the last of his beer.

Mrs Pinkletin began to shimmer slightly, and all of the small plants and shrubs on her body began to flower and grow fruit of all kinds and colours. Her arms wrapped around Stinkhorn the Great's body and pulled him closer; her hunger for food dipped as she filled with a satisfaction that was more to her than simple sustenance. It was unadulterated love.

"This is making me sick," The Traveller said.

Stinkhorn the Great pulled away from her and turned yet kept Mrs Pinkletin close to his side.

"My friends, for I am grateful for you bringing me to such beauty, for this, I shall elope with my one true love, and never again will my spores trouble your multiverse again. Of this... you have my word."

"Hold on," The Fixer said, feeling that as The Fixer, he had an obligation to uphold. "Can you just do us one more favour before you head off?"

"Anything!"

"Great." The Fixer turned and pointed at The Explorer. "Don't suppose you could get rid of him, could you?"

Stinkhorn the Great nodded. "But of course." He marched over to the Explorer who was backing away and holding his hands up in the air. Stinkhorn the Great grabbed him, opened up the back of the road sweeper and hurled him at the black hole without a second's thought.

"If tis all, I bid you farewell!"

"I think that's it… cheers!" The Traveller said with a wave.

Stinkhorn the Great gave a bow, pulled Mrs Pinkletin close to his side, pointed upwards and bellowed, "Our future, my love, we head yonder!"

And with that, Mrs Pinkletin uprooted herself and flew off with her new man back through the wormhole, disappearing forever.

"Well, that was eventful," God said.

"I enjoyed it," replied Norman.

The Traveller rubbed his eyes and felt tired for the first time in eternity, the effect of the giant mushroom head still sitting precariously on the platform was still choking their powers, and as such, all felt a little overwhelmed.

"Norman?" God asked. "How do fancy a promotion?"

"From what?" The Fixer asked with a chuckle. "Senior Berk?"

"I was a magic mushroom" Norman pointed out. "And I choked that giant fungal worm… poor thing."

"Well, whatever your post was, consider it behind you. I've got a new job for you."

"What is it?" Norman asked not even trying to hide the fact that his answer was going to be yes even if God had said 'Designated Beer Fetcher'.

"From now on, you'll be called The Janitor."

"Wow! Really?"

"Yep. No fooling. Do you want the job?"

"Of course!"

"Great, now, you can start by getting that road sweeper up and running and cleaning that bloody big mushroom away. Thing's giving me a headache."

"That could be the beer?"

"Don't be silly."

Norman, to say the least, was feeling pretty proud of himself now. He'd done many things in his fourteen-billion-year life, admittedly all in the last twenty-four hours; still though, he'd been through a lot. The places he'd been, the people he'd met, and now, The Janitor, God only knew where that job would take him. He sat in the familiar driver's seat of the road sweeper and started up her little engine, put her in reverse and backed the open doors all the way up till they came in contact with the mushroom head, and began to suck it all away. He had been one for smiling, not consistently throughout the entire story, but now he was sure that he would never feel a frown of unhappy thought cartwheel through his mind again. *The Janitor!* he shouted in his head. *What a name! What a title!* This was his chance to prove his worth, this was the beginning of a new life for him. Norman, the man, the myth, the legend.

God looked at his cards in his hand, and then at the river that lay on the table in front of him. Then at the nice clean stack of poker chips next to his yard glass that refilled itself whenever half-empty. The pair in his hands were indeed a pair of sevens; the cards on the table had no connection to either. So, being the almighty, trustworthy, and honest God he was, he changed them to a Royal Flush and felt no regret at all.

"You better not be cheating again!" The Fixer said sternly.

"When have I ever cheated?"

"When have you ever not cheated?" The Traveller added spying his own weak hand.

"Four million years ago, on the last hand we played, you turned my aces into hotdogs! I wouldn't have minded, but I got mustard everywhere."

"You're just a bad loser!"

"Bog snakes!"

"Any idea where The Finder is?" The Traveller asked flicking a few chips into the pot attempting to bluff his way to victory.

"Pretty sure Mrs Pinkletin ate him," God said casually.

"Oh," came the reply as his bluff fell through. He added more chips to the pile in desperation. "And The Keeper?"

“The who?” God asked. “The Keeper!” he recalled, “right… yeah, don’t know, don’t care.”

The intercom buzzed as Anne’s voice came through, “Are you boys still busy?”

“Hey snooky-wooky,” The Traveller said sickeningly. “We’re only on the second leg. Any chance you could bring us some more beers?”

There was a pause. “You can get your own beers!”

“Okay snuggly-boo-boo…”

“Crikey,” God said, “you still in the doghouse?”

“A woman never forgets.”

“I told you to give me that coupon for the Secret Gardens Retreat,” The Fixer added.

“I know, I know… but Miss Buttercup can be pretty convincing at times.”

“Especially with her assets,” Gad said, leading all three to bark like a pack of rampant dogs.

Anne coughed on the intercom. “I can still hear you.”

The Traveller slapped his head, “Okay bubbly-wubbly… sorry…”

“God” Anne’s voice replied with the cutting power of a heated samurai blade. “The Janitor is here to see you.”

“Aw, Norman! Send him in.”

There was a little tap on the office door then Norman came in looking down at his feet, with the look of a young boy who’d done something wrong and knew he was about to get the telling-off of a lifetime.

“How are you?” God said. “Come, sit down, have a cold one.”

“I’m sorry,” Norman said quietly. “I’ve done it again.”

“Done what again?” asked The Fixer.

Norman looked up and forced a smile. “Lost the black hole.”

The Traveller slapped his forehead. “Norman!”

Norman laughed, “Only joking… had you fooled though.”

“Great timing,” The Fixer said, “now sit down, take some cards and open a beer before God downs them all.”

God burped. “I’ve only had five crates.”

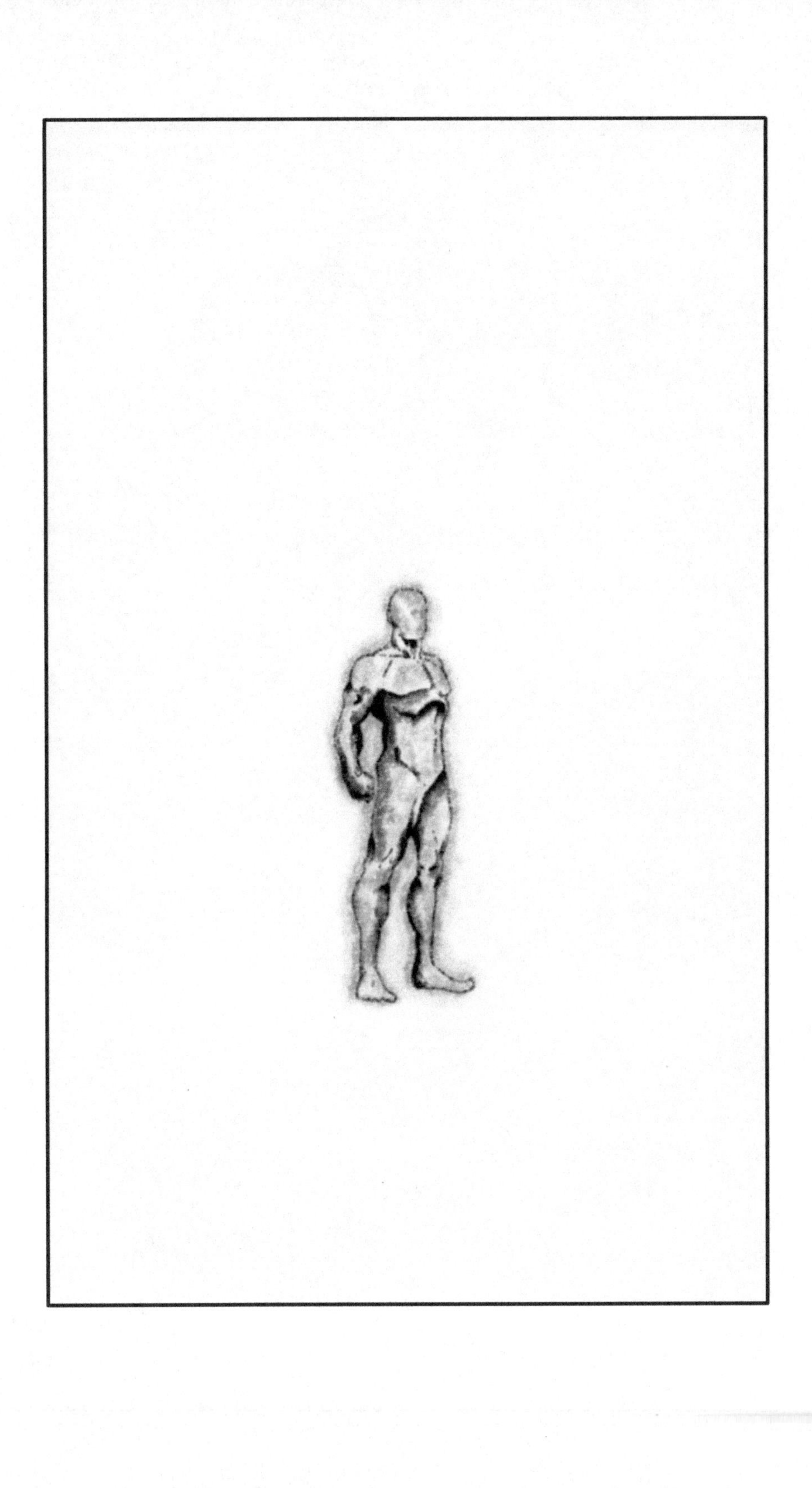

The Cosmic

During the frantic years between the rise and fall of The Fungal Empire, before the central black hole had been reset and the multiverse could recycle its universes correctly, a single universe had begun to cause problems of its own. A civilisation, located within the heart of a technologically advanced collective of planets had invented a way to traverse not only the expanse between galaxies, but the boundaries separating universes too.

A technology that would become vital in the coming days.

The Keeper saw this for himself from the confines of him storage room and decided that to save this universe from the all-reaching grasp of The Fungal Empire, he would rip it from the twisted multiverse, placing it inside a paperweight on his rock. Little did he know that his actions would unravel, causing the rise of a new and altogether different threat.

This universe watched intently from its paperweight cell the destruction Stinkhorn the Great unleashed, and knew that if the multiverse were to survive, new leadership would have to be formed. Uniting under a single banner of peace and understanding, this universe drew forth a plan. A plan to ensure the safety of the multiverse, existence and life itself, regardless of whether the means to an end were hostile or not.

Their goal to create a new God would become their only drive. A new God to rule all.

A new God to rival the old…

And so, sometime after the black hole was reset…

Norman whistled tunelessly as he shut the door to The Keeper's small, yet equally expansive storage room. He was the only person to visit it these days. Word had found its way across the multiverse that The

Keeper had journeyed to the all-female nudist Beach'n'BBQ planet of Jelly Wrestling Prime and attached himself with a small gathering of rebels who liked nothing more than to collect stolen items wherever they, um, well… rebelled.

They called themselves The Saturn Boom.

Even so, Norman thought that, having such a large multiverse to journey around and whatnot, The Keeper didn't need to store all his occult things in the storage room. He thought back to that time when he first came here, it was empty, save for the woven mass of the multiverse in the distance, and The Keeper's rock that he loved to sit on, tending to his broom. It was a simpler time, and a quieter and less hectic time. Now, however, you couldn't move two feet without knocking over a bronze fire pit, or a draping flag that unrolled with the smallest of touches. Tapestries and staffs seemed to congregate for small unheard meetings everywhere, the odd sacrificial table with ornate dagger stood waiting for the right moment to strike.

So, it was obvious that the storage room was the ideal place for Norman to sneak off to for his lunch break.

He'd just finished off cleaning up a star system in universe 71, where someone had forgotten to fully close the atmosphere of an ice planet and it had defrosted everywhere, when he'd got a call from God about a filament that was out of line due to a leaking gas giant spraying all sorts of gases over the sector. Norman hadn't really complained about sorting it out, he relished any job that he was given, though this sort of thing really fell under the duties of The Fixer, but apparently, he was busy with an imploding star that just couldn't wait. But Norman felt strongly about taking lunch breaks, it was where he really stood his ground.

He strolled past the large golden statue of a Saturn Boom deity — it looked like God, only with a rather strange smiling lizard head — and pulled universe 38 billion away where he'd hung it like a sheet from one chair to another and crawled into the small hidey-hole he'd made at the back of the room. Like a sort of pillow castle that you might make when you're a child, Norman had done the same, just with universes instead. He'd tied a few together to make a lovely ceiling that glowed a bit from time to time, picked three others up and leant them upright for the walls, and bent another into an arch to create a beautiful shimmering front door.

Throughout time and space and across all known and unknown dimensions, it was multiversally understood that everyone grows and learns, and comes to understand the relevant truths and things that others call the search for enlightenment, everyone, that is, except Norman.

The storage room might be the second-most complicated thing to exist in existence, that is, just after the central black hole. To have a storage room inside the multiverse that contains the multiverse, so it never gets lost, is a thing that has made many go insane with silliness, so you'd think that Norman may take a bit more care with the storage room contents, and if you really did think that, then more fool you.

He struggled with the clingfilm as he pulled it free from his sandwich, took a lovely bite and grimaced a little. He never liked pickle, thought it was a waste of time and whoever had created it needed to be sent to some disgusting prison somewhere. So, you'd be right in questioning why he put it in his sandwich's day after day. He scraped it to the floor and carried on eating, taking his chocolate biscuit out of his lunch box and laughing a little reading the joke on the back of the foldy bit — 'Why can't you hear a pterodactyl going to the bathroom? … because the P is silent.'

"Oh, my little biscuits," Norman said happily. "How you make me laugh."

Unfortunately, this was all too true, Norman in fact was such a fan of the jokes that appeared on the back of the famous chocolate biscuits that he regularly sent a handwritten letter to the company congratulating them on another fine example of humour.

This one was sure to keep him smiling for days to come.

Norman finished up his lunch and started to pack everything away again, taking his time to unfold the universe that he used as a pillow, blowing a few crumbs into the one he'd assembled into a bin in the corner. If he were a child who had all his friends over to look at his home-made castle, he would definitely be the king. Norman pulled universe 38 billion back over the chair again making sure that, on the off chance anyone did venture back into the storage room, it wasn't totally obvious that his little den was there.

"It looks pretty concealed to me."

"Do you think?"

“Yes!” said the man.

“Thanks!” replied Norman.

“May I ask you something?” asked the man innocently.

“Of course.”

“Did you make it all?”

“I did indeed,” said Norman smugly looking over at his little base proudly.

“Well then,” the man said as he pulled what looked to be a cheap sixties-style ray gun from his belt side and pointed it at Norman. “We have a lot to talk about.”

A green beam of light shot out towards Norman, blinding him momentarily. And then, with the smallest of whooshing noises, he and the man were gone. Leaving the storage room quiet again.

“I’m not saying it was the best thing I’ve ever done,” God said proudly, “but it was definitely up there. Top ten at least.”

The other members of the AA meeting all nodded and wondered if they’d ever get a chance to speak. It was well known by now that when the group came together God insisted on going first, and because of that he took up the whole hour of their time telling fabulous tales of drunken past times. Sure, it was entertaining, but the other members did actually turn up to get a bit of a release; the only release they got was when the hour chime sounded, and they could all go back to their local free houses and forget the past hour in a blur of fizziness.

“It was either me or him,” God continued, “I can tell from your expressions that you’d think I’d be first, but no! I took him down like a shot of Bengal vodka.”

The group’s coordinator coughed, shuffling his chair forwards with a squeal, moved his glasses back up onto the bridge of his nose and smiled.

“Well, that sounds, um, interesting. Maybe we could hear from someone else, perhaps?”

“If you want,” God said.

Nervous looks ranged over the space in the circle, no one really wanted to say anything. It was obvious by now that if anyone did say something, they would have to voluntarily make the choice to either come clean that they had a problem, and therefore bring the mood down, or tell an amazing story of a time they drank too much and make up a bunch of things because they got far too drunk to remember. And let God have the most amazing story, yet again.

"Susan?" the group coordinator said. "How about you?"

"Me?" she said shyly.

"Yes. Why not share a little?"

"Oh no, no thanks. Maybe someone else…"

"Come on Suzy!" God said happily. "I bet you're a wild one."

"No, I really don't think… how about Eric?" She pointed at a green blob who was trying to hide behind its bloblike hands. "Eric would like to talk."

"Are you sure?" the coordinator said.

Susan nodded. "Please."

"Okay," the coordinator said shifting his aim. "Eric? Do you have anything to share?"

God picked up his chair, spun it round and sat on it back to front as he sipped on a fresh cocktail he'd materialised from thin air. Eric, who seemed to wobble a little like someone had overfilled an invisible balloon began to speak.

"Uppy wuppy woo," he said, then spun a hand in the air like a helicopter. "Bang boom bong."

The coordinator nodded and wrote something down on his clipboard. It said: 'Need to find a translator.'

"Wow," God said, "that's bloody amazing. Maybe we could go out after this has finished?"

"That's not really why we're here" the coordinator assured him. "We need to…"

The hour chime went off and before he could finish his sentence nothing but overturned chairs and scattered dust surrounded the empty meeting room. God and Eric sat silently; the sucking sound of curly straws echoed in the quietness.

"Great time," God said to the coordinator, "really moving stuff. Inspirational. Really."

"You're not making much progress," the coordinator said standing, "I think that if you—"

"Sorry" God said holding his hand up. "Phone's going off. Excuse me a second. Fixer, my good man!" he shouted down the phone heading out the door. "What's up mate?"

The door to the small room swung shut and Eric sat quietly holding a half-empty cocktail that God had given him. "Downy doo-da?"

The coordinator nodded, bit his lip, and left without saying a word.

"So?" God asked happily watching the star-speckled view from the small AA building's carpark. "What's the news?"

"I've fixed what needed fixing."

"That's what I pay you for."

"If you ever did pay me, it'd be in half peanuts."

"C'mon mate, you're worth your weight in cashews."

The sound of The Fixer pretending to laugh was more than audible. "Very good."

"You got time for a cold one?"

"No" The Fixer replied angrily. "I take it these meeting thingies aren't going well?"

"Well?" God said loudly, "they're great! Bunch of wild ones, they are."

"Not too sure if you're missing the point there?"

God waved his hand in the air, knowing full well that The Fixer could see it from where he stood a googolplex light year away, "Never mind. So, no time for a drink, huh? What's keeping you busy?"

"This bogging multiverse of yours! If it's not a collapsing star, it's a fractured filament. I've just sorted out a comet that needed jump-starting, and now I've got to go and reset a planet's rings again. Do me a favour, next time you see those budgie-smuggling space giants of universe 9 trillion and 8, tell them to use a proper Frisbee, I can't drop everything to collect planetary rings from the neighbour's garden every other second."

God laughed, "Well that's what I pay you for."

"You don't pay me!"

Norman sat, quite happily too, in what he could only describe as a sort of spherical waiting room; a little table with a plant on it took the centre stage. On the other side of the sweeping chair that circled the ball, the man sat blank-faced, as if waiting for the right moment to kick-start things.

"Nice plant" Norman said eventually.

"Thanks," the man replied. He seemed nervous somehow, yet not at all scared, more excited perhaps; anxious, like waiting in line to get a signature from a famous singer. He very nearly passed out as he began to talk.

"I've been waiting twelve million years to meet you."

"Have you?" Norman said, "you could have called."

The man laughed. It wasn't a joke though, Norman held onto his phone like his life depended on it, and actually it did. 'Lose another phone and I'll deconstruct you' is exactly what God had said.

"My name's Norman," Norman said after another silence. "But I'm sure you already knew that."

"Actually no," the man replied shuffling a little. "We had called you by many names, but Norman was not one… I'm sorry if I'm staring. It's just a great honour to be in your company."

"Thanks… so. What's your name?"

"Thomas Moore," the man replied eagerly.

Norman frowned, recalling that he had heard that name before. Somewhere in the past twelve million years or so he had met a man with that exact same name. His bottom lip protruded with a wonder.

"You didn't have a road-sweeping company, did you?"

"I did," Thomas said, "but that was an age ago. How did you know?"

"I met another Thomas Moore just after I started my travels in the multiverse. He was one of the first I met. Took me fourteen billion years though." Norman winked. "Oh," he continued, "do you know about the multiverse? Or have I just given the game away?"

Thomas nodded flatly, "Yes, we know. And how is the other Thomas? Well, I trust?"

"I think he was eaten by giant pigs actually."

"How sad."

"I think the pigs were then eaten by a giant plant."

"How interesting."

"That used to be an old lady."

"I see."

"Do you?"

"Not really, no."

"Oh…"

"Quite."

"So. Where are we going?"

"Are you not curious about why I brought you here?"

Norman felt a little guilty for not asking, he had been trying to be more polite and engaging; The Traveller had said that he lacked in both departments. Now he just felt like he'd let Thomas down. "I'm very sorry, of course, yes, I should have asked at the start. I've been told I have poor manners."

"I don't think so."

"So where are we going?"

"It's a surprise," Thomas said.

"Okay. And why did you bring me here?"

"That's also a surprise."

"Right…"

By now the small plant began to jostle slightly feeling a strange tension settle between the pair, a combination of Norman's shocking underwhelmed response to an obvious kidnapping and Thomas's emerging doubt that he may have got the wrong person. The small fern, or whatever it may have been, only moved to slice the atmosphere, but ended up making things more apparent and congealed. Norman smoothed a crease on his trousers and remembered.

"I…" he hesitated, "I… sometimes get called The Janitor."

"Ah," Thomas said, looking a bit happier. "That's more like it. The Janitor, as in your ever-constant duties to clean things up and make things right."

"Exactly!" Norman said pointing his way, "only last week, I had to mop up a rather large X-ray spill that was threatening to bring an entire galaxy to a standstill. So many complaints."

"Wow, how interesting. Tell me, I guess you have an infinite number of amazing stories to tell. What's one of the strangest things you've created?"

"Created?" Norman quizzed.

"Yes. Created. As in what wonders have you filled the multiverse with?"

"Well. It doesn't really work like that."

"No?"

"No. The multiverse just sort of, I don't know, fills itself up really."

"I see. So, the randomicity is to an extreme then?"

"Yes." Norman nodded. He had an idea what 'randomicity' meant, though he also had a feeling that Thomas had made up the word and not told the relevant people. Regardless… "Once, years ago, I had to go over to universe 55 trillion and 2 and sweep up the leaking core of a planet."

"Do tell."

"It turned out that this planet was home to a group of people called the Flat-Hollowers. They thought that their planet was a flat disc, but also hollow. And the leader told everyone that he was a great prophet and could prove the doughnut world theory was real by the lava that came from volcanoes as simply a by-product of the super-heated core, which was really strawberry jam. And his mission was to create the largest can of whipped cream ever, and fill the doughnut's empty core with sticky sweetness."

"And I guess he did just that?"

"He did," Norman said sadly. "I used to like whipped cream, but the smell was on my clothes for years, and now I can't even touch the stuff."

The spherical waiting room wobbled slightly as a noise filled the air; the sound of what may have been landing gear entered Norman's ears. On one side of the round room the endless chair retracted back into the wall and one door-sized area of the wall pulled away, allowing light from the outside to pour in. Norman stepped towards the exit, covering his eyes from the blinding sun; he'd spent so much time travelling around space, staying in the atmosphere of planets, or remaining light years from star systems that he'd forgotten what it was really like to look up at the parent star from the ground, and feel its heat on his skin; his skin was clay, and this sun was quite warm, so fearing that he would soon become a statue he darted outside across what looked to be the top of a giant set of stairs and headed for shade underneath a vast column holding up an even vaster roof.

He turned and looked out towards the endless white city. The horizon seemed to just keep going, further and further, a cityscape like no other. Ivory buildings that looked heavenly in design, more like protrusions coming from the planet's surface than structures that had been artificially built. The air was so clean, clean enough to breathe, not like that old Chumpton air that Norman still remembered, nothing greasy and thick about this air at all. Between the huge buildings hung long vine-like bridges, glassy in appearance, ivory white walkways inside them. And at Norman's feet, a set of stairs at least a thousand strong, hundreds of yards wide, clean and untrodden. Behind him, a building so magnificent and mighty that only stairs like these could precede a grandiose palace like that. Doors that looked to be designed for giants guarded the facing front. Everything looked to have been made with expense and reason last on the list; nothing was in half measures here.

"Not bad," Norman said, looking around.

"We have everything here that you may need. You will want for nothing, and if you do, we can make it for you."

"Is there a video rental shop?"

"A what?"

Norman looked again and though obviously marvellous and astonishing, and a million other words that he found hard to spell, he couldn't help but notice that there wasn't anyone around. No one. Like not even a few. One would've been a relief to see. His total awareness of the absolute silence drummed at his brain, and now he was focused on it, it all became a little bit stranger.

"A what?" Thomas said again.

"A video rental shop. You know, so I can rent out some films and a bit of popcorn."

"Ah, right, I see. Mm, yes well, we don't have one of those. I'll have the team get right on it."

Norman went to talk and hesitated again, he didn't want to offend him.

"I don't want to offend you, but where is everyone?"

The Great Delight, or as we know him, The Keeper, sat at the end of a wooden desk next to The Masterful Wizard. Next to him sat The All

Knowing, and lastly, and most rightly, The Truth. They had each travelled a great distance from each corner of the Tadpole Galaxy to commence their next Saturn Boom meeting. And although at first, they might be seen as great and powerful entities, truthfully, they were elderly ex-golf enthusiasts that had too much time on their hands.

All four had taken their seats facing the crowd that had gathered, it wasn't the best turnout really, but they'd forgotten to send out the invitations, and not everyone could attend at such short notice; Bob, for instance, had wanted to attend but his wife was adamant that they had to visit the in-laws.

"Could someone please pass on the message to Bob's wife," The All Knowing said, "that we really enjoyed her last batch of Stardust muffins, and if she feels like it, we'd enjoy a weekly contribution."

The crowd nodded as one member swiftly jotted the side note on a scrap of paper and put it into his pocket. An elderly couple came in through the side doors of the town hall where the Saturn Boomers had decided to meet, and as a result a Mexican style wave of frowns flushed towards them.

"The sign says use the front entrance," one portly woman said bitterly.

The Truth coughed, clearing his throat as he held his little microphone with his hand.

"Now that's taken care of, I'd like to welcome everyone to the six hundred and first meeting of The Saturn Boom. It's nice to see you all again, I spot some familiar faces, and some new ones too. Always welcome here…"

"…Could we just make sure that if you are going to join you fill out the application forms properly," urged The Masterful Wizard. "We've recently been getting a lot of wasted forms that some people are using to doodle silliness on. This is a legitimate group, and we do not like to be seen as a club."

"Yes, yes," The Truth said happily, "I think we're all up to speed, David, don't worry."

"It's a matter that I must point out!"

"Okay. You've pointed it out… lay it to rest please."

“Fine,” The Masterful Wizard said grumpily. He was in charge of applications, and for all reasons, if there were any real ones that is, he took his job very seriously.

“Now,” The Truth said. “Matters at hand. Firstly, not only did Bob’s wife’s muffins go down a storm, but I hear that they’re expecting another child. So, congrats Bob. Secondly, and more importantly I might add, could we please, *please* get in the habit of restocking the toilet roll when we’ve finished in the WC. I think we can all appreciate that. No one likes to be caught short.”

“Could we get in that double thickness stuff?” The Keeper asked. “After Nigel was caught short outside and had to use sandpaper, I think he’ll appreciate a little comfort.”

“Good idea,” The Truth agreed. “Susan, remind me to send out a little get-well card to Nigel after this.”

“Of course, your Factual Truthness.”

“Can we please get on!” The Masterful Wizard said irritably.

The All Knowing covered his microphone with a palm and leant to talk quietly with The Masterful Wizard.

“I hope you’re not getting overexcited, David. If it’s too early for you to return, I understand. But you need to keep your temper to a minimum please.”

“I’m fine!” The Masterful Wizard said loudly. To which The All Knowing replied by glaring at him all-knowingly.

“…I’m fine…”

“That’s better.”

“So,” The Truth announced, “as you’ve all seen on the recent invitation, we would like to hold a vote on our next outing. We very much enjoyed the pencil factory tour that John organised for us, and I think I’m right in saying that we’re all very keen on something new to get our teeth sunk into. So,” he said picking up a small cardboard box from under the table that had been crudely decorated as if a two-year-old had got hold of some PVA glue and an open bag of pasta.

“All the votes are in, and I shall now commence the count.”

The Truth tipped up the box and scattered tickets across the tabletop in front of him, The Keeper then, with a flick of his hand, ordered them all into two separate piles in a half second. He still used his power now and again, though he'd been told that he was limited during all the outings and meeting, and whenever The Saturn Boom got together. That was only due to a few of the other members being a bit jealous.

"Forty-one against, fifty-six for," The Keeper said.

"Ah," The Truth said happily, "it is decided. So, can we all make an opening in our diaries, that next Wednesday, at exactly three o'clock, we shall gather outside the hall, and journey over to the Cardboard Box Design Studios, giving a big thanks to Mrs Higgins for giving us the use of her XL Minivan Plus."

There was a groan that followed as half the crowd who'd voted the other way slowly made their way from their seats to the front doors, pulling out cigarettes and other gizmos that helped pass the time during these white-knuckle moments.

"Marvellous!" The Truth said excitedly.

Deep within the central core of universe 3 and a half, inside a small star system that circled a glowing ball cheerfully named the Sun, on a planet that was half-green and half-blue, a tallish man named Thomas Moore took his wallet from his trouser pocket and handed a wad of notes over to a woman who had been dressed as a construction worker. Thomas at this moment was very much out of breath, bruised a little, though satisfied from doing things that legally I can't go into.

"Same time next week?"

"...Yes..." the woman said flatly.

"And maybe a goldfish? Like I have asked before."

"Maybe," the woman said coldly, "but it'll cost you!"

"That's okay," Thomas said happily.

"I ain't got no fish, so if you want to do something a little odd, you'll have to supply the thing."

"Okay." Thomas nodded, "funny story, actually, my friend owns a pet shop, and he's always saying how he's got too many goldfish to handle. Maybe I can — Oh she's gone."

The door to his small one-bedroom flat in the town centre of Chumpton slammed shut and the squealing sound of tyres racing off down the street could be heard. Again, after a rather noisy and expensive twenty-five minutes, the flat was quiet once more. Thomas quickly collected his clothes from wherever they had landed, folded them all and placed them in the washing basket, and took to the kitchen to find himself a drink. From one of the many empty cupboards, he pulled out a half-finished bottle of Corner Shop's Own Malt and dashed a large single into a glass — when I say glass, I really mean plastic… and when I say plastic, I really mean paper; it was all that he could steal from a birthday party he had been invited to last week. In all honesty, Thomas, in this universe at least, was not doing all that well.

He went back into his bedroom that also doubled as his bathroom, storage room, conservatory, pantry, gym, and dining area (it was a studio flat) and stood proudly in front of his wall mirror; this too may have been liberated, the embossed words *'Homestore 8 x 2 Mirror'* gave the indication that this was true.

"Ah Tommy boy, you are the man!"

He held up his glass and toasted to himself, then downed the lot. If it had been any half-decent spirit, it may have tasted a little harsh. He looked back up, and frowned noticing that his reflection still held a full paper cup of alcohol.

"I just drank that, didn't I?"

"No," his reflection said, "you just drank your own. This one's mine."

"Right," Thomas said considering the idea of outside help.

"You can have another if you like?"

"Can I?"

"Of course," his reflection said. "It's your drink."

"You're too kind."

"Plus, we're in no rush. I've still got to go and collect a few more before we head home."

Thomas went back to his kitchen and rooted around till he found another bottle of cheap spirit; it was right next to the floor cleaner, and though he was sure he would've noticed if he had drunk from a green bottle with a smiling duck on the side, he pondered if he had got them mixed up. Regardless, he took the alcohol and went back to the mirror to find his reflection standing there on the other side, happily leant up against the framework checking his nails.

"Have I poisoned myself?" Thomas asked.

“Don’t think so,” his reflection said, “we’d know about it.”

“We?”

“Yes. We.”

“We?”

“We.”

“As in?”

His reflection smiled, then took a large step out of the mirror and stood next to Thomas. “Do you want a glass, or will you happily drink from the bottle?”

Thomas looked at the drink in his hand, “Fine with the bottle, actually.”

“Good.” His reflection patted him on the shoulder, gestured with one hand towards the mirror, then, with a bit of force, flung Thomas into it. Both disappeared into the mirror’s world, leaving the small flat quiet once more.

There was a knock at the door a few moments later, and a woman’s voice came cackling through the letter box.

“I’ve left me pants in there! Fetch ‘em would you darlin’?”

Meanwhile, in universe 6 trillion, 9 hundred thousand and 2…

The Traveller tightened his grip around the shopping trolley handle feeling frustration that only a being with powers beyond imagination could feel. Throughout time and space, infinity and reason, he had done so much that would warrant him a title that any lesser being would call godly, although he would never take that title as God himself has been known to get a little jealous at times. From journeying across the known multiverse in seconds, to saving existence itself from sentient fungus, he had to say that this was the hardest thing he had ever done, or been forced to do, in this case.

“You can wipe that look off your face for a start,” Anne said as she flicked through the newly released summer carpet collection magazine.

“I don’t really see why I can’t just whoosh some energy about and make the best carpet for you.”

“You’re missing the point” came the blunt reply. “If you do that, what’s the point in doing anything at all?”

"What's the point in not doing it if I can do it?"

"Do I have to remind you of what you did?"

"It was twelve million years ago!"

"Yes," Anne said turning his way, "and I'm sure you can still remember all of their names who sat in the hot tub with you."

The Traveller looked at his feet and fell silent, he could indeed remember their names. He mumbled, "Sapphire Storm would let me create carpet."

"Which one was that again," Anne said coldly, "the one with three breasts or the one with four?"

"They all only had three."

"Dig deeper, why don't you! Shall we get a shovel while we're here?"

The Traveller bit his lip and fell quiet again. A heated red-faced stare from Anne was all that was needed to add a few more years to the sentence of The Last Upsetting.

"Sorry," The Traveller said.

Anne nodded, turned on her heel and proceeded onwards down the aisle of the local Carpet Centre. From the end of the aisle, a young and rather spotty little fellow emerged and headed their way. The Traveller had met many individuals in his time that resembled this boy, all with the same unwashed greasy youth, all semi-enthusiastic and totally above job titles such as Store Helper. The Traveller covered his face with a napkin he ushered into reality thinking about all the other youngsters that seemed eager, yet really only wanted to spit on you when pronouncing words correctly in an attempt to sound older than they really were.

"Hello. Can I help you?" the boy asked cheerfully.

"Yes," Anne said, "we're looking for something."

"Let me guess, carpet? Right?"

The Traveller moaned, "Very perceptive of you. You'll be running the place within a year."

Unfazed and obviously inexperienced in the art of sarcasm, the young boy smiled.

"I *am* running the place."

"Of course, you are."

"Traveller!" Anne bit. "Sorry about him."

“Not at all, ma’am. Is there anything you’re looking for specifically?”

Anne flicked through the magazine that the store helper at the front door gave her and pointed to a few designs and specs she had marked beforehand.

“I like these ones; do they come in a variety of colours?”

The young man asked them to follow him as he led them down a few more aisles and shelves, finally reaching a section of the shop that seemed over decorated with posh-looking ornaments and lights, and a man who stood by a small table like he was handing out free samples of alcohol.

“We save the good stuff for our best customers,” the youngster said. “Everything you see here is our finest wool. All these carpets are made from the wool that has been harvested from Atlantean Bubble Sheep. The wool is already cleaned at the depth where they feed. We shave it off, dry it, wash it, dry it again, put it through the extra fluffiness machine, then after it’s sat for 48 hours, we hand-clean it. Then dye it with an assortment of colours made from shells that have been collected from the Brasparia Beaches of Delicort 7. From there it is shipped in limousines straight to the weaving factories, where it is carefully bound together to create the finest carpets in all of sector 4b.”

“Very impressive,” Anne said happily.

“I knew you’d like it.”

“Can I ask a question?” The Traveller said.

“Of course, sir.”

“This carpet is saved for your best customers, right?”

“Correct sir.”

“But this is our first time here. So how can we be your best?”

“Sir, I was merely saying—”

“It’s just that you don’t know me or my missu — better half. Sorry. How can you be sure that we haven’t come here with some guns just to hold up the place? I mean, you’re not that big.”

“Sir. Um. Really, I just assumed. If money is a problem, then—”

“So, we look poor now, do we?”

“Of course not.”

Anne gazed wide-eyed at The Traveller who looked back at her, shook his head and went over to take a glass of Champagne from the man by the small table. Sitting down on the sofa, he crossed his arms in a sulk.

"Money isn't a problem," Anne said kindly. "We're looking for enough to do our downstairs. Six rooms in total."

The young man nodded and smiled.

"We have plenty of options to choose from, if you'd like to come to my office we can go through the paperwork. Will your partner be joining us?"

Anne looked back at The Traveller who had already polished off the first glass and was halfway through the second.

"No. He's better off here. Let's go."

All around Thomas little fragments of light sparked and flurried; in his left hand he held his bottle of booze and in his right, he held the hand of his reflective self. If this was another episode, then he was sure his guidance counsellor would need to hear about it. She said that the nightmares and vivid daydreams had had something to do with his father leaving at an early age, and though he had no degree in psychology, he had an inkling that she would find it difficult to connect this to any buried emotions from his past. The holding of hands he could put down to the curiosity he explored back in college when he and his roommate Dug got drunk one night and chose to experiment, but he thought he'd got rid of all that stuff after he paid Purple Desire to come around to his flat with the special equipment.

"I'm sure I'll wake up soon," he said softly.

"Wow!" the other Thomas said, "I thought you were asleep. Have you been awake this entire time?

"Um, yeah. Pretty much. I mean," Thomas coughed in embarrassment, "I may have passed out a bit with the initial shock of it all, but now I'm okay."

"Really?"

"Yes fine!" Thomas said in an uncontrolled high pitch. "Fine. Sure, it's not every day that you get pulled into a mirror by yourself, then find that a thousand fairies are dancing around you."

"Fairies?" Thomas questioned.

“Yes. The lights. Admittedly, at first it was a bit of a shock, but now I’m okay. Coolio—”

“They’re not fairies.”

“No?”

“No. Though now I’m starting to understand why I have a side note on your collection papers telling me to keep things simple. It might be easier if I were to just tell you they were indeed fairies… yes, actually, let’s go with that.”

“No, no. Come on. I may have a slight drinking problem, and a lack of basic social ability, but I’m not thick.”

A shimmer of light waved around them, like bioluminescent bacteria in water. The glow of something amazing, which was definitely not fairies Thomas had learnt, lit up for a brief second before shifting back to the ongoing sparkling. Very beautiful indeed.

“Okay. I’ll keep things as basic as I can,” Thomas said. “We are travelling between the filaments of space-time, from one universe to another inside a bubble of supercharged zero-point energy so that we do not disturb the balanced equation of existence itself. The reason for doing so? I am Thomas Moore of universe 37 googolplex, and I am with Collections. We, as in myself and around three billion other Thomas Moores, oversee collecting every other Thomas from every other universe and bringing them together. The reason for doing so…? I’m not at liberty to say. But at the very least you are now up to speed with the key parts.”

Thomas Moore, the alcoholic college dropout Thomas Moore, smiled, nodded, and eventually passed out, which, needless to say, was a little of a relief for Thomas Moore, the well-groomed, successful Collections Agent. One of the things that had been stressed deeply at the start of Collections duty was that at no stage should any Thomas Moore become emotionally involved in any of the lesser Thomas Moores that they may come upon. It wasn’t that they would feel sorry for them, or pity them in any way, of course not, but overall, all Thomas Moores throughout the multiverse share the same feelings towards others. And that is to think that no matter how well or how badly someone else is doing, they were doing better. The goal of the Moore Project couldn’t become hindered if any Collections Agents felt so much hatred and disgust towards a lesser Thomas that they would inevitably kill them off, and therefore this Thomas Moore who thought he saw fairies had just saved his own life by passing out in the nick of time.

The Thomas Moore from Collections huffed, moved his sleeping counterpart into a more comfortable position, and pulled a pen from his pocket to add to the side note of the collection papers: *'If possible, keep knocked out for long periods of time. Furthermore, do not feed alcohol.'*

Cigarettes were stubbed out on the cigarette bins that had been placed outside the hall after The Truth lobbied for weeks to acquire them, and a slow congregation of semi-enthused Saturn Boom members went back for the second half of the grand meeting. Most were quite entertained by the annual gatherings, although some just came for the free food; a large spread that showed off the best home cooking, which included fine homemade lemonades, homemade sponge cakes, and everyone's favourite homemade cucumber sandwiches that arrived by post by Anonymous. Everyone was on high alert after The Grand Wizard had mentioned that there would be a very large announcement and seeing that the proposed field trip to the box design centre hadn't been it, people were starting to wonder what else The Truth had in store for them.

"Sit down, everyone," The Truth said, "please, if everyone can find their seats again, we only have a few more bits to get through and we can all go home."

He looked to his side to see an empty chair where The Masterful Wizard sat.

"Have either of you seen David?"

The Keeper — sorry, I mean The Great Delight shrugged and carried on checking his nails. The All Knowing did much the same yet managed to add a half-arsed look around the room as if he may be hiding in one of the hall corners.

"Nope, not seen him either."

"The All Knowing," The Truth said emptily, "if anyone should know, it's you."

"I got the name due to my legal contacts in the local council. I just know people—"

"Okay, enough Steven," The Truth said.

"It's not like I actually know everything."

"I said enough!"

"Maybe me and The Great Delight should swap names?"

To that The Keeper showed a little more interest and shrugged again. He had found this small group of dreamers, activists and anarchists on the beautiful beaches of Jelly-Wrestling Prime and became so excited about the thought of joining something so meaningful and true, to be part of something bigger than himself. Though now it would seem that he had started to regret his choice. It wasn't because they never did anything corrupt since the Saturn hexagonal graffiti, it was just that... well, actually, come to think about it, that is exactly what had happened. The Keeper's dreams of revolting against evil companies and the like had been squashed by The Truth's insistence on field trips and bake sales. Beside the occasional undercooked muffin, there wasn't much rebelling to be had.

Finally, everyone sat down, and the hall fell quiet.

"I have received a letter from the Rigel School for Boys," The Truth said holding up a folded piece of paper. "Please sit and listen to what they have sent." He leant forwards to his desk-mounted microphone, wet his lips and began.

"Dear members of The Saturn Boom. My name is Keith Miller, and I am the headmaster of the school. I am writing regarding the upcoming summer Bake Sale Extravaganza that we hold every year, where all the profits go towards the church roof that always seems to leak, and what is left over we give to any local charity of our choosing."

The Keeper huffed heavily and stood up from his chair.

"I'm going out for a smoke."

"Okay." The Truth nodded.

Just then The Masterful Wizard appeared from outside. Placing his phone in his pocket, he nodded at The Keeper as they passed. The Truth continued.

"We would like to invite you and your members to the grand reopening of the school gymnasium." The Truth coughed and placed the letter down on the desk in front of him.

"Now, it is no secret that we as an organisation have a reputation to uphold. We all know this. However, unfortunately, in recent times, our reputation has been dumbed down a bit. I personally take part of the blame for that, I can tell just from looking around the hall that everyone is a bit sick and tired of the usual escapes to cloth museums and puppet shows, so here's what I'm thinking."

The Keeper had opened the side doors and stopped as he wanted to hear what great fun it would be attending a youngsters' bake sale… again. Part of him hoped for something more. The Masterful Wizard sat in his seat and looked up at The Truth who gave him an acknowledging glance, to which The Masterful Wizard became a little excited and jumped up and down on his seat.

"I think," The Truth went on, "that it would be in our best interests if we went there — every one of us, tooled up to the eyeballs — and robbed the place blind."

The Keeper, along with most other relieved patriots of the clan stood and cheered, feeling a wave of release flow outwards. The Saturn Boom had once been an organisation that people knew all about, looked upon like bandits of old; if news spread that The Saturn Boom were riding into town, the streets would empty, dust balls would roll across sandy roads, the faint crying of a baby would bring a foul mood that only gunslingers were happy to walk through. Now, however, The Saturn Boom were just a group of fattened elderly men who came together after the golf club had closed down, or the local pub lost its licence. The Truth, who had been a member for most of his years, had seen the change, noticed the steady downwards spiral that the group had taken from being active activists to the lazy mob they had become. He had at last acted, and The Masterful Wizard could not have been happier.

The day of the bake sale came around quicker than most realised, Bob's wife had forgotten all about the robbery and was now feeling quite guilty as she ran about the house looking for the keys to her husband's motorbike, while Bob shouted in panic trying to squeeze into leather trousers he'd bought when he was half his age.

"Found 'em!" Bob's wife shouted as she pulled the keys up from the back of the sofa (I mean, where else would they be?). "Are you nearly ready?"

"For heaven's sake, woman! Give me a chance." Bob pulled the button as tight as he could, sucked in his beer-fuelled abdomen, felt the clip lock in, and exhaled allowing his belly to sag over the top of his belt buckle. “Still fits!”

“That’s great. What are you taking with you?”

“Was thinking of this,” Bob said appearing from the stairs holding up a large baseball bat he’d used only once.

“A bit obvious, isn’t it?”

Bob frowned. “Well, what then?”

“A crowbar?”

“Where’s that then?”

“The garage, I think?”

Bob became a little flustered, feeling like a young boy again, he couldn’t turn up to a robbery with the wrong equipment; he’d just look silly. “I don’t have time to look in the garage! Paul’ll be here soon to get going.”

“What about a kitchen knife?”

“All in the washer…”

“Bread knife?”

“Same!”

“Mm…” His wife thought a while. “You would really stand out if you took the large salad spoon.”

“I’m taking the bat!” Bob said angrily waving it around in front of his wife. “Jesus! Why didn’t you tell me about this beforehand? I might turn up now for the robbery, and people will laugh at me because I’m not prepared!”

“Sorry. You look handsome. And the bat is perfect.”

“Well,” Bob said flatly as he watched Paul pull up outside the house, giving a few beeps of his horn. “Great. Well, the bat will have to do now. I’ll call you later when we’re done.”

“Okay. Good luck and have fun.”

Bob shook his head with embarrassment and darted out the front door quickly. He mounted his motorbike placing the bat on his knees, turned the ignition and revved the engine. Paul did the same, smiled, and held up a large salad spoon. “I knew I should’ve taken my bat!”

“So unprepared,” Bob shouted over the roaring engines, “wife’s been cleaning this for me for days.”

Paul's face fell a little with shame. He placed his helmet over his head, cursed his wife for suggesting a salad spoon, and both set off down the road heading for the front gates of the Rigel School for Boys. There they would meet up with two hundred or so other Saturn Boomer's from across the local galactic sector, all in high spirits, feeling like The Saturn Boom were somehow on the right path to become something great again.

Evidently, the turnout was less than awe-inspiring.

Less than fifty members squeaked as they walked — their leather trousers stretched round their inflated thighs from years of pie eating — as they made their way through the front gates of the school. Near the entrance doors, The Truth stood talking idly with the Mr Miller the Headmaster, both laughing and chatting small about meaningless trivial things such as the wonders of space and cupcakes. As the turnout of Boomers made their way inside, each nodded to The Truth with a little cocked smile. Partly due to the coming robbery where cakes, money and childish pride would be stolen, but mostly because so many other Boomers had not shown up; probably having the idea that an actual robbery was too good to be true; The Truth had steered the crowd off course for so long that many had already begun to defect to the Pluto Chills. No one knew why, all the Pluto Chills did all day was to sit about and hold meetings about how cold and lifeless life was, and that if Pluto was once a planet, then it damn well could be one again.

Half an hour went by as members took to their spots; inside, the bake sale had gone into full swing. Stands selling lemonade and red velvet cake populated the edges of the playing field while a large group of teachers tried their hardest to out-muscle a small group of boys at a long-lasting game of tug-rope in the centre. Neither was in the mood to lose: the teachers had too much ego to let a group of snotty teens trump them at a pulling contest, and the schoolboys were as you'd expect schoolboys to be — competitive and ruthless.

Keith Miller, the headmaster, took hold of a megaphone he'd been shining for days, and stood in a spot he'd picked out earlier for optimal acoustics. "Ladies and gentlemen. Please, ladies and gentlemen..." he coughed and waited for the buzzle of it all to die down till all eyes were on him. He wasn't really the kind of man who loved to be the centre of attention, it was just that Mavis the dinner lady had never responded to his advances and showing that he was the loud confident type might just do the trick to place him firmly on her radar.

"I would like to welcome everyone to our yearly sake bale."

"I think you mean bake sale, sir!"

A roar of laughter swept the crowd as Keith turned red. Mavis had been standing by the doors to the kitchen, and as he looked to see if she had heard his monumental cock-up, she had gone.

"Ha, ha," he went on. "Of course… bake sale. And to you, young Billy Perkins, I welcome you to after-school club for three weeks. Laugh at that!"

"There is no after-school club, sir" Billy Perkins said cheekily.

"Ah yes. Then I guess detention will have to do."

"Oh what… but sir!"

"Now then. I see we have a great-looking sale this year." He began to walk the field introducing the stalls as he went, "Chip! What fine scones you have. I hope you sell every one."

"Me too!" Chip said happily. "Do you want the first one?"

"Mm… better not." Though little Chip Fin was an enthusiastic baker, at only ten years old he still had a loose understanding on quantities and the use of ingredients. His marble cake had been deemed so well made that it still acted as the communal ash tray even after three years.

Keith nodded and carried on. "A lot of you may have noticed that we have a few guests with us today, and for the less learned of us, they are The Saturn Boom Club."

The word alone justified the robbery. 'Club.' The Truth bit his lip and recalled the many, many times David, or The Masterful Wizard, had argued and become violent at the very mention of the word.

"Can the club leader please come up here?"

The Truth shook off the horrid-tasting memories, looked up with a smile and went to his side. Keith looked at him happily and brought the megaphone to his mouth. "Here is a man that has moulded this club, shaped and changed this club. A club that has had its tainted history, but now a club that has changed its ways. What once was a club that people feared, has become a club that other clubs try to be more like. And now, if he is up for it, The Truth will invite you all to better understand the club that has club, club, club, club…

"The Truth," he finally said passing over the megaphone.

The Truth paused, huffed emptily, and said… "We're robbing the lot of you."

You wouldn't think that a bake sale could look like the ending scene from a horror movie, but then again, you've never seen The Saturn Boom in all its glory. If they'd never cared too much about vandalising the hemisphere of an entire planet, then making a small boy cry was child's play. Thankfully, no one had thought about being a hero that day, and as such it was only crème and strawberry jam that covered the playing field like a slaughterhouse floor. Little Chip Fin, on the other hand, was upset that it was only his scones that hadn't been stolen; they had in fact come in quite handy when the need to render parents and teachers out cold came to pass; no one was allowed to leave to alert the police.

The Truth rallied his men to the front gates as the last of them picked up any money tins or undamaged cakes. Keith Miller had been brave for all of two seconds, before he pushed little Gary Grimble out from his hiding place and took it for his own. Whatever chance he had had of becoming the Mr Mavis Dinner Lady was now as good as dead. Bob was the last to leave, he swung his bat high in the air as he smashed a lemon sponge to smithereens. If it made any difference, he looked very happy while he did it. He was just about to leave when he noticed one stall with a little girl standing behind it, all her delicate and beautifully sculpted cakes had gone untouched, and as such, he didn't use his bat, but simply squished his finger deep into the top of a white three tier cake and took off with the rest of his Saturn Boom vandals.

After receiving a long and apparently unwarranted stern talking-to, God gave into Sheila's demands. She wasn't a controlling woman, not in the slightest, if anything she had the patience of a saint. Usually if a woman asks her partner to do something, perhaps like putting up some pictures, it would usually take him roughly anything from one week to six months. God, however, once took so long to take out the rubbish bags by the back door that they had evolved over countless millennia, discovered inter-kitchen space travel and had started to colonise the shed in the garden.

So, you could forgive Sheila for looking smug; she had successfully manipulated God into not giving up on his AA meetings, and it had only taken her an hour.

"I don't see why I have to change groups!" God said. "The last one was working fine. Real bunch of goons."

Sheila huffed and rolled her eyes, "And that's exactly why. I spoke to your designated counsellor, and I know that you're not making any progress."

"Progress?" God questioned. "Love, I could be rolling blind drunk and still create life from a toothpick."

"That's not the point." Sheila reached into her deep handbag and rummaged around a bit, bringing back a small card that she handed over to God. "I've booked you in for a session with these lot. It's being held at the Alpha One Complex on Super Prime. The Cape Galaxy, universe 78 million and 4. It's starting in five minutes. No excuses!"

"But—"

"No. Excuses!"

God huffed and lowered his head.

"Please," Sheila said softly. "I'm not the bad guy here. I just worry. Look, if you go and you don't like it, I'll find somewhere else. But at least give it a go. For me?"

Eventually, after what seemed like a lifetime, God nodded. Not that enthusiastically, but it was a definite nod.

"If you go and give it a chance, when you get back, we can do the thing you've wanted to do for ages, and I promise I'll try to enjoy it."

God smiled, and a joyous look swept his face. "Really? Are you sure?"

"Yes," Sheila replied. "If that's what you want. I just don't see the attraction. It's not very ladylike, is it?"

"You should never miss an opportunity to try something new, once… twice sometimes. Three times at a push."

After a few minutes God had traversed unfathomable light years, roared through countless universes, broken all known laws of physics and changed into something rather fetching for his arrival. He came down outside Alpha One Complex with a very light landing and was instantly deflated. He'd expected that with such a grand name as Alpha One

Complex, Alpha One Complex would've been a huge, towering construct that took over the cityscape, its silhouette large and looming pressed up firmly against the green dawn sky of some alien planet. If you had thought the same then sadly, you would be wrong. As it happened, Alpha One Complex was just a small-town hall based in another small town. This was the Cape Galaxy, and the planet was Super Prime — planet of the Superheroes. And though misleading at times, everything had a name that over-indulged itself.

God made his way up the uneven path to the front doors, noticing a red, letter box overflowing with envelopes; the sign riveted to its front said, *"Capsule of Wonder, Destined to Transcend Time in The Fight Against Wrongful WIFI Connectivity and Respective Hearing. I Shall Stand till The End of Days, I Am More Than a Red Box, For I Am A Symbol."*

Inside, the usual circle of chairs sat round each other, with the eclectic scattering of people from all over the galaxy. God made his way to the nearest empty seat and sat down heavily. He had decided to do it for Sheila's sake.

"Hello everyone. My name is Mr Marvellous, and I have a drinking problem."

There was a brief applause from the other hopeless heroes as they commended Mr Marvellous for his honesty, then he continued. "It all started a few months back…"

Mr Marvellous flew through the sky faster than a man running from his ex-wife; the air itself tingled as his sheer amazement shot past. Ahead, a burning building stood amidst an emptying street, fire engines and police scattered everywhere on the road below. Their blue flashing strobes illuminated the black bellowing clouds against the cold, starry night. The sound of a young boy screaming from a top floor window fell upon the scene like an alarm bell ringing.

Mr Marvellous came to a hover above the expectant crowd while a few enthusiastic police officers snapped what pictures they could with their smart phones before the show began.

"'Stand back loyal citizens!' I shouted boldly, 'I shall save the child, and put out the fire.'"

A quick scan of the building with his thermo-vision made it obvious that it would only stand a few more minutes, plenty of time to save the young boy. Anyone would have thought that! It was Mr Marvellous, after all. He came to the window ledge where the young boy was, the flames of an ever-approaching fire behind him slowly eating away at the floorboards.

"'Take my hand!' I said…"

It was at this point in the A.R.S.E. — Association for Rehabilitated Super Entities — that Mr Marvellous began to break down, God saw this from his chair and kept quiet, bringing a glass of Champagne to his hand; an alcoholic's gathering like this he felt needed a bit of class.

"He didn't though," Mr Marvellous said with a choke, "he just stood there, pointing at me, holding a lighter in his hand and demanding that I go away and come back again properly, doing a few barrel rolls on the way."

"And how did that make you feel?" the A.R.S.E. counsellor questioned.

"…unappreciated."

"And?"

"Useless…"

"Anything else?"

"Well," Mr Marvellous said glumly, "I guess, not good enough either."

"That's perfectly normal Stuart," the counsellor said with a smile. "Here at A.R.S.E., we don't judge you, we try to let you see that even superheroes feel down every now and again. And as a side effect, drink often comes into play. My A.R.S.E. is a safe place where you can nestle into, feel comfortable, and let it all out when you're ready."

"Sounds wild," God said loudly.

"Ah," the counsellor said turning on his chair and looking over his register, "you're new today, is that right?"

God nodded and sipped his bubbling bubbly.

"I see Angus 500 has let us down again…" the counsellor said checking his register a second time. "For a speedster, he's always late. He's asked me to pass this on to anyone who wants it though, it's a coupon for… a Miss Buttercup? Apparently, it's for a 'special' in the

Crystal City Hot Tubs? He found it on one of his many, many…" the counsellor huffed, "many, late-night jogs to the Red Lights."

"I'll take it!" God said taking it happily.

"Now, if I've got this correct. You should be… God? Right?"

"Correct."

"That's a strange superhero name," The Amazing Flute Boy said.

"Yes," agreed Night Fear — Lord of Moons. "Talk about a big ego."

"God complex," War Maiden said. "We all go through it."

"Tell me," the counsellor went on, "why God? What is the meaning behind the name? And what powers do you have?"

"Well," God said leaning back on his chair, all eyes directed his way. "God is my actual name, it's on my birth certificate. And as for my powers, I can pretty much do anything I like, when I like, to who I like."

"Can we see?" War Maiden asked.

"Sure." God's hand sparked a little as a jet of energy flew from his fingers, turning Night Fear — Lord of Moons into a rather delicately carved shrub.

"Very nice," War Maiden said. "Can you fly?"

"Yeah, course."

"Have you ever seen battle?"

"Sweetheart, I invented battle."

"So, you actually think that you're really God?" asked the counsellor.

"I *am* God," God said. "I can prove it too."

"Go on then," The Amazing Flute Boy said, "tell me something that only God would know."

"About what?"

"I don't know. Something about me," The Amazing Flute Boy replied doubtfully.

"Right…" God scratched his chin and had a think, there were so many little nuggets he could choose from, so many small little things that Timmy — The Amazing Flute Boy — had done in his small life that it was hard to produce a single thing. "In year 4, back at secondary school, you were told by your teacher, Mrs Gunk, that you would never play the saxophone well. I remember that day cos you were so upset. You'd spent hours making posters that said, 'The Amazing Saxophone Boy' that now you'd have to throw away. In all fairness, The Amazing Flute Boy does sound better."

The Amazing Flute Boy turned red, and rightly so. 'The Amazing Saxophone Boy', I mean really. Such a silly name.

"Yes, well" the counsellor said. "Can we get back to the point of you being here? We all have stresses in our life. Mr Marvellous for example, he had an outstanding rep, till that fateful day he was laughed at, and turned to drink. War Maiden lost an arm-wrestling tournament with a Bularian Sand Lizard, and her choice of poison was kitchen cleaner."

"I find the cheaper branded labels have a better kick to them," War Maiden said.

"...So, tell me... *us*" the counsellor asked gesturing with his hands, "why have you turned to drink?"

God huffed, blew the glass of bubbly from his hand as if it were dust, rubbed his head, and began. "It all started about, I don't know, fourteen and a bit billion years ago? I'd just finished with the whole creation thing, and I guess the stress got to me. You know how it is. Life, existence, matter itself in one hand, and a wife that has so much belief in you in the other. After the first few million years, I just thought, do you know what? This drinking thing is pretty good actually...

"Same story everywhere really..."

For a while, The Amazing Flute Boy gazed at his fellow A.R.S.E. members, who in turn looked back in silence. There was The Human Man who could summon the strength of one really big man; he turned to eating toilet cakes after he was called a fraud. Killer Flea, the entity that could jump supreme distances in one leap had lost his mojo after he landed too close to a dog that was getting its vaccinations at the time, and his weakness had been shown to the world — One Spray Away, by Pet House Ltd — he couldn't go on; especially after the January sales had just started. Each A.R.S.E. member who had thrown in the towel began to reflect on their own stresses and reasons for turning to the bottle and came to a realisation.

"Yeah," The Amazing Flute Boy eventually said. "When you put it like that, I do sound pretty cool. Think I'll be off..."

War Maiden stood up lifting Night Fear — Lord of Moons under her arm.

"Me too. It was only an arm-wrestling game anyway. I'll take this shrub round as a peace offering," and she too disappeared out the door.

One by one every long-standing A.R.S.E. member stood, thought about how silly they had been by thinking that life was over due to some small little inconvenience, and left, never to be seen again. Finally, after a few minutes God sat on his own in the ring of chairs, sipping another glass of Champagne, while the counsellor ogled him with contempt.

"So," God said curiously. "What should I do?"

The counsellor shuffled forwards, frowned and replied, "I don't care! Everyone has left! My A.R.S.E. is ruined, thanks to you!"

"...You're very welcome."

Another small hall emptied, another failed meeting. This was becoming a weekly occurrence. Sheila would not be happy. And as if on cue, God's phone started to ring. He took it from the ether along with a curly straw that he hoped would spruce up his Champagne flute, but to his surprise it was Anne calling for the first time in God knows how long (and of course he did know: it was seven years three months and four days).

"Where is he then?"

The cold sharp no-nonsense tone of Anne's voice was a little icier than her usual pitch; this could only mean trouble.

"Nice of you to call," God said happily.

"Don't do that to me," Anne replied angrily. "Just tell me where he is."

"Who?"

"You know who!"

"...You would think that I, of all people would, wouldn't you?"

"So?"

"So... I don't."

"...Is that a question?"

God heaved backwards on his chair attempting to gain a bit of comfort, you would've thought that a planet of super entities would've been able to afford comfortable seats.

"I assume you're talking about our Traveller?"

"Correct."

"I haven't seen him."

Anne huffed angrily, “The man at the store said that another man holding some kind of knock-off ray gun took The Traveller away. I can only presume that this is some kind of, lads’… joke… prank thing. So where is he?”

“I honestly don’t know!”

“And if you did, would you tell me?”

“Of course!”

A short uneasy silence fell on the call as Anne went from angry to concerned.

“Look, you just make sure that when you see him you get him to call me right away. We’re meant to be going out to pick up our new wood flooring in an hour. Just tell him please.”

“Will do…”

The Traveller was well known for his quick escapes during shopping trips and times when the in-laws were due. So, it wasn’t a shock to hear about his departure from what sounded like a very interesting house renovation. Even so, history had shown that during these times of spontaneous escapism, God had been the Go-To safe house. A quick call would sort everything out, and perhaps, God thought, The Traveller may even have time for a quick pint… or two. Maybe three at a push.

Speed dial one pressed firmly, the name ‘Wing Man’ shone up on his phone with a picture of The Traveller in a hot tub surrounded by multi-breasted women, followed by the scrolling text on the screen saying, ‘out of area.’

Thomas Moore from Collections chewed the end of his pen as he started to run a head count. It hadn’t taken him long to gather up a handful of lesser Moores that had been passed his way by management. He’d found Thomas Moore from universe 68 thousand wondering hopelessly in the Ghaaba Sands of the Holiday Complex in sector 5; an offer of fresh drinking water and he was readily onboard. In universe 59, he’d rescued Thomas Moore just at the right time; he had found Private Moore and his platoon pinned down in a so-called red zone. The enemy were flanking his team; the demilitarised blue zones had all been captured; yellow zones were next to go. If it weren’t for the Collection agent’s perfect timing, Team Moore would've lost the annual Army Twisty Arm'N'Legs Championships for a sixth year running.

"Thank you, *sir*!" Private Moore shouted. "Orders, *sir*!"

"Umm," Thomas said unprepared scanning over his notes, "uh… at ease soldier."

"Yessir!"

There was Thomas Moore from the dwarf populated planet Hyper-Beast-Mode Centuri; a planet not compensating for anything. Thomas from universe 888, who understandably had lost everything to online gambling, and a handful of others that had argued little about stepping through a mirror or jumping in a ball of supercharged zero-point energy to traverse known and unknown space with their apparent doubles.

The small gathering of clones sat patiently inside the transit; a quiet mood fell about the cabin. Each Thomas eyed up the next, weighing them in, scanning them as if they sat against rivals or the enemy. All except Thomas who had brought along his second bottle of cheap whisky to throw back, he was well and truly not doing anything in the slightest, as he was unconscious, and snoring like a hibernating bear. After the long and very awkward journey through countless universal barriers, made even more awkward after the drunken Thomas woke up and tried to steal the dwarf Moore's battleaxe, mistaking it for a toffee hammer, the transport set down in front of the magnificent white building. One by one they took their leave and made their way out to what seemed like freedom, or at the very least, something close to it. A man dressed in ritualistic robes came to greet them all, took their names and jotted them down on a piece of paper that had numbers and boxes to tick, and escorted them all towards the grand white building at the top of the giant stairs. Down the road from where they were, just past a kebab shop and book shop that shared the same name — Greasy Fingers — The Traveller gazed through a window wide-eyed and curious.

"And you say that except for Norman and myself, there's only other Thomas Moores living on this world?"

"That's correct," Thomas Moore with the sixties-style ray gun said happily. And happy he definitely was. It took far, far… far (sounding rather deflated) too long for Norman to explain that he wasn't the one Thomas was looking for. Though in hindsight it may have been obvious,

obvious when thinking of his total uninterest regarding jokes that came on the back of chocolate bars, and obvious when considering his deep questioning about the meaning of life, and his unsatisfactory look when told, 'To clean the spills'. Now though, he was happy knowing he definitely, without question, had kidnapped the right man.

The Traveller took a seat by the window in the bakery. Moore 'n Sons was well known for its amazing baked goods, a foot-long sausage roll that had gone on sale put it firmly in the front running for Bakery of the Year Award. Coupled with the fact that they were the only place in the white city where you didn't need one of those silly little trolley coins to go shopping, it was near enough a guarantee they had the award in the bag.

"I've been to most places in the multiverse," The Traveller said gazing out towards the cityscape, "but I've never been here."

"We've been sort of cut off from everything," Thomas said taking a bite of his pastry.

Mm, The Traveller thought. "What I mean to say is, I know of everything in the multiverse, yet I haven't visited everything…"

"Takes a while, understandable…"

"…Yes, it does. But I don't know this place. What universe is this? You said you know of the multiverse, yet are we actually in it still?"

Thomas, in the most condescending way, laughed and shook his head, "Yes we are." He smiled. "But also no."

"So, what is it?"

"It's both."

"How could that be?"

"Don't you know?"

"If I did," The Traveller said through his teeth, "I probably wouldn't have asked."

"But" Thomas said looking puzzled. "You're God, right?"

"No."

"No?"

"No!"

"Oh."

"Yeah."

"So," Thomas questioned, "who are you?"

"I already told you! The Traveller! I travel."

"I thought that was some sort of code word for The Supreme Being. 'The Traveller', it has a mysterious sound to it, like you know everything, have the answers to questions that haven't been asked yet. Untold knowledge, limitless powers and so on…"

"Yeah." The Traveller nodded with a blank face. "I have all those things. But it doesn't make me the big guy does it? You could have asked at the start."

Thomas nodded in agreement; he'd made the same mistake with Norman. Had he have just asked outright without all the wise, mysterious riddles, a lot of time could have been saved.

"Right," Thomas went on, "any chance you could tell me where I'd be able to find him?"

The Traveller rubbed his head and began to eat his pastry. "Could be anywhere. I know he had some meetings; he may have had to go out of the offices for a bit to fix some quasars that were out of line."

"Shall I take you home too?"

The Traveller thought for a moment and began to panic. Anne! Oh no. She would not be happy in the slightest. She was already upset after the taps for the new bath turned up with the wrong pattern embossed on them, add to that, the paint that was picked out a week earlier, and discovering it was Sky Blue and not Lighter Sky Blue as intended, The Traveller's disappearance would surely plunge her into the abyss never to regain a sense of sanity again.

"Look," he said sharply. "Let's just skip a few things that I feel you want to tell me. I don't care where we are, and I don't care who you are, or, how you know so much about the multiverse, or even why there are so many Thomas Moores on the planet. All I need to know is: am I safe here?"

"We don't mean you any harm!"

"No," The Traveller said feeling that this was his chance to belittle his capturer, "obviously, I don't mean from *you* lot… the very idea!" he joked. "No, I mean can anyone find me here? Say, I don't know, an advanced being? An inter-dimensional monster, or perhaps, say… my wife?"

“If you wish to stay,” Thomas replied happily, “you’re more than welcome.”

After an hour or so…

Norman picked up another handful of popcorn and shovelled it into his mouth, not even noticing The Traveller taking the seat next to him in the small and quiet private cinema that had been built specifically for Norman.

“What are we watching?”

“Jesus!” Norman exclaimed, throwing a cluster of corn into the air, “frightened the life out of me!”

“Sorry…”

“What are you doing here?”

“…Hiding…”

“Popcorn?”

“Please.”

The Truth felt very good about himself as he sat comfortably in his little office counting all the money his savage cult had managed to steal from the children’s bake sale. It easily reached into triple figures. Why, the last time they had hit such riches The Truth was still ascending the ranks, the hexagon was halfway through being painted upon Saturn’s northern pole and tea was still Britain’s favourite hot drink. The ideas that rolled through The Truth’s mind as he pondered the unknown limitations of his cult gave his skin goosebumps and shivers. If a children’s bake sale today, then why not a teenager’s house party tomorrow? A quick glance on any social site and The Truth would know exactly when Big Pete’s parents would be out of town and where the rave would ‘kick off’. Or was this even too small a goal? When he was a boy, the previous cult leader had been a little less forgiving; he’d worked fiercely to create such a haunting reputation for The Saturn Boom, that The Truth could not help but feel a little inadequate.

He stood, turned to the window that looked out upon the thick woodlands of Mimas, third moon of Saturn, his stance wide, hands clasped together behind him. He was an iron man, a giant with an army at his back, and they would follow him anywhere… he hoped… Maybe.

“Mm” he pondered. Would they follow him anywhere? Thinking of his recent teachings and cult leadership, he felt a little shame regarding the direction in which he had steered them.

It was true … The Masterful Wizard was right … they had received a load of application forms back that had been defaced and brutalised. In years gone, people had been physically begging to join The Saturn Boom: “Better to join them, than go against,” that’s what the people used to say. And now what? Invitations to local bake sales. How could he be proud of that?

“I need to think,” he said as he took the locked money box labelled ‘Cult Funds’ from his desk drawer and placed the small amount of profit inside. Though not much for a cult robbery, it had been the highest profit from a bake sale the Rigel School for Boys had ever taken, if it weren’t for the robbery, that is.

There was a knock at the door then The Keeper appeared looking semi-happy as always. He somehow managed to have a perpetual look of boredom slung across his face, as if the monthly trips to the Orange Peel Recycling Plant, and the Wool Spinning Museum hadn’t flared his excitement.

“Great Delight,” The Truth said welcomingly.

“Truth.”

“Didn’t see you at the bake-sale heist. Something came up?”

“Mm… yeah.” Both knew that nothing had come up; nothing ever did. The Keeper had been an on- and-off Saturn Boom member for longer than The Truth knew. Longer than anyone knew. By the time The Truth’s great-great-grandfather was walking, The Keeper had already seen the Boomers rise and fall many times over. He’d been at the forefront of things when they took up arms against the hostile and often toxic Uranus Stings; he’d driven back the alien cricket swarms that came from beyond the Oort cloud. If history could speak outwardly then the very air that sat around The Keeper’s being would shout and scream at The Truth to move aside and let a real veteran take charge. Though The Keeper knew The Boomers needed new leadership, he couldn’t bring himself to do it. Godly he may have been, but God he wasn’t. If The Keeper really wanted to, he could take charge with a snap of his fingers. It’d be like taking candy from a sixty-five-year-old baby with dentures.

"So," The Truth asked, "what have I done to see you today?"

"Nothing. I just fancied a little chat. A catch-up, just to see how things were going."

"I'd be telling fibs if I told you things were grand."

"Really?" The Keeper said surprised. Even when the cult had been going through rough dry times, The Truth had always been upbeat about things.

"Yes," The Truth continued. "I may have lost my way."

The Keeper had indeed ventured over to his offices for a leisurely chat, though now his interest had spiked, and a genuine intrigue took hold of his mind. "Lost? How so?"

The Truth huffed, stood again and looked through his window into the distance. "I've been foolish to think that The Saturn Boom could've been anything else but a lethal force. I had images of us becoming part of society, helping out, giving aid to people that needed it." To which The Keeper rolled his eyes and sank into a chair. "Though I've come to realise that we give aid and help in our own special way."

"…Yeah?"

"Yes. You see, to all the people that wish to escape their normal, everyday lives, and become part of something truly huge, we are the answer."

The Keeper nodded. However frail The Truth's silhouette looked against the window, he spoke about the exact reason The Keeper had joined in the first place. The feeling of brotherhood, bonding and being goal-driven. The Saturn Boom had once had a sign hanging over their head office doors: *'Today Togetherness — Tomorrow, The Universe.'*

"It can still be like that," The Keeper said standing. "People haven't given up on the cult yet."

The Truth smiled. "I know. It's not the members I'm worried about, it's everyone else. What kind of savage battle-hardened cult gets invited to a bake sale?"

"You're right," The Keeper agreed. "That's very true… what are you going to do about it, though? Stand around waiting for the next 25% off voucher for the Tea Rooms at Donnington Derby to appear on your Voucher-World app, and book us all in for a cream tea? Or ride down there, take what's ours, and leave nothing behind… remember, it's not the robbery that counts, it's the togetherness that you're giving us, and them! We have to look to be the biggest entity to fear, so that the community can unite against us, and we need to give The Saturn Boom its reputation back."

"You're right," The Truth agreed. "It's so simple, really," he said cocking a crooked smile. "Today togetherness and tomorrow the universe. We could bring everyone together. Absolutely everyone. With your help."

"With my help?" The Keeper asked. He saw a spark in The Truth's eyes that hadn't been there before, some crazy notion had surfaced, and The Truth seemed to grow four times his size.

"Yes," The Truth said loudly. His voice had a sudden straightness to it. A bold certainty that took over the usual fragile tones. "Yes! Together, me and you, we could unite the universe. Bringing everyone together against The Saturn Boom, we could bring peace to the universe!"

"You're starting to sound much more appealing," The Keeper said happily.

"I can see it know. Such a beautiful sight. And I shall lead the charge, with you by my side."

The Truth took to his seat again picturing pure visions of unity and peace, the entire cosmos bound and bonded over the hatred of his own cult. He would become an unwritten anti-hero in a universe ripped apart by avoidance and an 'I'd rather not get involved' attitude.

"Multiverse," The Keeper corrected, sitting on the desk by his side.

"Excuse me?"

"I think you mean multiverse." The Truth became wide-eyed and visually seemed to vibrate on the spot. The multiverse united — now that was more like it.

"Fetch us a drink, we have a lot to talk about."

In every universe throughout the known multiverse, there are countless things to visit if you are in the mood for a little holiday. For instance, the planet called HAT-P-1, is by far one of the biggest planets in existence; sure, there are bigger, but this will do for an example. If it were any bigger, it would undoubtedly encroach star standards and begin a fusion reaction. This instability is one of the reasons that in universe 807, planet

HAT-P-1, known locally as Big Henry, is such a tourist attraction. The gaseous skies that wrap around the giant's core are filled from one hemisphere to the other with all sorts of strange and wonderful cities, bustling with markets and shops, drifting within the swirling purple storms.

In universe 39 million, the red giant star called Red Man, is very popular with out-of-work daytime television celebrities as it is a perfect place to catch a soothing tan. And of course, a large strawberry daiquiri too.

The Fixer, though not really a nasty sort of being, has little interest in any of these places. In his entire life he had only ever had time off on a few occasions; mostly ending in his inevitable imprisonment. He'd never like to admit it, yet for him, and The Traveller, it had become blatantly obvious that sorting out all the flaws and defects of the multiverse now rested on their shoulders. God, it seemed, had become far too busy attending to his own problems.

Scaffolding tends to pop up in the most random of places. If you took a stroll through the streets of London, I would put money on you coming across some metalwork on every other street where you would find little work getting done. The same story does not translate to the multiverse — except for one location.

God had found himself a little lonely after the falling off A.R.S.E., and though technically it wasn't his fault, he still felt the blame land on him. After he'd left Mega-Complex One, he had tried to locate The Traveller and failed miserably.

"So, I was your last resort?" The Fixer said cleaning lubricant from his hand. "Nice to know you still care."

"It's not like that, mate."

"Really..."

"Yeah." God sat at the bottom of the scaffolding sipping a fresh cocktail he'd picked up from Big Henry while on route. "What's wrong with it then?"

The Fixer took a seat next to him and tried to exhale the lump of stress from his chest. "Everything. Everywhere. All of it. I don't know... this multiverse of yours, it doesn't want to stay fixed."

Above where they sat, framework extended in all directions for three-hundred-million light years, creaking and swaying as the Boötes Void jostled slightly behind it. It was an ongoing problem, one that The Fixer was constantly attending to. The scaffolding had been up, keeping the void stable for nearly nine-billion years, and quite frankly, he was beginning to worry about wear and tear.

"You want a hand?"

"No," The Fixer said calmly, in a vague attempt to sound calm. "This is what I'm here for. The Fixer. I fix, therefore I am."

"Well said."

"Can I tell you something?"

"Of course."

"After all this time, I'm starting to think that the multiverse was a bad idea."

"Seriously?" God asked worriedly. "Why?"

"...Can you ever see a time when things won't need sorting out?"

God pondered. "I guess not."

Above them the sound of snapping metal chimed as one of a few thousand galaxies that resided within the Boötes Void collided with the scaffolding, sending a good few million years of hard work out the window. It was the same everywhere. The Fixer had just come from repairing a broken cosmic strand that had got stuck down a black hole; he'd described it as pulling Big Foot's shaven beard from a bath plug. Before that he'd been reshaping a nebula that had distorted itself into what only could be called inappropriate. It seemed, as both sat there drinking cheap alcohol together, that the fixing and ongoing maintenance of the multiverse would never actually end.

"Maybe you're right," God said eventually.

"Maybe... or maybe I just need a break."

"No," God argued kindly. "The multiverse was a great idea; it gave us all something to do. But I guess, thinking about it now, it may have been a bigger project than I realised. Hell, would I be drinking like this if we had just carried on playing cards?"

The Fixer laughed. "Yes."

"Mm," God agreed, "yeah, I probably would've. Let's make a deal," he continued. "We'll give the multiverse another few million years, and if things haven't changed much, I'll throw the bloody towel in, and return the bugger."

"If that's what you think," The Fixer replied sounding a little more cheerful.

"Well, unless you've a better idea?"

In the distance of the starry expanse, a comet streaked past followed by its icy white tail, arching over from one side of the universe to the other, coming and going without a hint of trouble.

"At least something works here. You know, in the last few days I've had to jump-start more comets, meteors and asteroids than I ever did in the first billion years."

"Yeah," God agreed, "those initial years were hectic. You remember that time when I couldn't unscrew the multiverse's pressure valve? Thing was going to make such a big bang. Glad I stopped it when I did…"

"Could you imagine?" The Fixer said. "There'd be matter everywhere."

"Right mess."

"And you'd have been mistaken if you thought I would've cleaned it up."

"No. That's what The Keeper's for. No one handles a broom like he does… saying that, you haven't seen him about, have you?"

The Fixer thought for a moment and shrugged. "I haven't seen anyone about in ages. Except for you, of course. I'm too busy with all the work. Traveller is probably knee-deep in wallpaper, and Norman. Well, who knows…?"

"Mm," God said. "Well, I don't," he frowned.

"No?"

"No. Anne called me up before asking where he was, said he'd disappeared. I've tried calling him but he's unreachable."

"Unreachable?"

"Yeah," God said bringing his hands up to gesture air quotes, "'Out of area' my phone says."

"That's strange," replied The Fixer, "I tried calling Norman recently. He was meant to be cleaning up a gravitational wave that'd swept dark matter everywhere, and when I called him, I got the same reply."

It wasn't uncommon for long periods to pass between them not seeing each other; take for instance The Finder's last birthday — may he rest in peace — the gang had gone to one of their favourite places, Weatherforks, and the time had come when The Fixer was up to get the next round in. It took him seventeen years to come back from the men's room, and even then, he had mysteriously misplaced his wallet. Still though, the feeling of this apparent disappearance had a slight ominous feeling to it.

"I better go and look for 'em," God said standing up from the scaffolding.

"You'll probably find Norman in the storage room. He goes there for his lunch break; thinks I don't know. But the evidence is quite clear: chocolate bar wrappers covered in shameful jokes littered everywhere."

"Crikey," God replied thinking that he hadn't been there in aeons.

"You ever heard of The Saturn Boom?"

God nodded and rolled his eyes. "The Keeper loves mingling with some strange characters, doesn't he?"

The Traveller and Norman followed the Executive Administrator for The Museum of Moore into the Great Hall. All around them, amazing paintings hung like historic windows, monolithic sculptures stood depicting various Moores, as if monuments to legendary figures that had once lived in times forgotten. The air had a heroic smell to it, dusty, yet mixed with the tell-tale scent of mythology and wonder.

"Who's that then?" Norman asked pointing at the Executive Administrator.

The Traveller huffed with repetitive boredom. "Thomas Moore…"

"Right."

The Traveller could see what was coming a mile off and counted to five.

"And who's that?" Norman said pointing to a statue.

"…Thomas Moore…"

"Gotcha."

Needless to say, the entire Moore Tour, Platinum version, hadn't really lived up to the hype. The extra money they paid to upgrade from the 'Gold Experience' had given them both a pair of 3D glasses and an audio tape describing the coming-of-age tale of a man and his road sweeper. Sure, it was funny, the odd explosion and rebellion uprising made for humorous listening, yet it never really seemed to pick up speed. The large skip by the far wall full of cassette players was all the evidence needed.

"We began the museum around ten thousand years ago, I believe," said the Executive. "We felt it was needed to document the evolution of things, as the Moore Project furthered its story."

"Brilliant," The Traveller said emptily, glancing at his phone.

"How big is this place?" Norman quizzed unfolding a seemingly endless origami map. "It's huge!"

"Yes," the Exec said, "we pride ourselves in having not only the biggest museum, but also having the biggest building in the universe. It stretches roughly two light years east and west, with the south wall nudging the fifth dimension."

"Amazing!" Norman replied.

"Quite," said The Traveller. "If it's all right with you, I think I might head back to the cinema really."

"What? Why?" asked Norman worriedly. "Are you not having fun?"

At that the Executive frowned and felt a little disappointed. No one ever in the history of life had become bored in the Museum of Moore. Though not a totally shocking revelation, as it had only ever been Thomas Moores coming to take in the sights; their narcissism was indeed legendary.

"Yeah," The Traveller said, "it's not that I don't like it here. Enjoying the whole Moore experience, for sure. Great stuff. All very, um, great. It's just that I hadn't finished watching that film that we started. And um, think I left my, um phone there? Can't survive without the thing."

"Which film?" Norman quizzed.

"You know… that one with the man."

"Which man?"

"The man… and the, um. He had that thing."

Both Norman and the Exec cocked an eyebrow and waited for the rest of the excuse.

The Traveller sighed, "You know what, actually I've got my phone here. And I just remembered we did in fact finish that film."

"Good," the Exec stated flatly. He had become quite out of sorts with The Traveller's ill-timed rudeness. To think he wasn't having a good time, the nerve!

"What film?" asked Norman.

"It doesn't matter."

"Okay…"

"Plus," the Exec said turning to carry on the tour, "if you had left now, you would've missed out the best bit. We'll leave this section of the walk-round for another day. Most of our tour's last a few weeks, but I can tell that you wish to see other things. From here we will head to the Moore Mines, then the Moore Door Services…"

"What happens there?" asked Norman.

"Probably something to do with doors, Norman."

"Correct," the Exec said icing over the sarcasm. "Front doors, back doors. Trap doors…"

"What about Labradors?"

"Witty."

"I do try."

"Then we will finish off with an in-depth look at the Moore Project, and how one man's dream to unite with the universe and become a god has nearly come to its final stage."

The Traveller paused, "Sorry?"

"Apology accepted. Although a little late."

"No. I mean could you say that again?"

The Exec nodded and began, "The Moore Door Company started three hundred and sixty years ago…"

"I mean the Moore Project!"

"Oh," Norman sighed disappointedly, "that sounded interesting."

"Curious, are we?" the Exec said slowly. The Traveller nodded, though inside a small knot began to twist, and something like female intuition started ringing alarm bells inside his mind.

"The part about 'becoming a god', what did you mean by that?"

"You could always get a refund on it?" suggested The Fixer as he tightened up a wobbling bracket. Above them the scaffolding heaved heavily with the constant strain of the Boötes Void, and its persistent non-weight pushing about for eternity.

"No," God said considering his options, "non-refundable. The Shop Keeper made it quite clear that I couldn't get my money back."

The Fixer summoned a wrench into existence and pulled on a bolt that had become more stubborn than the rest. "Store credit?"

"Nope," God shook his head, "it's practically worthless if we don't fix it now. Besides, what would I get in return? It wasn't as if they had a sale on Golden Fleeces."

"I was thinking that you could get something more useful than creation. You know, it's my birthday coming up, and being The Fixer, I could do with some new tools."

"Oh yeah?"

"Yes."

"And what exactly do you mean by new tools?"

The Fixer shrugged and scoffed as if he hadn't thought about the suggestion earlier.

"I don't know. Mjolnir? Can't do anything without a decent hammer."

"A hammer?" God chuckled. "You'd be all right with me trading in the multiverse for a hammer, would you?"

"Okay," The Fixer said, "what about Tyrfing?"

"And what do you want a sword for? I thought you were after new tools?"

"A sword is a tool!"

"For what?" God said, pulling the top off a fresh bottle of beer. "You going to whittle some good hands at our next poker game?"

"Funny. But I don't think I really need to, do you?"

"Undefeated."

"Correct."

They had worked for hours, chasing down broken metal piping, loose fixings and bent brackets. It was true, there would be no end to the maintenance. Far out in space towards the Virgo constellation, a small planet suddenly popped and streaked across the expanse like a balloon pooping air from its backside. The planet darted from left to right, deflating in a very uncomfortable fashion, coming to a gliding rest, flat and empty as an unsweetened pancake.

"Still haven't found my missing sheep, you know?" God said.

"No?"

"Naaa… just vanished without a trace. Too bad really, he was a good drinking partner."

The Fixer smiled as he attended to more bolts that'd wiggled loose while God stared out blankly into the starry unknown. "I should've picked something else. The multiverse wasn't my first choice."

"No?"

"No… they had loads there, actually. Boxes of them all lined up. Guess it serves me right for trying to save a bit of cash. I had an idea that I'd be happy with the Megaverse, but too expensive."

"What's that then?"

"The Megaverse? Think of a single infinitely huge, ever-expanding universe, only a lot bigger."

"Blimey."

"Yeah. They had loads to choose from. There was one, what was its name?" God thought trying to remember, "Ah yeah, it was a fair price, same as the discounted multiverse. It was the para-inter-fun-dimensional-wacky-verse…"

"Blah," The Fixer said sticking his tongue out as if he'd just been told the beer he'd been drinking for the last few hours was off. "Thank God you didn't get that. Sounds so boring and dull."

"Could you imagine? No, I don't know what to do really. Can't refund it, can't replace it. If there was some other way, I'd be willing to at least consider it."

The Traveller raced from the Museum of Moore towards the city centre; Norman huffed next to him trying to match his pace. Down every street they turned, every pavement they passed had become lined with Thomas Moores all standing in a single-file queue that seemed to stretch to infinity and beyond. On the horizon of the city skyline, a lonely building taller than the others flashed lights up its side in sequence; its roof an apparent beacon or transmitter, perhaps even a radio receiver, littered with metal dishes, cables and antenna. And the seemingly gigantic workforce of Moores who worked each dish into a specific place.

"What's happening?" Norman said between breaths.

The Traveller pulled at Norman's sleeve and took off into the air, "It's the Moore Project."

"Ah," Norman replied. Quite honestly, he hadn't been listening to most of what the museum Exec had said; he tuned out after being told about the gift shop, and the new sale on comical T-shirts and keychains. After that he'd lost all interest. "And what's that then?"

The Traveller, although not shocked about Norman's total obliviousness to things, felt another knot tighten in his innards. A feeling that told him that he and Norman could very well get to know the Moore Project better than they wished.

The pair came down with a smooth landing outside the large round swivelling doors at the foot of the building; the queue that had started possibly outside the city had made its way here, snaked inside and up the emergency staircase next to the lifts. The Traveller paced to the front trying to poke inside for a look, when a very well-dressed Thomas approached them. His earpiece, one-way glasses and no-nonsense hair cut had security written all over it.

"I demand you let me in!" The Traveller said flatly.

"Um," the security guard replied, "that's why I'm here, sir. I'm to take you to floor 420. It's where all the bigwigs sort out the meaning of life, and so on. They're expecting you."

The lift music was as you would expect; random sounds that had accidently formed into some sort of tasteless, yet not harmful tune that neither calmed nor irritated you. Expensive reflective walls stood around them, the high roof almost looked at them from the top of its nose. Though the guard was happily talking to Norman about all the heavenly things that he could've obtained from the gift shop, such as a Thomas Moore dashboard bobble-head or a Thomas teapot with matching Moore mugs, between the laughing and jesting, he was giving The Traveller the coldest of glances.

"And you can get those T-shirts three for a tenner."

"Wow," Norman said happily. "We're going to have to swing that way when we're done here."

The numbers raced on the small lift floor indicator. Quicker than The Traveller wanted, they had completely missed out double figures and found triple digits. The numbers slowed; the feeling of dread rubbed at his shoulders. It was not something that any omnipotent being really experienced; when you had been there when Death took his first steps, could name all the colours and learnt to tie his own laces, you never really came to fear him that much. Yet something, maybe distant, just beyond his infinite reach told him that whatever lay moments away would not bring anything good.

Bing the lift popped.

The doors slid sideways effortlessly opening to a room covered in fine carpet, oak inset on everything and a quaint little fountain in the corner. In the centre a huge thick oval table seating ten Thomas Moores, all sipping water with sliced cucumber, turned their way.

"Our guests," Mr Security said shunting them both inwards. "Would that be all, or have you anything else you need?"

"No," the closest Moore said fingering the top of his water glass. He had the same sense of entitlement that came with every Thomas Moore, you could find this show of cockiness in each one. Even the Moore from universe 75 million and 4, where everyone was homeless, had an inflated ego after somehow creating the world's first multi-storey cardboard box house; the underfloor heating was just showing off.

"You may leave, Thomas. Go and join the rest in the unification centre and become one with your brethren."

"Thank you, sir."

The door shut softly, and the room fell quiet. Ten sets of eyes landed on The Traveller and for everything he was, and had been, he felt a little uneasy about it. He stepped to the empty chair in front of him, he didn't need to be a genius to know this was for him. Took his place by the table and leant back into its groove. As chairs went, he had to admit it was by far the most comfortable he'd ever sat in; somewhere between a jacuzzi full of Playboy bunnies and a Saturday night watching the Crystal City Women's Athletics on TV.

Norman looked about for another seat and found nothing. He thought about turning the small fern in the corner out from its pot and using it as a stool, but mud would get everywhere, and having only just heard about fengshui he didn't want to upset it. So, in the end he just sat on the floor.

Thomas Moore at the far end of the oval table coughed.

"You are not God?" he said. He seemed to have the appearance of an older man, more years than the rest.

"No," The Traveller replied.

"And you?" he asked the top of Norman's head. It bobbed from side to side. "We have been searching," he huffed like a chain-smoker, "for God…"

"Well. I'm not him."

"We know, who you are… you are The Traveller."

"Yes," The Traveller replied narrowing his gaze.

"And you," Thomas pointed at Norman's head. "You are, The Janitor. Norman, The Janitor."

"Oh," The Traveller said holding up his hands. "Believe me, it sounds cooler than it really is. Tell 'em Norman, tell them what you do…"

"I sweep."

"He sweeps… and cleans. He's the equivalent of that cleaning lady over there by the…" The Traveller stopped realising it was just another Thomas Moore in a maid's outfit wiping down the sides. "…Maybe he's a little more vital than that."

"It matters not. We have what we need."

"Right," Norman said happily starting to stand, "we'll be off then."

"No," Thomas replied.

"No?"

"Are you sure about that?" The Traveller asked boldly. "If you know what, and who I am, what makes you think I won't just leave?"

Thomas took a hanky from his pocket and cleaned his withering lips, pulled at a small drawer by his side and thumbed a concealed button. The wall next to The Traveller that had a painting of *The Last Supper*, only with Thomas Moores, lurched on hidden brackets, and slowly sank into the floor revealing a large room behind a sheet of thick glass. Inside, much to The Traveller's horror, Stinkhorn the Great and Mrs Pinkletin were fixed in chains, hung up like pigs ready for the slaughter; a nasty analogy, but rest assured no one ever, *anywhere*, would even consider eating either of them.

"Oh… my… God," The Traveller said.

Norman waved. "Hello."

"As you can see," Thomas said weakly, "you won't be going anywhere."

"But how?" demanded The Traveller. His thoughts of doom were, well, dead on the money. And on top of that, if he managed to find his way out of it all, whatever 'it' was going to be, he would still have to handle the wrath of Anne.

Thomas leant back in his chair heavily and sipped at his cucumber water.

"Many years ago, before we were born, our universe transcended to peace. During this time, it had been noted that outside of our existence, the multiverse was under stress. We saw as you and your, 'God', did what you could to fix things. Bhaa…" he croaked, "you struggled with every step. We knew that if it were to survive, we would have to take control. But we couldn't do it alone."

Norman nudged one of the other Thomas's with his elbow and whispered, "Have you got any crisps?"

"No… shhh…"

"This universe came together, from every part giving up their physical being and joined to create a new idea. But it wasn't enough. We needed to bring in others from outside our own paperweight universe to finish the job, but not wanting to upset the balance of life, we chose to use only one individual: me."

"Why?" asked The Traveller. "What made you so special?"

"I know," Norman said snapping his fingers, "you're super intelligent in this universe."

"Well thank you, but…"

"It's got to be something to do with all Thomas Moores, Norman."

"No," Thomas said lifting a finger. "It's—"

"Hold on," Norman said, "did you win a competition?"

"No" Thomas said, "I—"

"A competition?" The Traveller scoffed. "Like what?"

"I don't know." Norman shrugged.

"The best self-obsessed being award?"

"...Thank you..."

"Yeah," Norman laughed, "first, second and third prize."

"Ha. Maybe he won the most boring museum guide. You could've at least given out some free samples."

"Look," Thomas said getting a little tense, "it's nothing to do with—"

"Actually, I started finding it a bit boring too" Norman added, "and the audio tape was not all that great either."

"Look!" Thomas shouted, "firstly, we had to get an intern to do the audio tape as our usual man was sick."

Thomas dabbed his mouth with a napkin and calmed himself. "It was many years ago," he went on. "I was drinking myself to oblivion in a nightclub located in a city called Chumpton when I met God the first time. He told me how he was looking for a black hole and a sweeper... and so a plan was hatched after listening to him spill more than he should've."

"His pint." Norman nodded.

"Details!" Thomas said. "Details man, what's wrong with you?"

"Ignore him," said The Traveller to Thomas.

"...Anyway. I vowed to never again fall or fail. I made it my life's work to build a multi-billion turnover sweeping company. I obtained the rights to everything. Including the rights to advanced top-secret tech that I used to break through universal boundaries, journeying on my own to this paperweight universe, bringing forwards the Moore Project. We had begun to collect other Moores from the multiverse to boost the project, all their consciousnesses were bound and bonded under fusion reactions, using our unification engine. We had hoped that God would come and find us, so that we could tell him not to bother any more, but you were here first..."

"Not through choice!" The Traveller said angrily, "I was happy picking out carpets... well, happy-ish."

"We can now stop collecting Moores, as you will supply us with all the energy we need. We saw your power drained near Stinkhorn the Great, many years ago and a plan to trap you was made. You have no idea how happy I am that our goal has finally become a reality! You will be immortalised forever!"

The Traveller backed away towards the door kicking over his chair, "I already was immortalised, by myself, too. Norman!"

Norman dropped his packet of crisps and came to his side.

"What do we do?"

The Traveller wondered. Beforehand he could've wondered and pondered, analysed and made corrections within half the time it takes to ignite a gas-lit outdoor BBQ.

"Any ideas, Norman?"

"We could go to the gift shop?"

The Traveller should've expected that.

"Maybe later… for now, probably best to run."

Universe 4 thousand, 1 hundred million and 9 was a mess, not all of it, but a fair chunk. The Keeper had been held back, put on hold and told not to be so naughty with his godlike powers for so long that, much like a bottle of fizzy pop laced with Mentos, he had exploded with a built-up pressure of omnipotent force. The Truth, The Masterful Wizard and The All Knowing couldn't believe their eyes. From the small vessel that The Keeper had conjured into reality they watched as he threw his frustration around a helpless galaxy. What once was a beautiful spiral, with star-laced arms sweeping outwards for trillions of miles, had been mercilessly warped into a possible balloon animal.

"It's got to be a dog," The Truth said.

"No," The Masterful Wizard laughed, "it's obviously a giraffe. The long neck gives it away."

The All Knowing shook his head. "Whatever it may be, gentlemen, does not matter. The fact is, is that we have unleashed a being of true power upon this galaxy, and it had done no harm to us!"

Both rolled their eyes and shared a glance, "I'll have you know," The Truth said, "that he told me that for our sake, he'll show us what he can do with a galaxy that has little worth before moving onto the big stuff. We're not monsters."

"Not yet anyway," The Masterful Wizard said.

"So," The All Knowing continued, "what ghastly beings resided in this poor helpless galaxy?"

"Ticket inspectors," The Keeper said as he floated back to their vessel. He rubbed his hands together feeling a buzz that had been missing for far, far too long.

"Ticket inspectors?" The All Knowing said disapprovingly. "I'll have you know, my brother in-law is a ticket inspector, and a fine one at that!"

"Didn't he have your new Jag impounded last Christmas for parking on a double yellow?"

"Yes," The Truth added, "and the year before that he had it towed for parking five minutes over the time limit."

"That," The All Knowing said flatly, "may be true, yet you have successfully proven my point."

"So, what then?" asked The Keeper. "You want me to put it back to how I found it?"

The All Knowing had been very much on board with the new idea. Mass violence and corruption on a multiversal scale. It had all been so attractive and fun. Except, in reality, he had honestly thought that it had been The Truth going off on a tangent again, rattling off some crazy ideas about what he was capable of, and how he'd bring fame back to The Saturn Boom once more. Prior to this latest outburst, it had all been just talk, fun and enthusiastic talk that The All Knowing safely knew would lead to nothing. But this?

"This is too much. You have crossed a line!"

"I have crossed a line that needed to be crossed."

The Keeper passed through the wall of the small vessel and solidified in front of the three. He had spent countless aeons sweeping up the multiverse, letting it jiggle for a while before cleaning it back up again. Billions and billions of years had come and gone as he sat on his rock in his small storage room, watching God, The Traveller and the others go off and have fantastic adventures together, while he sat, fondling his broom handle. He had been teased and taunted, mocked and made fun of by his equals for not being completely equal. Well! Enough was enough.

"The Saturn Boom welcomed me in," he said. "And I'm very thankful. But now is the time when I will give something back, and you, you little fragile being, will not stop me."

"Couldn't you just give us something that we could all enjoy though?" The All Knowing said softly, "like a lifetime supply of toilet paper? Or the results to the lottery? Why does it have to be violent?"

The Keeper lifted his hand and smiled; he hadn't changed anyone into a plant for over a million years, and the thought alone made him tingle. "This won't be violent, and it will not hurt."

The All Knowing closed his eyes and was turned into a foxglove.

"This is but a small example of what I can do."

"I for one am very excited to see the rest," The Masterful Wizard said, "it's about time we started being a bit evil."

"Indeed," The Truth nodded, "gather the troops."

The Traveller had made an honest go at running, though a little out of breath, and tired of answering Norman's relentless questions regarding the gift shop and where babies come from, he had finally worked out that running had been nothing short of hopeless. His true powers had gone, no thanks to Stinkhorn the Great, again, and as such, he had been forced to look at every wall map in the building, spending a few minutes each time locating the 'You are here' message followed by an arrow. In the end, after a few more failed attempts, he had dragged Norman into what looked to be the changing rooms for the company gym and squished himself and Norman into a locker.

"It doesn't smell that nice in here."

"You're welcome to go if you want."

"Are you sure?"

The Traveller huffed, "Just be quiet and say nothing."

"Okay."

The door to the changing rooms opened as a small group of Moores came in, laughing and joking about some meaningless trivia. All was well until a sweaty pair of boxers fell from a top shelf above Norman and landed on his head. The smell, and regrettably, the taste, made him heave. He stormed from the locker, and pulling open the gym bag of the gym goers, emptied a half-decent portion of crisps and chocolate bars inside.

Needless to say, Mr Moore was not happy. Both were abruptly marched to the lifts, taken forty-three floors down, and strapped into the unification engine.

Unlike the high quality of the office chairs on floor four-two-zero, they were both sat down on two chairs that came straight from Death Row; the whiff of charged electrons hung in the air like gone-off mistletoe. Their arms and legs were strapped securely, with probes stuck to every part of skin available. Behind them stood a huge glass barrel at least one hundred metres high, with metal struts standing up from the floor holding it in place, while inside a whirling bright multicoloured vortex of energy surged like a huge pint of Guinness unwilling to settle. All around them gantries shot here and there, staircases ascended between the spaces, and on all stood the queue of Moores that had started miles away. The Traveller turned his head as much as he could, and as much as the head strap would allow, spotting the end of the line as it headed into a doorway at the bottom of the gigantic glass barrel. As each Moore ventured inside, their bodies faded to nothing while their consciousnesses filtered inwards.

"Excuse me?" The Traveller asked one Thomas who seemed to be in charge. "Any chance we could just join the queue? It's just that I've never really been one for pain."

"This won't be painful," the older Thomas Moore from floor four-two-zero said, as he exited an opening lift door. He stood above where they sat, grasping the railings with both hands — probably for stability; he was pretty old, after all — and signalled for things to start.

Clunking began, softening out into a smoother whir; the engine roared into action, and The Traveller promptly came to the realisation that this may very well be the end of things. A strange emotion for any immortal. It started with a tingle, or maybe a tickle, in his legs climbing over his knees and up his spine, soon the pinpricks covered his head, and all at once he jiggled in the chair.

"More power!" Thomas shouted from the railings.

Another surge of energy burst up his legs, and the roaring engine became a scream.

The Traveller had had a very good life, better than most in fact. He'd visited nearly every place in the multiverse and sampled all the street food and drink he could. He'd fallen in love and got into copious amounts of trouble for doing so from the wife. So, I guess he couldn't really complain. Norman went out smiling, as usual, though it may have just been wind…

I would dare say that most people in their lives have at some point seen a picture of The Pillars of Creation. Huge dust columns situated in the Eagle Nebula some six to seven thousand light years away from Earth. They are a staple and hallmark of natural beauty, a symbol of amazement and wonder. They have formed due to the erosion from newly born stars and will continue to change shape for ever more. Each pillar, an immeasurable length, far beyond the grasp of human minds.

"So, why are they now sticking the middle finger up?"

The Fixer shrugged, "Coincidence?"

"Mm," God said suspiciously. "Don't reckon so."

If it was a coincidence, then it was a very unpredictable one at that. The odds of it naturally occurring were mind-numbingly small. Plus, the words *'You Suck'* written in gaseous dust underneath couldn't have happened by mistake.

"You know, call me crazy" God said rubbing his chin, "but you think that whoever did this, also had something to do with the cosmic strand we just untangled?"

"We?"

"…Yeah."

"I think you mean me," The Fixer pointed out, "you've never been any good with reef knots."

Both thought deeply; chance was ruled out. This, for sure, had to be man-made; well, not man-man-made, but super-man-man-made. If that makes any sense.

"The Builder?"

"Na," God said, "he does kids shows now."

"The Sculptor then?"

"Not his kind of work."

"The Insulter?"

"Too obvious."

"The Talker?"

"...Too dead."

The Fixer smiled and shook his head, "The Keeper."

"My thoughts exactly."

A billion or so light years away, and three universes over to the right, The Keeper had just finished working his magic on a small planet that had previously only ever done good to others. The bounteous planet known as The Field of Dreams — nothing to do with baseball — had had a longstanding contract with the local galactic theatre chain, specifically the distribution of popcorn. The planet had been the right distance from its parent star, enabling the infinite field of corn that stretched the entirety of the land to grow perfectly, then pop on its own. It was then packaged and distributed the same day. 'Fresh or your money back'. However, now, thanks to The Keeper, the planet was in a state of orphanage, having been flicked several billion miles from its system; and let's face it, no one wants to eat cold popcorn.

"Great job," The Masterful Wizard said worriedly. "Just... great."

The Masterful Wizard had always been the type to scream and shout, bawl and moan about being treated unfairly, or complain about some meaningless thing. The sort that would gladly pipe up in the company of others, yet when cornered on his own would be quiet enough; a troublemaker, or, as The Truth once noted, a real pain in the backside. The Truth, unfortunately, could no longer note anything, or even have an opinion, as The Keeper had grown weary of his need to control things, and had eventually turned him into a small *Allium cepa* (an onion, for those not in the know). As cowardly as he was, he had skilfully managed to assure The Keeper that his services would be needed for things like handling bags or taking notes.

"Really great job on the rest of them, too," he went on, pointing towards the vast minefield of onions floating behind them. The Keeper had little need for The Saturn Boom, and as such had turned them all into salad fillers.

The Keeper took his set of keys from his side, unlocked a spatial doorway and stepped through, pulling The Masterful Wizard with him. Universe 1 billion had no idea what was to come.

"Where to, your Absurdly Ruthfulness?"

The Keeper frowned, "I don't like that. It makes me sound bad."

"Right," The Masterful Wizard said wondering how long he could go before he became a carrot. "And of course, you are not bad."

"No."

"I mean sure, you did kind of set off that supernova that wiped out an entire galaxy. But I can't see how that might be translated as bad…"

"Exactly."

"And sure… there may have been a few trillion species that lived there. But it's their own fault."

"I'm glad you see that."

"May I just point out, that perhaps next time we could just, I don't know, *scare* a civilisation? You know, instead of performing an act of total genocide, we just make them fear us a little."

The Keeper rubbed his hands together and set off to the most populated section of the new universe, leaving behind him a lonely parsnip to bob through space for the rest of time.

The Traveller's mind was still his own. It swirled around the barrel like an oil unwilling to mix, determined to stay single in a vessel of communitive oneness. Every now and again another unique thought passed his own, it had a smile and seemed to be laughing, it could have only been Norman. The collective shouting from a billion Moores echoed all around his own mind, all chanting in sync, howling deafening words, climbing over one another like ants clambering up a high wall. Outside the barrel, the eldest Moore shook hands with the last Thomas that had been waiting weeks to become one with the others, they exchanged final words before he headed inside, joining with the vortex.

The unification engine geared up again, churning out power like there was no tomorrow, drawing strength from the planet's core. The pressure around The Traveller's mind grew thicker.

The voices chanted on, "We are Moore… we are Moore."

The Traveller braced himself, feeling the walls buckling around his mind.

"We are Moore," they continued to sing. "We are Moore."

The Traveller couldn't hold out much longer. "We are Moore," he said. "We, are, Moore."

Old Thomas took to the railings above, he stood in front of a control panel looking down at the great glass barrel, watching as the last fragment of The Traveller's mind merged with the rest. This was it, the time when a mere Moore-tel became a god.

His hand struck down on the large, and totally clichéd red button, igniting the unification of souls. First came a blinding light, then a roar of heat, followed by a crack that snaked up the barrel's side. Then another, and another. After seconds, the glass shattered into a million shards covering every gantry and staircase in glimmering snow. The blinding light began to subside; Thomas blinked, his eyes fighting for sight. At the epicentre, a silhouette stood. It took one step forwards, then a second. The light died, and the new being strode out.

Thomas gasped. In front of him stood a man made up of an entire new universe, his body a platter of stars, galaxies and glowing threads. Something like the diagram you see in surgical books showcasing the nervous system of the human body, only this was so much more.

Old Thomas fell to his knees. Not to pray, just because he was incredibly old. And started to weep.

"I am The Cosmic," the being said gently.

"Oh Cosmic, tell me, please! What is it that you desire?"

The Cosmic blinked the two galaxy superclusters that formed his eyes; he could see an existence that no one else could. He felt the meaning of everything, and knew the multiverse was ready for his presence. His purpose was clear, his direction true.

"I will find God and give him relief."

Old Thomas looked puzzled, "Do you mean to say, you'll kill him?"

"Sorry," The Cosmic said. "Yes, that sounded a little rude…"

"No, no. I knew what you meant. I just…"

"…Yeah" The Cosmic replied rubbing the back of his head. "Right, I'll be off then."

The Cosmic, a name that he chose for reasons only a million-billion Thomas Moores could justify as 'about right', looked upwards, clenched his fists and ascended into the air. He rose like a bubble, weightless and silent. The ceiling above him parted, morphing and distorting, sealing back behind him. Through the outer wall of the building he flew, upwards into the warm bathing light of an alien sun. He picked up speed heading into the clouds, vapour trails at his feet, the feeling of unlimited power running through every cosmical part of his body.

Behind him the planet shrank quicker than a round of Jäger bombs at a works Christmas party; Old Thomas left alone for the rest of his years knowing with confidence that his legacy would live on. The Cosmic increased his speed: planets slung past him, stars, dust clouds and more came and went. Soon a galaxy swept behind him, a hundred thousand light years travelled in seconds, and yet he carried onwards.

A trillion infinite spaces traversed with thought alone, his will a godly power: his cockiness an inflating balloon. Ahead lay the great unknown barrier of the paperweight universe. A wall that, in all other universes, did not exist, though a challenge that he knew from his first conscious spark he would have to break through to meet his maker.

"For the multiverse!" he cried.

And just like that, he collided with the barrier, giving him what could only be described as the worst headache a cosmic entity could ever have to deal with.

"Jesus!" he said clutching his head. He hadn't even made a scratch. Just a faint *ping* noise you might hear when an insect hits your window while driving.

The Cosmic shook off the embarrassment and drew every amount of power he could from the universe that created his very being, every pulsar and every neutron star; every fusion reaction and every swirling conscious mind that had something to hit with answered his call. This time he wouldn't fail; he backtracked taking a run-up further than lateral time itself extended, pulled his energy together and with gusto, shot off a million times faster than anything had ever travelled before. he collided with the paperweight universes edge, and *ping!*

"Bollocks!"

In the vast vacuum of space, God heaved a sigh holding two pieces of a broken broom in his hands. He'd searched three quarters of the endless multiverse and had come up with nothing, only a scattering trail of what The Fixer had called 'childish behaviour' that The Keeper had left behind, as he zoomed from one universe to the other making a mess of everything. As The Keeper had left universe 11 and a half, he had not only swapped all the salt for sugar and put clingfilm on the top of all the toilets, but he had also turned all the lights off, meaning that everywhere beings of all kinds were soon to get sticky feet, a bad aftertaste from their morning coffees, and ultimately broken toes as they stumbled around knocking into unseen furniture looking for mouthwash and wet wipes.

"Is there no end to his madness?"

"Sarcasm never suited you."

The Fixer scoffed. "Well. I did warn you this might happen."

"When?" God asked doubtfully.

"Before! Ages ago. Back when you just gave him his broom."

"You never said a thing."

"I did!"

"Go on then," God asked crossing his arms after throwing the broom to one side, "when exactly did you tell me he'd go nuts?"

The Fixer rolled his eyes, "Come on. You'd just given him his broom, shown him the storage room, and I distinctively remember asking if you were sure about that."

"...Right."

The Fixer stood up and shrugged.

"That's it?"

"I did tell you."

"You think that you asking me if 'I'm sure', is the same as telling me that my wife's ex-pet hamster would at some point lose his marbles and break everything?"

"Well," The Fixer said. "Close enough."

A billion light years away against the backdrop of stars, a bright flash of light exploded. Then another, and another. One by one, hundreds of supergiant stars began to burst and go supernova, like a line of Christmas lights popping in a row. The Keeper had moved them all into place leaving a glittering word, far too rude for me to write down, written in space for all life forms everywhere to see.

"Childish," The Fixer said shaking his head. "How can he misspell a four-letter word... and one so frequently used."

It would be entirely fair to say, that after a good few hundred years, the audience had become a little tired of waiting. Barry's great-great-great-

great-grandson had just come back from his four hundredth bathroom break to find an empty stage, and to top it off, the man who was selling the peanuts and beer had died from old age.

He made his way down row seven towards his seat, knocking over a few decomposing bodies and a skeleton still with its ticket in hand, and sat down next to his wife.

"Still hasn't started then?"

"What?" Marge asked cupping her ear. Her hearing had worsened over the past few years. When she had first taken her steps down the theatre stairs with her mum, she had had such excitement and wonder about all the large pictures and canvases that hung around the stage. Now, however, she could barely see them as the last threads gave way to age and gravity.

"I said," Barry Jr-Jr-Jr said loudly, "they still haven't started yet?"

"No. At least, I don't think so."

Barry Jr-Jr-Jr huffed, "We'll give it few more years, till Barry the 4th can walk, and then we'll head home."

Behind the large draping wall of material on the stage, Rot the Thing peeked out towards an audience of a hundred-thousand strong, all eyes, and empty sockets, staring back at him. His father, Stinkhorn the Great had told him that if it came to it, just start the show without him. It had been more of a request than an order. Rot the Thing was the oldest offspring, he had roughly a million brothers and sisters that Stinkhorn the Great and Mrs Pinkletin had spawned, and if remembering each of their names was hard enough, Rot the Thing had been charged with taking care of the lot of them till his mum and dad returned.

"What's it like out there?" the second oldest fungal-plant-esque lifeform, Gag the Kinda'Nasty said with excitement. "Are people still out there?"

"Mm," Rot the Thing pondered, "a bit."

In the wings it was becoming restless; a thousand small sludgy bodies were becoming impatient. The play, which should've started roughly eighteen hundred years ago, entitled *The Rose That Could*, was meant to start with a mass slaughter. Stinkhorn the Great had hand-picked his best actors to perform the first act. A swarm of bees would fly in a frenzy in a flowering field, ravishing petals and stamens, leaving only one small rose standing alone in a barren wasteland. As you could imagine, a thousand fungal-plant-esque type bodies, all wearing bee costumes, all fitted out with stingers, and all crammed into a small space would soon become a little uncomfortable.

"Look," Gag the Kinda'Nasty said, "I think we should make a start."

"No!" Rot the Thing replied. "I know Father said to start without him, but this was his big dream. This is the reason why we're here."

"I'm not doubting that, oh brother of mine, but we don't need father until the third act. Plus, Muck the Stain has been standing out there on the stage for nearly two thousand years dressed as a rose, and I think he's starting to get back problems."

"Then tell him to stand up straight!" Rot the Thing barked. "Father said to us, just before he went off with Thomas Moore, that he'll be back soon. You know why he had to go, and well, the audience numbers speak for themselves. So, please, just tell the hordes to wait. They've been patient this long, I'm sure they can be for another two thousand years."

"And what about the audience?" Gag the Kinda'Nasty pointed out. "Should they wait too?"

"Yes! They reproduced for this long. And when the new punters are old enough, just start handing out the programme again."

"As you wish."

Far on the other side of the multiverse, an ageing Thomas unclipped the fake shackles from Stinkhorn the Great and Mrs Pinkletin, allowing them to stand freely and stretch.

"Ah," Stinkhorn the Great said rubbing his wrists, "by far, tis my finest hour. Though be it not stage bound, fooling a man to one's face, tis quite the example of skill."

"Is that you Alfred?" Mrs Pinkletin asked.

"Tis I, my honey glow. How are your… arms? The restraints were not too tightly wound I trust?"

"They were fine Alfred. Fancy a cup of tea?"

Stinkhorn the Great smiled, and simply looked at his wife with awe. Everything about her he enjoyed. From her mossy covered body, her festering compost bottom, to her decomposing face that only a few hardened shrubs grew upon. He had been truly blessed to have met such a beautiful being as her. *And to think,* he thought to himself, *she had allowed me to root myself in her, and she in return gave me an army to which I could convey the greatest show the multiverse had ever seen.*

"Yes" he said happily, "tis I, Alfred."

"And is Alfred your real name?" Old Thomas said as he sat down in front of his laptop, "or shall I just put Stinkhorn?"

"Please, sir, Stinkhorn the Great, and Mrs Pinkletin."

"Of course."

Stinkhorn the Great made his way around the large oval table in the centre of the room admiring all the posh classy assortment of things that lined the walls and shelves. He wished that one day, maybe soon, he and Mrs Pinkletin, along with the rest of The Cucumber Sandwich Theatre Company, would be able to afford such delicious overpriced and exotic things as these.

"Right," Old Thomas said standing as he gestured to his computer screen, "have a look and tell me what you think. If you don't like it, I'll change it."

Stinkhorn the Great strode over, pulled the chair away and rolled it to the room's edge, and bent forwards focusing on the bright screen in front of him. It read: *"The Rose That Could, a review by T. Moore. My expectations for the night's play were not high, yet I forced myself to attend. To say that I was completely wrong with my original thoughts would be a total understatement. I found that Stinkhorn the Great, and Mrs Pinkletin have an overwhelming grasp on the persoonia and personal life of the plant, and the character building throughout the fourth and fifth acts were undeniably realistic, and really hit home when conveying a sense of family and imminent danger. Therefore, I implore everyone to go and watch The Rose That Could at least four to five times. Trust me, you will never be disappointed!"*

Stinkhorn the Great smiled and nodded, "How long till it is on the website for everyone to see?"

"Straight away," Old Thomas said.

"Then please," Stinkhorn the Great asked.

"Right away." A few clicks on his keyboard and the review had been uploaded to every mainstream site that got the most hits.

Old Thomas held his hand out for Stinkhorn the Great to shake.

“I would like to thank you, on behalf of life forms everywhere. Because of you, it has been possible to create the ultimate being.”

“It was nothing,” Stinkhorn the Great said happily. “I would gladly help any being out, if needed. God knows, I would not be here if it weren’t for The Traveller and his kin. Where is he, by the way?”

“The Traveller?”

“Yes.”

“Dead, thanks to you.”

Stinkhorn the Great, for a time, felt a lump of something awful grow in his throat, then swallowed it. It sat heavily in his stomach and did not taste good in the slightest.

“I beg your pardon?”

“He’s dead,” Old Thomas said uploading the review to another website.

“You told me,” Stinkhorn the Great said, changing his overall tone from joyous to downright angry, “that The Traveller would not be hurt!”

“And he wasn’t; he felt no pain.”

“You did not inform me that you had schemed to kill him for this, ultimate being!”

“And I needed not, either!”

“Sir, you are a scoundrel and a thief. If I had known your true intent, I would have not been so eager to help.”

“You wanted reviews. You wanted an audience. I gave them to you for a small cost.”

“The cost was a friend!”

“Bah…” Old Thomas said, waving his hand.

“Tell me,” Stinkhorn the Great said flatly, “what is it that this ‘ultimate being’ will do?”

Old Thomas smiled, “He will kill God, and take control of the multiverse.”

To that, Stinkhorn the Great felt little regret in picking up old Thomas by his ankles and eating him bit by bit so that the pain he felt made up for the pain he’d caused. Since years beforehand when Stinkhorn the Great had eaten The Talker and became the thing he was today, he had experienced a multitude of feelings, yet it was only now, today, on this quiet little planet of Moores that he truly understood the feeling of betrayal. Oxyn the Big had come close to what he felt, yet only a Moore could've pushed it to this limit.

He grabbed Mrs Pinkletin round her flourishing hips, and looked upwards.

"To the stars, my dear! We have a God to save!"

The Cosmic sailed straight past frustration and was now heading for a little town called Positively Unhinged. He had flown at the great paperweight barrier at light-speed, he had flown at it at over light-speed, he had clawed and punched it, he'd bitten and bashed it. He'd done everything that a being would do to crack through to the other side. At one point he nestled down next to it holding his knees in his hands and whispered sweet nothings to it in an attempt to pass through as its guest; though due to his ego he'd never tell anyone about that part as it would be far too embarrassing.

He'd just emptied a lungful of profanities at the damned thing, grown cosmic strands on his head only to rip them out, when a small wobbly distasteful shape appeared in the distance heading his way. At first, he thought it may have been some random lump of rubbish floating through space — you know how things can turn up when least expected — yet as it came closer it was obvious that it was indeed a giant mushroom holding onto a giant plant.

"Good luck," The Cosmic scoffed as he hid behind a passing comet to watch the pair struggle to escape. Mrs Pinkletin floated towards the great glass wall, her reflection a thing she never came to see, giving her a little fright that was totally justified. Stinkhorn the Great, being the gentleman… mm, no, gentle-shroom? Stinkhorn the Great, being the gentle-shroom he was, took one swing at the barrier with his hardened club hand sending an almighty wobble in all directions. A crack appeared, then another, and soon a huge chunk of glass began to float away into the universe behind them, allowing his fair and stagnant better half through first.

The Cosmic boiled under his spatial skin, feeling fusion react in a way that was most displeasing. He stood, with the intention of giving the giant overgrown pair of weeds a good thrashing, when he heard, "Wherever you are, ultimate being, I, Stinkhorn the Great, am coming for you!", and subsequently hid behind the comet again feeling a little worried for his life.

Outside the infinite confines of the paperweight universe, Stinkhorn the Great escorted his fair lady outwards finding himself standing in the storage room. A place that he had no knowledge of. They stood in the middle of what looked to be a crazed hoarder's living room; sacrificial tables and furniture with torturous daydreams that, in his younger years, he would've been only too happy to use.

"Alfred?" Mrs Pinkletin said lifting her branched arm upwards.

Past the maze of littered things stood The Keeper. His gaze was latched firmly on them with an intent so obvious that no words were needed.

"I will do away with you both," he said deeply.

Stinkhorn the Great furrowed his brow, placed a hand on Mrs Pinkletin's chest and moved her backwards behind him. "Take safety my love." He flexed his shoulders, cracked his neck; no one would get away with threatening his beloved. "Move not until I have finished, sweet blossom."

Mrs Pinkletin smiled blissfully and began eating the remains of a mummified cat she found in a sarcophagus lying next to her.

"This would go beautifully in a sandwich."

"Come on then," The Keeper said flatly. "You are merely two obstacles I have to overcome."

Stinkhorn the Great cocked a smile and moved towards him, his giant figure shifting everything from his path like a cruise ship breaking through ice. He picked up a bronze statue with one hand, took it between both palms and snapped the thing in two, throwing them idly to his feet. The Keeper didn't move.

"You have no power over me," The Keeper said. He met Stinkhorn the Great's eyes with furious stubbornness, never flinching or reacting to any of the great mushroom's shows of intimidation.

The two stood metres from each other, The Keeper barely reaching Stinkhorn the Great's waist. He was smaller, though he knew ultimately that no matter how strong his opponent was, he was neither godly nor omnipotent.

"Thou forget," Stinkhorn the Great said like a volcano ready to explode. "Your name be The Keeper I presume?"

"Yes…"

"I know you," he went on. "You were an ex-hamster. Pet to a god. Changed for the task of sweeping."

The Keeper gritted his teeth.

"You are omnipotent, though not by choice. You were a mere rodent, spinning plastic wheels for an eternity."

"Pick your next words wisely."

"You know me?" Stinkhorn the Great asked blankly.

"I do…"

"…Then tell me, imp. What happens to an omnipotent being when face to face with Fungal-kind?"

The Keeper thought momentarily, bottom lip protruding while his now mortal brain whizzed and fizzed, eventually coming to the realisation of his situation.

"Well," he gulped. "Umm… I…"

"Thou do forget," Stinkhorn the Great said boldly. "Tis you that has no power over me!"

"Just one bite will do!" Mrs Pinkletin said as she came racing round Stinkhorn the Great lifting The Keeper off his feet and high into the air with an outstretched vine.

"I'm sorry!" The Keeper wailed. "Ahhh… don't eat me!"

Stinkhorn the Great laughed hysterically watching with grand enthusiasm his one and only, Mrs Pinkletin, coil her vines around The Keeper's body, bringing him closer to her mouth; her tongue vigorously jolting from one side to the other throwing saliva everywhere. It was times like this when Stinkhorn the Great truly felt blessed to have met someone so beautiful with table manners he could appreciate.

Down came Mrs Pinkletin's jaws, crunch came the sound, blah came the response…

"That tastes like gone-off pork" she said with disgust. And immediately threw The Keeper forcefully to her side. He crashed into a pile of spears propped up against a pinball machine and came to rest in a heap on the floor.

Stinkhorn the Great took Mrs Pinkletin's hand and knelt before her.

"You are perfect in every despicable way. Shall I bring him with us so that you can feast on him later?"

Mrs Pinkletin became docile, the flowers on her back opened in response.

"It tasted like gone-off pork" she said softly.

"Then we shall leave it be... come on my love," he said turning to the multiverse in the corner, "we must gather our spawn."

Moments later in a universe yet to be numbered...

Globule the Sticky, one of the youngest of Stinkhorn the Great's spawn, slimed over to where Rot the Thing stood with a look of impatience slapped across his face. He, along with two hundred of his smaller brothers and sisters had been in costume for three hundred years, waiting for their 'big chance to shine', as their father had put it. They were to be part of a large set piece in act nine; an emotionally challenged compost heap that would later become the rose's best friend, guiding it through the troubles of friendship. And by now, Globule the Sticky had had enough.

"If you do not start this play!" he shouted, waving a furious arm around in front of his older brother, "then I am going to take the rest of us outside, and ruin this play for good!"

Rot the Thing glanced at Gag the Kinda'Nasty and received a look that was much the same.

"Look," he said flatly. "I want to start this as much as you all do. But you know Father. He did say to start without him, yes. But honestly, he really said, 'you start without me, and you'll end up like Squish the Flattened'. And we all know what happened to him."

"I don't care!"

"Me neither, actually," Gag the Kinda'Nasty admitted.

"You see! We should start."

"Look, little brother. Give it a little longer, and then we can—"

"No!" Globule the Sticky shouted. "You start now. Or I walk!"

Rot the Thing feared the worst, and knew full well that Globule the Sticky, though small and unassuming, indeed had the support of most, if not all of the lower ranks of the family tree. What he lacked in size, he made up for in motivational speaking, and stickiness.

"Mm, fine," Rot the Thing said eventually, "but you'd better explain yourself to Father when he gets back. I'm not bailing you out this time."

Rot the Thing gave the nod.

The theatre lights descended.

All went dark, and the casual chitter-chatter from the audience members slowly faded; half were relieved that things were about to kick off, the other half had suffered memory loss in their old age and had become panic-stricken not really knowing what was going on.

A single spotlight beamed down at the stage, illuminating Muck the Stain as he stood there in all his red, blooming glory. His costume handmade by the finest tailor in the multiverse — The Tailor; for reasons I won't go into, he owed Stinkhorn the Great a favour and had agreed to make all the costumes; presumably, it had something to do with him not wanting to be eaten alive.

Muck the Stain cleared his throat, took a lungful of air and readied the song he had practised in his mind for a thousand years. This was it.

"A million bees be buzzing a—"

Boom! went the double doors at the back of the theatre.

Stinkhorn the Great and Mrs Pinkletin stormed through and down the centre stairs as the theatre lights shot back on, cutting off Muck the Stain mid-sentence.

"Dad, I just started!" Muck the Stain said angrily. He would be even angrier if he knew that a talent scout had come to watch him sing.

"Play's cancelled," Stinkhorn the Great replied. "Ready the horde, we're leaving!"

Muck the Stain stood there, open-mouthed, in a state of hesitation. "Can I not just sing a little?"

"Ready the horde!"

"Maybe just a line or two?"

"Ready! The! Horde!"

"We won't ready anything!" Globule the Sticky said flatly as he emerged from the wings, followed by a shifting compost heap of anger.

Stinkhorn the Great turned and stood over his youngest spawn.

"Oh," he said, "is that right?"

"Yes," Globule the Sticky said, staring up at his father; a being easily a million times his own size. "I've taken control now, you hear!"

"Really?"

"Yes. And we're going to—"

Stinkhorn the Great's foot came down on Globule the Sticky. The last thing he saw were the remains of Squish the Flattened stuck to his father's big toe. And much like Squish the Flattened, Globule the Sticky would remain stuck to Stinkhorn the Great's little toe till the end of time.

"I think," Muck the Stain said cheerfully, "I'll go and ready the horde."

Behind the failed mutiny, Mrs Pinkletin had felt an empty growl in her stomach, and had started making her way through the audience one elderly man at a time, not even stopping to add any seasoning at all.

"Flowering buttercup of my heart," Stinkhorn the Great said, "save some for me, my dear."

"One more time!" The Fixer said shaking a Frisbee at a rather flustered-looking space giant. "One more time you lose this over next door's fence, and I'll be keeping it for myself. You understand?"

"Yeah," bellowed the space giant taking the planetary rings from The Fixer and heading back to the sandy nebula known locally by the natives as 'Relax Dude'.

As he turned, the lovely view of a buttock-hugging pair of speedos a few miles wide greeted The Fixer at eye level.

"Blah…" he spat, "space giants. They know too much, and care too little."

"Maybe I should idolise them," God said softly. "I used to enjoy everything you know, the whole 'creation' thing."

"Why did you air quote, 'creation'?"

God shrugged, "It's more destruction nowadays."

"What's got you so glum?"

A heavy sigh came from God's chest, it was a sound that The Fixer hadn't heard since their old local free house rang the bell for last orders and the queue was already too long to even consider standing in.

"Pint?" The Fixer said, holding a fresh glass of lager in his hand. "My treat."

"No…"

"No?"

"Na."

"You're saying no to a drink?"

"Yeah."

"Good God what's wrong?"

"I've come to a decision. Regarding the multiverse."

"Right… and that is?"

"I'm not going to take it back. But I can't keep it the way it is."

"Meaning?"

"Meaning, it'll have to change."

The Fixer rolled his eyes. "Meaning? … I don't have the patience for riddles, you know."

"Meaning," God smiled, "it'll have to be reset."

"Can you do that?"

"Of course," God replied. "I'll have to check the instructions, but I'm sure we can do it."

"We?"

"Yes, we," God stated, "you're my fixer."

The Fixer nodded; he couldn't argue the obvious. "So, what do we do?"

God pulled the instructions from the ether and sat down on a rather comfortable armchair he materialised from thought alone.

"Where's mine?" The Fixer asked.

"Make your own…"

… And he did.

God began flicking through the manual a page at a time while cracking open another cold tinny he took from the armrest fridge. The thought occurred to him, that if he had simply read this at the beginning, things may have gone a lot smoother. It took him a while to get to the page he was looking for, there was so much babble that, like most instruction manuals, didn't need to be included. Plus, a thick segment of the manual had been graciously translated into every language there was, which obviously didn't help the matter.

"Can you speak Fungal?" God asked.

"Not after I sacrificed my throat for a joke I didn't even understand myself!"

At the top of the page, the words 'So you want to reset your multiverse?' were printed in red. Underneath, surprisingly, there was not, as you may have thought, an endless list of checks, rules or points, but instead a simple and short instruction that read, *'To reset multiverse, using control panel supplied: press and hold pound sign for ten seconds, then turn off and on. Reboot will be started.'*

God nodded, "Easy peasy… Let's go."

The Cosmic lurched and darted from one strange-looking sacrificial table to another as the multiverse sparkled like cheap Halloween spider-webbing in the far corner of the storage room. He nestled down next to a large fire pit that looked to have been only recently used, the smell of 'herbal' remedies thick in the air. He could still see over by the desk the small paperweight holding his own universe inside, and guessed that wherever he was, must be the great beyond; for a being called The Cosmic, he wasn't really that smart.

Next to him, resting against the leg of the fire pit, stood a small dagger with the words *'Happy Birthday Fixer'* inscribed on the handle. He took it, though he didn't really see why, it was just a feeling of security that he was after. If he were to ever see Stinkhorn the Great again, he knew he wouldn't be able to match him with strength alone. Even though his own being was a construct of an infinite number of lifeforms and minds, Stinkhorn the Great was sentient mould, and unless he had extra-strong bleach to hand, he was sure he would need a knife.

He stood, gaining a little confidence, and turned.

"Who are you?" he said, sounding a little more fragile than he would've liked.

The Keeper stood with his back towards The Cosmic, a thick heavy cloak hung over his shoulders; a stiffness running the course of his body gave him the appearance of a tall, dark and mysterious foe. He reacted with nothing, simply staring into the speckled mass of the multiverse.

"I said," The Cosmic added, "who are you?"

Nothing. The Keeper did nothing.

The Cosmic straightened his posture and raised the dagger in the air. Yet remaining safe behind what looked to be a heavy Saturn Boom Pinball machine; if it came to it, he was sure he could throw it on its side for cover.

"I said…"

"Are you a God?" The Keeper asked. He remained still.

"I am!"

"No," The Keeper replied softly. "You are not. I am the one true being." He turned to look at The Cosmic, his eyes a fierce depth, his demeanour controlling. "What could you possibly do to hurt me?"

The Keeper raised his arm, and with a flick of his wrist sent a burst of energy towards The Cosmic, who immediately turned into a pumpkin. The dagger fell to the floor, bouncing a few times for good measure. The Keeper cocked a smile and continued staring at the multiverse.

The pumpkin wobbled a little, then burst into fragments of slush and seeds, reforming once more. The Cosmic stood tall, flicked a little lump of pumpkin flesh from his shoulder, and took the dagger in his fist.

"I am The Cosmic!" he shouted, to which The Keeper turned, puzzled about the current standing. "You had your chance! And you blew it! It's time for a new owner, one who'll succeed where you have failed. One who will build where you have fallen. Step aside, false God! Lay down, and surrender!"

The Traveller and Norman's consciences sat back watching the terribly cringe-inducing monologue unfold, both covering their metaphorical eyes, unable to watch the tragically bad villain's speech unfold.

Jesus, The Traveller thought, *this guy is just awful.*

I like him, Norman thought.

Of course you do.

Do we have any popcorn left?

Here, The Traveller thought, passing over the idea of salted popcorn.

Thanks.

The Keeper laughed, quite villainously too.

The Traveller slapped his forehead. *Here we go.*

"Your little tricks won't stop me!"

"You can turn me into any vegetable you like," The Cosmic said, "but I will continue to come back for more."

"Then I shall turn you into many types," The Keeper threatened, "and make a stew of you, that I shall eat with gusto!"

"Then I shall give you the gift of heartburn, and if it comes to it, the trots."

"You will not stop me. Neither will the runs. I shall make you into a million peas, and cast you to every corner of existence…"

"Aha!" The Cosmic said, pointing a finger to the air. "Then I shall be everywhere and take my lead from the shadows!"

Jesus, The Traveller thought.

Yes, Norman added. *He is pretty bad at this, isn't he?*

Bad? I've heard more threatening dinner ladies.

A hundred miles from the nearest town, Brown Bears troop leader Skip dangled over a cliff edge in the middle of The Great Forest, located on Super Prime. His second in command, Mavis, held his ankles tightly while rooting round for a decent foothold.

"Jonny!" Skip shouted angrily, "just jump up and grab my hand, for Pete's sake!"

"No!" little Jonny said flatly. Little Jonny had somehow found himself on a small rock shelf halfway down the cliff side; inches from his feet, a thousand-foot drop descended below.

"For God's sake, Mavis," Skip said coldly, "I told you to watch Jonny. You know what he's like."

"Sorry."

Little Jonny smiled taking in the amazing view. As far as he could see, green trees spread out towards the mountainous horizon, small flocks of birds swooped in the warm air while fluffy clouds glided idly here and there.

"Jonny," Skip said after calming down a bit. He did well, seeing how he was hanging upside down, a head full of blood and near death facing him from below. "Look, if you take my hand, we'll go back to camp, and have a good old sing-song. What do you say?"

"No."

"For God's sake, Jonny!"

"I can't," Jonny replied innocently, "at least, not yet. Mr Marvellous hasn't turned up yet."

To that, Skip's blood boiled within his veins. "That layabout? You'd be better off waiting for The Human Man."

"I promise you," Little Jonny said with hope, "he's coming!"

Skip looked up past his middle-aged portly midsection at Mavis, "These bloody heroes, do nothing but sign autographs and eat free meals."

"I think he's quite cute."

"Don't you start."

Just then, a sonic boom rattled the air followed by the sound of birds flapping out of harm's way, and the casual background noise of heroic music filled the sky. A faint blur shot across the tree canopy in the distance, a white vapour trail curling behind.

"It's him, it's him!" Little Jonny shouted happily. "I told you!"

"…Great," Skip mumbled.

And it was indeed.

Mr Marvellous sped towards the cliff side like a raging bullet, coming to a hover right by Little Jonny as he looked back in pure delight. A super hand reached out.

"Come on, son. Let's get you to safety."

"Mr Marvellous!" Little Jonny said excitedly, "I'm your biggest fan!"

"Of course, you are… now, let's get you off this rock, huh kid?"

"I've got all your magazines and books. And your limited-edition playing cards."

"Mm, that's good. Shall we?" he replied opening his hand for Little Jonny to take.

"We're actually okay here thanks," Skip said dangling upside down just above them. "You can go if you like."

"It's really no trouble."

"No, we can do it," said Skip, "Jonny!"

"Look," Little Jonny said, "here's the picture of you when you did that sea rescue last year."

Mr Marvellous huffed, "Thanks. Let's go…"

"No!"

"No?"

"No!" Little Jonny said flatly. "I've waited a long time to see you. And I'm going to make the most of it!"

Mr Marvellous rubbed his face feeling a little flustered. In the distance, his super hearing picked up the cry of a bus full of nuns, as his arch nemesis, Evil Nigel, unfolded yet another dastardly plot.

"Look kid. Just take my hand so I can get going, yeah?"

"Is that Evil Nigel?" Little Jonny asked. "I know it is. I called him a few minutes ago. I thought that we could rescue the nuns together?"

"What?"

"He's always doing this," Skip said wobbling from side to side in the breeze. "Last week he forced Professor Neutron to take him fishing. Sorry."

"Please, please don't tell me you climbed down here voluntarily?"

Little Jonny looked back at Mr Marvellous blankly. "Well, maybe a little bit. Skip? Will I get my climbing badge now?"

"Jesus, Jonny!"

The Fixer finished off his can of beer and threw it over his shoulder as God opened the door to the storage room.

"I hope you're going to pick that up?"

"Aren't we here to reset the multiverse?"

"Yeah. So?"

"So, it doesn't really matter does it?"

"Mm, I guess not," God thought emptying a Bag for Life full of empties by his feet.

"Litter bug."

Inside, God was rather shocked to find out just how much stuff The Keeper had collected over the years. He remembered at the beginning, the storage room was as full as a Scottish comedy open mic-night, now it was packed from wall to wall.

"Where's the control panel then?"

"Well," God said at a loss. "It used to be over there." He pointed.

"Where the statues of the four horsemen are?"

"Yeah," God said. And laughed. "I could teach them a few things about destruction."

"Quite…"

The pair began to search through all the things that The Keeper had deemed worthy of a place in his collection. A lot of it was stuff he'd been given from The Truth to look after; Saturn Boom memorabilia that was as cheap as a DVD you'd buy from the local street market, and just as fuzzy. The Fixer made his way through a large desk that had been littered with all The Keeper's drawings he'd done while waiting to sweep things up again. One picture was a crude stickman portrait of all the guys standing in a line, with The Traveller missing, and a smiling sun in the corner.

"Bloody hell," The Fixer said, "looks like a four-year-old's drawn this."

He tossed the picture to one side and ventured into a drawer. He couldn't believe it, words escaped him; he'd found exactly what he'd been looking for. He called God over in a hurry of excitement.

"You found it already?"

"No," The Fixer said. "Even better, I lent him my entire collection of nudist bottle openers a few billion years back."

God looked at The Fixer and literally had nothing to say. "I literally have nothing to say."

The Fixer laughed, "You don't need to say anything."

In the background, two very distinct voices began to shout and bawl.

"Can you hear that?"

God nodded.

"Follow me."

By the multiverse in the far corner of the cornerless storage room, The Cosmic and The Keeper had moved a table and two chairs into position and had set up a small game of battleships to sort out their differences. And by the looks of things, it was a very heated game.

"You just sunk my last frigate!"

"It's not my fault if you choose to place all your ships in every corner. It's a bit of a rookie mistake."

"Shut up," The Cosmic said. "B4."

"Miss. D6."

"Goddamn it! Can you see or something?"

"D7."

"Stop sinking my ships!"

"Or you'll do what?"

"Or I'll julienne your head!" The Cosmic said waving the dagger in front of him.

God nudged The Fixer and gestured over behind where the two were playing; a large silver box that looked like something a first-grade art student would've made in his spare time stood happily. Painted across one side it said, *'Control panel.'*

"Bingo," God said.

In a universe, not so far, far away, Stinkhorn the Great, Mrs Pinkletin and their immense horde had been very keen on finding God, and aiding him with his continuing living situation, when they realised that they had been followed and tracked down by a huge fleet of ships, commanded by none other than the Spork child, seeking vengeance for the consumption of his entire race.

'He who could lift solids and liquids together, would one day bring forth peace.' The Prophecy had been true, just not on the right planet. After a time spent alone, the Spork child had brought all the Chopstick Tribes together, leading to the end of the Noodle Wars. The ocean tribes of the western sea had met with the mountain tribes of the east, and spoke words of peace and harmony, and put an end to violence itself. It was then that the Spork child took charge and led the Chopstick people on a hunt for Mrs Pinkletin in the name of vengeance and blood.

Stinkhorn the Great took hold of the leading battleship, ripped open its hull with a deafening bellow, and tossed a few hundred Chopstick foot soldiers into the vacuum of space. Further down the frontline, Rot the Thing headed a gallant charge at a large squadron of Chow mien Tia Fighters, while Mrs Pinkletin wove her vines tightly around a heavy troop carrier, squeezing it till it creaked into two fragments.

The sweet, and sour — sticky at times — conflict raged on; hundreds fought bravely and thousands came to rest.

With his last dying breath, Stinkhorn the Great spotted the Spork child's vessel, surrounded by a small battalion of ships; he would finish off what his beloved had started, and devour the Spork child once and for all; well, not for all, the battle had made him quite hungry, and he was not in the mood for sharing.

God pulled open the front of the control panel, and found that it really was made from cardboard, blue tack and a bit of tape. Inside lay a small keyboard, a light on its top flashed red every now and again. It too had been securely fixed with electrical tape.

"Whose job was it to put this together?"

"Not mine," The Fixer said casually.

"Mm," God replied. "Where's the hash key, then?"

"Pound sign, I think you mean."

"Right, pound sign… Here we go…"

God pressed down on the button and waited.

Eric the blob had finished work for the day and was heading home to his wife and son. He had the air of a winner, the confidence of a king. It had been several weeks since he had touched a drop of alcohol, and he could feel the benefits of it. If he could, he would've thanked God personally for putting him straight, and making him see the errors of his ways. Everyone at his office had been delighted to finally welcome him back again. Blob, Blob and Watkins, a legal firm, had tried to do the best they could in Eric's absence.

Eric opened the front door to his company house, the drifting smell of freshly baked, well… something close to bread, filled the air. His wife, Sodium Citrate, hugged him wildly as their son, Potassium Cyanide, came racing down the stairs. A happy family, they surely were.

Not only had Eric just finished his first day back at his law firm, quit drinking for good, but unbeknown to his close friends, Eric was also a very cunning investor, and had recently sunk money into a new digital currency called Slopcoin. He'd sold at the right time and made such a profit on his stake that he, his wife and son could live the rest of their life's debt-free.

"Nothing's happening, mate."

"Give it a minute," The Fixer said.

"It's meant to take ten seconds! My finger's getting achy."

"Hold on." The Fixer did what he did best and kicked the side of the control panel. "Anything?"

"...Nope."

Little Jonny gripped onto the side of the cliff with everything he had, for such a small boy; Mr Marvellous was truly stunned at his unusual strength.

"Let go!"

"No!" Little Jonny shouted, "you haven't even done a barrel roll, or fought a bear yet!"

"Stop messing around Jonny!" Skip said from above, his face as bloodshot as a fingered eyeball.

"No!"

"If you don't let go, I'll have to pull down this entire cliffside, and take it with me when I go," Mr Marvellous said angrily.

Little Jonny thought about that for a moment, "Okay," he said, "that would be cool to see."

"Don't you dare do that," Skip shouted in a panic, "you can't just rip up a mile or two of earth to save one annoying boy!"

"What if I jump?" Little Jonny asked. "You could fly after me really fast, saving me at the last minute."

Or after the last minute, Skip thought.

"Look, kid! While we've been messing around, four nuns have been skinned alive. I can't afford to let any more than, say five or six meet their end, I have to go!"

"You shouldn't let any nuns meet their end!" Skip shouted unhappily. "Call yourself a hero?"

"I didn't ask to be born this way!" Mr Marvellous said.

"You have responsibilities, you know."

"As troop leader, your current situation makes it hard for you to argue that."

"I have enough problems!"

"Weeeeee..." Little Jonny said as he jumped to the air.

"Great," Skip said flatly, "you see what your meddling has done?"

"Do you want me to save him?" Mr Marvellous said sarcastically. "Or shall I let him plummet to his death?"

Skip shrugged, "Do want you like…"

"I said pound sign!" The Fixer chuckled, "you've been pressing the star sign."

"Ah, right. Sorry."

Behind them, The Cosmic and The Keeper had given up with their quiet game of battleships and had begun to scuffle and roll around on the floor. Every second or two The Cosmic morphed into a turnip then back again.

Ten seconds began counting down.

Eric sat down in front of his laptop, pulled his wallet from his pocket and held a lottery ticket in his hand. He thought that there could be no way he would win the Blobbery jackpot. It had been a triple rollover, and the pot had reached an all-time high. The highest in the planet's history, a jaw-dropping amount of seventy-four Blobbelines. Granted, converted into Earth currency, it would only be enough to buy a small second-hand car; however, it would be enough to see Eric through to retirement.

He typed in his email address and password — 1234 — on the global lottery site and scanned in his ticket's barcode.

"Sodium!" he exclaimed! "Sodium! Get in here, quick!"

The control panel started to shake a little, a puff of smoke plumed from its top, while a small fire lit at one of its cardboard corners.

"Is it meant to do that?"

"She'll last another few seconds!"

Little Jonny smiled, feeling the rush of air pass through his untrimmed hair, his untied boot laces flapping about as he roared towards a canopy of trees. The cliff edge was inches from his face.

"Wheeeee…!"

Stinkhorn the Great picked up the Spork child in his tightened fist, the young revolutionary beating at his chest rhythmically, shouting and chanting as he came closer to a mouth full of teeth.

"Choke on me! Choke on me! Choke on me!"

Eric threw Potassium in the air, kissed his wife with passion, having just won the global Blobbery, funds already transferring to his account.

And then, as if nothing had ever happened, Little Jonny fizzed from reality, Stinkhorn the Great became nothing but nothingness and Eric wobbled from existence.

The multiverse trembled, individual universes sparked and popped like bubbles one after another. God and The Fixer turned and watched as the web-like mass in the corner of the storage room dissolved, receding back on itself.

The Keeper stood up. "No!" he bellowed. "What have you done?"

"Sorry," God said emptily and flicked a finger in the air lifting The Keeper off his feet, hurling him backwards into the swirling implosion.

The Cosmic grabbed the knife from the floor next to his feet, posed himself upright and drew up the blade. "You!" he commanded. "You're God?"

"Me?" The Fixer said.

"No, him!"

"He's not even looking in your direction," God said laughing.

"And how can you tell? He's got what look like galaxies for eyeballs. He could be looking anywhere."

"Fair enough" God admitted. "Yeah… I'm God. Who are you then?"

"I am The Cosmic. And I have come from the paperweight universe," he said pointing over to the small paperweight sitting atop The Keeper's rock. "I have come to rid you of your title!"

"If it's not fungus trying its luck, it's something else," The Fixer tutted.

"Right," God replied, "off you go." And with another flick of his finger, he lifted The Cosmic off the floor, spinning him chaotically backwards into the paperweight universe, sealing its cracked outer glass shell for good.

"Where do these clowns come from?" God asked.

"No idea… does it matter?"

"I guess not."

Both started racing around the storage room picking up and tossing every bit of The Keeper's collection into the vanishing multiverse before they ran out of time. As it became smaller and smaller, the entire storage room started to shake violently.

Both stood, sipping large cocktails with small umbrellas in, and waited for the quaking madness to subside. Eventually, there was nothing but darkness itself everywhere. In the absence of existence, a passing thought came to God as he remembered he'd told Sheila he would be back soon after leaving for milk and bread; that was three weeks ago.

"Bollocks!" he said. "She won't be happy."

"She'll be fine, she's been good to you, and you'll have plenty of time to make it up to her."

"I bloody hope so."

"You've only had to reset creation itself, it's not like you've taken her girls' night away from her."

God looked at The Fixer and bit his lip. "Susan and the rest of her girls were coming over tonight to watch the finale of *I'm a Carbon-Based Life Form, Get Me Out of Here*."

The Fixer scoffed and shrugged, "Good luck."

And on cue, a blinding light exploded around them, a trillion, billion, gazillion tonnes of matter and antimatter blew out from where they stood in all directions. Piece by piece, atom by atom, a universe formed, split into parallels, grew to infinity and split again. Timelines span out, paradoxes and coincidence, déjà vu and synchronicity churned out and washed over everything. Dimensions and quantum singularities popped and fizzed, and the sound of God slurping the last of his Long Island Ice-Tea through a straw echoed for eternity.

"Think you've got it all," The Fixer said bluntly.

God lifted a refilling jug. "Not from this one."

Protons swirled, wildly colliding with neutrons as electrons began to spin around bonds that were forming on microscopic scales. Hydrogen atoms birthed, followed by Helium; soon elements of all kinds tore into reality, and vapour became dust that soon became dust clouds. Stars appeared, and before long, lumps of matter formed the start of rocky worlds and gas giants.

Out of the chaotic dance of creation, The Traveller fazed into life. The Finder came next. Soon Norman appeared holding a bag of popcorn. A moment later, and a moment too soon, The Keeper emerged from the swirling void, and was immediately turned into a potted anthurium that The Gardener would later plant, only for it to be devoured by a ruthless gang of slugs. Eventually, every omnipotent being that had ever taken a holiday in the multiverse was resurrected from the sweeping wave of life itself.

The Transvestite smiled and flashed a thigh.

The Talker opened his mouth, refrained, and simply nodded.

The Dancer wiggled and The Laugher giggled.

The Nudist blushed, and The Pickler pickled.

This new and improved multiverse would be correct, it would be better, and above all, it would be fungal free.

"Though saying that, I will miss old Stinks," The Fixer said thoughtfully.

"Yeah," God agreed, "he was okay really. If you ignore his merciless craving for the total genocide of everything…"

"Oh yeah, if you can see through that, he was a nice guy."

"All right Norman?" God said cheerfully.

"Hello," he smiled in return.

"Took your time," The Traveller said, "what happened?"

"A lot," The Fixer replied. "Where've you two been?"

"Hiding mostly," The Traveller admitted wondering if Anne had managed to find the right carpet without him.

"And eating popcorn," Norman added.

The Finder came over and stood with them happily. "I had some godawful dream about being eaten by a giant plant." He looked over his shoulder and watched as existence rolled away from him like the lowering tide, unveiling everything that had ever wanted to be. "What happened?"

"A lot," The Fixer said again.

"You won't get a better answer from him," The Traveller said.

"A lot has happened though," The Fixer said obviously and added, "Look, there's Anne."

The Traveller grimaced as the idea of carpets and bath taps curdled in his mind, questioning if a quick bolt for the paperweight universe would be a better option.

"Face the music," God said, smiling. "...This should be interesting..."

Renovations

The multiverse flourished wildly for the next sixteen billion years after its reset, yet inevitably it would indeed fail once more. Even with God's helping hand and The Fixer's never-ending maintenance runs, and even with the black hole set in place recycling universes properly, the multiverse would never truly become settled and still. It would forever drop to a chaotic and frantic depth that only another reset would fix.

The Shop Keeper warned God repeatedly that it would never work unless its stand was found or replaced with an equal part. The stand that had been lost was the key to the multiverse's survival; its very existence and ongoing life span rested on this one vital element.

It was true that for sixteen billion years life had found its way once more. Across countless universes it had risen from the primordial soup, evolved and transcended through the ages of time. Yet it would never be enough to satisfy the maniacal onslaught the multiverse would embrace; no number of higher beings or galactic civilisations could halt its maddening. The stand was the multiverse's counterpart, its equal and its opposition. The multiverse was complexity itself. Tangled dimensions, interwoven realities and more. Yet the stand was pure simplicity. It was not basic, and it was not plain, it was simply fundamentally raw. Everything that the multiverse was, the stand equalled it with less. It counteracted the insanity, bringing only prosperity to its being.

Without the stand, life, existence, and every conceivable reality would fail. One way or another, the multiverse would either die a crazed beast, or live onwards, only if the stand were found.

And so…

… In a universe not so dissimilar to our own…

Grog Thunderbottom sat underneath his bridge, quite miserably too, gazing up at the starry night pondering where on Pux 4b his dad had gotten to. It had been four hundred and seven years to the day since his dad, Nigel, had said they'd be back soon, and Grog was beginning to question his honesty. As a nine-foot troll, he'd never really found a place on Pux 4b to call home. Yes, of course at times his general size came in handy; mostly to fix light bulbs or reach the really high up cobwebs that most of us struggle with, but it never really satisfied his happiness.

He'd been all around the small planetoid a good four times already and had always been asked kindly to move on; something to do with house prices in the local area decreasing soon after his arrival. He wasn't a bad troll, not in the least; in fact, most people that had met him said he was a very kind soul, though it was more out of fright and the urge to not be eaten alive.

Earlier that day he'd changed into his most presentable outfit and walked into the village. People had screamed when they saw him plodding down the high street. Windows slammed shut; one man started a small fire in his shop as a kind of defensive tactic. After knocking several times on the front door of the council building, Grog folded up his handwritten letter, posted it, and plodded off back to his bridge.

"Well," Council Leader Sam Samson said, "that was a close one."

"Did you see his eyes?" his wife said worriedly, "they were like two fire balls."

"Indeed. I heard he once tore a farmer in half for not letting him eat his eldest daughter."

"It's true!" old man Jones, the local Baker said, "I seen it wi'me own eyes."

"Golly!"

The small crowd of council men and women huffed a sigh of relief and took to their seats. As Council Leader, Founder of the Flower Society and all-round weasel, Sam Samson bravely picked up Grog's letter by the front door and took it upon himself to warn everyone that what he was about to read could either be a list of violent demands, or the remains of Grog's last meal. He coughed to clear his throat, and began:

"Dear Council members of Butts Trollop, I, Grog Thunderbottom, would like to ask a few things. Firstly, please, please, please, could you

stop sacrificing your nuns and priests directly over my bridge, to what end you see I don't know, but I have great difficulty getting red blotchy stains from my bed sheets, it's costing me a fortune in washing powder. Secondly, can someone please tell the local farmer that his gates are open. Every night I find a sheep standing on my bridge, somehow chained up. In the last two months I have rehomed ninety-one sheep; the rest now live with me. If this continues, can someone from the council please take a look at my planning permission application form, so I can at least build an extension to allow room for my new pets? Yours sincerely, Grog Thunderbottom."

"Golly," Sam Samson's wife said, "what should we do?"

Old man Jones lifted his hand and stood, "I can call the Church in Bodwhiff. Ask 'em if they've got any spare nuns they don't need?"

A mumble of agreement waved around the room. "Please, Jones," Sam Samson said, "and call the farmer, see how many more sheep he can give us too."

Grog slumped down into his large armchair he'd fashioned from a nearly dead cow as his best friend, Bernard the sheep, came down and sat next to him. The popping of burning wood cracked in the small room, while the tasty smell of the farmer's eldest daughter came from the oven, wafting about the under bridge.

"Aye Bernard," Grog said fulsomely, "what would I do without you?"

Bernard fixed his gaze on the fire; the embers dancing around like fireflies. "Bhaaa..."

Grog smiled. "Yeah, I guess. You are wise beyond your years."

"Bhaa," Bernard replied.

"All right... don't go on."

The sky turned red as the Barbarian frontlines shot their flaming arrows upwards; a thousand or so spikes arched higher, curved and came down fatally upon the helpless troop men. Captain Casper Von-Huxby raised a sword to his soldiers who had avoided an unfair death; he was met with cheers of applause. Over thirty million men and women had answered the call to war, and by the Gods of Asteria itself, Captain Casper Von-Huxby would lead his army to victory. He would lay down his life without question so that even the weakest may live, and he knew that all in his ranks would do the same.

Far beyond the snaggle-toothed mess of the frontlines, the Barbarian leader, Fang, beat another defector to death with his bare hands. It mattered little to Fang how many would have to die in order to secure the win, he would sacrifice everyone if it came to it. He would be the one to take back the battle-scarred planet of Orkla, the prophecy had said. And with everything he had, Fang would make that prophesy his life's work.

The Fach-iawn War raged on for many years after that day; billions died, and an entire generation was lost to bloodshed. Orkla became such a distasteful world that the planetary system's trade deal that had stood for over five hundred years crumbled, leading to global chaos; an economic downfall led to worldwide hunger, and soon it didn't matter if the war was over or not, people would suffer greatly.

Commander of the free world, Na'Fal Kabharr sought peace, coming to understand that Orkla could not survive. In an historical event, Barbarian-kind signed a peace treaty and Orkla could finally begin to heal.

Of course, none of that really mattered, as their entire civilisation was microscopic, and Norman just swept them up in his dustpan and brush and threw them in the nearest bin.

"Ah," Norman said, "a good job well done."

"Shh!" the library Curator hissed from her desk. She pointed up towards a large sign that hung behind her that also said, *'Shh!'*

"Sorry," Norman said loudly.

"Shh!"

"Sorry," he whispered.

The Curator looked blankly and went back to whatever was keeping her busy. The Library of Gods, in universe 4 million and 13, was the largest library in the entire multiverse. Except for The Traveller's in-depth categorised photo album from his visit to the Crystal City, The Library of Gods had collected the most amount of data regarding everything. If there were a list of 'Wonders of the Multiverse', the library would surely be in the top three; only beaten to the number two and one spot by the assets of Lady Suds-Pearl, curator of the famous hot tubs located at the Crystal City.

Norman began to whistle and went back to sweeping. Somehow, he'd found himself here and couldn't remember why; like a lot of other discoveries Norman came upon, it was always by accident. True, he technically was meant to be carrying out Explorer duties after The Explorer had been deleted from existence, and for all reasons he had done just that. Norman had flown here and blasted there. He'd explored many places of the new multiverse and taken note of all the really worthy places, and after a few hundred years he'd ended up here. He enjoyed bumbling about the multiverse like some kind of carefree hippy.

Though Norman's old duties were still very much a large part of his life. He had spent countless years as The Janitor, and after giving such a long time to one job, it's hard to cut all the ties. Cleaning now was more like a hobby; he always kept a notebook close by so he could jot down everywhere he'd been and spruced up.

One fond memory he recalled was on a planet called The Dust-Ball. It was a young planet; its people had only just discovered the means to traverse the space between worlds. Their technology was still, however, a bit Wild Westerny, you might say. On the first trip from The Dust-Ball to the neighbouring planet, Silicon Gate, the wooden coach convoy simply fell apart during re-entry. Thankfully, all the horses were wearing full-body space suits with enough air to see them through a year or two. It took Norman five days to find and bring back all the cattle they'd been moving on route, though a tricky task. He was rewarded with ten pieces of silver and his pick of women.

Norman pulled a brown-and-white photo from his pocket and thought back at that amazing night he'd spent with Mary-Sue.

"Ah," Norman said, "no one plays backgammon like you, Mary-Sue."

"Shh!"

"Sorry."

In the vast halls of the library, hundreds of voices echoed like spirits of a lost age. Bookshelves started at one end and carried on to an unseen distance a million miles away. Stairs spiralled upwards, dotted randomly here and there taking people to the upper floors like well-educated steel tornadoes. And even higher up, towards the rooftop, clouds and mist congregated to discuss the habits of simple mortal men. Birds flapped softly, insects buzzed, and the three o'clock flight from Science-Fiction to Historical Events boomed passing overhead.

It would've been easy to spend a lifetime in The Library of Gods; its size, and structure easily seen from the universe next door. And although Norman had a timeless existence, he could've stayed till the very walls collapsed from old age, yet he knew that at some point he would have to carry on into the new multiverse, and further his exploration. He took out his notebook, scribbled down some coordinates and points of interest, packed up his dustpan and brush, and left.

God sat comfortably on his chair while Sheila sat the complete opposite, completely opposite from where God sat, so, in other words, bolt upright, and looking very, very angry. Between them, the marriage counsellor jotted down a few points on his pad, clipped his pen back onto his shirt pocket, and joined the silence once more.

After a few minutes, God began to say something. He opened his mouth and Sheila gave him the old 'I bloody dare you' look, and as if by magic, his mouth closed shut.

"Sheila," the counsellor said shifting forwards on his chair, "this is a safe place, if God wants to…"

… And he morphed into a slice of Battenberg cake.

"Why did you do that?" God asked. "He was one of the nicer ones."

Sheila scoffed. "You know, they all take your side. It doesn't matter what I say."

"Ah, come on now love, you know that's not true."

"Last counsellor we saw, at the Couples Retreat on Monogamy Prime, can you remember what you told him?"

Of course God could remember what he had said. Or at least he thought he could. "Of course!"

"…and that was?"

God hesitated.

"Well," he fumbled, "it was something to do with your birthday?"

"Are you asking me?"

"I mean our anniversary?"

"Pardon?"

"Christmas?"

Sheila trembled a little, huffed and thought back to the breathing techniques her yoga instructor, Breaking Wave, had told her about. She'd been by God's side ever since the very beginning before the whole life thing had started. She was, by definition, a great catch. She was independent, strong, confident. She could repeat God's favourite drinking song 'The Butcher Found His Wife in Cahoots with the Postman', out loud just from memory, and she could drink an entire yard glass of 9% Jovian Ale in under four and a half seconds. Once, she even ran from one end of the multiverse to the other, just to bring God his lunch box on his first day of work after he'd left home without it.

God stared at her and saw every little moment, every second of every day they had spent together. And after a million-billion-years with the same woman, God was happy that Sheila still was able to hoist his mainsail.

"What I do remember," God said eventually, "is the first time I saw you. I'd been out with The Finder all day, and we came into that small pub feeling thirsty, The Book Maker."

Sheila laughed, "That was a bookmaker."

"So, you say… anyway, we tried to order some pints, but the guys behind the bar said that they didn't serve beer. God knows why."

"Because it was a bookmaker!"

"Sure. Sure. Anyway. Suddenly, there's me feeling like I had everything I ever wanted, then this amazing, young, beautiful girl comes wandering in."

Sheila smiled and looked coy. "I didn't look that good."

"Ah you did. I'd never seen such a beautiful looking girl ever before."

God leant forwards and placed a hand on Sheila's leg, and in turn she placed hers on his.

"Come on, we don't need to be here, do we?"

Sheila chuckled and squished God's fingers gently within hers.

"Look. If you can cut back on the drinking, we don't need to come back here, okay?"

"Okay."

"I mean it," Sheila said firmly. "I worry. And I don't want to see you drink yourself into oblivion. So, if you can cut down…"

She left it at that. God nodded and tossed a bit of energy towards the Battenberg, reshaping the counsellor once more. The door shut behind them, and the counsellor sat, wondering why he could suddenly taste marzipan in the back of his throat.

Meanwhile, in a completely different universe, The Traveller wasn't having such luck. Granted, he had at last managed to get the new carpets down after Anne had insisted that he used only real, legitimate tools to do it. Now, however, it had been decided by the boss that the kitchen wall had to come down to make way for an all-in-one kitchen-diner.

"Anne," The Traveller said emptily, "I could make you a dream house with thought alone. If you wanted a rainbow for stairs, or a bloody hippo for a dining-room table, I could just think it into existence. So why on earth am I using a bloody hammer?"

Anne stood by the half-deconstructed wall with The Fixer as they both sipped fresh coffee.

"You're missing the point," The Fixer said.

"Exactly," Anne agreed.

"You were meant to be coming here to help me!"

The Fixer shrugged. "Was I? I thought it'd be more of an advisory role than anything else."

"Did you now?"

Anne dunked a digestive biscuit in her coffee and sighed. "You better finish it before my parents come around."

"When was that arranged?"

"Months ago," The Fixer said. "Debby and Mark are coming around at half three for late lunch."

"I'm glad someone takes notice," Anne said.

The Traveller gripped the hammer in his hands and growled under his breath, "Are you going to help me… or are you going to stand there doing nothing?"

The Fixer shrugged again, sipped his coffee and smiled. "Yeah. You definitely need a bigger hammer."

The hammer ended up in the far wall as The Traveller brought a huge sledgehammer into reality and begun pounding away in rage at the open brickwork. "You! Stupid! Silly! No good! Wall!"

"Now you're getting somewhere," The Fixer said.

"Be a good boy," Anne added, "and try not to make a mess."

The sledgehammer landed next to the smaller hammer as a large wrecking ball morphed into shape.

"That'll work."

Grog awoke to the sound of music. Not at all good music, in fact, I'd say it was more chanting than anything else. A sort of rhythmical, repetitive sound that you might hear when visiting a village shaman, or witchdoctor to get rid of a boil. He threw the bed sheets off him, pushed his large feet into his slippers and made his way to the front door. Bernard woke too and came to his side to see what all the commotion was about.

Outside a small gathering had formed just up the bank from his front door under his bridge. A small fire had been started and a few of the villagers were prancing about moronically. At the front, a holy man stood. I say 'holy man', but to be honest it could've been any village idiot; he had some kind of coloured robes around his shoulders and held a large book with both hands that he read from. Every now and again he'd look up at Grog, gauging his mood.

Grog picked up Bernard and stroked his head and he started to purr; he loved his ears being tickled. It wasn't every day Grog was sung to. It wasn't even his birthday. Not even close.

"Beastly creature!" the holy man shouted, "be gone I command you, be gone! Take your ugliness and leave!"

"Ugliness?" Grog said to himself.

"Be gone I command you! Be gone!"

"Bhaa," Bernard said.

"Beastly creature!"

"Umm… excuse me?" Grog said holding a hand up. "Excuse me?"

The holy man, who turned out to be Sam Samson, stopped chanting and stood silent. His wife and the rest of the Flower Society carried on prancing around unfazed.

"Uh, yeah. Are you talking about me?"

"Yes! Beast!" Sam Samson said firmly. He had to remain as firm as he could, not only to look dominant and powerful, but also because Mrs Samson had promised that she would do something for him that she only rarely did and usually on his birthday.

"I command you, Beast, be gone!"

"I have a name, you know?"

"Bhaa."

"They are being rude, aren't they Bernard?"

"Bhaa..."

Sam Samson opened a small bottle of what must've been holy water, and started to flick its contents towards Grog, who raised an arm to shelter his face from any splashes.

"Hey! Do you mind?"

"Go back to the realm of dankness, and rot!"

"Rot?" Grog asked flatly. "I've had the building inspectors over five times this year. I'll have you know there's no rot or dankness, anywhere in my bridge house!"

Sam Samson paused, "Dust?"

"Nope."

"How about cobwebs?"

"On my to-do list for the day."

Sam Samson closed the book in his hands and stepped to Grog while his wife led the dancing behind him.

Quietly he said, "Look old chap, I'm sort of needing you to clear out. It's nothing personal, you see, it's just that we've got the annual Village awards coming up, and well, it won't look good having a troll living under one of our bridges."

"Really?" Grog said rhetorically.

"Yes. Plus, well, Mrs Samson has said that she'll let me watch a documentary later about the rise of affordable fire-resistant concrete. I watch it every year. Even though it's not my birthday." He chuckled with excitement.

"Concrete?"

"Yes."

"Affordable concrete?"

"And fire-resistant!"

Grog calmly placed Bernard on the floor by his feet, who sheepishly ran back into the house. "So, you want me to, 'clear out', so you can watch this show of yours?"

"Ah," Sam Samson said happily, "I knew you'd see the light."

Grog frowned, took Sam Samson by one leg, lifted him off the ground, and began to shake him angrily.

"Look here! I'm not going anywhere! I've been round Pux a million times and it's always the same. I like Butts Trollop, even if I'm not welcome. So, give me one good reason why I shouldn't throw you in the oven next to the farmer's daughter?"

"I told you!" old man Jones shouted as he danced around behind Mrs Samson; one of the Flower Society members had the flu that day, so old man Jones volunteered to fill the spot; he thought the silk dress was especially comfortable.

Sam Samson cried in horror; it was Grog's breath more than anything that was making his eyes weep.

"So?" Grog said. "What'll it be?"

"Please! I'm too important to be eaten alive!"

"I'll swallow you whole if it helps?"

Grog closed the front door and made his way to his armchair where Bernard sat. It hadn't taken much convincing for Sam Samson to apologise and run off with the rest of the Butts Trollopers. He was equally happy that not only had he been 'allowed' to stay, but Mrs Samson had made it quite clear on the run home that her husband would definitely, one hundred per cent, not be watching any documentary.

Grog unfolded the village newspaper that Sam Samson had handed to him as a sort of pleading chip. It was a good read most of the time but came into its own when Grog ran out of toilet paper. The fine double thickness of the pages seemed to soak up everything that other brands couldn't.

"Let's see what's been going on then, shall we Bernard?"

"Bhaa."

"Doris has had twin boys, it says here. And the Alpha Persei School for Girls are having a bake sale. They better watch out; the Mercury Mobsters are on the move again." Grog laughed.

"Bhaa…"

Grog flipped a few pages uninterested in most of the usual drivel that had been deemed newsworthy, picking out bits that caught his eye.

"Terry Jones the mechanic is selling his 1984 Ford Buick, he won't get that much for it! And oh," Grog said unhappily. "The Last Orders have conquered and enslaved Pux 4e."

"Bhaa," Bernard said worriedly.

"Me too," Grog agreed. "It won't be long till they're here to do the same."

"Bhaa."

The Last Orders, Bernard thought as he settled down on Grog's lap for a nap, *that means trouble.*

The last time Bernard came face to face with The Last Orders, he'd been drinking with his old friend Bud, when a tactical squad of Last Orders gunmen came bursting into The Pen; a shady back-alley nightclub where all the Continuum bovine gathered.

The Last Orders, Bernard thought, trembling. *We'll have to leave.*

Bernard had been inside the multiverse longer than most. When he left the safety of God's garden, and ventured the cosmos, there had been so much to see and do. He'd outlived and survived the Fungal Empire and steered clear of The Cosmic, he even somehow made it through a multiversal reset. But The Last Orders, they were tenacious and stubborn, like a weed that wouldn't submit.

God walked into the shop after visiting the pizzeria next door, whistling quite tunelessly. He made his way to the counter at the back, just past the out-of-date electrons and half-price Nebulas and was a little shocked to find a giant of a man standing at the till waiting for him.

"Um," God said, "am I in the right place?"

"Most definitely," The Shop Keeper said happily. "Excuse my new appearance. I've had a little reworking done."

"A little?"

"Yes. I got tired of looking like such a frail being, so I decided to change my look for something a bit more threatening. Robberies have dropped overnight."

"Understandable," God said.

"Can I interest you in anything while you're here? A new project to get stuck into? Perhaps a Quantum Realm, or a Binary Star System?"

God pulled an empty glass from the air and filled it with beer, making sure that its head was just the right size. "Not at the moment. Maybe another time."

"Are you sure?" The Shop Keeper said hurriedly. "We've just got some new cosmic string in, and we're having a sale on gravitational waves; buy two and get a complimentary surfboard."

"Na," God said chugging down his beer in one, "I'll pass."

"You know, a sharpened pencil is always ready to draw," The Shop Keeper said wisely. "One wouldn't want to see you, uh-hum, lose your edge. Sir."

"Imposhible!"

"Imposhible?"

"...Impossible," God corrected, then hiccupped.

"Sir. I hope you don't mind my asking. But how are things? In general."

"Great! Just grand. Living the dream." God filled another glass and this time sipped it carefully, as if nursing it back to emptiness. He looked idly around the shop, rustled about his pocket with one hand and nodded at The Shop Keeper. A moment passed. God finished his drink again and poured himself another.

"Excuse me, sir..."

"Jesus, sorry, where are my manners? You want one?"

"Sir."

"Here," God said lifting another glass to the countertop.

"Sir, really. I'll pass."

"No, you won't. Just have the one."

"Sir, I must insist."

"Go on..."

"Sir!" The Shop Keeper said angrily. "I said no."

God looked a little upset as he dematerialised the glass and went back to gazing about the shop.

"I hope you're not just here to escape someone, sir."

"Course not," God said. "Burrp... oops, sorry. Tequila Slammer?"

The Shop Keeper huffed and frowned. "I'm going to have to ask you to leave, sir. This is a shop for the all-knowing, not a brewery for the all-singing."

"Ah, come on, I'm only having a laugh."

"Sir. Please."

Reluctantly, God made his way from the shop, hanging his head lower than it had been on the morning after The Traveller's annual get-together at the all-Platinum Lace Bar in universe 69. This, he'd decided, was far worse than the walk of shame.

The impressively large Cathedral Ship sat down just outside the capital city of Yon, located on Pux 4e, sending a wave of dust bellowing outwards. The smaller troop carriers landed around it; their doors opened as a million Last Orders footmen scattered, heading towards the city centre. Panic spread through the streets, like butter that hadn't warmed up enough, tearing holes in your bread; an analogy that alone sends terror down the spine. Overlord Dave looked through the window from his private quarters, high above the ground in the tallest spire of the Cathedral Ship. If it hadn't had gained a reputation for being a place of horror, pain, suffering and agony, it would most definitely be considered as one of the prettier looking ships in the sector. Shame really.

It had been a rough night for Overlord Dave; not only had he had to stay up late scanning over slave party documents and execution notices, but when he finally managed to get to bed, his pillow hadn't been fluffed up properly and the air conditioning wasn't fully working. It took him hours to get to sleep, only to wake up an hour later with cramp in his foot. He sat down in front of the window as a maid brought over his breakfast; Chocolate Hoops seemed to always set him up nicely for the day, plus, the little game on the back of the box kept him entertained for a while.

"Here's your warm milk, too, Overlord Dave."

"Ta," he replied. "No bickies?"

"…I shall fetch them immediately!"

"Thanks. Oh, do me a favour…"

"Anything, Your Overlordness."

"Get yourself down to the execution wing and send up another maid please. Preferably one who won't forget my custard creams."

The young maid quivered a little.

"Okay." Then ran off in tears.

Overlord Dave smirked. "Classic."

He munched down on his cereal happily, enjoying its chocolatey goodness, staring blankly at the back of the box trying to work out today's riddle.

Mm, he thought, *it's a tough one.*

The door to his quarters slid open as a fresh maid came striding in.

"Ah," Overlord Dave said, "come over here, I need your help."

"It's Margery, Your Overlordness," she said eagerly, "I'm at your disposal."

"Margery? What a pretty name. I shall call you maid, from now on."

"Of course…"

"Of course, what?"

Margery rubbed the back of her hand and looked a little worried, "Of course, Your Overlordness, I mean. Sorry…"

"That's quite all right. Now, take a seat and have a look at this please."

Overlord Dave turned the cereal box around and passed it over the table to where she sat and awaited an answer. Margery looked at the box, it read: 'What has hands, but cannot clap?'.

"Oh," she said. "I think it's a clock, Your Overlordness."

"A clock? Are you sure?"

"Most definitely."

"Mm," Overlord Dave replied. "I thought it may have been a slave found stealing bread from our kitchens. He'd wind up with no hands."

Margery nodded. "Yes, Your Overlordness, but it says here, 'What has hands'."

"Yes. A slave would need hands to steal the bread, of course."

"Yeah…" Margery replied, at a loss. Then bravely said, "but this one does have hands."

"Yes. But after the stealing, we'd chop them off, you see."

Margery looked blankly at Overlord Dave, "Of course," she finally said. "How silly of me." She took another look at the back of the box and nodded. "Yes, I see now, it is a slave that's been found stealing. My mistake."

Overlord Dave smirked again as a fresh maid made her way into his room after he'd sent Margery off to the execution wing. It had become such a regular thing that working as a maid on the Cathedral Ship had become the highest paid job going, especially when considering the hours actually worked. Margery had started at nine o'clock in the morning and was all finished by ten past; her husband and four children had been set for life.

"Your new slave count," Bol said as he walked in. He was a horse of a man… well, some kind of being, anyway. Bi-ped for sure. His origins were not really that clear to Overlord Dave, though from the looks of him he was somewhere between a towering orangutan, and a six-week stint of steroids. He placed the large folder down on the table and grabbed the cereal spoon and bowl from Overlord Dave.

"Do you mind, I hadn't finished that!"

"Shut it," Bol said slapping Overlord Dave round the back of his head. "Respect your elders."

"Sorry."

"Any bickies?"

Both looked at the new maid who huffed and nodded.

"Execution wing?"

"Please."

"I'll send another maid in."

"Thanks."

Bol flung the empty bowl to the table and picked up the cereal box, looked at its rear and said, "It's a clock."

"Are you sure?" Overlord Dave asked, "just that I thought it may have been…" Bol gave him the usual look when he was being undermined and raised an eyebrow. "…Yes, it's a clock isn't it."

"So?" Bol stated loudly slapping his hands together, "what's on the agenda today? The usual?"

"Yes. We'll enslave as many as we can, drain the planet of its resources, and move on. Hopefully, all done by tomorrow teatime."

"Right," Bol said, "I'll be off then." And with that, he thrust the large window open and jumped out on to the spire, flinging himself downwards, jumping from one gargoyle to the next, reminiscing of past times when he was just a young-beast, frolicking joyously with his equally hairy friends through the jungle home world of Gwallt Major. Weeks he would spend away from home, exploring and venturing out to untold lands. He recalled the words his beard-wearing mother always used to tell him as he returned, 'This ain't a hotel you know!'.

Overlord Dave shut the window behind Bol and fastened it tightly, turning to tend to his small cacti and plants that sat on the window shelf. Besides his love for execution, he was quite the gardener.

The Traveller's tape measure wasn't really what he remembered. It had the length, of course, just not the rigidness. Every time he extended it outwards with both hands, it fell limp; possibly age and over usage had worn it down.

"Grrr," The Traveller growled tightening his teeth around his carpenter's pencil. He'd been trying to take the dimensions of the kitchen wall where at some point he had planned — 'he' as in Anne, and 'planned' as in told — the washing machine and tumble dryer would go.

Again, he had been instructed to use absolutely zero powers and use only real tools to do the job. And again, The Fixer stood by the doorway watching as his increasingly frustrated friend began to lose his rag.

"Why don't you use a laser point?"

"Grrr," The Traveller growled again, and dropped the pencil from his mouth, "either go away, or help *damnit*!"

The Fixer scoffed. "Fat chance. I'm far too busy to get involved in that nonsense."

"Busy?"

"Far, far too busy," he replied as Anne passed him a small plate with a slice of cake and fork on. "Thanks."

The Traveller stared blankly back. Breaking Wave had told him to count to ten every time he felt stress building up. Apparently, it was a great yet simple way to realign his chakra and boost internal healing powers. A few years back, God made the decision to employ a spiritual yoga/guru type fellow to help everyone remain as happy as possible. It had nothing to do with a sly attempt to keep everyone busy so he could dash off and watch the horse racing without being caught, although, in the end, he did indeed get caught. That being said, Sheila agreed that Breaking Wave, a handsome, chiselled, well-groomed, young, athletic man who had a constant problem forgetting to put on a shirt, would be perfect for a weekly slot for everyone.

"Feel better?" The Fixer asked finishing off his cake.

"Not really."

"Personally, I don't think he's worth the money."

"Don't think he does it for the money."

The Fixer smiled, "I don't even need to find my life's path!"

To which The Traveller laughed and felt a little better about himself.

"Yeah, in fact, out of all of us, you're the one who most definitely does need some kind of direction."

"What? Cobblers…"

"Don't lie to yourself," The Traveller replied flatly, "a wrongful lie to oneself will ultimately damage the internal life energy of the sentient mind."

"I'll damage your internal sentient mind," Anne said walking in with a drink, "if this isn't done soon."

"There's no way I can finish this in time, snuggly-boo."

"Blahh," The Fixer whispered.

"Well," Anne continued, "you're going to have to do your best. And make sure that everything is tidy and clean, I don't want to see any dust or paint anywhere."

The Traveller nodded, and though feeling a little under pressure and overwhelmed with the constructing and building of household appliances, he relaxed a bit thinking that at the very least The Fixer was here to oversee it all, and make sure he didn't mess things up too much.

"Well, I'd better be off then" The Fixer announced.

"What? What, why? Hold on."

The Fixer laughed, "I told you, I'm far too busy for this silliness."

"But I literally have no idea what I'm doing. I'm The Traveller, not The Ultimate Handy Man."

"I know that," The Fixer replied, picking up the carpenter's pencil from the floor and passing it over, "he's waiting for me in universe 81 trillion, we've got a Nexus rift that needs sealing. Don't worry, you'll be fine with a washing machine."

"But what if I accidentally plug the electric into the water?"

The Fixer laughed. "You really are useless at this."

"I travel around critiquing bed-and-breakfast venues and places of interest, I have never in my life picked up a hammer or screwdriver…

except that time we were playing crazy golf and I had to defend myself from that crazed rhino that escaped from hole seven, next to the little windmill."

"Ha. Yeah, good times... well, anyway, I'll be off..."

"No please!" The Traveller said.

"I have to go!"

The Traveller panicked and began to foresee a flooded kitchen, or a house fire caused by some sort of washing machine disaster. He'd plugged the cables in back to front and upside down, and on the first spin a pair of socks had been sucked up into the mechanism and caused the whole thing to explode in a fiery ball of confusion, leading to the house collapsing into a pile of dusty rubble, with only the front door standing. At that very moment Debby and Mark stood outside, holding the doorbell as small bits of concrete and brick showered them with dirt, ultimately leading to the notion that Anne should definitely move out, leaving The Traveller to lay in the chaotic messy bed he had made.

"Everything okay?" Anne asked standing at the kitchen door watching a glazed look move across The Traveller's face.

The Traveller nodded, and focused. "Me?"

"Yes. Are you okay?"

"Fine" he replied and tried to look casual. "Pretty fine. I'll have this done in a jiffy," he said, spinning the screwdriver in his hand looking like a well-seasoned cowboy. As Anne disappeared into the living room his confidence morphed back into frustration as he sunk behind the tumble dryer whispering bloody murder at his carpenter's pencil.

The phone rang in the middle of the night as Sam Samson wiped the dribble away from his bottom lip, pulled his face mask from his eyes and made his way downstairs to the array of telephones that lined the table by the front door. He flicked the light on as his old hound walked over from its bed.

If the white phone was ringing it usually meant that old Mrs Davenport had wandered outside and fallen in the duck pond again. If it was the blue phone, it could've been one of two things: either the town hall was on fire, or the butcher's had unfortunately run out of sausages; either had been deemed a council emergency. Green was for 'village rivalry' matters that had become an ongoing problem; the folks from Tumbly Crust down the way always tried to boycott the local fete. Orange was for the Flower Society, and purple was specifically for old man Jones.

Lightning cracked, and thunder followed as Sam Samson stood over the black phone; his hound backed away towards its bed howling a little, just to thicken the mood.

The ringing became louder. Sam Samson moved his hand towards the receiver; another whip of light bolted the front porch and rain popped against the front door. Mrs Samson had now awoken and she stood on the stairs behind them holding the banister tightly. A bedroom window banged from somewhere upstairs, a draft of sudden wind whooshed down the stairs blowing her nighty in a whirl.

"Sam?" Mrs Samson called in fright as he went to pick up the relentless phone.

He nodded back.

"It'll be okay," he assured her.

"Please…" she replied worriedly. "Be careful…"

He shone her a smile as a third lighting strike hit somewhere out in the fields, casting shadows of wheat upon the back walls. Sam Samson lifted the phone, wettened his lips and braced himself for the worst.

"So?" Sam Samson said emptily, standing in a wet field in the middle of the night roughly an hour later. "They're all gone then?"

"Yup," Farmer Collins replied.

Mrs Samson trudged over in her wellies while doing her best to shelter herself from the casting rain with her brolly. There were only a few things that would get her out of bed at one in the morning; most of the time it was Brad the stable boy.

"I can't see any forced entry."

"That's what I said," Famer Collins added.

"Indeed. What sort of time did you notice they were missing?" asked Sam Samson, trying to conduct the beginnings of his investigation.

Farmer Collins rubbed his nose and tried to think. "Well, I was just heading out to do my nightly rounds and such, first I got to check how the hemp's doing behind the razor wire just past—"

"Yes, yes," Sam Samson said rolling his hand in the air quickly.

"Ah, right, I mean, 'corn'," Farmer Collins winked, "anyway. I was making my way back to the 'ouse, when I see an empty field, where I would usually see my flock of sheep. And there they were, you see, gone."

"And that was roughly when?"

"Oh, I don't know. Maybe eleven fifteen?"

"Tumbly Crust?" Mrs Samson quizzed.

"Mm," Sam Samson replied, "don't think so. I mean sure, they did take responsibility for that car fire last month, and they did indeed steal all our garden gnomes, but come on. We're talking about five hundred sheep here. All missing."

"Yup," Farmer Collins said, "and one and a half tonne of hemp."

"...Good God!"

Grog felled another small tree, lashed two together with woven vines and placed it down across Trollop River for a makeshift bridge. Bernard herded the flock over one by one. Behind them, way off in the distance, a howling storm swelled above the village as house lights all over began to flick on, and the siren geared up and belted into action. Only twice had the village alarm been active; once during the great storm of '86, and the other when old Mrs Davenport first fell in the duck pond; on both occasions she was soaking wet.

"Bhaa," Bernard said to the others.

"Bhaa?"

"Bhaa!"

And the speed of the crossing grew.

Grog didn't really know where they would go. He knew that the scattering of villages to the south wouldn't take them, and he'd been barred for life from the villages in the north. To the east lay Tumbly Crust; they wouldn't be pleased with his arrival, they were still bitter after taking the blame for the missing gnomes. They could move west, though the journey would be long and hard, strewn with difficult choices, tests and lots of other things that would perfectly fit in a story that was happier with hobbits and wizards.

The last sheep skipped over thc bridge with blissful unawareness, and so Grog collapsed the bridge hurling it into the raging torrent. The storm had moved away from them now and everything was damp, the smell of the earth after a shower wafted in the night air. Five hundred sheep crowded around Bernard looking for help. Like a woolly Moses, Bernard had, sort of, crossed the red sea, and now his flock looked to him for answers.

"Bhaa," Bernard said flatly. Which roughly meant, "Trollop River isn't really red, it's just the discarded velvet cake that no one wanted after Mrs Davenport's one hundred and fifty-first birthday that had been thrown away."

Grog came to the centre circle, met Bernard's gaze, and knew that for a while, at least, the old disused mine a few miles south would provide them some shelter. It had once been a hive of activity; a non-stop-all-hours-of-the-day mine where most of the men and burly women had found work.

"Let's go," Grog said.

"Bhaa!"

The Shop Keeper squared off a couple of boxes on the shelf behind the till, dusted above the door and started to turn off all the lights. A faint glow came from a few packages that housed Hyper-Giant Blue and Red stars from the back room.

Things were usually quite slow in the shop. Every few billion years or so, a being of great unmeasurable power would wander in, look for some new creative outlet, get ripped off, and leave without knowing any better. Yet in the past four years, God had stumbled in more times than the local drunk stumbles into the side of the fish 'n chip van. The Shop Keeper knew that it didn't really fall under his duties, yet he couldn't help but to worry a little about the state of God's liver. On every occasion God had come to visit, he'd been holding some sort of beer, or cider, or spirit, or any drink that would fall under the category of alcohol.

The Shop Keeper turned the last light off and locked the front door, making sure that the small group of youths wasn't lingering around, ready to smash his windows again and make off with some galaxy clusters.

"All right?" God slurred from the ground. "Fancy a cold one?"

The Shop Keeper sighed and looked at God as he lay in a puddle by his feet. "What are you doing?"

God hiccupped. “Relaxing.”

“On the floor?”

“Yep,” God said, “you know what you’re getting with the floor.”

“Do you, now?”

“Bloody right you do.”

“Explain,” The Shop Keeper said coldly.

“The floor’s cold. It’s hard. Uncomfortable. It never tries to be any better. It’s consistent,” God said patting the floor with a wobbly hand. “Gets my vote every time.”

“I see.”

Fortunately, The Shop Keeper had morphed into a huge thundering brute from the withering elderly gentleman he once was, and so was able to easily lift God and carry him back inside over his shoulder. God’s legs swayed from side to side, and a burning feeling entered his throat from the last rum mixer he’d polished off.

“Jesush,” God slurred, noticing a few spiderwebs hanging from the roof beams, “you need to clean this place up a bit.”

The lights flickered on in the back room behind the front desk as God was slumped down on a chair and faced the right way. From below the desktop of a tall standing table, The Shop Keeper brought out a rolled-up blueprint he’d been saving for the right time.

And God burped again.

“Can you just sober yourself up, please?”

“Ah come on, I’m enjoying myself!”

“Indeed. Tell me… what did you do with the Aquaverse I sold you?”

It was a silly question really; I mean, knowing God’s drinking habits, what else would he have done with the Aquaverse, other than adding a copious amount of sugar and yeast to it?

“Tell me that’s a joke?”

“Nope. It’s fermenting in my living room as we speak.”

“An entire universe?” The Shop Keeper asked rhetorically.

“I call it, ‘God’s Own’. It’s a bit sharp but sells by the bucketload in the Continuum.”

“Indeed,” The Shop Keeper said rolling out the blueprint across the tabletop. “Can I tell you something?”

"Of coursh!" God said accidentally pulling off the best Scottish impression the world had ever seen.

"Please remove all the alcohol from yourself…"

Yes, it had been fun relaxing on the floor outside the shop, and even more fun creating the crazy antics of how he ended up there earlier that day — a story that included a few barrels of wine, a BBQ utensil and a small gathering of bullfrogs — God in the end decided to flush his system, detox and materialise a large latte in his hand.

"Thank you," The Shop Keeper said with honesty. "Tell me, how are things with the multiverse? I've been meaning to ask…"

God sipped his latte and thought it needed more sugar, and of course more alcohol. He huffed, "Fine."

"Just fine?"

"Yeah…"

"I think that you're a bit bored, you know."

God nodded and downed the rest of his coffee and took a closer look at the rolled-out blueprint.

"What is this, anyway?"

The Shop Keeper smiled and said, "Let's make a deal. You stop the drinking, and I'll give you this blueprint."

God became obviously intrigued, looked down at the blueprint noticing dotted locations of wormholes he knew of in different universes, with arrows and lines joining up everywhere…

"What it is?" God asked suspiciously.

In a small, town hall, located on the peaceful planet of Sooth Delta in universe 50, the sound of breaking waves came from a small radio in the background, with the sound of Breaking Wave grunting heavily in the foreground. Sheila was equally flustered. She had gone from Downward Facing Dog, to Mountain Pose straight into a rather complex Sirsa Padasana, and she now felt more flexible than an intern when discussing their potential working hours.

She rested in the Plank for a breather while Breaking Wave stood over her, taking her firmly by the hips to readjust her posture.

"How are you feeling?" Breaking Wave asked softly.

Sheila wobbled slightly and mumbled, "More excited than a schoolgirl going to see her first rock concert."

"What was that?"

"Good thanks!"

If it wasn't the rotating hips that got her revved up, it was Breaking Wave's constant prancing around, shirt off, glistening abs, perfect long hair and incredible natural musk; somehow, even after an hour of stretching and jostling, he still smelt of sensitivity and puppies.

The small timer in the corner by the radio buzzed signalling the hour was done, and Sheila felt a little dead inside.

"You have done very well today."

"Thanks," Sheila replied patting a clean towel across her chest, in the most unprovocative way. "I feel that maybe a few more attempts at the Gandha Bherundasana would help me move forwards."

"Ah," Breaking Wave replied, "my favourite position."

The back door swung open as the next client came in. The Finder stood holding a flying carpet for a towel, wearing a headband that used to belong to a tennis enthusiast.

"You could've tried to be a bit late," Sheila said bitterly.

"Sorry."

"Please," Breaking Wave said happily, "come in and set yourself up, my love."

"...Um, okay." The Finder didn't really mind attending these so called, 'much-needed sessions'; in fact, he'd discovered that he was quite a pro at the old yoga. No, what bothered him a little was the unstoppable touching and staring that came whenever he moved into the Bridge Pose.

"So," Sheila said flatly, "shall we say same time next week?"

"What? Oh, yeah... sure" Breaking Wave replied casually. "If you think you need more sessions."

"I could do with a few more," The Finder said.

"I shall book you in for another ten."

Sheila left without saying a word; Breaking Wave's attention for The Finder may have only bothered The Finder a little, but it definitely bothered Sheila a whole lot more.

The Shop Keeper looked at God, who in turn looked at the blueprint, and waited for an answer.

"So?" he finally said. "What do you think?"

God smiled. "I bloody love it."

"Good. I thought you would."

"Why haven't you shown me this before?"

"Well," The Shop Keeper said, "I wasn't too sure if it was your type of thing. I've been talking to my colleagues, and well, it's no secret that you've got a special connection to the multiverse I sold you. You took a few other products since, and always returned looking a bit, I don't know, sad? Maybe."

"You've hit the nail right on the head there. I've been looking for something to fill the void since fixing that damned thing… well, continuously fixing the thing. Nothing I put my hand to satisfied me. Not even the Insulting Beast of Upya Miner you asked me to tame did the trick. Blooming thing just compliments me all the time when I'm in the shower…"

"Well. I had a word with the guys, and after a lengthy talk, I finally got a green light. If you want it, it's yours. But! I would insist that you really do take a look at the instructions before starting construction."

"Trust me, I won't make the same mistake as last time," God replied opening a fresh beer.

"Mm," replied The Shop Keeper doubtfully. "Maybe cool it down on the drink this time round?"

"…I'll consider it."

Bol flung a few resistance fighters into a shop window with one arm, while finishing off a packet of chocolate-covered peanuts with his free hand. After the terrible, and near heart-breaking news that none of the maids outside Overlord Dave's quarters had thought to bring biscuits with them, he'd gone out in the hectic streets of Yon to look for some sort of naughty snack. And of course, to enslave the natives.

"Blaa," Bol cried throwing the empty packet to the floor, "call them peanuts? Disgusting."

Behind him, Last Orders footmen moved through the streets in step, clearing the side alleyways and arresting anyone who had been verbally against the enslavement; so, pretty much everyone; it wasn't as if they hadn't been given fair warning though. Overlord Dave was, perhaps, a bit of a child when it came to his behaviour, but he did have his redeeming traits. Earlier that week he'd sent out a small scout ship prior to the invasion, to airdrop five hundred tonnes of leaflets expressing his sincere apologies for the coming appropriation of Pux 4e. Printed in the blood of the leaders from Pux 4d, the words, *'Join us or die. Tickets for the Raffle on sale after lunch'* lined the front page. To make things worse, the grand prize was a lifetime of payless work, foodless meals and total abolishment of all basic human rights; the flip side was that everyone was a winner.

"Charge!" a small group of Yon warriors shouted, running towards Bol. They landed in the shop window with the other resistance fighters.

Bol pointed up the street, a hairy finger stretched out lifting towards the single tall building in the distance, "Get the mayor!" he shouted, "and someone get me some blooming cashews!"

"Aye sir!"

Overlord Dave watched from his window as the takeover unfolded, sipping his hot chocolate through a sparkly pink straw. He spied his troops swarm the city like an invading army of termites below, who'd been consistently taking orders from an irritating genocidal teenager; there was a definite release of anger in the way his men were fighting.

The small star system of Pux had been a relatively easy system to overthrow, with only a handful of resistance fighters meeting The Last Orders in the heat of battle. Unlike the previous system of Stubborn Gamma that simply wouldn't budge.

The new maid took Overlord Dave's empty plastic safety mug from him and went to wash up, as His Overlordness jumped onto his freshly made bed, pulling out his favourite comics from under the mattress: *Mr Marvellous — Issue Four — The Travelling Circus*, a story of tall people, small people, and a lot of brownies; though not the fun type, as in the ones Farmer Collins usually baked.

Overlord Dave had the largest collection of Mr Marvellous comic books in the entire galaxy. He'd been a fan from a very young age, and mostly thanks to his friend who had found surviving comics after the multiverse's reset, he'd managed to grow his collection over the years. It wasn't just Mr Marvellous he followed either; really, Mr Marvellous was simply the flagship hero that promoted Grand Comics, and Overlord Dave thought he got in the way of the true 'heroes' of the stories: the villains. *The Travelling Circus* story had Overlord Dave idolising every great moment, inevitably leading to him spotting obvious parallels with his own life. Often, Bol would have to give him a reminding slap over the back of the head.

"You're nineteen years old!" he'd shout angrily.

"And you'd make a rug fit for a king," Overlord Dave would say under his breath.

He jumped up from his bed and stood, opened the comic to page fifty-one, and began his most prized monologue he'd memorised early on in his comic obsession. "I will finish your very being, Marvellous man, or should I say, marvel-less man. My lions will feed on your flesh, their claws will…"

"You're nineteen years old," Bol said flatly as he clipped Overlord Dave round the back of the head. The great Sasquatch-like being, who had ripped a man in half for being called a Sasquatch, threw the Mayor of Yon to the floor and took a spot next to Overlord Dave's window looking down upon the battlefield.

"Please!" the frightened mayor sobbed on his knees, "whatever you desire! Your ruthless enslaver, just ask!"

"Where'd you find him?" Overlord Dave asked placing his comic back under the mattress.

"Council building. Was hiding in a filing cabinet."

"Was he on his own?"

"It was a filing cabinet, not a walk-in wardrobe."

"I mean were there any others in the area?"

"There was a large desk in the corner, a chest of drawers by the window."

"I mean people!" Overlord Dave shouted. A look sharper than cold gin returned his way. "I mean people… sorry."

"Yeah," Bol said flatly. "Took most down to the execution wing, brought the mayor and a few others up 'ere."

"And what of the city?"

“Practically empty. There’re a few pockets of resistance, nothing noteworthy. The Drainer has finished with the planet’s core, it’s on its way back to the fleet. The population of Yon is onboard, going through conditioning now.”

“Great,” Overlord Dave said happily. “Good stuff.”

Commands were sent to every Last Orders ship in the fleet and take-off commenced. In the sky above them, the spherical shape of Pux 4b hung like that one Christmas bauble you’ve had your eye on since last year, and after waiting for the hours and days to pass, till the decorations were dusted off and the queues outside the local Bargain-buy shops were at their most volatile, you took it home and hung it with pride. Pux 4b was the last planetoid in the system to fall, and by the hand of Overlord Dave, he swore it would fall with force.

Overlord Dave smiled picking up his comic book from under the mattress as Bol gave him another deserved slap round the back of his head.

“You’re nineteen years old!”

“Sorry…”

It’d been a good few hours since Norman had set off from the main reception area of The Library of Gods, and though his investments were in the exploration of the new multiverse, he had to admit that, well, quite honestly, he was lost in the vastness of things. Somewhere between ‘History’ and ‘Crime’ he’d made a wrong turn, missed the clearly painted blue and yellow signs on the floor leading to the exit, and now found himself knee-deep in ‘Sports’. He first suspected he’d gone off course when a rogue golf ball came hurtling past him.

He’d ducked out of its path and landed heavily, accidentally knocking into one of the smaller bookshelves, sending a book entitled ‘Theoretical Portals of Sizes’ to the floor; obviously, someone had misread the title reading it lazily as ‘The Problems with Off-Side.’ The book hit the tiled floor, and without warning, Norman fell into it, finding himself standing in the midst of a rather hostile gathering at Arcturus Football Stadium, horn and beer in hand, screaming at the top of his voice totally out of tune, “His name is Zynx Worble-Tron 3rd, and he watches from the stand.”

Did Norman know why? Of course not! Did he know who Zynx Worble-Tron 3rd was? Another silly question. Did he enjoy himself... well, yes, actually, he did rather enjoy himself. That was until a librarian picked up the book of portal sizes, shook Norman out of its pages, and took it away to its rightful home. Norman, a little shaken, sat on the floor, football scarf wrapped round his neck, the smell of man crusted on his clothes and an empty cup in his hand.

Grog pulled away the last hunk of wood that'd been bolstered across the mine entrance years ago. In fairness it had done its job well; even Grog, a nine-foot troll, had had to activate some muscle to rip off the screws. The chance that power from Butts Trollop Nuclear Plant was still running through the old wires was a bit of a stretch, but hoping for the best Grog reached for the light switch, and as if luck was on their side, one by one the hanging lights flickered on, illuminating the mine shaft as it gradually descended downwards for an unknown depth.

Grog waved over to a small bush a few yards from him, signalling for the flock to get inside quickly. Sheep, in every part of the multiverse, except Bernard of course, had a real problem with the concept of judging scale. It was an issue that, if you had the time for, you could link all the way back to the relationship between their stomach and their eyes. A sheep once died from a grass overdose, at least, that's what all the young lambs were told around Halloween. Grog looked over, and the huge mound of wool that'd formed after five hundred sheep had hidden behind a single foot-high shrub slowly fell apart, and one after another each sheep happily bounded into the mine.

"Bhaa!" Bernard said to Grog, hearing footsteps coming their way.

"Yep," Grog replied, "I could smell them too."

They plunged down the mine entrance out of sight as Sam Samson and Farmer Collins came into view. It came as no surprise that the pair had tracked down Grog and the sheep. Farmer Collins had, due to his 'corn' field he grew inside the razor-wire pen under the cover of darkness, begged the council to pay for some courses that he said were vital. Courses that involved hand-to-hand combat, weapons training, negotiation and hydroponics for beginners. Tonight, however, he had brought forward the skills he learnt in his tracking course. The council of

Butts Trollop had been wangled into forking out for an SAS-style week of non-stop arctic survival for Farmer Collins, and until this night, they had sworn it had been a waste of money.

"Told you it'd come in handy."

"Yes, yes, very good…"

"Don't be like that," Farmer Collins said coldly, "I lost a brother out there."

"No. The instructor died of frostbite and you ate him."

Farmer Collins nodded and bravely said, "You got to do what you can to survive."

"You were at a training camp for Brown Bears!" Sam Samson said shortly. "Seriously, didn't the instructor just fall in the lake?"

Famer Collins bit his lip, shrugged and said, "They're in there," pointing at the mine entrance.

Bernard peeked his head around the corner looking out into the night air; the silhouette of the two men was obvious against the black, star-speckled night sky. Behind him, the rest of the flock skipped downwards out of sight. He knew that they would be safe for the time being. Not just from Butts Trollop, but from everyone. Grog stood over Bernard and joined his gaze, he too knew that they couldn't just stay there, waiting to be dug out like tick heads.

"Bhaa," Bernard said wisely.

Grog agreed.

The night air was fresh, cool but not cold; the light buzz of unseen winged things venturing out after the storm lifted the quietness of the surrounding fields, somehow bringing a homelier feeling to the air. Grog stood out, stopping just short of Sam Samson and Farmer Collins, the moon on his back, and Bernard by his side. Between them a readiness oozed in. Farmer Collins eyed Grog up from head to toe. His training told him that a well-aimed flying knee followed by a rear chokehold would put him down for good; though his gut told him 'Jesus look at the size of that troll!'

"Sam Samson…"

"…Grog…"

"…Bernard."

"Bhaa…"

"What did he say?"

"He said don't even try it," Grog replied. Farmer Collins looked at Bernard, who somehow pulled off a suspicious narrow gaze, or something close to it; the facial structure of a sheep won't permit too many detectable emotions; it's usually an 'I'm hungry' look, or an 'I'm full' look.

"He looks hungry," Sam Samson said in a worried tone. "Tell me Grog, is he dangerous?"

"More than you know..."

Bernard growled, bared his teeth and tried to look fierce.

"He's definitely hungry," Farmer Collins said.

"What do you want?" Grog asked impatiently. "We're not going back to the village."

Sam Samson rubbed his hands together and hoped that Farmer Collins hadn't forgotten his self-defence training. He was quite a portly fellow, if needed Sam Samson could easily outrun him, or use him as a human shield.

"Look Grog, we're here for the sheep. You and your little pet can do what you like, but I must insist that the flock is returned."

"And the hemp you stole," Farmer Collins added.

"Firstly, you'll find a mound of 'corn' outside the council building in Tumbly Crust... not our doing. And secondly, the sheep stay here!"

"But yes, the thing is... Sheep Nationals are coming up next week, and well, we've invested quite a bit of the budget in them."

He turned to Farmer Collins looking for assistance.

"Bhaa!" Bernard interjected.

Grog nodded, "Aye, if you haven't kept up to speed with things, The Last Orders are on their way to Pux. How long till they're here? Weeks? Days?"

Sam Samson laughed the notion off as he did the rumour of the over-amorous stable boy. "Rubbish... old man Jones writes the newsletters, and ninety per cent of it is made up. You'd be a little foolish to believe everything he says..."

"Though," Farmer Collins added, "he was right about the farmer's daughter being eaten by Grog."

"Mm," Sam Samson said, "true. Sorry about that by the way..."

"It's okay."

The thundering boom came as a small scout ship buckled through the atmosphere; its forward shielding glowed brilliantly becoming the brightest spot in the night. All four stood and watched as it cracked again, breaking through the higher clouds, leading a vapour trail to a lower altitude, settling out its pitch and slowing its speed. Bernard's gut told him to run, or at the very least hide; or, at the very, very, least, run and hide. Famer Collins' gut simply told him to get some cakes; the shortage of red velvet had become a crisis.

Grog eyed its underbelly as it sped overhead. The Last Orders insignia was crudely painted on its hull. Its heading was back to the village.

Sam Samson's phone began to ring in his pocket to the sound of Mrs Samson singing her heart out in a completely ear-screeching tone.

"Let's just pretend we didn't hear that," Grog said.

"Bhaa!"

Sam Samson nodded and mumbled to himself. He took the call that came from a very worried Paul Samson, his brother and self-appointed council leader of Tumbly Crust. He'd heard the small ship breaking through the night and awoken with a jump; his own array of phones had not stopped since.

"Bhaa!" Bernard said pointing a hoof towards Butts Trollop. The scout ship had begun its leaflet spreading; its back hatch had opened, and a billion scraps of paper fluttered through the sky, reflecting the moon's brilliance the same way small polystyrene balls do while dazzled in a strobe light at a below-board party.

"So, we've hours then," Grog said bluntly.

Sam Samson put down his phone and looked as pale as his legs did during his annual holiday to the Pux Beach Complex. "Well," he began, "Paul says he's talked to the observatory on Tumbly Hill, it's spotted a huge fleet heading our way."

"Well, yes," Grog said, "we already knew that."

"What's the plan, then?" Farmer Collins asked lighting a suspiciously long cigarette.

"He wants to meet… all of us. Not just with Butts Trollop, but Odd Smudge, and Bodwhiff too. All the villages are meeting," he said becoming very serious indeed. It'd been a long time since he'd seen any of his brothers, all of whom were now village leaders.

"Good luck with that," Grog said. And turned back to the mine.

"You're not coming?"

"Of course not! This isn't my problem, I have to look after the sheep, make sure they're safe."

"You really think you'll be able to last, hiding down there?"

"I'll make it work…"

"Bhaa!" Bernard said to Grog.

"Not you as well?"

"Bhaa!"

Grog huffed and rubbed his head. "Is that what you really think?"

"Bhaa…"

"And you've known for how long?"

"Bhaa? … ish…"

Sam Samson tucked his phone back in his pocket and questioned if there was any real conversation going on at all between them. The concerned council leader in him instinctively thought that if there was a way to talk to sheep, if it were possible to break down and translate their language, Butts Trollop would definitely have a good chance of bringing home the gold at the yearly Sheep Herd-Off; it was the most watched show last year, a close second to *Farmers Gone Wild.*

"Fine," Grog said reluctantly, "but if I have to do any flying, you're coming with me."

"Bhaa," Bernard smiled, though really, he just looked full.

"He looks hungry," Farmer Collins said.

The small pendulum clock next to the fireplace ticked away worriedly, only half enjoying every second it could before the inevitable happened; that being The Traveller finally breaking under the weight of his father-in-law's disapproval of everything he'd ever done and losing his marbles in a totally unwarranted rage leading to the death of a completely innocent clock via the upstairs window. A bead of sweat came from the clock's face as it noticed The Traveller shake a little after Anne's dad simply said "Mm" after the news of his heroics, saving the multiverse.

"I fought a giant mushroom," The Traveller said sharply.

"Mm," Mark replied sipping his black coffee.

Debby smiled, though her understanding of The Traveller's job was a little unclear. She patted Mark's leg and nodded. "Did you hear that dear, a mushroom… very, um, impressive, isn't it?"

"Mm," Mark muttered and narrowed his gaze across the room.

"He also saved God from a rogue employee," Anne added. "Go on love." She nudged The Traveller. "Tell them what happened…"

"It's really nothing."

"As I expected," Mark said swiftly. "You may have saved all of known creation, gone from one side of this existence to the other, but tell me, bucko! Have you ever held down a full-time job?"

"Dad!"

"I'm just saying. He travels around, visiting places, leaving his mark, probably indulging in what the locals have to offer, then he's gone again, off to some other part of this multiverse of theirs. I tell you; a hippy is what he is!"

"Dad!"

"I'm not a hippy!" The Traveller said.

"No? Tell me," Mark said leaning forwards, "what's more important, a decent job, or love?"

The Traveller could foresee the outcome already. He bit his lip and knew he'd come to regret it.

"Love," he said.

"Ah… there you have it!"

"Love is important," Debby said, trying to find some neutral ground to perch upon, "though a job is also quite important."

"Very wise, Mum."

"I didn't work fifteen-hour shifts down the Continuum pit, every day of the week just to see you settle down with some love-induced layabout. You should be with someone important, sweetheart, like a doctor. Or that other fellow you used to see, now he was going places."

"I can cure anything a doctor can!"

"Yeah," Mark said emptily, "cure it with hugs and peace."

"I could create a brand-new virus from nothing and cure you in the same microsecond."

"Don't though, yeah?" Anne said softly.

"I heard you couldn't even take my daughter carpet shopping without running off."

Mark looked The Traveller up and down, sneering at his entirety. Mark had never liked him. The few times he'd met The Traveller when he came to see his daughter at the Continuum warehouse, he'd spotted The Traveller taking unplanned naps and snack breaks, and had him down as a half-hearted individual on the spot.

"A hippie, I say!"

"Oh dear," Debby said searching for something to say, "um... very nice... um, coat rack." She pointed.

"It's not a coat rack," Anne said, "we got it when we visited universe 9 hundred and 34 million. It's actually an Angarsium Waiting Sloth from the planet Toom-Plum." Debby looked closer, and what she had thought were rounded hooks for placing jackets and such were actually big, curving claws, meeting a very thin body. The sloth stood upright, then gently wobbled over to where she sat.

"What's it doing?" Debby said hysterically nearly knocking Mark's coffee from his hands.

"Jesus, woman, calm yourself!"

Anne huffed with embarrassment. "You've called it over now; it thinks you need it to take your jacket."

The tall Angarsium Sloth creeped over to Debby as she screamed a little more, furiously trying to take her arm from her sleeve as the sloth began to lick her cheek kindly.

"Help me, Mark!"

"Stop messing about, woman!"

"Jesus, Mum," Anne said cupping her face behind a hand. "Just give it your jacket."

Mark placed down his coffee on the table, tore Debby's arm free and tossed the jacket at the sloth. "This is exactly what I'm talking about! Instead of simply thinking up a coat rack like normal Continuum folk, you've had to get a mobile one that licks and walks, and God knows what else. I don't care if its species is fading out, or you and your mooshy-wooshy 'green peace save the rain forest' toff are giving it a chance to live. If you want a coat rack, get a coat rack!"

"It *is* a coat rack!" The Traveller argued.

"You said it wasn't, though?" Debby asked.

"It's not, it's a sloth!" Anne said.

"That lives as a coat rack," The Traveller replied turning Anne's way.

"Whose side are you on?"

"Next, you'll be telling me that the washing machine is a tortoise, or the bath is a shark," Mark said angrily.

"Don't be silly!" The Traveller argued. "The bath is from Continuum Plumbing, and the washing machine is from Calm Beach."

"I've never even heard of a shop called Calm Beach!"

"No, Calm Beach located off the coast of Relacksus Lot in universe 361."

Debby leant back on her chair and peered through the doorway into the kitchen and saw something that resembled a giant Leatherback Turtle folding a few freshly washed bed sheets.

"Need I say more?" Mark said flatly.

Throughout time and space, there have been a hundred trillion people stuck behind the wheels of their cars, frustrated, angry, possibly verging on what may be considered as a total effing breakdown, and all due to the fact that always (and I mean *always*) there is a hundred miles of traffic cones for apparent 'emergency' roadworks, and *always* one yellow-dressed man holding a broom that had also lost all interest in its initial job.

GTM (Galactic Traffic Management), the company who had been contracted by God several times in the past to complete various closures, went bankrupt due to their fleet of trucks, or at the very least, due to one truck in particular. Famously, it had been the only truck to ever be put on trial by the cosmic courts; the historic 'Body Shaming Trial' set records throughout space, after one portly employee walked behind the reversing vehicle and it abruptly shouted 'Caution! Object Detected!'. Surprisingly, it had nothing to do with dipping into pension funds or asking for bailouts, which is the usual now.

"So," The Fixer said doubtfully, "this is... a plan?"

"It's a great plan!" God said excitedly. "Bloody great, great plan, it is!"

"And he gave you this for nothing?" asked The Finder who had only recently come from his yoga session with Breaking Wave and hadn't had the time to change from his spandex.

"Yeah," God said necking a cold beer happily, "well… freeish."

"Freeish," The Fixer grunted. "Those Continuum Merchants, nothing's ever free."

God nodded, "There was a little negotiation involved if I'm honest."

"As in…?"

"Weeell… free pass for life, a few star systems named after him… the usual."

The Fixer ran his hand across the rolled-out blueprint of the concept plans for the 'Expansion' God had been given for freeish. There was a criss-cross of lines, dots, circles and other shapes on it that hadn't yet been invented by modern man.

"It looks pretty," The Finder said, "but, what is it?"

The Fixer and God looked at each other and smirked; The Finder had never really had a mind for engineering. While he was at school with the others, when he was only half an infinite-years old, he would be chasing seven-dimensional butterflies round the school fields, cataloguing the various gamma clouds overhead, and working out why you never saw moles above ground, while the others were experimenting with primordial soup in the kitchen and being chased by the overweight dinner ladies.

"Come on," The Fixer said, "it's simple."

"Explain it to him then," God said.

"You bought it! You explain it."

"No, you said it's simple, so you tell him."

The Fixer looked at the blueprint closely, scanned it and took in as much data as his omnipotent mind would allow, and said, "Yeah I've no idea."

"Knew it," The Finder laughed.

"You guys are embarrassing," God said abruptly. "It's a design blueprint for wormhole extension."

"Exactly how much more extending can you do in a wormhole? They literally go everywhere. From one side of a universe to the other." The Finder didn't know much about construction, but he knew all too well about wormholes and where to find them. “Only last week, I went out to get my yearly supplies of digestives, I used wormhole 24 in universe 10, it’s had an extra lane added to handle the extra traffic flow. If any more civilisations become interstellar, we just push the wormholes out a bit.”

“Push them out a bit?” The Fixer laughed. “That’s the technical term for it, is it?”

“That’s your job, not mine.”

“Still. After a billion years I’d have thought you’d take some sort of interest in my work.”

“When was the last time you asked about mine?”

“Ladies,” God said, “back to business. This isn’t to expand them wider, or to, ‘push them out a bit’. We’re going to construct interdimensional bridges, so that beings will be able to travel freely from one parallel existence to another.”

“Is that wise?” The Fixer said worriedly. “You remember The Cosmic? That was interdimensional meddling at its finest.”

“True. But we can police it, regulate travel. We’ll sort something out.”

“Your casual approach to things has always made me feel better.”

“Only one issue,” The Finder added. “No matter how powerful we may be, that’s an awful lot of work. And GTM have gone into liquidation. Body-shaming scoundrels…”

“How’s the diet going?”

“No comment.”

God rolled up the blueprint and grasped it with both hands. “I’m leaving it up to you to find me a workforce to carry everything out,” he said, pointing at The Finder. “When it comes to locating things, you’re my main man.”

“You’re joking.”

“Na… straight up.”

The Fixer laughed. “Utilised to your fullest.”

“I can’t spend my time looking around for a few million people to help us. I have things to do, you know!”

“Like what?”

"Well," The Finder said, "lots of things. I've got my session with Breaking Wave next week, can't miss that, you've told me I have to go!"

"Consider yourself available."

The Finder frowned. "What about logging all the new universes that are created every second? Someone's got to name them."

"What number are we up to now?" asked The Fixer.

"Universe septillion to the power of 9 million and 4."

"So," The Fixer said, "I'd say septillion to the power of 9 million and 5 would come next, right?"

"Great!" God said happily, "so you can take over the old numbers game while The Finder here sets off and finds me some grafters."

"I want to log in the records that I am formally complaining, and I want extra pay for my troubles!"

"Beer?" God said, passing a cold one.

The Finder huffed, snatched it and skulked off. "It's a start!"

The council hall fell quiet as Grog followed Sam Samson to his seat, who was simultaneously followed by five hundred sheep. Not once in a thousand years had a troll set foot in the Communal Hall, and rightly so; a few hundred council members became slightly anxious. Whispers rolled around the vast room like a prickly wave of cowardly sighs; everyone had an opinion yet not one had the bravery to stand up and voice his or her distrust; or indeed, disgust.

"A troll," a floating voice said.

"Is that allowed?"

Grog stood, cracked his fingers, flexed his shoulders and smiled, "Anyone got anything to say?"

A brief pause followed, then another voice piped up over the dead silence. "Cup of tea?"

"Any sugar with that?"

Sam Samson took to the small stand at the front, and although he had always been one for the limelight, recalling his almost perfect rendition of Farmer Collins in the yearly village panto, 'My Corn has Tumbly Crust on It,' he couldn't help but feel a little nervous standing in front of so many villagers from so many villages.

The day that so many had said wouldn't come had come. Most thought that either the stories of The Last Orders were simply fake, or, at the prospect of them being true, their hostile fleet would never get to Pux 4b in their lifetime; they took the same line of thought when it came to rubbish disposal and tax returns. All these villagers had come from far and wide to hear the council leaders speak, to hear that their common worries were misplaced, and that the small planetoid had some kind of contingency plan in the works. Sam Samson cleared his throat, gazed down at the scrap of paper in his hand that, other than the printed titled that read, 'In case of emergencies…' was completely blank, and felt the life drain away through his boot souls.

"Bhaa," Bernard said breaking the tension.

"Yeah!" Grog seconded, "get on with it." A small polystyrene cup came over Grog's shoulder filled with what may have been tea. "No biscuits?"

"…Sorry."

"As you may already know," Sam Samson began, "a scout ship has dropped leaflets upon us, explaining the coming invasion. Now, I can't say I speak for everyone here, obviously not, but I would like to say that I for one welcome our new overlord and hope for a long and healthy life as a nameless slave.

"The chair is now open…"

Paul Samson stood up and leant against the stand, bringing the small microphone higher so that his deep voice could be heard at the back; he liked his own voice a lot, he'd even gone as far as to record and upload it to his Satnav so that he could always hear himself speak.

"Greetings from Tumbly Crust."

Sam Samson sat down next to his wife who had become a giggling mess as Paul looked down at her, slinging her a wink and a smile. She'd always thought that she'd chosen the wrong brother; Sam's good looks were nothing compared to Paul's devilishly charming smile, perfect hair, and what Mrs Samson had called his best feature, his lovely big hands.

"My brother here thinks that we should just roll over and let The Last Orders take our land without a fight. I, personally, do not agree in the slightest. Who remembers the Giant Slug Plague of '67? That was a dark four years, but we knuckled down, stayed strong, eventually driving out the slimy beasts! And who can recall the historic battle of Pux 4b, when the invading force from Quiveron Delta came, with their troops of bus-pass-holding nudist pensioners settling on our shores, taking residence in our fields? We beat them off fairly, and without mercy! Who here can say that now, today, here right now, they will do nothing as a fleet of savage slavers make their way towards us, with their unrivalled firepower, weapons of mass destruction, ships so advanced that hope flees from their very arrival? Who here can say that they will not stand! Fight! And battle for what's theirs!"

"I'm okay with that," Farmer Collins said from the back row.

A few other heads nodded in agreement. "Any idea what their dental plan's like?"

"Anyone know if they're in the pension scheme?"

"People, please!" Matt Samson said standing up sharply from his chair. "We at Bodwhiff have to agree with my brother, we can't just sit around doing nothing!"

"And what would you suggest!"

"We can't fight them! We'd all be killed!"

"Ladies and gentlemen, please" Rod Samson said also taking a stand, "Odd Smudge will of course side with whatever the four villages decide. But we cannot fall into a state of panic. I think firstly we should consider the options."

"Which are?" Paul asked from the stand.

"Which are, obviously, number one, we stand and fight…" which led to a jostling of unpleasantness and worry. "Number two, we try to negotiate with them, see if we can come to some sort of deal. Maybe try to make them an ally." And again, there was a large amount of disagreement and condemning. "And our third choice, which I'm sure we have all already decided on, is to evacuate Pux, and run."

"I'm not running anywhere!" Grog bellowed.

"Ah," Paul said smoothly from the stand, "our resident troll. And what would you have us do? Maybe you could lead us to victory?"

The hall fell into soft laughter as the very idea of a troll having any kind of authority hit the funny bone just right. Grog had been pushed and kicked all over Pux 4b, ran out from one village only to be rejected from another.

“I’ve got more fight in my little toe than any of you have in your entire body,” Grog said confidently.

“Is that so?” asked Paul.

“Aye, it is…”

“Then let the troll prove his worth!” Matt suggested. “If this creature truly believes he is of worth, send him to the fighting pit… I shall have my champion beat him roundly.”

Rod scoffed and shook his head. “Your champion isn’t worth the money you paid for him. My gladiator will rip this beast limb from limb!” To that the entire turnout of Odd Smudge bellowed with a cheer. “I shall make him a coward!”

After the lengthy discussions had gone on into the night, way past Sam Samson’s bedtime, everyone had gone back to their homes, slept well, awoken to a fresh day and made their way down to the communal fighting pit where Grog had slept all night. A gathering of two hundred strong came to watch Grog battle the village’s champion; their eagerness to witness an overconfident troll get beaten was a thing that barely any could truly hide.

Only moments after Bernard had been nice enough to throw Grog together a breakfast, he was standing in the centre of a sandy arena; seats ringed the circumference as if he were a gladiator from times forgotten.

The cheering crowd bellowed with excitement as trumpet players blew their tuneless wails, signalling their unbeatable champion to enter the ring.

Paul Samson knew little of his gladiator, only that he came from somewhere near the Panthium System. He’d acquired the monolithic man from a passing interstellar market freighter, swapping several tonnes of ‘corn’ for the fighter: Brootox the Slayer of Races, the Eater of Continents. The man with steel fists and blood of venom. He carried his name with pride. When stationed on Panthium 3, he’d faced off against an entire battalion of enemy worriers singlehandedly and won. For a warm-up he’d rendered most of the other champions unconscious whilst waiting in the wings. Nothing he’d faced before this day had even come close to rivalling his strength.

Paul Samson sat back in his chair high above the sandy arena watching his giant pace towards Grog. He held a cool drink in one hand while Mrs Samson torched his hair and big hands uncontrollably.

"So, you're the champion, huh?" Grog said unimpressed. "I've wrestled with bigger toenails than you."

Brootox cocked a smile, swung his shoulder back, pivoted on his back heel and balled a fist into a steel lump aiming for Grog's chin. It hit Grog with the strength of a hundred men, yet Grog stood motionless, his body still. The roar of the crowd dropped to a sudden silence. Brootox creased his forehead, took a step back, curled his arm round again and struck Grog squarely upon his chin once more. Yet still Grog stayed on his feet unflinching.

"Do you mind?" Grog said flatly. And with that belted Brootox clean off his feet. The huge gladiator that had been championed by so many hit the side wall of the fighting pit, landing in a pile of arms and legs in the sand, kicking up a cloud of debris.

"Anyone else?" Grog shouted.

… About an hour later.

"I did try to tell you," Grog said tucking into the farmer's daughter's arm he'd brought from home.

"Yes, very good," Paul said rather hurt. "Well done…"

"So, it's decided then?" Sam Samson asked, "Grog's going to take a group of resistance fighters, and lead a charge against The Last Orders?"

"Mm?" Rod questioned, then turned to his villagers. "Hands up who wants to stay and die? … Okay, and hands up who wants to run off and live a bit longer?"

All hands shot up as was expected. The same happened when Matt asked the Bodwhiffers, and so too the Tumbly Crustians. After a few minutes, the hall was empty, except for Sam Samson, Mrs Samson, Farmer Collins, Grog, Bernard and five hundred sheep.

"Well," Sam Samson said emptily, "that's us, I think."

"Bhaa," Bernard said wisely.

Paul led his brothers and the villagers from the eastern region of Buck Leg, towards West Bucket Chug where the airfield lay waiting. Meanwhile, all the other small gatherings of towns and hamlets from everywhere else on Pux 4b had, not surprisingly, chosen to do the same. What seemed like the biggest army of jelly backboned natives flooded the various hangars, making their way up the stairs of each carrier that would fly them to safety; or at the very least, give them some sort of first-class comfort before Overlord Dave forcefully put them all to slavery. One by one, the huge, bloated airships took to the sky, steam ejecting from huge exhaust pipes as their spacefaring engines began to churn, kicking into life. The first airship wobbled slightly, its nose end veered upwards to the clouds, its simple propellers whizzed furiously keeping its gigantic weight bolted in the air, till finally Paul gave the order, and the rocket assembly took control. The airship popped loudly and shot off space bound, closely followed by a hundred more ships carrying a hundred thousand more Puxians.

Grog stood outside the council building with five hundred sheep crowded around him, waving goodbye to all the people who had ever told him to 'move on', 'please leave' or asked him 'could you at least take a bath?'. Behind him, Sam Samson sat on the cold stairs of the council building, sobbing into his hands while his wife shared a smoke with Farmer Collins; their choice to stay was admirable, though a little foolish.

"So long!" Grog shouted happily, "hope you all fall into a neutron star."

"Bhaa!"

"Ah… come on. I'm only joking."

"Bhaa?"

Grog shrugged. "I don't know, hadn't really thought about it. What do you think?"

Bernard winced and thought deeply, "Bhaa… Bhaa!"

Grog nodded. "Aye, a drink to get our heads straight does sounds good. Come on, we'll go to The Duck, down in Bodwhiff, they do the best house beer."

"I'll have you know!" Sam Samson said managing to halt his sobbing momentarily. "The Busty Vicar has won best house ale for four years running." He then wailed, "Butts Trollop has always had the best pubs!"

Grog rolled his eyes at Bernard and shrugged. "Whatever… are you coming? Or stopping here with your friends?" Sam Samson nodded and blew his nose on Farmer Collins' shirt as he and Mrs Samson giggled childishly.

Bol sat on his hammock that sprawled from one side of his room to the other, high above the floor where there lay no furniture. The floor always gave him nightmares; as a young… um, hairy, monster-type thing, his parents took it upon themselves to take note of how the Bostial Birds roosting in the next tree taught their young how to fly, and as such had hurled Bol and his eight siblings out of the tree canopy in the hopes that they would somehow learn something from it; they did, they learnt that parents on the whole, though a necessity, sometimes had the worst ideas when it came to good ideas.

He reached over to his weapon stand that hung next to his bed, as did the rest of his furnishings, and ran his fingers over the various daggers, clubs, axes and spikes, pondering which one he would use when conditioning the Pux natives into submission. He'd always taken a fancy to his most vicious club, a four-hundred-kilo brute that seemed to always do the damage required. It had the greeting power equal to a man that'd been on an all-day session with his friends, who had finally found the men's room in one of the nightclubs that always seemed labyrinthian; nothing would stop it from doing its duty.

Yet today it was Skiver, his favourite jousting rod, equipped with a two-foot spike that twirled round to cause the most brutal, and most definitely illegal, harm to its victim. The laws of war were always quite a grey area for Bol, he knew that there were many things that were seen as 'bad form' when immersed in combat. You never took a man's life while they were unarmed, or even more so, from behind. Skiver was a weapon that Bol had picked up from an old war museum located on a planet they'd ransacked a few months ago. It had been kept in a glass box with an assortment of other weapons that had also been labelled unethical for war. His parents had always wanted Bol to be a doctor — one of the only real smart suggestions they'd had — and although the law of war stated that you never took the life of a medic, Bol had always been more intrigued with the idea of savagely beating his rivals than taking care of them.

Skiver sat down on his lap as Bol took out a cleaning cloth from his side dresser that swung back and forth from the cool breeze coming from the aircon and began to polish its length. It had always been bad timing with Bol, even when he was a child, someone was bound to walk into his room when he began to polish something.

And…

"Bol!" Overlord Dave's voice thundered through the intercom. "Bol!"

"Jesus."

The used cloth was slung down to the floor to sit with the mounting pile as Bol threw Skiver to one side, as gently as possible, he didn't want to damage it before it had a chance to kill (it was an antique after all) and clambered down the wall fixings to the ship's intercom.

"I told you not to disturb me!"

"Bol, I need you up here," Overlord Dave said, "there's a jar of peanut butter that I can't open."

Bol sighed with frustration. "If I come up there, I'll be unscrewing your head from your neck."

"…"

"…Do you understand?"

"…umm…"

"Well?"

"…I'll get my maid to do it."

"Don't bother me again!"

Overlord Dave gulped as he let go of the two-way button on the intercom, and graciously passed the stubborn jar over to his new maid. The new maid, who had gone through months of training, sat through countless lectures and listened intently to all her tutors as she came ever closer to finishing her ND in Advanced Maiding, clasped the jar with a heavy calloused hand, grit her teeth and turned the jar lid counter-clockwise as if her life depended on it; thankfully her enthusiasm wasn't wasted, her life was indeed resting on whether she could open it or not.

Pop! came the relieving sound as the lid came off; her life was spared for another day.

"Do you mind?" Overlord Dave said passing her a jar of jam; one of many in fact. The new maid looked over Overlord Dave's shoulder and saw an entire cupboard full of jars of jam, peanut butter, pickles and possibly what she thought looked like the insides of an old long-dead king. And the thought that Overlord Dave wasn't even hungry came to her, and so she ventured…

"Are you testing me, Your Overlordness?"

Overlord Dave smiled and placed the jar in her open palm. "Open this, and I'll let you go home, a free lady. But!" he shouted, "fail, and you'll be turned into glue by the end of the day."

Susan, which was the new maid's name, not that it mattered, dried her clammy hands on her dress, rubbed her palms together and began to tug the jar with everything she had. From side to side, she wrestled it to the floor; clamping it between her knees, she brought both hands to the lid and squeezed the thing roughly, like a lid from a mouthwash bottle that has the anti-child thingy. Eventually, Susan triumphed, she stood up, sweat dripping from her face, her dress damp and sticky. She passed the open jar over to Overlord Dave and felt pretty damned good about herself.

"Well done," Overlord Dave said happily, "but you took too long…"

"What?"

"Go on," he said with a gesture of his head, "off to the execution wing with you…"

"…But I—"

"No, no… off you go…"

Overlord Dave felt pretty good about himself too. It'd been an hour since he'd executed anyone, and his hands were starting to shake.

God travelled back to the Continuum to find an empty home; a house that was clean and tidy, a house that someone had spent time cleaning, a house that was quiet save for a tuneless whistling coming from the back garden: it was, of course, Sheila. History has shown that this could mean either one of two things: a clean house and a tuneful hum was the sign that Sheila had had a good day, or that God had forgotten something crucially important and was being set up for an almighty chewing out. And being God, he thought he had a fifty-fifty chance, but knowing

Sheila and the minefield of marriage, he had more of a twenty-eighty chance.

Outside, Sheila rolled up her yoga mat and lay back on the cut grass as she listened to her favourite rock, blasting through her radio. A clean untouched wine glass stood next to her as she set down the half-empty wine bottle and smiled as she saw God wander timidly outside through the kitchen doors.

"Everything all right, love?"

"Fine," Sheila said happily and somewhat wobbily. "Come and sit with me."

"You been doing the garden?" God said as he noticed the mowed lawn and trimmed verge bushes. "You know, we've got people to do that for us."

"Not any more!" Sheila said raising the bottle in the air, "sacked them both. Had to!"

"Bloody hell, Sheila, why?"

"Found them both rolling around in the pool house with nothing but fig leaves covering their shame. Plus, I think they've been stealing your fruit and veg down in the allotment."

"I bloody told 'em the other week about that… probably for the best. All Adam ever did was stare at Eve's buttocks…"

"I can understand that!" Sheila burped, "found myself staring a few times too. Did she ever show you her snake tattoo?"

God bit his lip and thought that the best advice he was ever told by a road worker called Terry 'Big Stack' Jones, was to deny everything. *Everything!*

"…You hungry, love?" he bypassed.

"Na… not really. Come and tell me what you've been up to; bring us another bottle too."

God flexed his power and materialised a fresh five-litre wine barrel on the grass next to Sheila and set himself down comfortably.

"I've found myself a new job" he said, "something that's got me busy, and something that I hope will be good for everyone…"

Sheila summoned a long curly pink straw into existence and was merrily sucking the life out of the wine barrel.

"The boys and I are building interdimensional bridges to allow more traffic and space exploration through the multiverse. We think—"

"Have you ever been able to do the Downward Dog?" Sheila blurted out slurring her words. "You should grow your hair I think."

God paused… "Can't say I've tried."

"You'd look great in a loud flowery shirt, you know!"

"Maybe," God smiled, "anyway, I think I'll be busy for a few million years building these—"

"Come here and give us a smooch."

"Sheila," God laughed, "what's got into you?"

"Nothing yet," she winked and began to roll up her sports top. "I don't care if the neighbour seesush… let them look!"

God laughed again, and though in our reality he was the eternal living consciousness, the true undeniable meaning of reason, thought, space-time and the four unquestionable forces of nature, he was still a man in his own reality, and as such didn't argue with Sheila when the chance for some boisterous canoodling came around.

Mr Morris next door had been happily rifling through his stamp collection by his bedroom window when he saw the quite frankly confusing positioning of bodies twisting outside, and not one to be outdone, pinched Mrs Morris on the bum as she reached down for her slippers by the bedside.

"You can cut that out for a start," Mrs Morris said shortly, "not on a Wednesday!"

Later on, after God had relieved himself quite well with the help of a slurring, over-confident Sheila, he'd met The Fixer by one of the largest wormholes in universe 47 thousand back in the multiverse. Deemed by the local deep space travelling natives as The Big Wormhole.

A truly inventive and unique name it is.

Both God and The Fixer stood by its swirling vortex, its gaping mouth a few trillion kilometres wide, sucking time and light inwards, ejecting matter far across the universe a billion light years away. The Fixer had to hold down his hat briefly as quite a strong current nearly knocked it off his head.

"Why that hat all of a sudden?"

The Fixer shrugged knowing that it would come up in conversation.

"I'm dating a girl and she thinks I look sophisticated."

"Mm," God said in a questionable tone, "it's a top hat."

"And?"

"You're wearing overalls."

"…And?"

"You're wearing overalls and a top hat?"

"Yes," The Fixer said bluntly, "your point being?"

"You don't even have a cane or monocle."

To which The Fixer brought both into reality and looked for some kind of return. "Happy?"

"Always… but for now, mate, how about just the overalls?"

The Fixer frowned and threw the top hat, cane and monocle away; they went twirling into the vortex, never to be seen again. It wasn't a massive loss however, as a small intelligent rodent from the planet Cabbar found them years later buried in a sand dune and went on to become the face of a huge peanut company.

"So," The Fixer said, "what's the plan?"

"The plan," God replied, "will be to trial one bridge on this wormhole. See if it actually works."

"You could've picked a small wormhole to test it out on first."

"Ever heard of the phrase, 'go big or go home'?"

The Fixer laughed. "This isn't a Winter Olympics snowboarding contest. Unless you're expecting me to do some flippy-whirly-gig stunt on the crest of it. This is a matter of precision, understanding. Working out all the variables, double-checking them, logging stuff, trial and error. If this fails, we'll be disrupting an entire sector's travel plans."

"People should always check their route before leaving home," God said as he began to sip a lager top.

"Has that got lemonade in it?"

"It sure does."

"Good God!" The Fixer said in shock, "what happened to you? You used to be cool."

"I'm still cool," God said, "I've just cut back a bit."

"There's cutting back a bit and then there's that. Lemonade for Christ's sake… next you'll be having gin after lunch, and not before long you'll only have a sherry at Christmas."

God nodded, saw his point and transformed his pint into a yard of Guinness followed by a brandy chaser. "Any better?"

"A little," The Fixer replied, "though sharing wouldn't go amiss."

"Make your bloody own… besides, I'm meant to be the only one judging people round here."

"By all means," The Fixer said open-handed, "judge away, but don't expect to have nothing said when you start drinking like a teenager."

"I'll have you know teenagers are probably the worst for drinking."

The Fixer smiled and couldn't help but agree. "Yeah. The girl I'm dating turns twenty next month and she pounds the beers away."

"Twenty? Bloody hell, have you told her how old you are?"

"I'm ageless you buffoon. How can I be old when I'm eternal? I'm neither middle-aged nor in retirement. I've been here since always, and cos of that I have no age… so, if you ever meet her," The Fixer said calmly, "do me favour… I'm twenty-four and still live at home."

"Can't you just settle down with a normal girl? You know, a girl that is at least a few billion years old, had a bit of experience at least."

"You have your tastes, I have mine."

"Jesus," God said chuckling to himself, "twenty…"

"So… here'll do fine then?"

"Yep, crack on."

The Fixer took a hammer from his belt side and started to knock in a huge yellow sign into the fabric of space. On it, it read, *'Work starts here from six weeks to seven billion years — expect delays'*.

Anne filled another round of mugs with coffee (it wasn't actually anything like coffee in the slightest, but to keep her father happy she sold it to him as Continuum's Best-Ground, when really it was a strange herbal blend from the Trip-out Nebula Complex in universe 37), and brought the drinks back into the living room, setting them down on the table.

Mark took his quickly, being the type of old-fashioned chap of the kind that couldn't sit still if he didn't have anything in his hands, and stood, taking a walk over to the nearest hanging canvas that had a very lifelike picture of an overly oval bare-breasted lady sitting on a tree branch.

"Mm," he grumbled feeling the Phantasm Cactus extract as strange, beautiful colours flashed in his eyes.

"You okay Dad?" Anne asked watching as he went cross-eyed.

"I'm fine!"

The Traveller smirked.

"Perfectly fine." He rubbed his face then his chin trying to stay wobble free and upright, "coffee's a bit strong…"

"I can fix you a beer if you'd like?" The Traveller asked.

"It's not even seven o'clock… can't say I agree with this sort of artwork," he said nodding at the naughty nude canvas.

"It's not art," Anne replied emptily. She already knew what her dad would have to say. "It's a Hairless Lubricious Ape from the forest moon of Endall."

"Endall?"

"Yes… Endall… it's just down the road…"

"Oh…" Mark said as the Hairless Lubricious Ape squawked madly and set off in a crazed rush. "Why have you got it in your house? … in fact, don't tell me. Something to do with giving it a home, or some toff…"

The Traveller jolted from his chair and closed the drapes over the glass window to the ape pen in the living room and frowned with irradiating hatred. Anne daren't look at him, not solely because her father was being a bit tricky, but also fearing she may gain a small tan from The Traveller's radioactive glare. Debby sipped her coffee, and though she too was suffering slightly from colourful hallucinations, she felt good having something else other than a butler sloth, a cleaning turtle or a hairless ape to concentrate on. And so, she downed her drink and asked for — or in fact demanded — another.

The Traveller followed Anne into the kitchen as the neutron-powered kettle boiled and wondered how much longer her parents would be staying.

"Excuse me?"

"I'm sorry… if I had asked you would've said no."

"Two weeks?"

"It's not all bad… think you're working dad down a bit now."

"…Two weeks!"

"Only till their house's been fumigated—"

"Two poxy weeks though!"

"With any luck, it'll only be one."

"One's long enough. I don't know if this hasn't been obvious, but your dad and me aren't really finding any common ground."

Anne shrugged and reached for a packet of biscuits she'd been hiding in the back of the cupboard for a rainy day.

"So that's where my custard cream went…"

"…Sorry. I was going to eat them on my own," Anne confessed, "but I think I should give them to Mum. They'll help soak up some of the hallucinates flooding her veins. You don't want her overdosing on our sofa, do you?"

The Traveller waved his hand dismissing the idea. "Your mum grew up in a different time, pretty sure that stuff is weak compared to some of the things she used to do. You're probably better off giving them to your dad."

"Do you think?"

Anne followed The Traveller's finger as he pointed back to the living room where Mark was trying to catch invisible nymphs as they flew round his head, playing violins and enjoying a healthy game of 'Got-Your-Nose.'

"Mm" Anne said, "you're probably right… look, I'm very sorry, I really am. I wanted you to meet my folks under better conditions. All I told them was that you were an older man who'd travelled a lot."

"Seriously?" The Traveller asked stunned. "So, they know nothing about my actual job?"

"Well," Anne said softly, "they know you used to work at that warehouse. And that you had a great deal to do with it all… creation and stuff…"

"But…"

Anne hesitated. "But none of that really made my dad think you were good enough for me."

"Blimey," The Traveller said resting against the countertop. "If none of that impressed him, nothing will."

He felt for the first time in a while a slight gut wrench at the thought that he and Anne's folks would never see eye to eye. I mean, sure, it's a long-standing joke that you never really get along with the in-laws, but come on, The Traveller having done what he has for the multiverse had to have given him some brownie points at least.

"Did you tell him about the time I saved that entire race of Pizzha People from being devoured by the House of the Drunkan-Few?"

"Yes" Anne nodded, "both times."

"What about when I beat The Master at a game of Cosmic Chess, which spanned four thousand years?"

Anne grimaced. "He said you were probably trying to get out of work."

"Jesus," The Traveller replied.

"I know…"

"Digging water wells for the Sandmen?"

"For your ego…"

"Finishing the meal made by Mannekenpix?"

"…Greedy."

"Slaying the Nemean Lion?"

"Just plain wrong!" Anne said. "Firstly, killing is bad, and secondly you stole it from Hercules."

"Hey!" The Traveller said lifting a finger, "you wanted something to hang on the wall in the downstairs toilet, and I provided."

"Well, I don't like it and I never have."

"Fine, I'll take it down," The Traveller said sulkily, "I'll have to dig out the nine-headed Lernaean Hydra."

"When did you kill him?"

The Traveller gulped. "I'm only joking. He's fine."

"He'd better be! We're going around his for Sunday dinner next week."

And The Traveller gulped again and made a mental note: *'Resurrect Lernaean Hydra'*.

"There is something you could try," Anne said positively.

"Oh yeah… and what's that?"

Anne bit her bottom lip and smiled. "You could take him with you to work?"

"Oh no…"

"Yes! I think that's a great idea!"

"No, no, no..."

"You could show him all the things God has you doing. Take him around the multiverse a bit, show him the sights."

"Show him the sights?"

"Yes."

"No."

"You're doing it."

"No!"

Anne plunked her mug down on the countertop next to him and cocked an eyebrow. "You're doing it." The Traveller huffed and feared for a second visit to the eternal doghouse.

"Are we understood?"

"Yes darling... custard cream?"

The Busty Vicar had always been the talk of Butts Trollop, her ample exterior, obviously ageing slightly, was always met by thirsty men who'd just come from the local cricket game looking for a bit more excitement. It wasn't rare for her to be overloaded and packed out with inebriated men, fighting for space, knocking things over and roaring with blue-collar jollies, especially when the darts team were in town. For an old pub, The Busty Vicar was a prime example of how a brewery should be run.

Grog struggled to even fit behind the bar as he made himself another stein of ale. It'd taken him half an hour to find a stein glass; a pint glass was more of a shot glass in his hands, and after the first twelve he felt entitled to get a larger drinking cup.

"Dry roasted, or a packet of crisps?"

"Bhaa," Bernard said hungrily.

"Can you eat pork scratchings? Isn't that basically cannibalism?"

"Bhaa!" Bernard frowned.

"All right, all right... no offence intended," Grog assured him.

Sam Samson rubbed his nose as he slumped over a table by the fireplace sobbing a little into his sleeves. "Prawn cocktail and a wine spritzer please."

Grog looked at Bernard and shrugged. Neither knew what a wine spritzer was, though it didn't stop him from trying.

"How about you two?" he said pointing at Farmer Collins and Mrs Samson who were both resting against one another by the fruit machine. "Anything for the lady?"

"Ah, I could do with a big fat sandwich," Farmer Collins said feeling the hunger that only came with smoking corn substitute. "Is the kitchen still open?"

"Bhaa," Bernard said as he skipped through the doors into the kitchen, followed by five hundred sheep. I guess, as Grog had lived with Bernard for so many years, it hadn't occurred to him that Bernard's ability to cook Michelin quality food was at all strange. Neither was it at all weird when Grog had caught him on more than a few occasions watching *Food Fanatics* on catch up. You see, an omnipotent sheep has to, at some stage, find something to keep himself busy. After Bernard found that he could trans-warp the cosmos like some free-thinking woolly space jockey, little came to entertain him. So, food, and of course the cooking of said food was really the only option he had to pass the time.

"Bhaa?" Bernard shouted from the kitchen.

Grog turned to Famer Collins, "He said do you want a warm lobster in a summer preparation with a side of braised red cabbage, or pie and chips?"

"Pie and chips please," Farmer Collins and Mrs Samson said together.

"You hear that?" Grog shouted into the kitchen.

"Bhaa!"

"Language!"

"Oh," Sam Samson wailed hopelessly, "what's the point of it all?"

The sound of falling pans and cutlery came from the kitchen as Bernard's tone became quite irate. He took only a few things seriously in life: the softness of his woolly hide, the ongoingness of his general living, and the cooking and prep-work that went into every meal. A few seconds later a few sheep exited the kitchen looking rather sheepish; obviously…

"We're all doomed," Sam Samson cried as he opened his bag of crisps. "As if being abandoned by my own brothers wasn't bad enough,

I'm spending my last night on Pux drinking my last drink in the company of a troll."

"Hey," Grog said unamused, "don't blame me if you didn't go with 'em."

"I guess I'll be forced to work, day and night," he continued, "without food, water. Or even the most basic of needs... a bed, a pillow..."

"I sleep on a pile of bricks," Grog said.

Farmer Collins waved his hand in the air. "And I sleep on the floor most nights."

"At least you don't have to put up with his snoring," Mrs Samson said, pointing at her weeping husband. "For a man who looks after himself you don't half sound like a car engine when you're sleeping."

"Bhaa!" Bernard shouted from the kitchen.

"I do not snore!" Grog argued.

"Bhaa!"

"Language!"

Farmer Collins heaved himself up and made his way to the bar, and even after Sam Samson tried to make him understand that the house whisky was only meant for royal visitors, the cap was inevitably spun off and a tumbler was filled.

"Here's to slavery!" he said, and necked the entire glass, then filled another.

"Do we know anything about The Last Orders?" Grog said snatching the bottle of whisky from Farmer Collins for himself and taking a seat by the fireplace.

"Well," Farmer Collins ventured, "...I'd say, they must be pretty bad. What with all the hostile planetary takeovers and what have you."

"Right," Grog nodded, "anything else? Something perhaps a bit more in depth?"

Mrs Samson staggered over and sat next to her husband who had opened another bag of prawn cocktail, and she began to rub his back kindly.

"All I've heard," Sam Samson said moanfully, "is that their leader, Overlord Dave, is a ruthless man."

“Man?” Farmer Collins said, “he’s in his teens! Why, when I was a teenager, I was out shaving sheep, picking crops, making connections overseas. I had nothing to do with any such dictating and so on.”

“Well, teenager then,” Sam Samson said, “regardless. They say that after the leaflets are dropped, a huge monstrous ship descends from the sky, and an army that could flatten Mt Trollop floods the land… we’d be better off burning everything of value and running off with the rest of them.”

Grog frowned and thought that the idea of running was rather cowardly. He’d been running his whole life; not in a scared, too afraid to face his past sort of running, more like an unwanted, please not here sense of the word. Though the idea of becoming a slave was neither that much of a tender thought. He couldn’t see himself as a slave, not that anyone could, mind, it was simply that the idea of moving about, doing stuff for other people, especially people he didn’t know bothered him a little.

“Can’t say slavery would fit me,” he said eventually.

“Would it fit anyone?” Farmer Collins asked.

Grog nodded. “He’d make a good slave,” he said pointing at Sam Samson.

“Really?” Sam Samson replied cheerfully, “do you think?”

“Oh yeah, definitely,” Grog replied. “I could see you moping about your masters, getting them drinks and food in between shifts.”

“You’re not just saying that?”

“No,” Sam Samson’s wife said happily, “you’d be the best slave they’d ever seen.”

Sam Samson cleaned his damp nose with his hand and smiled. “Thank you. I know you’re just being kind, but I appreciate your words.”

The kitchen door swung open as Bernard trotted out holding a tray with a steaming pie on it; it leaked smooth glossy gravy everywhere on the plate. Chips, peas and other assorted veg became small lifeboats in the tiny Oxo tsunami. It came down on the table in front of Farmer Collins with a thump, and for a moment, Farmer Collins thought he’d died and gone to puff pastry heaven. It didn’t take long before Mrs Samson prioritised her husband’s back-rubbing to a number two spot and tucked into some lovely crispy chips.

"Anyone for a game of pool?" Grog asked.

"Can't," Sam Samson replied. "Arthritis in my wrists."

"Dominos?"

"I'm colour blind…"

"Darts then?"

"I'm a pacifist!"

"For Pete's sake," Grog said, "is there anything you can do?"

Sam Samson perked up with a smile and replied, "I could get the pub quiz sheet out from the till? That'd keep us busy for a bit."

A communal groan moved over the empty pub, even the Butts Bandits fruit machine managed to let out a little deflated moan of its own at the thought of one more pub quiz. They all seemed to have the same format: a string of easy general knowledge questions, followed by a few sports-related puzzles, ending with the round that no one ever in the history of pub quizzes either enjoyed or got right: foreign politics.

The debate on how to spend their last evening together went on into the night, and by the unofficial call of last orders, roughly half one, it had been decided that The Last Orders were in fact a bit of a bad bunch; what with all the hostile planetary takeovers and the like.

In the morning Grog woke to a stinking hangover and the sound of coins dropping in the winnings collection tray of the fruit machine. Bernard hadn't slept, he never really did, and had spent the night winning and spending what coins he found that had dropped down the back of the various chairs and holes in the old uneven wooden floor.

"Argh," Grog said holding his thumping head, "what time is it?"

"Bhaa…"

"Right… any breakfast going?"

Bernard nodded and gestured over to the table underneath the darts board where everyone had already taken their seats. Full plates of English breakfasts sat on place mats steaming, wafting smells of all kinds around the roof rafters.

There is nothing, and I mean nothing, that has the curing power of a full English breakfast.

Grog's knife and fork were slung to the side as he chose the fire poker as a more suitable means to tackle his hash browns and bacon. A stein of ale substituted the hot coffee by his side.

"A bit early for that?"

"Hair of the dog," Grog said fuzzily.

"No," Sam Samson replied, "that's Tail of the Weasel. Hair of the Dog is the house ale of The Naughty Maid in Bodwhiff."

"The Naughty Maid is in Odd Smudge, darling. You're thinking of Vengeful Pony," Mrs Samson said.

"The Vengeful Pony?" Farmer Collins queried, "they have The Jumping Frog."

"No," Mrs Samson replied, "The Jumping Frog is our house cider, The Vengeful Pony has The Morning Runs."

"For God's sake!" Grog shouted feeling confused and frustrated, "I don't care how many jumping ponies there are! Just let me drink my drink!"

"Sorry..."

"Bhaa?" Bernard asked as he handed over a box of painkillers.

"Thanks." Grog threw them down his throat and tucked into his breakfast. It'd been a long time since he'd eaten anything that you might class as human food. Before he'd been dragged away from his house, Bernard had planned to turn the farmer's daughter into a lovely goulash, so the taste of baked beans on fried toast was something of a nice change.

"So," Sam Samson said cleaning a few crumbs from his mouth with a napkin. "I hope everyone is ready to welcome their new masters." He picked up his glass of water and lime, and toasted, "to our new life!"

"Aye," Grog said, "I've been thinking."

"Is that wise?"

"Careful now," he said, followed by an altogether satisfying burp. "You said last night, while you were crying your eyes out like a little princess, that we should just burn everything of value. Do you remember that?"

"Well... I may have been a bit over dramatic... but yes, I remember."

"Right," Grog said, "I think that's a good idea."

Farmer Collins choked on his bacon. "Are you serious?"

"Bhaa?" Bernard asked.

"Aye. I do. I love Pux even if Pux doesn't love me, but I'd rather burn everything instead of becoming a mindless number on someone's clipboard… I was thinking, the mines that are around the area, they go quite deep. Some very deep in fact. I'm no expert, nor claim to know a lot, but Pux is only small, and I know that some of those mines go right down to the planetoids core. That's why some of them were shut down, too dangerous."

"And what's your point?" Sam Samson asked bluntly, "reopen them, dig a little deeper and let some hot molten rock run out?"

"Not really," Grog said walking to the bar and fixing himself another drink. "Our local famer here knows a lot about explosives and stuff. I've seen you prance around the village showing your medals to the girls…"

"I've never been the confident type," Farmer Collins admitted.

"We've noticed," Mrs Samson said.

"So, what then?" Sam Samson asked, "blow up a few mines and cause a bit of damage?"

"No," Grog replied as he looked at Bernard. "I say we wait till The Last Orders have landed and blow up the whole planetoid with 'em on it."

"Bhaa!" Bernard shouted in agreement.

Bernard liked that plan; his fluffy tale began to wag.

"Careful now," Grog said happily.

Farmer Collins looked worried. "He looks hungry again."

The Finder had been floating around the limitless expanse of the multiverse with zero success. His mission was simple: find a workforce skilled enough to carry out the duty of God. This line sounds like something you might find in an old dusty Bible, when really it meant find a workforce willing to shut down major routes through multiple universes for extended periods of time and have millions of life forms hurl abuse their way as the question 'oi mate, what's the road shut for?' is asked again, and again, and again.

He'd visited the dwarfish system in universe 10 million and 3, their labouring skills were unmatched and were able to dig under any mountain in only a matter of hours. Unfortunately, when the Dwarf King was told that they'd be digging through the barrier between two realities of converging cosmoses, he quivered and turned the offer down. It might've been the realisation that gold played no part in the eventual goal; nevertheless, The Finder had to look elsewhere.

After leaving universe 48 trillion, having been told much the same by the famously tenacious and hardworking Giant Despotic Ants of Armello 5, The Finder ventured into universe 12, the Rap-verse. He'd never been one for rap, his music taste did indeed incorporate a lot of different sounds, but regrettably, rap wasn't one of them. Champ'N'Bubbly, a rapper who had monopolised the cosmos with his famous line of fizzy alcoholic drinks had amassed such wealth and glory that his entourage was around five-billion strong. Whenever he went on tour, entire cities had to be rented out just so his groupies and dietary requirements could fit in. Yet, unfortunately, even though Champ'N'Bubbly had told The Finder 'For shizzle we can quizzle the fizzle', The Finder felt that they weren't really the sort of men and women he was looking for.

And so, the search went on.

Far away, in a completely different universe, Norman had gone from simply lost, to unfathomably lost. He'd followed the red arrows that should've taken him to the reception area of The Library of Gods, yet somehow ended up in the Brexit section. He'd tried to maintain his hold on the orange arrows, but somewhere along his path he'd looked at the floor and saw only green squares. Finding anything in The Library of Gods had become a real nightmare.

After misreading a sign that said Hip-Hop which he swore blind said 'Gift Shop', he gave in, found a small bench at the bottom of one of the many high-standing bookshelves and took out one hard back to read. The cover was speckled with stars and planets, and a green skinned man standing with his legs apart and arms crossed stood in front of a gold heading that said, *'Champ'N'Bubbly — The Rise of a Star'*.

Champ'N'Bubbly's entire life had been a whirlwind of chaos, a roller-coaster ride of shrewd investments, music collaborations and crazy week-long parties. He'd travelled the Rap-verse, discovered new planets, explored galaxies that others knew nothing of. There were ups, there were downs. There was trouble and there was peace. Norman could barely believe the sorts of things that Champ'N'Bubbly had got up to in his short-lived career. It was by definition unbelievable.

Yet somehow completely relatable.

It was like reading the story of someone you knew, your famous next-door neighbour that had always been kind enough to lend you some sugar.

"Mm," Norman murmured, turning to the last page. "What's a ghost writer?"

The Finder set himself down feeling the strain of it all. Finding had come easy for him, in all the many, many years of finding he had behind him, the experiences he'd gathered and consumed, the many ways he'd learned to identify clues, patterns and small details left behind by things that never wanted to be found, he could've been one of the top three detectives to ever live. However, finding a suitable workforce was becoming a problem.

His desk stood in front of him, piled up with stacks of paperwork; each assorted into mounds of mixed-up, completely useless names of organisations and individuals who he'd deemed unworthy for the job.

God knocked on his office door and came in with a smile.

"Since when have you had an office?"

"Since I entered the recruiting sector."

"You don't have to sound so down about it."

"And why not? Isn't this a job for The Recruiter? Or perhaps The Employer? Or some other entity with another ridiculous name?"

"Ah come on now, you don't have to be like that!"

The Finder shook his head and waved his hand over the mountains of paperwork.

"Looks fun!"

"It's not…"

"Any that stand out?"

"No."

"We also need to find someone who can dig us a hole to install the bridge," God said casually adding another duty to The Finder's list.

"A counsellor wouldn't go amiss."

God laughed. “Already got one, thanks. No, we need someone who is great at digging.”

“Wow,” The Finder said, “now there’s a thought. Digging! If only I had thought of that before! Digging. See, when you told me I needed to find people to dig these interdimensional bridges for you, I assumed you were in the market for some circus clowns, or maybe a trained juggling bear!”

God laughed again. “Already got one thanks.”

The Finder cleared his desk with a sweep of his hand, transforming all the redundant work into a small box of ham sandwiches and two glasses of wine. “So, we need someone who is good at digging… mmm…” he said rather sarcastically.

“Yeah,” God agreed. “Someone who takes to digging like a duck to water. How about The Excavator?”

“There’s a thought,” The Finder said peeling off a crust from his sandwich.

“Or The Miner?”

“Yeah… maybe.”

“Or, perhaps, The Burrower?”

“Or The Exhumer?” The Finder suggested wondering why the obvious hadn’t come up. “May I ask,” he continued, “are you still not talking to The Digger?”

“Who?” God said, protruding his bottom lip. “Can’t say that name rings a bell.”

“Are you sure? It’s just that I recall this guy, when was it now, must’ve been a few years gone…”

“Never heard of him,” God said, cutting him off.

“Seem to remember you and he were quite close at some point.”

“Nope.”

“Quite a good friend,” The Finder winked leaning back on his chair. “Quite a close, good friend…”

God turned and looked everywhere round the office bar The Finder’s direction. “Great space you’ve made yourself here.”

“You’ll have to call him!”

“Nice bookshelf,” God continued. “Solid shelves.”

"Or meet him face to face. That'd probably be better. You know, after what happened…"

"I don't know anyone called The Digger and whatever you heard about me and him is all made up!"

"Not according to The Fixer."

"He's the worst for making stuff up. He once told me he thinks you're terrible at your job and have bad hair."

"I do have bad hair… Sheila told me the same thing. About The Digger, not my hair," The Finder said brushing what hair he had left after his stressful morning. "You know as well as I do, that when it comes to digging, The Digger is the only one you could trust."

God took hold of his wine glass and huffed emptily. "I haven't spoken to him in at least seventeen billion years."

"Well then, maybe he's forgotten all about it!"

"If I haven't, he hasn't."

The Finder waved his hand. "Ah come on… you were at university, you were both young, and needless to say drunk as well. Things happen."

Both reminisced the morning after that rather eventful party. It had been in full swing for six thousand years and was getting to the point when authorities would have to get involved. God had found his way up to his room to find The Digger passed out on his bed, and instead of moving him off, or taking The Digger's bunk, he simply curled up and spooned for what must've been a restful slumber.

"There was muck all over my trouser bottoms."

"You don't help yourself, do you?" The Finder laughed.

"It was just a friendly nap! A comradial snooze. A brosome doze. A…"

"Just go and see him," The Finder said calmly. "Go and tell him about the multiverse and what we've got planned and tell him that you need his help. I'm sure he'll be more than happy to help out."

God lifted his wine glass, sank the lot and turned to walk out.

"He already knows about the multiverse, anyway. A few billion years ago he asked if he could holiday here for a while."

"Really? So, you have spoken to him then… briefly, that is?"

"Very briefly!"

"Any idea where he is?"

“I know exactly where he is, unfortunately.”

The Finder smiled. “Any chance I could come with you when you see him?”

“Fat chance…”

The Kardashev Scale, for those who don’t know, relates to a civilisation and its advancement in terms of power. At present, it is thought that mankind from Earth in universe 1, will gain Type 1 status in the next few hundred years; that is, if they don’t blow themselves up first. Type 1 on this scale indicates that a civilisation can harness the full power and energy available on its home planet. Type 2 tells us that a civilisation has harnessed the total energy from its parent star, having possibly created a Dyson Sphere; a huge spherical structure that circles the parent star, or something similar. Type 3 is the strength to harness an entire galaxy’s power; type 4 the entire universe, and type 5, which The Digger has become extremely frustrated over, would be able to manipulate a universe in any way they wished.

“Why are we playing this ruddy stupid board game anyway?”

“You offered,” replied the small mole sitting opposite him.

The Digger picked up the dice and tossed them with care. “A four and an eight? A four and an eight? This isn’t fair!”

“Hey!” the mole said calmly, “we both found this magic spice stuff at the same time, and we both wanted the last gram of it,” he said nodding over to a small clear plastic container. “But you seem like a very powerful sort, like myself, I must add. We could’ve thrown omnipotent bursts of lighting and so forth at each other all day long till our faces went blue, but this is the right way to do it. Trust me, I had a very similar experience with an omnipotent sheep once over a game of cards.”

The Digger crossed his arms and pouted. Kardashev — The Ultimate Board Game Experience, didn’t really sit well with him, especially now he’d landed on the mole’s biggest hotel sitting proudly upon the IC 1101 square.

“You owe my type 3 civilisation… Four hundred billion space bucks,” said the mole happily.

“That’s nearly everything I have! I’ve only got that house on Pluto Avenue, and a few bits of change.”

"You could always remortgage?"

"Never!"

The mole picked up the dice and dropped them casually upon the board watching as a pair of sixes rolled into view. "Ah. Community Chest."

"...Great."

"Wow. I've come first place in a beauty competition, collect one hundred thousand space bucks from every other player."

"It doesn't say that!"

"It does, look."

The Digger took the card from the mole's paw, looked at it with feverish eyes, and threw the board in the air, telling the mole in no uncertain terms to clear off before he reduces him to a worm.

The planet Deshurt, that The Digger had found most delightful, had a sand content of nearly one hundred per cent. He had spent many years on holiday here building sandcastles and vast networks of cave systems. Sure, the Deshurt worms, irritable moles and the occasional long-winded rebellion at times made things a little difficult, but up until now he'd enjoyed all of it.

Beyond him lay a dry ocean of endless sand dunes. Whirling grains swirled from the tops of each peak as the sun roasted the dirt; air currents picked up and lofted what they could into amazing shapes and spirals. As far as The Digger could see, he saw nothing, except a small solid silver playing piece and a discarded game board flipping over and over at the foot of a sandy valley.

His drilling rig sat behind him, toasting under the heavy sun. It's bulk slowly sinking into the soft ever-changing sandy waves of the planet. It came with him everywhere. And though huge, cumbersome-looking and clunky, the rig was his masterpiece, a state-of-the-art drilling machine that not only bore down through dirt and rock, but through space-time fabric and multi-dimensional realities. Its immense power came directly from the Magnetar embedded inside the core of its engine. With this single highly magnetic star driving its force towards its target, the rig was able to rip through anything it desired, or, in this case, anything that The Digger desired.

The Digger had only two passions in his life. Firstly, and most obviously, was his love for digging. And secondly, was his great fondness for board games.

"Bloody moles," he croaked with sadness.

With a flick of his hand his rig shrunk down to the size of a matchbox, and with the care that he gave Scrabble letters forming a winning hand, he placed his machine in his breast pocket and shot off towards the stars in search of his next excavation site, and perhaps, an opponent that would be more inclined to lose graciously.

The cage slammed shut behind The Traveller as he grasped his shield and spear tightly. The crowds of onlookers with their cracked and disfigured faces cheered and screamed watching as the foreigner took his stand against the mightiest fighter. Mark waited uneasily watching the brawl unwind out in front of him from the stands. A behemoth of a man stood out from the other side of the cage; a hammer clasped in his palm twice the weight of The Traveller — he was no stranger to the Battle Cage of Thunderon 2.

Down came the first blow of the mighty hammer, billowing clouds of ash around The Traveller's feet. Up came the second hit, knocking him clean off his feet. Rolling thrice, The Traveller sprang back to his stand. Taking his spear gladly, he thrust the length of its handle between the giant's legs, heaving his body upwards and over, bringing the brute down headfirst onto the dead ground. A cheer followed.

Wasting no time, the mightiest fighter was pounced upon, taken from the back of the neck, the spear under his throat gripped tightly.

"Yield!" raged The Traveller. "Yield for the sake of Thunderon 2."

"Never!"

"Then I have little choice."

The Traveller threw down his spear, gave up his shield to the wretched floor of the Battle Cage, and turned the brute into a cabbage.

"Ah, now," Mark said blankly. "That's cheating!"

"You heard him," replied The Traveller, "he was never going to give up."

"How do you know? You fought him for thirty seconds. That was barely an argument."

The Traveller felt a little frustration pound the inner side of his temple. He'd taken Mark from one corner of the multiverse to another, freed princesses from tyrannical beings, saved helpless civilisations from stars going super nova; he'd even talked down The Pickler from destroying Alpha Prime, yet nothing seemed to impress his father-in-law.

"And a cabbage?" Mark said flatly. "Call me old-fashioned—"

"You're old-fashioned."

"...Call me old-fashioned, but that's not much of a hero's death, is it? A man like that surely would've wanted his head chopped off, or boiled alive or something. No, no. Turning a man into a cabbage seems like the easy way out."

"But the people here are now free! They're no longer slaves! I offered out the dictator's prize fighter, made a deal that would see him gone if I won, and I've done it."

"Yes," Mark agreed. "But in a very cowardly way... Shameful."

The Traveller rolled up his sleeves, with the frustration that only came from unimpressed judgemental in-laws, took Mark by his wrist, and shot off in a fizz of electrons to another space in space-time, hoping that soon he would win his father-in-law's acceptance... Maybe.

The skies above Butts Trollop grew darker as ominous shape-shifting clouds drifted overhead, a light spatter of rain drizzled upon the wettened ground, scattered bolts of lightning flashed backlit shadows in the horizonal distance. The morning had come where a small group of unsuspecting heroes would claim back their land by doing the only thing that they knew would potentially work: blowing up their home planet.

But first.

The barn door rolled open unsteadily on rusted tracks hitting the framework with a satisfying clunk. Inside, Farmer Collins' collection of old-timey tractors and farm equipment sprawled randomly from wooden wall to wall. Pitchforks and hoes hung on metal hooks, craving for a day they'd be used again. Grog followed Farmer Collins inside, making their way through, zigzagging between the maze-like collection, stopping at a back door fastened with a padlock that seemed more suited for a giant's chastity belt. A bronzed key fetched from around the farmer's neck came forth, slid into the padlock and twisted.

"Um…" Farmer Collins said hesitantly. "Grog, um, look. I keep my array of explosives in here, see. There's quite a bit. But do me a favour, and don't judge me."

"Why would I?" Grog replied. "That's why we're here."

"Yes," Farmer Collins said rubbing the back of his head, "right. I kind of mean if you see anything else. Don't think of me as a strange sort, okay?"

Grog nodded impatiently. "Okay."

The padlock lay down on the bench besides them as an even larger hidden room inside the barn opened up to Grog. He stepped in, marvelling at the vast assortment of high-powered, and quite frankly high-tech weaponry. From sticks of dynamite by the box load, to large neutron bombs placed upon one another. Grenades piled up like giant rabbit droppings, landmines stacked like pancakes, nuclear bombs irradiating carelessly, and women's dresses on coat hangers in every colour imaginable.

Grog coughed fighting the urge to smirk.

"You said you wouldn't judge me."

"Never said a word, sweetie."

"Stop it…"

Farmer Collins' tactical training had obviously not been wasted, the patchwork on his Peacock Wedding Dress was second to none.

"I said stop it!"

"I'm not judging!" Grog reassured him. "I'm admiring your handiwork."

"I just feel a little more relaxed when I'm setting charges, when I feel pretty, that's all."

Grog smirked this time and couldn't care less about it. "Whatever works for you."

Farmer Collins ushered Grog along, taking a second to unwrinkled his Shimmer-Shell Dinner Dress; it was his prize favourite after all. Grog stood eyeing from top to bottom a goliath contraption that sat in the middle of the carefully placed hanging dresses. Its large spherical shape loomed over him, flashing a scattering of small bulbs and gauges one after another.

"I'd hate to know how much you spent on that washing machine," Grog said sounding as genuinely interested as possible. "I mean, the Peacock Dress alone must've set you back over a million in expenses."

"And how do you know how much a peacock is? Like dressing all fancy too?"

Grog laughed. "I'd sooner clean my nostrils with it than wear it, and just because I'm a troll doesn't make me uncultured. I watch the Oscars every year."

"I see... well, between me and you, I spend nothing on them dresses, what with my stealth skills and what have you. And that there is no washing machine, it's a bomb."

"A bloody big bomb!" Grog admitted. "What's it for?"

"I built it a year or so back, took me a while. I'd smoked too much, um, corn, and spent a night in the shed putting it together. No idea how it works, or what sort of power output it gives. But the morning after I found this note that I'd written in my hazy state: *'Use only if scenario one comes up, or if Bodwhiff attempt a midnight poaching session'*."

Outside, Sam Samson, his wife, Bernard and the sheep watched as Grog heaved the huge bomb out in front of them, followed by Farmer Collins waddling out dragging a small pallet truck carrying a multitude of explosive devices.

"Blimey Colin!" Sam Samson gasped. "What is that thing?"

"Bhaa?" Bernard asked.

"Aye," Grog agreed, "your name's Colin Collins?"

Farmer Collins nodded with reservation. "It is..."

"That's not the strangest thing about him though," Mrs Samson said.

"I know," Grog replied.

"Bha?"

"I'll tell you later."

"Look," Farmer Collins said defensively, "yes, my name is Colin Collins; I'm a highly trained explosives expert with survival training, and I like to wear women's clothes! There's nothing wrong with that."

Mrs Samson raised her eyebrows in surprise and said, "I was going to say about your ability to wiggle your ears, actually. But that seems pretty small in comparison now."

A moment passed, then Sam Samson said, attempting to break the awkwardness.

"I liked the Velvet Bone Garment worn by the Skull-Witch, Queen of Thunderon 2."

"Can we please just get to setting these bombs?" Farmer Collins replied, hanging his head in shame. "Let's not get distracted away from this plan."

"Come on," Grog said patting him on the back. "Let's show The Last Orders who they're messing with."

Farmer Collins smiled and nodded. "I know by the day's end they'll be regretting setting foot on our home!"

The vast Collins Farm rested on the outskirts of Butts Trollop, having the small village at the foot of its land, easily seen from the living room window so that any time Farmer Collins sat in his favourite armchair, a freshly rolled corn cigarette in hand, he could watch from a distance the community that he helped grow and defend.

The ride on Old Masie, the longest working tractor on the farm, took a while to reach the closest mine shaft still accessible via lift. The journey was loud due to the vintage engine's thirst for fuel, uncomfortable due to the lack of seats available, and very shaky due to the lack of any real suspension; Mrs Samson thanked the relentless vibration, having not felt so invigorated in years.

"You seem happy my love?" Sam Samson asked innocently watching his wife's eyes roll backwards.

One by one the boxes of dynamite were unloaded and shipped down the lift shaft, greeted by a string of sheep passing the sticks one after another until they reached the dead end a few hundred feet down. Grog, knowing the interlinking mines well enough from his previous runs-in with the pitchfork and torch-wielding mobs, planned to use an evenly distributed number of dynamite sticks at each mine shaft that went a few hundred feet.

"And what of the neutron bombs?" Farmer Collins asked dusting his hands off on his trousers outside the mine entrance.

"How many have we got?" Grog asked.

"Eight. Do you want the sheep taking them down as well?"

"No" Grog replied. "These mine shafts are only shallow compared to others. We'll blow these first to thin the inner mantel and place the heavier bombs deeper to kick-start the planet's core exploding. Hopefully, it'll spread to every corner of Pux."

"You seem quite sure about this plan," Mrs Samson pointed out.

"Aye, well, yes. There's been plenty of times I've wished this to happen, just to get rid of you lot so I could live in peace," Grog laughed.

The neutron bombs were set down at eight specific shaft ends that went a few miles straight down under the planet's crust. Sam Samson was very satisfied setting up the remote detonator on the bomb that sat directly under Tumbly Crust.

A few miles away, in a cave system that had only been known by the most adventurous Pux explorers, Grog led the party down a winding, cold, close tunnel that went deeper than the rest. Running water could be heard from some far-off stream; droplets of moisture fell from the freezing stone ceilings as the air became thinner, and scarcer to breath. Headlamps were flicked on as the light from the outside faded from dim to pitch-black. Sound travelled like a wasp trapped in a glass jar; every breath and footstep echoed a thousand times chiming as crisp as a winter's morning naked swim.

After a time, just long enough for Sam Samson to become worried at the thought that Grog was indeed leading them to their doom, an orange glow illuminated the craggy walls up ahead, with the air around them warming with every step they took.

"My goodness!" Mrs Samson shouted stepping out on to a small ledge at the cave's end, covering her eyes from the blinding light.

The swirling core of the planet sat floating before them. White-hot elements of nickel and iron cooled and melted at the same time. Small bursts of flame shot out; random black spots of material waved for a second then sank under its boiling surface while its entirety rotated gently. The core of Pux 4b may not have been the biggest core, yet its veracity was powerful. And with the help of a large enough explosion, its own explosive ways might just be destabilised enough to jump-start a planetary breakdown.

"And that's where your homemade bomb comes into play," Grog shouted over the bellowing sound of the core.

“Scenario 1,” Farmer Collins said rhetorically. “I’ll go back and fetch it.”

“No need,” Grog said, “Bernard here can just teleport it down.”

And so, without hesitation, the mystery bomb appeared next to them all, balancing precariously on the ledge’s end.

“Why on earth have we been shipping down each individual bomb by hand?” Sam Samson asked bluntly, “if your pet could’ve just done that in the first place?”

“Mainly because I wanted to see how committed you were to the plan. But mostly because I could… and it was a laugh, of course.”

Later that day, there was a succession of rumblings from the bottom.

“Grog!”

“It’s the dynamite, you bloody moron.”

The ground wobbled and shook as each plot of explosives detonated a few hundred feet under the ground; a shuddering quake tore around the planetoid’s equator as small plumes of dust rocketed skywards above the selected mineshaft entrances. The outer mantle’s thickness had thinned, and while The Last Orders set their Cathedral Ship down sending their foot soldiers dispersing throughout the land, the secondary wave of neutron bombs would blow, bringing down the rocky barrier between the core and the cavern around it. Finally, the mystery bomb would fire off, bringing the planetoid to a total cataclysmic event, destroying the dictator and his slave ships for good.

“Yes,” Sam Samson said raising a finger, “a solid, sound plan indeed Grog. Though, may I ask, where are we when this all happens?”

Grog protruded his bottom lip expressing his short-sightedness clearly. “Well… Umm…”

… A short rumbling from the bottom followed.

A billion miles away in the distance of space, a dark shadow lofted silently within the vacuum, blocking out speckled starlight as it drifted towards Pux 4b. The Cathedral Ship, in all its menacing glory, threw full exertion to the engines, making its heading, its full and only priority; life support would be knocked down to minimal importance within the slave camps. Overlord Dave knew with one hundred per cent certainty that his workforce would be restocked by the day’s end. And just maybe, somewhere on the small planetoid of Pux 4b, there he would find a maid worthy of fetching his biscuits at lunchtime.

The Finder sat at his desk questioning whether he really did give Champ'N'Bubbly his business card or not. An unexpected knocking came from his office door as a small gathering of rappers had appeared without invitation, and even though he could've easily flicked them far across the galaxy, he'd thought that hearing them out would give him a little break from the monotony.

"And you say you can supply the workforce we need to begin works as soon as possible?"

"Fa'show..."

The Finder never bothered learning the rap tongue that was widely used throughout the Rap-verse, he'd never seen the point in it. It seemed like a language that was so close to English that changing only parts of it had been a waste of time. Even so, he became worried that he'd somehow misinformed Mr Champ'N'Bubbly regarding what services he had been after. He'd not mentioned a show or gig, or whatever it was called, not once.

"Fa'show?" The Finder finally asked.

"Yea... No doubt. Listen Fizzle, we can smack down anythin' your wanting, as long as the greens be coming our way."

Six of the famous rapper's entourage who stood behind the leading man shared some healthy palm slapping, and 'whoohed' every time 'greens' had come up in their talks. The Finder assumed that greens must've meant money, and naively asked, "How long will it be till I can get a price up for the job?"

Champ'N'Bubbly smiled showing all of his gold teeth. "We can talk about greens all day long!"

"Whoo..."

"Yeah!" another henchman said high-fiving his friend. "Whoo."

"Quite," The Finder noted.

Champ'N'Bubbly stood and told his fellow rap members to wait outside The Finder's office while he and 'The Big Dog' settled over the so-called greenery that would be required for the works to begin. He shut the door behind them, rubbed his eyes and took his seat, slumping in heavily.

"Oh, my goodness, Finder, my old chum, may I please have a drink if you've any to offer?"

"Pardon?" The Finder asked blankly.

"A drink," he responded, "if it's not too much of a bother?"

"No. No bother at all."

A glass popped into reality on the desk and began to fill with a bubbly headed golden beer.

"Oh, I'm sorry to be a pain, but may I please have a wine? Beer makes me go all fuzzy."

"Um… sure."

"And apologies again, I am a bit of a stickler about these things, but a flute of crisp red wouldn't be too much of an ask, would it?"

The Finder shook his head and exchanged the beer for wine; a few bubbles floated idly, landing on the desk next to the crisp clean wine glass. Champ'N'Bubbly took his beverage gently, sipped it with the care of a connoisseur and exhaled, releasing what sounded like the weight of a thousand worlds from his chest.

"Please forgive my chums," he continued, "but these sorts of things, discussing major planned works over a fine wine, well, you see they mean well, though they haven't really the brainpower to see it through."

"Quite," The Finder said collecting what confusion he had, piling it up into a little heap, and throwing all prejudgements he had out the window. "I have to ask, but what happened to all the fizzles and smack down big dog stuff?"

"Ah… Beneath the show of showmanship, there lives but a simple man."

"I'm sorry?"

"The Poet from the Sorrow System, I believe."

"Correct," The Finder replied, leaning back into his chair bringing a glass of the '74 into reality for himself. "I'm assuming that 'Champ'N'Bubbly' doesn't really exist?"

"Oh, but he does. Maybe not right now. Not here, within these walls, but out there, outside, all throughout the Rap-verse, Champ'N'Bubbly is a real, living, breathing person… I've been projecting for so long I sometimes forget what it's like just to be me again."

A sadness fell upon the rapper's face, a look that revealed a long-distant truth that somewhere in the past, a former life had been cast aside voluntarily so that fame, wealth and what The Finder had come to understand as 'booty' could be acquired.

"Tis a lonely life at the top…"

"I'll second that… so, if you don't mind, can we talk business?"

Champ'N'Bubbly nodded placing the nursed wine glass upon the table, not before setting a coaster down, and gestured for The Finder to proceed.

"You understand the project that we need from you?"

"I do," he confirmed, "the ins and outs of what you and your fellow partners are doing is neither here nor there to me; I can give you a million plus operatives that are willing and ready to work. From my understanding, from what you've told me, it's a simple long-term scheme, closing an outer section of the internal wormhole so that your works can be carried out? We can close down a few selected sections of high traffic areas, diverting the flow temporarily while you do what needs doing. Furthermore, I can have crews on each intersection where diverted traffic is sent, ready to stop the flow in the incident of any accidents of works overrunning. I can easily get hold of the correct equipment, vehicles and so on."

"Fantastic," The Finder said happily, "and the price-up for the job? When can you get that to me?"

Champ'N'Bubbly scoffed and waved a hand in the air. "Don't worry about the cost old boy."

"I have to pay you and your entourage something."

"Leave them to me… I'll pay them myself. I've amassed such wealth that my bank accounts are literally bottomless. Last week I purchased a planet just so I'd have somewhere to park my cars. And besides, this whole thing will give me a chance to step away from going to venues, concerts, bloody birthday party appearances for the royals. Oh, blimey, how tiring it all gets."

"I'd have thought that it being a choice to get into the rap game, you'd enjoy every bit?"

“Choice?” Champ’N’Bubbly asked rhetorically, “have you ever visited the Rap-verse?”

“Only once,” admitted The Finder, “it was for a nephew’s christening.”

“Well, let me re-inform you then, friend. I come from the planet M.C., located in the system of Beats, located in the Bopping Galaxy. Do you honestly believe I ever had a choice? I grew up thinking that maybe, if I tried hard enough, I might one day break the shackles of destiny and toss my Hip-Hop future to one side so that I might become something new. You see, I always enjoyed classical music. But I was always picked on for being different.” He huffed, a tired soul, and stood, sipping his wine one last time before placing it back upon its coaster, and headed for the door.

“You have my number,” he said pointing to a card he’d placed on the desk. “I’ll have everything ready for our planned operation in a day.”

The Finder nodded and thanked Champ’N’Bubbly for his help and honesty. Looking like a man exhausted from a lie that had got way, way, way out of hand, the rapper held the bridge of his nose, closed his eyes emptying a last lungful of air, set his mind right and opened the door to a small gathering of his entourage standing outside the office.

“Don’t trip fool,” he said to The Finder cursing every false word. “Champ’N’Bubbly and his crew go’n be on point for ya’ll works. Hit me up one time.”

The Finder could tell that he died a little bit more inside.

Upon the snowy summit of Mount Moira, two violent foes stood opposing one another. Their greed a thirst that never truly died, a hunger that outlived even time itself. Here, on the rooftop of infinity, a battle of brawn would take place, away from even the most fearsome of breeds; history was willing to turn its eyes away so that monsters of monsters could rage for one last dying spell before victory was set.

God cracked his knuckles, his gaze fixed against the steely stance of The Digger. His nemesis was surely a truly powerful and cunning adversary.

“You agree then,” God said flatly against the howling wind torrents.

"I do," The Digger replied. "You win, me and my rig will come with you."

God nodded, "And if I lose?"

"Then," The Digger smiled, "you leave me be. Just let me dig where I wish, no questions asked."

"Agreed!"

God knelt, sinking into the snowdrift; The Digger the same, both taking hold of either side of the board… "Ready?"

"On three!"

"One, two… Go!"

In the history of mankind never had a game of Hungry Hedgehogs been so violent and raw.

"I can't remember this being so fun!" The Digger shouted tapping furiously on his pink steed's tail, snapping its small plastic mouth wildly.

"Shut up and concentrate!"

Small white balls pinged and ponged about the tiny battlefield, quickly scoffed up in the beast's jaws. Fingers ached, sweat glistened on foreheads and before long the board was empty, save for two blue and pink hedgehogs smiling blissfully at each other.

The Digger jumped to his feet with gusto. "Eight to six. You lose again!"

"Ah that's not fair. I got snow in my eyes!"

"Excuses, excuses. Well, well… where should I go next? Ah, I know, anywhere I bloody like!"

"Shame though" God said casually, "you would've enjoyed the job. Probably just as well, mind. Your rig wouldn't have been able to cut it anyway."

"Fiddlesticks… there's nothing my rig can't dig through. It's a beast!"

"Na. Not this. I'll get hold of The Tunneller, or The Mole. They'd be more useful than your machine."

"They're rookies!" The Digger assured God sternly. "Don't ask them for help, for crying out loud, I'd rather do the job myself."

"Are you sure?"

"…What's the job?" The Digger asked emptily.

"Not much really. We're just going to dig through the side cavity of a wormhole, opening up a dimensional bridge for interdimensional public access. Probably something you wouldn't be interested in."

The Digger thought for a moment; his name held not the best reputation within the Continuum at present, and neither did his machine. "I'll tell you what… I'll come and help you out, and we can pen this game down to a friendly."

"Are you sure?"

"Yes, yes. it's fine… Fancy another round?"

"Hedgehogs again?"

"What else!"

Meanwhile, in a completely distant universe, in a totally new space-time reality, the amphitheatre came alive with the sound of echoing cheers; a standing ovation met The Traveller while he stood on stage in front of the vast chalkboard scribbled with complex symbols and large mathematical equations; a variety of flowers and underwear were tossed at his feet.

Mark sat in a chair on the stage, arms folded and upright, and totally and unsurprisingly unimpressed.

"Thank you," The Traveller said expressing his gratitude for the applause and celebration. "Thank you. You're far too kind."

Upon the chalkboard, the single most valuable and ingenious formula was written. Using multiple techniques, algebra, standard and quantum physics, and a few crafty equations that only omnipotent beings should know, The Traveller had successfully worked out how the Lampin people of Rog 4 could convert all the natural sunlight coming from their parent star into a permanent food supply, and a limitless source of power that would hopefully take their rather primitive civilisation into a new era of living.

Mark's expression showed he was not impressed at all.

"What's wrong?" The Traveller asked emptily.

"Isn't there some sort of code, or something, that prohibits you from getting involved with this sort of thing?"

"Like what?"

"I don't know… interfering with the primitives. It's cheating."

"It's a helping hand!"

"Well, needless to say, you can't just go running around, with me in tow I might add, and alter the course of an entire species' destiny. You've no idea what you've done."

"What I've done, is save a species from destruction, and I've done it without any hippy-wippy magic, as you put it..."

From the stage's side, a small cluster of men wearing black suits and glasses walked out, surrounding The President of the Lampin people. He beamed with pride as his outstretched hand met The Traveller's welcoming palm, shaking it firmly being the only truthful way he knew how to show his appreciation.

"Thank you," the Lampin President said and turned to the packed amphitheatre. "My fellow people! Listen, listen now. We have been given a gift, a gift from God!"

"Oh Christ..." Mark said holding his head in shame.

"A gift," the president continued. "For years now, we have strived to tackle the ongoing problems of this world, rid it of past viruses and ailments, but now, now thanks to this man! This being! We can finally have the power to traverse space and fight back and destroy those pesky people from our neighbouring planet once and for all!"

Mark coughed. "Told you so..."

"Wow," The Traveller said holding up a hand, "I thought you said you needed it to enable your people to survive?"

"I did," The President confirmed, "and now, thanks to you, we'll no longer have to sign danged peace treaties with those rotters from Rog 5."

The Traveller, feeling a little embarrassed and ashamed of himself, waved a hand at the chalkboard changing a seven to an eight in one of the many lines of the complex equation. Months later it would be confirmed by the Lampin scientists that the equation had been a fake, after the first attack vessel had readied for take-off, and as the ignition was started, 'Jiggle'em Chains' by Champ'N'Bubbly echoed through the cabin to the surprise of two hundred Lampin warriors.

"Now what have you done?" Mark asked standing up from his chair.

"Come on," The Traveller said close to defeat, feeling broken and empty.

"You'll have to try better than that," Mark said feeling pretty good about himself.

Breaking Wave's breaking wave soundtrack had run its course over the last hour yet again, and yet again Sheila felt that her flirting, obvious show of interest and outwardly vocal chit-chat about how muscular and hansom Breaking Wave deserved at the very least some credit. Of course, Sheila was and always had been a faithful woman, she had loved only God and God only. Even so, the sight of a Herculean specimen with a man-bun, flowery open shirt and a smile that could stop a bull elephant was hard to fight against.

Regardless…

"Is it the noises I make when I'm stretching?" Sheila asked bluntly. She'd patted her sweaty chest four times already to absolutely no response.

"Is what the noises?" replied Breaking Wave. He rolled up his yoga matt and began to tidy up his equipment clearing the small, town hall for the next visitors.

Sheila frowned. "I've been coming here for weeks now, weeks! And I've been reducing my outfit quite clearly over that time, if I come again, I'm pretty sure I'll be wearing floss, and I'm starting to think that you may not find that quite your cup of tea."

"I don't know what you mean."

"Come on now," Sheila said stepping his way, "what's wrong with me? Am I not good enough for you?"

"No woman is good enough for me…" Breaking Wave said softly.

"No woman is good enough for you? What do you mean by…? Oh…"

"I'm sorry," he said looking at his feet shamefully. "I've not meant to lead you on."

Sheila stood up and became quite guilty for reasons she found hard to justify, and said, "It wouldn't make any difference if I threw myself at you, would it?"

"No. I'm afraid there is another." From his gym bag Breaking Wave pulled out a small diary and opened the pages randomly. Weeks and weeks flipped past with only The Finder's name scribbled down repeatedly. "He doesn't even know I like him."

"Um, I'm pretty sure he does."

"Yeah?" he said with the smallest ray of hope.

"Yes, definitely. But it wouldn't make any difference either. You see, he's kind of got a secret girlfriend. You'd be better off going to see The Finder personally and telling him that you're not interested."

"Why?" he said defensively.

"Well, as much as he likes coming here, it's strictly for the workout and exercise. He told me apart from that he feels a little awkward being here on his own with you. Not that he has anything against that, of course! You like who you like!"

"Mm," Breaking Wave thought, "I don't want to make him feel uncomfortable."

"I didn't think so."

"Maybe I should go see him then…"

"I think it's for the best."

"Go see him and tell him I can't be without him."

"Um, no…"

"…Yes," Breaking Wave said, his eyes jolting crazily from side to side. "Go see him, proclaim my love for him. For his withered experienced body, his greying stress-ridden hair."

"Pardon?"

"I think that's a great idea!"

"Um," Sheila coughed attempting to retrace her steps, "no, no. Really, I don't think that's a good idea. Maybe just zing him a text?"

"No, it has to be face to face!"

"Perhaps an email would do?

"He can't say no if I'm there."

"Maybe a handwritten letter would do the trick?"

Breaking Wave began to stuff his gym bag with his scrunched-up towel and gym shorts furiously with the excitement of a miscalculated show of affection you wouldn't be shocked to find at a teenagers' Prom night.

"Maybe we need to calm down and reflect a little?" Sheila said calmly.

"There's no time!"

"I could pass on a postcard for you?"

He zipped his bag up eagerly and flung it over his shoulder as he stepped towards Sheila gripping her hand tightly with both of his and shook it fervently.

"I can't thank you enough! Thank you, thank you! I feel so free and vulnerable."

"Okay…"

"Please. Please. I'm going now to find my man; if you see him first, please don't say anything. I can't wait to tell him and make him aware that it was you who told me I should throw myself on the fire, put myself out there even if my heart would break."

Sheila fumbled for words. "I- I- Well…"

"It was you who told me," he continued, "that I should expose everything I am even if it means I am rejected! Of course, if it is rejection, I'll have no choice but to hurl myself into the nearest sun, vaporise myself turning into nothing but ash, taking all that I hold close along with me!"

"Umm… Really, please don't!"

Breaking Wave's calm persona fell off him like slightly melted chocolate falls off a slightly warmed up choc-ice. Leaving only a hysterically laughing, wide-eyed delusional yoga instructor. He laughed a little longer than what would be deemed as usual behaviour before turning and rushing out the door, climbing in his small space transport, heading for the stars.

"Ah," Sheila huffed quietly in the empty town hall. "Bollocks."

The multicoloured aura shimmering from The Big Wormhole's spiralling mouth flung galactic light and debris thousands of miles outwards into space. God and The Fixer stood gallantly staring into the spatial chasm pondering the future while the constant hum of ships, freighters and other cargo vehicles flew overhead. Ever since the news broke at the galactic council building that God and his co-workers were planning to open up The Big Wormhole to interdimensional space travel, the inhabitants of universe 437 thousand were excited to say the least.

"They know it's only a trial bridge though, right?" The Fixer asked.

God shrugged, “I guess so. All the info is available at the council building, and online. If there were any complaints, I’d know about it… left my email address for contact.”

“Really?” asked The Fixer. “I’d have guessed you’d be flooded with hostile letters.”

“Well, when I say my email, I really mean The Finder’s. Dealing with unhappy beings, not really my sort of thing.”

They turned away from The Big Wormhole as the rising sound of engines pricked their curiosity coming from a nearby construction nebula. Champ’N’Bubbly and his armada of traffic management ships, headed by The Finder, slowly warped in their direction. Above the roaring engine noise, the unfortunate sound of Champ’N’Bubbly’s number-one hit single blasted out for all to hear. ‘Booty in my Boot Space’ had sold a trillion albums in its first two days throughout the Rap-verse and had gone on to win Best Lyrics at the RV Oscars; having lines such as ‘Booty in my boot space, girl you got a cute face, see you back at my place, make sure you bring your toothpaste’, you can truly understand the genius that is Champ’N’Bubbly.

A billion yellow-flashing beacons spun in their cases upon the roofs of a hundred million modified Galactic Traffic Management trucks. Each vehicle was carrying five thousand plus traffic cones, sandbags, metal signs and sub-woofers with enough bass to blow the ears off of a charging Cosmic Bugle Beast.

“Fair play,” said The Fixer, “he actually found people to do it.”

The Finder exited from warp speed with his hair a little untidy, and a face to match.

“My email is for work purposes only!”

“This is work,” God replied.

“Having to deal with Mrs Thompson from the Garillion System, complaining every few hours about how a three-hundred-and-seven-year-old woman won’t be able get her cats to sleep due to the planned construction is not part of my work.”

“But you’ve got great people skills,” God insisted. “I’m sure you put her mind to rest.”

“I would’ve been better off simply putting *her* to rest, indefinitely.”

“Someone’s a little cranky,” The Fixer joked.

"I've been busy like never before, interviewing thousands of potential builders and construction contractors to carry out this work. I haven't even had time to sleep."

"You don't sleep though…"

"…Beside the point. And while I've been doing that, what have you been doing? Nothing, I bet!"

"Wow, steady on," The Fixer said defensively. "I've been busy too, you know; it's not easy keeping count of all the new universes that are created every second. I lost count a good ten times."

"Please tell me you're joking."

"No, I mean, I know whatever number I'm up to now, there's an eight in it."

"Seriously?"

"And a five. Definitely septillion Googleplex eight something-something, five something…"

The Finder stood visibly shaking, massaging his temples with his fingertips while feeling a headache set in.

"Don't get angry," he told himself. "Anger is the root of hate and can only lead to negative energy… calm down…"

God smiled and sipped at a fresh Manhattan. "I knew those Breaking Wave sessions would work."

The Finder exhaled deeply and nodded. "They do… though I think he's taken a liking to me."

"Hey, congratulations," The Fixer said happily. "Do I hear wedding bells?"

"Don't be silly. He's a good yoga guru, but that's it. Plus, do me a favour, if he asks, I've got a secret girlfriend."

"No worries, mate."

"Anyway," The Finder said turning to Champ'N'Bubbly who had dismounted his metal chariot and now stood with them, "this is Mr Champ'N'Bubbly, from the Rap-verse. He's agreed to lend us the use of his entire entourage to carry out the works."

"Wos'up big player?" Champ'N'Bubbly said attempting to fist-bump God.

"Um… I'm good, thanks."

"F-Dog told me and my boys you needed help, yo. We'd be happy to assist."

Champ'N'Bubbly smiled a golden smile at God and gestured to the small gathering of entourage that crowded around him to go and double check the vehicles and equipment. High-fiving before leaving, of course.

"So sorry, old chap," Champ'N'Bubbly whispered to God, "can't speak much, but look, all in hand, safety briefings ready to start, Champ'N'Bubbly just a front, will meet up later for gin and sandwiches over brunch."

God nodded. "Totally understand…"

"I knew you'd be drinking gin soon!" said The Fixer loudly. "I knew I should've slapped that lemonade out of your hand the moment I saw it."

"He had lemonade?" asked The Finder.

"Yeah, in a lager top!"

"…Good God."

Blunt Spoon, Champ'N'Bubbly's right-hand man, held a folder in front of him while a large gathering of hand-picked entourage members who had been assigned lead roles came to await orders. Blunt Spoon had always known about Champ'N'Bubbly's true nature, and although a good friend, blackmailing his way to the top seemed like the easier option. Regardless…

He flipped open the folder and began.

"Listen up!" he shouted. "We got ourselves a long day ahead of us, but if we do it right, we're going get paid real good, soon. So quiet down and listen up. My main man Nuff' Said will head up the initial install. Ya'll be installing a wormhole closure on the seventy-eight outside lanes of this here wormhole. It's going get real busy real fast, so keep your eyes open, and watch each other's backs. Nuff' Said got all the drawings and paperwork, so any questions ya'll got, go ask him.

"Nuff' said," he said, turning away.

"Word, Blunt Spoon."

"You got a hundred thousand men at your disposal, so don't get all worried about delegating or nothing, you want something done? Then get it done."

"Nuff' said," said Nuff' Said.

"Word. Now listen ya'll, my cousin, Spare Change, will set up the diversion route; after that, he and his crew going set up traffic lights and stop-and-go boards. There going be a lot of travelling public stopping asking for directions; we don't want that, we don't need that, so if ya'll get any problems, you just tell them they need to follow the signs and that's it."

"Where's the diversion going?" God asked curiously.

Spare Change unfolded a map and handed it to God. "We goin' send them towards the Phoenix Dwarf Galaxy first, then straight over to IC 1613. From then on, it'll be a nice easy journey to Pegasus Dwarf where they'll re-join the exiting wormhole traffic."

"Right," God said seeming quite impressed, "and how long should that journey take?"

"No longer than two million years," Spare Change said happily.

"That's quite impressive, not that long really."

God nodded, handed the map back to Spare Change, and patted Blunt Spoon on the back for a job well done.

"Hello everyone," he said to the growing crowd. "My name's God. As you may or may not know, my friends and I are going to be testing something out. I've got plans for an interdimensional bridge that will cross over into a parallel universe. With any luck, universe 47 thousand and 1." He paused to take a swig from a fresh beer. "I understand that payment has been dealt with by my colleague The Finder, and your fellow Champagne Bubbles."

"It's Champ'N'Bubbly," Blunt Spoon said in God's ear quiet enough to not embarrass him.

"Right, sorry, Champ I mean. Well, if all goes to plan, I'd like to extend the offer, call it a bonus. In the event that all goes well, I'll give every one of you a free travel-pass through the bridge for life."

A communal nod of agreement Mexican waved across the crowd in front of him.

"Great… I think that's it?"

Blunt Spoon coughed and said, "Before I forget, if any of ya'll have an accident or something, the nearest hospital is eighteen light years away. Spare Change and my main man Nuff' Said got maps to hand out."

The gathered entourage slowly scattered and made their way back to their individual traffic management space trucks, signing into their own briefing sheets given out by their individual lead hands. There was a buzz of anticipation in the air, a feeling of excitement and uncertainty. Of course, in the past, the entourage had got involved in many building contracts and schemes; for instance, four years ago on planet Funk, the entire southern hemisphere had to be dug up and rebuilt so that a single stage could tolerate the stress of Champ'N'Bubbly's backing dancers.

Yet this was different.

This felt like real graft for everyone, as it would not only benefit themselves as money hungry 'hustlers', as Blunt Spoon had once called himself, but it would be a monstrous act of community service that would aid and hopefully improve an entire universe's gain. And for some, it would count towards their Community Service.

God shook the hands that were closest to him, thanked Champ'N'Bubbly for his help and arranged to meet him later for gin and sandwiches, as The Finder took a seat looking weary and fatigued.

"We're only just getting started, mate."

"Maybe you are," The Finder said heavily, "but my work started already."

"It'll be a while before it's all shut down anyway," God said, "time to relax and have a beer, I guess."

"Since when do you need free time to drink?" The Fixer asked. "I once saw you create an entire spiral galaxy on twenty shots of tequila."

God smiled. "Yeah, but the tracking was out, thing wobbles all over the place to this day."

"Did you find The Digger?" asked The Finder.

"I did," God replied, "he's in the site office…"

"Familiarising himself with the work detail?"

"Na… playing Armoured Chickens and Ladders. We've got time for a few more rounds if you're interested?"

"I'll pass thanks."

"Space Snap?"

"No…"

"…Hide-and-seek?"

"…Go on then."

Mark had slated The Traveller more times than he had fingers and toes, and no matter where The Traveller took him throughout the multiversal plane of existence, nothing seemed to prove his value.

Accepting the challenge to navigate the Labyrinthine Forest of Gollen 4 to retrieve the long-lost gold of King Vox the Destroyer concluded with a disheartening sigh of anticlimactic wind escaping Mark's chest. Taking on the eighteen Grand Seventh Dimensional Chess Masters at once seemed to pull Mark into a dozing state of affairs; nothing, it seemed, would work.

And so, the journey continued…

Meanwhile, lost yet not forgotten, though maybe a little forgotten with regards to anyone remembering enough to care, Norman was still in The Library of The Gods. He had found himself in the Educational Section. A librarian took *The Nine Steps to Spaghettification* from him and proceeded to take it back to the Health Section where it ought to belong.

Had it been years he'd been trapped here? Norman didn't know, though it hadn't stopped him from building a small makeshift tent from some Earth Road Maps he'd found and some disused bookshelves as kindling for a fire.

He nestled down inside his camp under the watchful eyes of the West Midlands and thought back to when he sat quite similarly in his tent within the storage room of the multiverse. It was a happier time, a quieter time; a time when chocolate bars gave him laughter and sandwich rappers came apart without the need for a pre-workout.

Throughout all his adventures and travels, all his fortune and misfortune, everything he'd done and accidentally walked into, Norman knew he had somehow grown as a living being, yet he felt saddened to think that he still lacked the intelligence to escape a simple library. He gained a status, a right to regale stories to his friends whilst drinking heavily round a table. His own history had shown that he was not merely a being from a box made from clay, nor was he a road-sweeper driver or a magic mushroom; he was alive, living the multiverse as it should be lived. Experiencing things as and when they came, all under the banner of The Explorer.

Not that anyone really called him that. Much like someone who never gets called their real name due to their nickname taking precedence, Norman never was called The Explorer because, well, he was just Norman, and that had been universally decided.

"There's got to be something in this place that can get me out of here," he muttered to himself flipping open a Gwallt pop-up book he'd found discarded.

Then, just as sudden as his birth, a thought expressed itself inside his clay mind. An idea so magnificent that he stood tall, jumping to his feet.

"If I can learn more stuff," he began, "by reading more stuff," he connected, "I'll be able to do more stuff," he painfully strung together like a disjointed elbow, "and that means I would find my way out of this library."

Protruding his bottom lip, he frowned. "Now all I need is to find some books…"

The Last Orders had now arrived. The swarm of smaller, more agile attack ships flew wildly about the gargantuan Cathedral Ship like scavenger fish moving around a great white shark. Above the outer atmosphere of Pux 4b, within the star-speckled night sky, Grog and Bernard gazed upwards: high beyond the scattering of clouds the blinking lights of the impending invasion force revealed itself, like opening the attic door only to be greeted by a tangle of Christmas lights staring back at you, both Grog and Bernard knew there was trouble to come.

Farmer Collins moved aside allowing Sam Samson to peer through his telescope he'd set up upon the top of Trollop Hill. The air cold, a breeze wafting what remaining leaflets there were into small puddles and gutters.

"Blimey," Sam Samson said, viewing the Cathedral Ship in all its glory. "I mean, for a dictatorial vessel feared by millions, it's quite pretty."

"Too bad it's going to get blown up then, aye?" Grog replied.

"Bhaa!"

"Yeah. That too."

"Can I see?" Mrs Samson asked pulling a sheepskin jacket tighter round her shoulders.

"Bhaa!"

"It's fake," she replied. "God only knows what I'll do the day this buffoon can afford real fur."

"Flower organising and council work is a morally satisfying job," Sam Samson defended, "it has nothing to do with money."

"Aye," said Grog, "but I'm sure if you'd known that earlier you would've chosen your vocation more wisely."

"…Maybe."

"It seems to me," Farmer Collins added, "that this here Cathedral Ship is where they'd put all their new slaves. What with all the pillaging and rape that would happen."

"Um," Grog said, "maybe not the latter."

"Well, even so, what I mean to say is that after you invade a planet, or planetoid in our case, if I were in charge, I'd land my Cathedral Ship down and start getting all my new workforce on board."

"Seems reasonable," Mrs Samson agreed thinking back to every young stable boy she'd encountered.

"Yeah…" Farmer Collins said, "but that's just it, isn't it?"

"What's it?"

"No thanks, I've got some cheese'n'onion…"

"She said what's… it!" Grog laughed.

"Right sorry. I can't see that huge ship bothering to land if their new workforce consists of me, you, Bernard, Mr and Mrs Samson and a few sheep. I mean, Pux is empty, ain't it? Since everyone else left… of course."

All at once the feeling of solitude and isolation fell upon the small group of unsuspecting heroes. Their fellow men and women had left like rats leaving a sinking ship, and now the realisation that they all stood on a ghost planet brought goosebumps to their skin. To the east, south, north and west, empty abandoned towns lay wasting away. Possessions collected by generations, handed down to children by their elders thrown idly away were now bound to collect dust for years to come.

"Well not really years," Grog said with a smile, "as we'll be blowing it up soon."

"But" Sam Samson said thinking about all his valuables back at the house, "so many things, never to be used, loved or cared for ever again."

"So bloody what! I've been on my own all my life..."

"Bhaa!"

"...*Most* of my life. I've got a lot of things that I'll miss too. But you can't start feeling homesick now. Especially now!"

"Right," Famer Collins said nodding at Grog. "We've got a big problem now, and it has nothing to do with your flower-arranging stamp collection. Somehow, we've got to get that big ship to land. I hope that they're not going to see that Pux is empty and move on. We can't let that happen!"

"Any suggestions?" Mrs Samson asked.

"I completely forgot about my flower-arranging stamps," Sam Samson murmured sadly to himself. "And my assortment of Brootox ties."

"Aha!" Farmer Collins said, "we could turn all the power on in all the residents' houses, make it look like everyone's still about?"

"Won't they have some sort of scanning equipment? They'll be able to see that it's just us."

"What about if we use a giant harpoon?" Mrs Samson said, "we could pull it down?"

"Do we have a giant harpoon?" asked Grog.

"No," she replied.

"Right..."

"Seems to me that we'll have to go up there ourselves," Farmer Collins said gazing upwards at the distant ship, "and bring it down from within."

"Do we have any ships still lying about?"

"Mm... maybe one or two?"

"So, we fly up there," Sam Samson said. "Then what?"

"I guess we storm the castle," Farmer Collins replied. "Fight our way through what I assume would be an army of guards, footmen and so on. Finally making our way to the engine room after potentially losing a few of us in battle. Sam Samson would most likely die first..."

"...What?"

"…Then we blow the engines, bringing the huge ship into free fall, eventually crash landing, and that would force the smaller ships down too. With any luck there'd be at least one of us still alive to trigger the bombs, igniting the planet to blow, sacrificing yourself for the greater good."

"Right," Grog said, "or Bernard could just transport us up there?"

"Bhaa!"

"Right," Grog continued, snapping his fingers. "That's a great idea. We could pile up lots of explosives in a ship, fly it up there, let them take it onboard willingly, then blow it up while Bernard transports us out just in the nick of time."

"And the chances of me dying first, doing it this way are… smaller?" Sam Samson asked.

"Aye, much smaller. You might not die at all!"

"Well… I like those odds."

Beyond the twinkling lights of Butts Trollop, the air hangar lay, a scattering of small aircraft still remained grounded. With any luck one would be big enough to house enough explosives to make an indent in the Cathedral Ship's ability to remain in orbit. The explosion would have to be strong enough to damage its engines, yet not so strong to simply blow it up all together.

"And why not?" Sam Samson asked. "Why not just blow it up in one hit?"

"The Last Orders may be a dictatorially run empire," Grog replied, "but if anything happens to the Overlord, there's always someone new to step into their shoes."

"And how do you know that?"

"It says it right here in the leaflets they dropped," Grog replied handing one over, "back fold, it's all under the title *'What to Expect as a New Slave'*."

Sam Samson took it happily and began reading it as if it were some sort of homework to study.

"There'll be a test later…"

"…Very funny."

By the time Space Snap had sped into its fourth round inside the site office, Champ'N'Bubbly had supervised the closing of most of the lanes inside the wormhole. Traffic had come to a near standstill, moving only one fifth the speed of light, with tail backs reaching nearly four light years back; extra signs had to be erected.

C. Money, a close friend to Nuff' Said and backing vocals to Easy P-zee leant down as a little old lady wound down her driver window with a look of confusion draped worriedly across her face. The forty-eight-way traffic light set-up was in full swing stopping and starting drivers continuously.

"Excuse me, young man?"

"Word… how can I be of assistance?"

The little old lady hesitated and had obviously taken a wrong turn somewhere.

"I'm so sorry" she began, "I'm just on my way to see my daughter. I'm eighty-six, you know? Anyway, I'm travelling from Ceres trying to get to Earth. Somehow, I've ended up here? Can you point me in the right direction please?"

"Yeah," C. Money said with a kind smile, "what ya need to do is simple. Turn yo'self about, head straight for Canes Dwarf. You should pick up signs for the Milky Way pretty quickly. Try to head for a hundred and eighty degrees in the Orion arm, you should see park'n'ride signs for Alpha Centauri A… Just keep going, you can't miss Earth."

C. Money smiled again tapping her roof, feeling like a good job had indeed been well done as the small modified 1952 Austin A40 trundled off star bound, with a little old lady blissfully smiling behind the wheel, never to be seen again.

"Your diversion's a joke pal!" a driver shouted angrily as he rolled past in a brand-new BM-Double-U, "been round four times!"

"Enjoy the fifth!" C. Money advised.

A few million miles away, deep within the enormous swirling mouth of the wormhole, the last few cones were being dropped off the side of a spacefaring traffic management vehicle, finally closing down the wormhole so that work could begin.

The large convoy of trucks, ships, entourage buses, groupie minivans and so on lined the closed down section of the wormhole. A trillion amber-flashing beacons spun in their shells, and much like the roadworks that crust the M25 every night like an unstoppable case of athlete's foot, there seemed to be a billion kilometres of cones laid out before any real work was actually seen by human, or in this case non-human eyes.

"Right," God said waving his hands about in front of him as if portraying some unknown wise knowledge, staring up at the cascading wall of the inner wormhole sweeping up and away from him for miles and miles. "This is the spot where we dig!"

"You sound so confident," The Fixer said admiring the drilling rig in all its rusted glory.

"Are you sure?" asked The Digger as he cracked his fingers feeling on point after a winning game of blind charades. "You've done your research? I mean, as much as I trust you, you know that digging one millimetre out might distort the very fabric of space-time?"

"Of course," God said rolling his eyes, "plus, we're three million miles inwards from the entrance. If everyone sticks to the speed limit, they'll have about thirty seconds to get in the right lanes."

"Again," The Fixer said, "my confidence in you is near full capacity..."

"As always," God replied.

Champ'N'Bubbly and a few of his handpicked crew strolled over, stepping to the beat of 'Shaking an' Money Making'. It was yet another of his own masterpieces that broke record sales.

"Sup, big player?"

"Me?" asked The Digger pointing at his chest.

"I think you misunderstand the term 'player'," said The Fixer.

"But I do play," replied The Digger naïvely. "Like... a lot. I mean, playing board games and digging are the only real things I enjoy."

"Still... don't think he was talking to you."

"How's everything, Champ?" God asked.

"Cool on the worm-front. We all locked down, ready to start popping some dimensional barriers up in here!"

"Yeah!" his small entourage group shouted communally, and then high-fived.

"Lanes are closed, and traffic's froze. Except from one little sweet old lady driving the wrong way towards oncoming traffic, we all good."

"Great!" God said happily.

From the site office, three million miles away towards The Big Wormhole's mouth, The Finder stretched his arms to the metaphorical sky, arching his back and felt a little rested after resting a little. It had been a long and heavy few days for him, and having even a few hours of doing nothing was the break he most definitely needed.

And with a whoosh and fizz of charged particles, seconds later, he arrived standing next to The Digger.

"I feel much better," he announced to his friends. "Sorry if I was a little cranky back there. I was burning the candle at all three ends and didn't even realise it."

"So, we can prod and make fun, and you won't bite our heads off?" asked The Fixer.

"That'll be the day!" God laughed.

"Long time no see," the Digger said, shaking The Finder's hand happily. "You been well?"

"As well as I can be. You still digging?"

"Yep."

"And playing board games?"

"Yep..."

"...Anything else I should know?"

"Nope. Think that's it."

"Pleased you two could have that heart-to-heart," God said, "really brought a tear to my eye."

"You may jostle me at will," The Finder said smiling, "but I feel revitalised."

"Um," the Fixer said pointing to a small space transport flashing its headlights wildly within the queues of disgruntled wormhole commuters. "Is that Breaking Wave?"

The Finder wobbled. "Oh God..."

The Fixer smiled. "This should be interesting."

"What should I do?"

"Weeell," The Fixer replied knowingly. "I can't let myself get involved in any personal business that you may have..."

"Stop messing about and help me!"

Shaking hands gripped the silver dinner tray as the new maid brought Overlord Dave his bowl of rice snaps and the latest edition of The Pickler. At present, she was the tenth new maid in the last four hours, and though her immense pay had successfully been wired to her account, now knowing that her daughter's university scholarship had been covered, she still felt a little hesitant when entering the young overlord's chambers.

"And where have you been?" Overlord Dave asked suspiciously.

The bowl hit the floor with a ping as she ran off in the direction of the execution wing; tears streaming from her eyes.

"…Send for a new maid!"

"You can't just keep slaughtering your staff!" Bol advised in a very un-advisory way. "We don't have a limitless supply."

"After we've raided this little planet, we'll be restocked."

Bol sighed, and for the third time said, "For the third time, there's no one down there!"

"…Are you sure?"

"There's no one down there!"

"…Not even a few cleaners?"

"…No!"

"How about some kitchen staff?"

"No!"

"Plasterers?"

Bol, who was famously a naturally barbaric and utterly hostile killing machine, drew strength from some deep part of his hairy self and held back the urge to dissect Overlord Dave limb by limb.

"I told you," he said calmly, "there's no one down there, and you've got two stowaways on board."

"Since when?"

"There standing right there!" he shouted kicking the emptying cereal bowl with enough force that it became part of the wall.

Overlord Dave flinched and gave up the idea of rice snaps and slaughtering maids and noticed the two stowaways standing by the back wall.

“Um…” he ventured, “any chance either of you are maids?”

“Jesus!” Bol shouted storming from the chambers. “Sort out your own bloody invasion!”

“Unfortunately, no,” The Traveller said. “Though I could quickly straighten everything out for you?”

“Oh, that would be a lot of good, wouldn’t it?” Mark said flatly, “brought me halfway round known reality to clean up some spilt milk? How impressive.”

“Only for starters!” The Traveller replied. “We’ve just got here. I don’t know whether he needs help or he’s up to no good.”

“Have you asked him?”

“…Well, not yet. No.”

“As I thought, too busy with your own business… such a layabout.”

“You know, I’m really trying here,” The Traveller said emptily.

“No,” Mark replied shaking his head. “I’m sorry, but all I’ve seen so far is a jobless layabout that doesn’t deserve my daughter’s affections. Take me home please!”

“Ah come on,” The Traveller said desperately and turned to Overlord Dave.

“What’s going on here? I mean, are you trying to, I don’t know, murder loads of beings, set some free? Maybe have a problem with a Farlon Wombletron?”

“You already dealt with a Wombletron two universes ago,” Mark pointed out. “Poor thing never stood a chance.”

“Okay… look…”

“…Overlord Dave,” Overlord Dave said.

“Look, Overlord Dave,” The Traveller continued. “Forget the Farlon Wombletron. It doesn’t matter. I gather from your title you’re a little ruthless and tyrannical?”

“Weeell, would you look at Mr Detective here,” Mark said. “Quite the sleuth.”

“I class myself as a little ruthless,” Overlord Dave said with the slightest hint of smugness. “But I only do what needs doing.”

“At least you’ve got a job,” Mark said with a nod. “Quite stable, is it?”

“Yeah, stable enough.”

"Are you seeing anyone at the moment?"

"Hey," The Traveller said, "don't start offering Anne out like that. I'm standing right here!"

"Standing, doing nothing with your hands in your pockets. As usual… Tell me son, what's your job entail?"

Overlord Dave thought for a moment. "Well… I mean, I run the biggest empire in the galaxy, having taken over and enslaved thousands of planets and civilisations, and of course I own the biggest fleet of star ships, warships, battleships and slave ships. I've conquered solar systems and slaughtered entire races in the name of The Last Orders. And on top of that I have the biggest collection of comic books this side of the sector."

Mark paused and nodded. "Okay," he told The Traveller. "You might need to do something…"

"Oh," The Traveller replied rolling his eyes. "Giving me the green light, are you? How very kind."

"If you don't, I will."

"No, no," The Traveller went on. "I'm sure I can manage it."

"Can't say I'm that surprised that Sam Samson refused to come with us," Farmer Collins said. Behind him a heap of explosives sat as deadly as a dormant cow pat, ready to explode all over someone's wellington boots.

"That's a very farmer-specific analogy," Grog pointed out, hunching down behind the pilot's seat. The small transport vehicle wobbled from side to side unsteadily while its white-hot engines blasted it skywards.

"It's all I could think of."

"Bhaa!"

"Yeah," Grog said, "there's that too."

The small outline of Sam Samson and his wife, and five hundred sheep standing next to the hangar doors became dots against the hazy details of the ground as they jetted upwards through small pockets of random cloud cover. Mrs Samson was a loyal woman, trusted and a real fighter for those she held closest to her, so of course she felt bitter about staying behind with her husband.

"I just had a bad feeling about all that dynamite."

"Don't worry," she told her husband. "Not everyone likes heights."

The transport vehicle zoomed and forged forwards, tearing through the upper layers of the atmosphere; with a shuddering rattle, it broke through into lower orbit. The vast swelling of a thousand troop carriers misted around the huge Cathedral Ship's bulk dead ahead.

"It's bigger than I thought," Grog said. "I hope we've got enough explosives for it."

"Size doesn't matter. It's how hard you hit the nail, not the size of the hammer."

"You hear Mrs Samson say that?"

"Once or twice," Farmer Collins replied.

"Thought as much."

Farmer Collins took hold of the guidance stick in front of him pulling the transport out of autopilot. It had been an age since he'd flown any kind of spacefaring vehicle, aside from his training of course. He had to admit he was a little rusty with the stick; he was of course a lot happier taking himself up to The Last Orders' mother ship, rather than having an omnipotent sheep that talked to trolls, mind-beam him up there.

"It's perfectly safe," Grog said. "It feels sort of nice."

"Having each atom torn apart, jetted thousands of miles instantly and then reassembled one by one by a clever farmyard animal doesn't sound nice and safe."

"Bhaa!"

"Aye, exactly. He's not a farmyard animal… he's Bernard."

"Even so," Farmer Collins said, "I feel much better doing it this way."

The outer hull of the Cathedral Ship loomed. It was, if nothing else, what you'd expect from a cathedral. At least from the outside, anyway. Of course, there had never been reports of one uprooting from its foundations and traversing space, and you'd be hard-pressed to find a single hunchback inside this one, even so, if you could picture Notre Dame with colossal engines strapped to its sides, and roughly a million times bigger, you'd be getting close to what the Cathedral Ship looked like.

"Ay up," Farmer Collins said worriedly, "something's wrong. I've lost all control."

"Yeah," Grog replied, "but we all knew that years ago."

"I mean I'm not flying the ship any more."

"Were you really doing it before… looked like guesswork."

"We've been caught in some kind of tractor beam."

"I'm not a farmer; I've no idea about field equipment."

"Good day," Overlord Dave's voice whirred through the intercom on the dashboard. "We have taken control of your ship and are currently moving you to one of our flight decks. Do not attempt to escape or flee, as we have weapons locked onto your engine core. We currently have two of your crew held hostage… your diversion has failed. Furthermore, please let me know if any of you have cleaning experience, as I have rice snaps and milk everywhere."

The static pop of the finished transmission left only a quiet hum inside the transport vehicle.

"Well…" Farmer Collins said, "any ideas?"

"I'm not worried… Bernard's here. He won't let anything happen to me."

"What about me?" Famer Collins asked.

"You don't need help from a farmyard animal now, do you?"

Breaking Wave stood on top of his transport; the blocked traffic stretched for countless light years behind him; horns beeped as loving hand gestures were thrown out the window. In his hands he held a boombox above his head playing 'Burning Loins' by Spare Change, his gaze fixed on The Finder.

"Well, this isn't awkward," God said.

"I think it's cute," The Fixer noted.

"Please don't encourage him," pleaded The Finder.

Champ'N'Bubbly thought about selling him his new album 'Cosmic B'donkadonk' while Breaking Wave felt his heart pound in his chest.

The Finder huffed, and reluctantly walked over to the transport to try and bring Breaking Wave to his senses.

"Hey," Breaking Wave shouted over the deafening music, "I've something you need to know!"

"I'm sorry," The Finder replied. "You're a very nice yoga instructor… but…" he said as his voice trailed off.

"Say something!" shouted Breaking Wave. "Tell me I haven't waisted my time."

"Look… you're a very nice, um, yoga instructor… but. But uhh… Oh! Look, here comes my girlfriend."

He ran over to where a modified 1952 Austin A40 sat purring, pulled open the door and helped a sweet little old lady out onto her feet.

"He's not, is he?" God said opening a fresh can.

"Oh yes, he is!" smiled The Fixer.

"No…"

"Sorry about this," The Finder said softly to the old lady. "Ah," he said loudly, "came to give me my, um, packed lunch did you, darling? You always think about me and my darn lunch."

Breaking Wave frowned and lowered the boombox to his chest. "Who's that?"

"This?" said The Finder, "it's my blooming girlfriend."

Kissing her on her soft, almost empty tissue-paper-like cheek was a risk he was willing to take. "Wow… I love this blooming lovely lady person."

"What's her name?" Breaking Wave said coldly stepping down to the road.

"It's Adelaide," she said happily, "I came from Ceres you know, heading to Earth to—"

"Yes, yes," The Finder interrupted, "I'll just get my coat and take you home."

Breaking Wave grew obviously upset; he was visibly shaking and angry. "You're lying to me."

"Now, Breaking Wave," The Finder said cautiously, "calm down. Think happy thoughts."

Bol thrusted his second favourite sword, lovingly named 'Mr Stabby', into Farmer Collins' back, pushing him, Grog and Bernard down the hallway towards the interrogation room. Their ship had been brought down comfortably in the flight deck; the back door ripped clean off while a small army of foot soldiers wrestled all three to the ground.

Not even Farmer Collins' hand-to-hand combat training seemed to help.

The mound of explosives had swiftly been jettisoned from the flight deck out the airlock without thought; a thousand sticks of dynamite and lumps of C4 twirled majestically in the vacuum of space.

"Keep moving!" Bol said, prodding Grog's back.

"Hey!" Grog replied, taking Mr Stabby from the great ape and snapping it in two. "Prod me again, and it'll be your legs."

Bol nodded wide-eyed, looking up at Grog who stood a good few feet taller than he.

"Do you mind walking a bit faster, please?"

"Aye, not at all."

"Bhaa!"

"Exactly, manners cost nothing."

Whoosh sounded the doors as they parted. Inside Overlord Dave stood; a few Last Orders interrogators rested on either side of him. The room lighting was dimmed to cause unsettling thoughts and worriedness. Mark sat on a chair while The Traveller picked his fingernails next to him.

"Bhaa!" Bernard said with a smile, or at least what constitutes as a smile on a sheep's face.

"All right Bernard!" The Traveller said recognising his from the Continuum. "What a surprise to see you here."

"I'd advise you all to keep your mouths and tongues quiet," Overlord Dave said flatly. "Your plans to blow up the ship have failed… you will all suffer a most un-grandiose end."

"Un-grandiose?" Grog asked.

"Beg your pardon, your… um… Overlordness. But is that a real word?"

"What would a farmer know about words!" Overlord Dave asked defensively.

"I'm only saying…"

The Traveller coughed. "It does make sense. I mean, it sounds a little strange, but it works."

"Are you going to do anything?" Mark asked The Traveller bluntly. "Or just talk with your hippy friends all day long?"

"You will not do anything, nor try to escape," remarked Overlord Dave, "and FYI, in the newest edition of The Pickler, issue seventy-nine, he says to The Grand Iceman, when he's just about to melt him over a large vat of slightly temperate water, you will soon be Un-Grand-Ice… Man."

Grog and the others nodded, the interrogators both saw the funny side too.

"Fair enough," The Traveller said, "that's quite good writing, I guess… for a comic book."

"Thank you," Overlord Dave said.

"Can you please do something!" Mark said frustratedly.

The Digger pushed forwards with his rig. The immeasurable power of the Magnetar inside the engine's drive chain took hold of the inner wall of the wormhole; sparks and small lumps of space-time debris flew everywhere while the focused electromagnetic beam pulled the smallest of openings wider; safety glasses and hard hats were handed out.

Everything began to shake.

Everything began to rattle.

"We're rolling now!" The Digger said.

As if Breaking Wave's awful and downright selfish parking of his transport hadn't caused enough traffic jams, what traffic that had now began to move soon slowed down to watch the only piece of machinery in a million miles kick into action. The brightest of lights momentarily blinded every living thing in a million-light-year radius; sun-visors were pulled down.

"What's the problem with me?" Breaking Wave shouted holding his hand up to his face. "We could just be friends if that's what you want?"

"It's a nice offer!" The Finder replied as loud as he could as the drilling rig roared onwards behind them. "But honestly, I've just got a lot on my plate right now… here," he said taking something from his trouser pocket.

Breaking Wave opened his palm, there lay a small biro with the words *'Interdimensional Bridge Construction Honorary Member'* on it. "What's this!?"

The Finder smiled and waved his hands about helplessly. "Just a little sorry gift."

"I gave you my heart and you gave me this?"

“I’m sorry,” The Finder continued. “I’ll book more sessions if you like. How about I pay you double for your trouble?”

“Like some kind of eye candy? You can just pay for my time and leave!”

“It’s not like that!” The Finder said grasping for anything helpful.

Breaking Wave’s cool exterior broke down completely. Throwing his hands in the air and realising there was no other choice, he flung himself into a racing charge. Passing The Finder, he flung God out the way, pushed The Digger from the driver’s seat, sat himself down on the rig and unleashed the full devastating fury of the Magnetar outwards from the wormhole’s entrance. The beam thickened, drawing power from every last element inside the devilish star-drive.

“If I can’t have you, I’ll rip this universe in half!”

The unstoppable beam of light bore through the universe like an earthworm on concentrated adrenaline, pulverising planets, butchering galaxies and crushing entire cosmic planes of existence. Through the fabric wall to the next universe it burst, breaking through a second universal wall… a third, a fourth. Multiple realities shattered. Life throughout a trillion star-systems ended in the blink of a celestial eye… Into the next universe it cored; a billion miles onwards, Pux 4b sat idly, the Cathedral Ship with its fleet of troop carriers in high orbit.

“I’m just saying,” Overlord Dave carried on, “that The Pickler is far superior to any hero you’ll find anywhere.”

“Now, that’s simply not true,” argued The Traveller.

“Bhaa!” Bernard announced worriedly.

“Aye,” Grog nodded, “I can hear it too.”

Pux 4b stood no chance. Again, the beam passed through its tiny mantel and thin core, hitting the mysterious bomb Farmer Collins had made in his hazy state. The explosion of the planetoid’s core doubled the frenzied chaos pouring from the bomb’s devolution riggings.

“Ah!” Farmer Collins remembered at last, “that’s what it does. Devolve stuff…”

“What?”

Pux 4b’s land mass and small oceans belted outwards, destroying the small home world decimating its entirety, which came as a relieving moment for Mrs Samson as her husband had just started his rendition of

‘Can You Smell a Bodwhiff in Here’. The explosion rocked the Cathedral Ship tossing it like a giant demon tired of religious views. A shockwave of pure devolution energy expanded in all directions. Anything it came into contact with it threw backwards in its own evolutionary time scale. Bernard, as the quickest, sharpest and fluffiest of all omnipotent animals, encased Grog and himself in a bubble of none-space, protecting them both from the blast. The others, however, were not so lucky.

Overlord Dave was reduced to a small toddler; still dictatorial though, as most toddlers are. Bol shrank to a former organism in his ancestry chain; angry, cuddly, he appeared like a koala bear woken from a short nap. Men and women from every deck morphed into chimps and Neanderthals.

The energetic distortion wrapped around everything. Mark sat on the chair, screaming absurdities at The Traveller who felt the omnipotence drain from him like a dream after waking up. He could feel nothing, except the self-loathing love that a tour guide feels at the end of a busy day.

And yet the shockwave continued.

On every planet, in every solar system, in every galaxy, in every universe, beings of all kinds began to change and regress backwards in time. Entire civilisations were struck by the shockwave of time reversal. Multi-planetary peoples from everywhere were abruptly thrown backwards by a few million years. The various colonies of nomadic space giants fizzed into run-of-the-mill twelve-foot-tall behemoths and every omnipotent being that resided within the confines of the multiverse, whether on holiday or not, was reduced to a university level physics teacher.

Car alarms raged on within the wormhole as God watched Champ’N’Bubbly and his entire entourage devolve into former life forms only able to rhyme three-letter words. Breaking Wave wobbled on the ground as a gelatinous pool imbedded with relaxing and calming thoughts.

“What happened?” asked The Finder. His mind, once a complex network of memorised maps of the multiverse, now a vast empty space.

God hesitated, tried to materialise a pint in his hands, failed, and felt devastation run through his now mortal being.

"Nooooo!"

Apart from Bernard and Grog, every sentient, living, breathing being in each corner of the discount multiverse now faced the exact same fate, all, except one.

Norman frowned as he tried to get to grips with it, nothing written in *Terror Forming for Beginners* made sense to him. He'd only picked it up from the shelf due to its fancy cover, pretty pictures and fun-looking cover font.

"What does, 'after reassembling the genesis planet's primordial elements, and conversing with all theories, in regard to biological outputs and variables, it's now time to seed the ground with hydrogenic foundations' mean?" he murmured. It all seemed rather confusing to Norman.

The look of puzzlement on his face only deepened when he saw the energetic shockwave race down towards him flinging books from their shelves. Norman closed his eyes and braced.

The Hand of Grog

After a combined existence of thirty-one billon years, from its creation to its reset to present day, the multiverse had arguably in its own right become a sentient living organism. Every race, culture, civilisation and being that'd transcended to a higher form had added to this fact, and as a whole, made the multiverse the hive it is.

Though trouble dawned…

The devolving blast spread through each and every universe, and as such, sentient life in its trillions regressed bringing the multiverse to its knees. Yet through this fall came a hero.

A hero unlike any other before him.

The blinding light that'd enveloped the ship's decks and halls faded; the unsettling ringing that left Grog disorientated seemed to die down as his senses rose to their feet again. All about him, small creatures unknown to him plodded innocently here and there, all similar except for a tiny angry looking baby draped in Overlord Dave's clothes.

Grog shook off the last of whatever had hit him, noticing Bernard talking furiously to a bald man with a backpack strapped round his waist. The Traveller waved his hands in the air, shrugged repeatedly, trying to explain to Bernard that it didn't matter how loud he bleeped, he no longer understood him.

"Yes. No! I've no idea!" The Traveller said flatly.

"What happened?" Grog asked holding his head in agony.

"Don't ask me," replied The Traveller. "Seconds ago, I could tell you the square root of infinity, now I can only tell you the best place to get a sports massage. Something terrible has happened… I can't think straight!"

For the first time, in a while of course, since the last time something bad and shocking had happened, The Traveller genuinely panicked, pulling his rucksack from his shoulder and riffling through it looking for something that might aid in his recollection. There was something that he knew and there was something that he'd forgotten — in fact it was a lot of things he'd forgotten, or at least something that had been taken away.

The Digger, who knew everything there was to know about everything, had only the knowledge of a well-seasoned digger driver. So too The Fixer, who could now easily replace the spark plugs on say, a standard 1954 Austin A40, yet would be lost when sewing space fabric together. The Finder, now an anorak-wearing beach-wandering metal detector enthusiast, and The Traveller an experienced tour guide. As it transpired, for those beings living in the multiverse that came from the Continuum itself, they were now simple, basic, and un-omnipotent.

God himself had been transformed from the creator of it all, to a man holding a can of beer whom you wouldn't be surprised to see shouting at pigeons.

"Bhaa!" Bernard said with a slight hint of anxiety.

"Aye!" Grog replied, "I'd forgotten about the Samsons! Well... Turned out he did die first after all."

"Bhaa!"

"Ah, come on. It's a little funny. Think about it, we stopped The Last Orders from taking Pux, and probably saved the universe from enslavement too."

"Bhaa..."

"Multiverse?

"If the multiverse has been totalled," The Traveller said worriedly, "then... then..."

"Then what?" Grog asked.

"Then... um... I don't really know" The Traveller replied curiously. "Now then" he continued, looking about him. "Mark?"

"What have you done!" Mark said angrily. "And why can't I do anything any more?" Mark was indeed angry. Angry and confused, and without admitting it, a little scared too, and as such, raced out of the interrogation room arms flailing dramatically in the air.

"What about Farmer Collins?" Grog asked, "surely not him too?"

"Listen," said The Traveller. "I don't know who you are, but Bernard seems to like you. You need to understand, before all this I could've told you exactly what happened, but because of what happened, happened, I now can't tell you, except that things are bad, very, very bad. Now I have no idea of anything, except that the B&B in Greater Farashy on planet Sprax, has free breakfast buglets and universally enjoyed side orders of pang-chinx… And I have no idea what that means!"

"Maybe you need to calm down?"

"How can I?" The Traveller said worriedly. "All I can think of is facts about landmarks, train time schedules and planned bus routes!"

First there was a clang, then a ping, which abruptly turned into a bong. A loud crashing metallic sound such as a great orchestra would conduct rattled the walls of the Cathedral Ship, rising like an earthquake's tremble. A deep warbling climbed till ears were covered and panic stations were helmed, and then, just as suddenly as it came, the tremor vanished, leaving only a tiny glimmering portal, like a crease in time, floating silently in front of Bernard, Grog and The Traveller.

"What's that?" Grog asked, pointing.

"I don't know," replied The Traveller obviously. "But the House of Twelve Drunks is the biggest pub in—"

"Okay, all right!" Grog said holding a hand up, "save me the headache."

From within the tear, a silhouette appeared, a familiar outline that The Traveller had once known. The shape of a man that he'd been quite close to, joined with and travelled the multiverse with, yet was it a man? Or was it…

"Norman," The Traveller said happily. "It's Norman!"

And yes, indeed it was.

Yet Norman had become something else, something new, and dare I say it without sounding too clichéd, somewhat improved. He held himself taller than before, somehow more upright; his posture had left behind the curved and slouching village-idiot stance of old; his facial expression had grown and surpassed the moronic, each and every part of him had become *Norman*! And Norman, it would be said with a certain amount of reservation, ceased to exist.

"Yes… it is I. Norman."

"Norman," said The Traveller, "I can honestly say it's good to see you!" Where have you been? What are you doing here and—"

Norman did not need The Traveller's questions; he muted his words with a single flick of his finger.

Norman turned to Bernard and smiled. "Bernard… you and Grog must come with me."

"Hey…" Grog said stepping back, "I'm quite happy here, thanks pal."

"There's nothing to fear," Norman said calmly. "You. Me. Bernard. We are the only three beings left undamaged in existence."

"Bhaa?" Bernard asked sheepishly.

"Yes," replied Norman, "there is much to discuss. It seems that the fate of the entire multiverse now rests upon us… again. I mean, this is nothing like when The Fungal Empire began taking over, or that time when The Cosmic, or The Explorer were a little bit revolutionary. You know," Norman continued openly, "this is actually quite serious, really.

"Anyway" Norman coughed and said mystically, "you must come with me."

"Aye, you said that already."

"Right, sorry. Can you come with me then?"

Grog nodded reluctantly and picked up Overlord Dave.

"Ah, I'm afraid he'll have to stay here," Norman said.

"You can't just leave a baby on its own," Grog argued. "I mean sure, it's a barbaric baby, a killer and enslaver of planets… but look how cute and tiny his feet are."

"Bhaa!" Bernard said flatly.

"Of course I know there's bigger things going on," Grog said defensively, "excuse me for trying…"

Overlord Dave was set down with a rattle in his hand next to baby Bol and surrounded by a high wall of sofa cushions for protection, as Norman led Bernard and Grog to the only place where he knew they would be safe.

"Goo blahh whaa blaa!" Overlord Dave shouted at Bol; he would rule the cushion castle with an iron fist.

There was simply nothing. Not even empty space. At least with the spaces between planets and galaxies, the vacuum of the cosmic golf, there are blips and spots of energy popping in and out of existence, yet here, wherever 'here' was, there was just nothing, it was devoid of nothing.

Grog gazed upwards at the vast expanding emptiness of it all, and said, "What's that then?"

"That," Norman replied, meeting Grog's gaze, "is the time stream."

The Continuum itself. The reason for everything that had been, was, would be and may ever be, spanning out like a giant endless cylinder above them. It was where God and the rest of his civilisation had called home forever, and not just 'forever' as in a long period, literally forever. Since always. A million years ago and ten-billions of years in the future at the same time. The Continuum was everything.

"And here we are," Norman smiled, "existing outside of the time stream."

"Um..." Grog said scratching his head, "is it safe?"

"Existing outside the time stream?"

"...Yeah."

Norman thought about this and nodded. "Perfectly safe. Realistically, we neither exist or do not exist, we are simply here, and not here. The Continuum is everything that has been and will be, yet we are a little bit extra."

"Right," Grog said emptily, "clears that up nicely."

"Bhaa?" Bernard asked, and rightly so.

"A good question," Norman replied, "and one that needed asking. As far as I'm aware, the shockwave rampaged through everything in the multiverse, devolving as it went. The Continuum seems undamaged." Norman pondered and continued. "Regarding myself, I didn't actually evolve from something. I began as nothing, a lump of clay, then with the help of a black hole, I was a man, falling deeper into the multiverse."

Norman clasped his chin and paced up and down as thoughts and complex imagery manifested in his mind.

"The shockwave had a strange and unexpected effect on me, evolving me past any known state of mind."

And this was true.

Bernard was indeed an omnipotent being; thought alone could bring about the creation of whatever he desired, yet Norman, now, was what you may consider to be a god's God. He was life itself, the meaning for it all. The multiverse lived in his veins; the time stream sparked in his neurons. He was more than omnipotent, he was, technically, the next step in a deity's evolution.

"Great," Grog said slapping his hands together, "so you can just fix everything with a snap of your fingers, and we'll be on our way."

"If only it were that easy. You see, yes, I could just bring everything back to how it was, or at least how it should be, but…"

"Bhaa…"

"Exactly. Nothing about the multiverse is how things should be. On a basic level, it's a broken product. One that should be shelved."

"Shelved?"

"Yes," Norman said, "shelved. Put to rest. Destroyed."

"You can't destroy it!" Grog said angrily. "It's everything! It's where life lives, trillions of beings, countless bridges that haven't been slept under."

"Far beyond trillions," Norman said. "Don't see me as a monster, Grog. But it can't go on existing."

"I won't allow it."

"There's nothing you can do…"

"Maybe nothing I can do, but I'm sure you can do plenty!"

"I can do everything and more," Norman replied. It was a strange and new feeling for Norman. Not once did he accidentally spit or trip over his own words when he talked.

"So, do something then!" Grog shouted.

Above them, the pulsing time stream glowed, it's physicality only existing due to Norman's very existence. "If I could not be here, looking up at it, as we are, it would not have any definitive shape."

"Brilliant," Grog said flatly.

"Perhaps there is something," mused Norman, "a small chance that we could take, to try to bring things to a close resolve."

"Bhaa?"

"Exactly… you see." Norman pointed further down the time stream. On the horizon, a branch of sorts divided from the main root of it all; this could only be one thing.

"And that is?"

"This small branch is the multiverse," Norman said.

"It's not that big, is it?"

"And how big do you think an hour is? A few inches? As far as time's concerned, a second and a year can both fit into a small glass of water."

Grog looked up at the small secondary time stream; it was thinner than the main flow, yet it consisted of what looked like small chaotic flashes of electricity popping from within its frantic motion. Norman paced back and forth rambling on about quantum physics, chaos theory, probable outcomes and chocolate bars. He told Grog that it would be very tricky — tricky being the lightest of all words that could be used; he'd thought about saying insurmountable, preposterous and impossible, yet thought against it as Grog seemed like a very friendly, yet simple, troll.

"You could also say inexecutable?" Grog added. "I'm not a simpleton, you know."

"I'm sorry."

"...It's quite all right... carry on."

Carrying on...

Norman ventured further, explaining to Grog that they could not simply flash things back to as they were. Bernard nodded understanding it all very well as was to be expected. They would, as Norman continued, essentially operate on the new time stream branch. Much like an open cut, or a complex heart transplant, they would join the time stream at a certain point, change small parts that must be changed and pray to God — whoever that might be now — that the new third time stream branch that would be created would be right and perfect.

"So, you're saying we'll time travel and fix things?" Grog said fairly unimpressed.

"Um..." replied Norman. "I guess you could say it's time travel; we will be going back in time, but we're not really travelling anywhere. By definition we would need some sort of vehicle or machine to 'travel' with, and as you can see, we're simply jumping in and out of the time stream."

"Yeah," Grog said, "simply. It's all so simple... like getting some milk from the shops. Just popping out for a bit."

"Bhaa!"

"I'm not being sarcastic!"

“That’s all right then,” said Norman innocently.

“So?” Grog continued, holding his chin in a pondering manner. “Where’s the best place to change time from? Maybe just before the explosion?”

“Perhaps a little further back than that,” Norman suggested. “We want to be sure that not only does the devolution damage not happen in this new time stream, but we need to be completely sure that it can never happen.”

“And how can we do that?”

Bernard came to Grog’s side, already visualising what had to be done; a face only a troll could truly understand looked up at him…

“Bhaa,” Bernard said having never really taken anyone’s life before.

Grog frowned. He knew that it had to be done. For all the goodness, well-meant and kind things Farmer Collins had done and said, Grog understood that if this dreadful situation were to be bypassed, Farmer Collins would have to be taken out the picture. Dispatched. Extirpated. Expunged…

“It means killed,” Norman said.

“I know what it means!” shouted Grog.

“…Sorry…”

Five hundred pairs of eyes lit up the mist-covered ground of the back fields. The moon high in the clear dark sky, the air cold, but not too cold; it wasn’t the sort of night where you’d have to put on an extra jumper, not by a long shot, it was simply a little chilly. Regardless… Farmer Collins made his final sweep of his rearmost field on his tractor, made his way past the small pond by the wheat and potato crops, and finally drove by the high electrified fence that surrounded his prized ‘corn’. His personal crop brought in most of Butt Trollop’s income. Amazing really when one realised that the entire operation was run strictly by himself and Mrs Samson; her husband hadn’t the mind nor the lungs to guide such activities.

His sheep were also an award-winning flock, having beaten off rivals such as the Bodwhiff Sheep Curling team of 86’, and the Tumbly Crust Woolly Wanderers, who, before Farmer Collins became team manager, had won every cup game for thirty years.

Farmer Collins was indeed a staple of the community, a man whom many saw as wise, worldly, perhaps even an extremely good judge of character. His input into the village could never be ignored, nor could it ever be taken away. In fact, the word was, down in the happy clean streets of Butts Trollop, it had been the farmer himself who had put the village on the map.

"I had lots of maps before Farmer Collins came on the scene," Grog said, "and Butts Trollop had always been there."

"I mean in a kind of meaningful way. Like before it was just a village, now it's a nice popular village."

"Bhaa!"

"Yeah, you mean wealthy."

"Perhaps," agreed Norman.

"Look," Grog said lowering himself down behind the rolled-up haystack. By the hedge side, against the shadowy gully that ran the field's length, they watched as two shady looking individuals lurked in the night's darkness. Norman could barely see what they were doing — of course, really, he *could* see everything, obviously he could see, hear, smell and taste everything that was happening right this second, he was essentially the god of all gods, but just for atmosphere and the validity of the story, for now he struggled to see as Grog and Bernard sneaked their way along the electric fence, removed the outer casing from the fuse box, snipped the wires and made off with half a tonne of Trollop Kush.

Not to smoke, you understand, this isn't that kind of story. It was more a kind of fraternity type thing. A plan, or prank, if you will.

"Aye," Grog said shaking his head watching himself place the wire cutters back in his pocket and scamper off towards his bridge in the dead of night. "I completely forgot we did that."

"Bhaa!"

"No bloody way was it my idea! You sell yourself as such an innocent sheep."

"Bhaa!"

"Right," Norman said making a move from behind the hay bale. "We go and do the deed."

"What? Right now?"

"Yeah" Norman replied blankly. "Right now. The sooner the better."

"I thought you said time, no matter the scale, is all the same."

"So?"

"Couldn't we just do it in a bit? Like tomorrow? Or maybe the day after?"

"Bhaa?"

"I'm not having second thoughts!" Grog told Bernard defensively. "I mean… I don't know. It just seems wrong. Farmer Collins was the only one out the lot of them that I actually liked. We can't kill him to save a few people…"

"We'd be saving the entire multiverse," Norman pointed out.

"Even so… I liked him."

For whatever reason, those three words seemed to hit some deeply buried archaic root, down inside Norman's chest somewhere. He remembered how The Traveller, who had become one of his closest friends, had transformed many a life form into plants and other fauna types, just as he had started to like them too. He fully understood now the meaning of relativity. For Norman, time fluctuations and probable outcomes of infinite time streams may be just like colouring a kid's menu at a Carvery, but for Grog, his complexity came from taking the life of a man that he had come to… tolerate I guess, on some level.

"Okay," Norman huffed, "perhaps, maybe, we don't have to kill him. Maybe we just, I don't know, find his notebook with the plans for this bomb and change a few numbers round. Say, instead of devolving everything, it makes everyone enjoy country music for an hour."

"Can we do that by changing a number?"

"Yeah. I can do whatever I want."

"And you're sure he's got a notebook with sketches and plans and stuff? It's just that I never saw one with him."

Norman looked at the entirety of Farmer Collins' farm, swept his gaze over every brick, doorway and wall, searching for a notebook; like a doctor who needed to X-ray a former patient, fearing they'd dropped their favourite pen during a gastric bypass operation.

"Anything?" Grog asked.

"Yeah, I think so. There's a small book covered in glitter and cut-out paper cows and horses, stashed in a wall safe."

"Bhaa!" Bernard bleeped. He closed his eyes, and whoosh, the book lay fizzing momentarily in Grog's palm.

"Bhaa..."

"Maybe he just prefers cows and horses, Bernard," Grog said kindly. He began to flick through Farmer Collins' notebook. It was like opening a writer's book of unused ideas that had been scribbled frantically down at three o'clock in the morning when great story points came in dreamlike fashion. Half were barely readable, the other half a mix of fantastic food mixes and weapon designs.

"Anything good?" asked Norman curiously.

"Aye," Grog said, "there's this." He showed Norman and Bernard one specific page. "You wouldn't've thought chocolate finger sandwiches were any good, but he gave it five stars."

Norman nodded and mentally jotted that down. "Anything about the bomb?"

"Hold on..." Grog passed up the opportunity to mentally remember some of the really good recipes that stood out and carried onwards deeper into the hazy rambling of a corn-fed farmer. "Here we are. The Devolution Bomb."

"Right," said Norman. "Let's have a look."

The mathematics behind the riggings seemed quite basic and easy to grasp, that being said, it was clear to him that Farmer Collins somehow was able to unlock some hidden intelligence buried deep inside his mind when conducting himself in a way that would be seen as most improper. Norman drew a pen into reality, cunningly changed a 1 to a 7, and gave the notebook back to Grog. "All done."

"Is that really it?"

"What did you expect?"

Grog shrugged. "I'm not really too sure. Something a little more, dramatic, I guess?"

"...Sorry..."

Norman flexed his brainpower after Bernard had returned the book and pulled them all from the time stream back into the safety of the empty nothingness, realigned himself, Bernard and Grog with a time not two weeks after the explosion had happened, and threw himself back into the multiverse.

“Is it me,” Grog said suspiciously, “but does this all look a little wrong to you?”

“Bhaa!” Bernard agreed apprehensively. They stood where Pux 4b once lay, yet space as they had known it was far from anything familiar. The Cathedral Ship sailed by, flags and banners presenting The Last Orders motif moved little in the vacuum of space. All around them a hive of unstoppable activity seemed to race on. Norman gulped and knew within the time it takes to realise that that bottom burp you so readily expelled had been so much more in hiding. His mind’s eye tore through the local universe, ventured through the now many finished interdimensional bridges that Champ’N’Bubbly had helped finalise, and saw only flags and banners proclaiming the dictatorial standing of The Last Order.

“They managed to take over multiple universes already,” Norman said. “We failed.”

“Bhaa!”

“Surely, we can try again?” Grog asked.

“We can try an infinite number of times, though, I must stress, doing so will create an infinite number of time streams. A result that would completely disrupt the nature of things and how they should be. Potentially it could cause a total onset of carnage, breaking all the laws of physics on every dimensional plain. We could bring about the end of time itself, for without time, creation has no starting point, no reference to begin from. Every new-born time stream would mean going back, time and time again, fixing and correcting our wrongs, making right what had been damaged by our very meddling in the first place! We would be ordered with an endless life of cleaning our mistakes; till death took you, Grog, you would be a slave to the time streams we created!”

“Really?” Grog said wide-eyed and panicked.

“Naaaah…” Norman replied smiling. “Only joking. Come on… I know where to try next.”

“Bhaa!”

God stumbled into the shop, drunkenly of course, The Shop Keeper was standing happily in the back room, rummaging through some lost products he’d been saving for such an occasion.

"Aha!" he said and presented God with a rolled-up paper. His face as excited as a toddler when finding one last fizzy sweet buried in the corner of the sticky innards of a sweet packet.

"Please, do me a favour, and sober yourself up a little," he asked God kindly.

God, never being one to take orders on the whole, brought an Irish coffee into existence and drained the last blurry cocktail from his veins ready for the new caffeine-fuelled mixture.

"Thank you," The Shop Keeper said.

"No worries."

"Now," he continued, rolling out the paper upon the back-room's desk. "I have here something that you may find interesting. Something that may give you some zest once more."

"Plans for a new drink, is it?"

"...Far from it!" The Shop Keeper said a little insulted. "Though they are blueprints. Blueprints, that is, to an interdimensional bridge, from one universe to another..."

"Aye," Grog said standing outside the new time stream watching as the events unfolded. "We've seen this before. I thought the idea was to stop it from happening?"

"It is," Norman replied. "Stop the devolution of everything, and if possible, stop The Last Orders from taking over. The thing is, we don't want to change lots of things, if we can help it, that is."

"Bhaa?"

"Correct," Norman said. "I've changed the location of the bridge to somewhere in the Carnival Supercluster. The supercluster is in a distant region of space, in this specific universe that God had already built the bridge in the previous time stream, yet not yet in this one."

"Right," Grog said again feeling completely lost.

"We'll jump forwards a little bit, say to when Champ'N'Bubbly is gathering his equipment from the construction planet of Bildorup. It'll be right next to the new construction site."

"Bhaa," agreed Bernard.

"Right," agreed Grog. Again, only out of politeness.

"...Here we go..."

Norman recalled many years ago how he had suffered from travel sickness when he and The Traveller were racing across existence together; the blurring of stars and galaxies as they whooshed by had a sickening effect on his bowels, but now, quite frankly, he relished any chance to zoom from one space to another at the speed of thought. It was a delight knowing that he had full control over everything.

Grog, on the other hand, had never reached such speeds; he had always maintained a perfectly good walking pace, or, if he was really pushed, he would reluctantly force himself into a kind of monstrous jogging movement.

"Bhaa?"

"Ahh…" Grog mumbled holding his gut. They had travelled a million light years in the time it took Overlord Dave to end the lives of seventeen maids.

"I'm okay" he grumbled again, "could do with some milk though."

"No time for that," Norman replied placing a cap over Grog's oversized head, "we're here."

Grog stood up straight, tidied his Bildorup staff uniform that Bernard had issued him on the flight over, and welcomed the next customer heading his way inside the frantic tangle of bodies moving here and there in the Bildorup warehouse.

"Excuse me?" a vis-vest-wearing multi-armed being said, flicking through the company catalogue. "Do you do any discounts on working gloves?"

"This is a builder's yard, not a high street retailer."

"I mean have you got any sales going on?"

"Look pal," Grog said feeling his bowels twirl in his midsection, still unsettled from the journey. "If it's in the catalogue, I've got it. If it's not there, don't bother asking."

"Okay," replied the being, "it's just that this catalogue is from last month, it's got a buy-one-get-one-free deal on pairs of gloves; the new catalogue doesn't have that deal… so are you still running it?"

Grog huffed. What could only be described as a show of professional hostility echoed throughout the giant warehouse, up past the high stalls of measured wood planks, past the endless boxes of taps and joints and through to the outside garden pots and water features.

"That may have been a little too much?" Norman quizzed watching as the being wobbled off towards the exit. "I mean, you made him cry, Grog."

"Well... what do you expect? Ask silly questions, get angry answers."

Outside the largest of all the builders' yards on Bildorup, the first traffic management vehicles stopped in the car park. The sound of 'Ain't nothin' But a Bubbly Thang' came from the custom-fitted speakers. Champ'N'Bubbly and The Finder were in deep conversation as they came striding through the main entrance, followed by a good-sized group of entourages; all dressed in bright yellow clothes, hard hats and safety boots.

"And all I have to do is name drop you and they'd do whatever I wanted?" asked The Finder wide-eyed, hearing tales of fantasies given by Rap-verse concubines that would've been illegal in fifty-five other universes.

"Of course," replied Champ'N'Bubbly.

"Well, I may have to pay them a visit at some point."

"I thought you had a girlfriend, old boy?" Champ'N'Bubbly whispered, "or was she just a guile?"

The Finder shrugged. "She's about as real as Champ'N'Bubbly is," he smirked.

"Ah..." he whispered under his breath, "any benefits though?"

The Finder laughed. "Last time I said I was looking for someone to date, God set me up with a Fatalian Battle She-Hound. She thought that serving me the drained blood of her enemies inside the skull of her last kill was romantic."

"Good heavens..."

"...Yep. She didn't even put one of those tiny cocktail umbrellas on the side."

"Modern women!" Champ'N'Bubbly replied. "There was a time when courting a fair lady was like a game of chess. Back and forth, the understanding and mutual agreement that you were hers and she was yours. Now, well, now you can't even date a girl without having to bring your own cocktail umbrella."

"It's madness," said The Finder.

"Madness!"

Grog leant against the customer service desk as naturally as possible — stiff, upright yet somehow slouching — and made himself as approachable as he could.

"Hello" he said bluntly.

"Wad up," replied Champ'N'Bubbly. "We looking for some equipment to manage traffic."

"Yes. Traffic management equipment, in fact," added The Finder. "Signs, antimatter sandbags, spatial cones. Things like that."

"Afraid we're all out of stock."

"We'll take quantum spec, if you have it?"

"All gone."

"Thermodynamic spec?"

"The last one's just left."

"Rolls of red tape, then?"

"All out."

"Well, what *do* you have?" asked The Finder a little flustered.

"Nothing for you!"

Grog's manner was somewhat unconvincing, even Norman thought he was a little rude.

"Look," said The Finder emptily. "These plans have been up for quite a while now. I know that there's a lot of you that have certain reservations about opening up bridges to other universes, but this work will be going ahead."

"Excuse me?" asked Grog, a little off guard.

"You've had plenty of time to voice your opinions. Especially now, while the anti-bridge marches are going on. Right outside, too."

"Yeah," Champ'N'Bubbly agreed. "You can't stand in the way of progress."

From the back room behind Grog came Bernard in an equally fetching Bildorup staff uniform, with matching cap, and stood on his hind legs resting on the till side. "Bhaaa..."

The Finder frowned, thought back to a time he'd very nearly forgotten and said, "It's Bernard, isn't it?"

"Bhaaa!" he replied.

"Well, well. Last time I saw you, you were trimming God's back garden. We all wondered where you'd gotten too. Did I hear that you, Bud and Massie the cow were knee-deep in Gwallt jungle mud stealing secret recipes for the Smut Brothers?"

Grog turned and gave Bernard a disbelieving look; a look that carried with it the sad admission that even though Grog had been friends with Bernard for years, Bernard was indeed, as far as Grog knew, thousands of years old, and Grog really only knew a small part of his life.

"You never told me about that," Grog said, a little heartbroken.

"Bhaa," Bernard replied sensitively.

"Aye… but still. I'd tell you if I'd stole secret recipes."

"I'm sorry if I got in the middle of something?" asked The Finder.

"Bhaa."

"I guess there's a million other things that you've done and not told me about," Grog continued emptily. "Probably a handful of other cattle-based friends you've got that you've enjoyed antics with."

"Bhaa!" Bernard said sharply. Even without a translator, the cut of his voice made it obvious that 'Not now!' was the response.

"Bhaa?" he asked turning to The Finder.

"Yes, sorry," The Finder replied opening the catalogue in his hands, "we just need these bits. A billion cones, here's a list of signs we're after."

Bernard left the till and escorted The Finder and Champ'N'Bubbly to a transport bay where a few small, motorised vehicles sat patiently waiting to become helpful. They hopped on one and disappeared out of sight, turning down aisle eighty-four, Traffic Management Equipment. Not once did Bernard look back, and Grog, standing lonesome at the front desk, felt like he'd done something wrong.

"What was that all about?" Norman asked coming to his side.

"Nothing," Grog replied a little blue.

"We can't let these things happen. We need to fix the time stream, not get jealous or upset. Do you understand?"

"I said it was nothing!"

"Okay," Norman replied calmly, "it was nothing. Okay. We we're only here to reinforce changes that we already made. Hopefully changing the location of the bridge will be enough."

Grog rubbed his nose with the back of his hand clearing his sheepish thoughts.

"Shall we go then? Back to the present?"

"Let's wait for Bernard first," replied Norman, and then asked, "would it be worth stopping off somewhere on the way for a bottle of something and a packet of biscuits?"

"Excuse me?"

The present was much the same. And although changes had been made, the location of the new bridge relocated and for all the sabotage that Bernard attempted on the equipment he sold to Champ'N'Bubbly and The Finder, they arrived in the new time stream's future with everything just as it had been.

The devastating devolvement had spread throughout the multiverse once more like daytime TV; every corner of existence was now inhabited by prehistoric beings.

Norman's huge mind concluded that, even though the future is not set, and destiny on the whole is marginally unscripted, it appeared that wherever the bridge was to be built, and however many defective cones and leaking antimatter sandbags there were, Breaking Wave was always going to lose his cool, take control of the rig and fire its beam of unstoppable might outwardly towards Pux 4b, always finding the target and always devolving the cosmos.

"We've created three new time streams now," Norman pointed out standing under the mesmerising glow of each as they flowed like giant white neon lights, hanging in the nothingness that was.

"You could be right then," Grog said flatly. "We could be spending an eternity fixing our wrongs."

"Bhaa?" Bernard asked curiously.

Norman shook his head. "We can't just go and kill The Shop Keeper. Firstly, it's a bit naughty, and secondly, I don't know how. He's omnipotent."

Grog coughed and delved into a small plastic bag. He handed Bernard a bottle of Apple Sours and a packet of chocolates.

"Here," he said to Bernard, "I got you these. As a kind of sorry."

"Bhaa?"

"It's a hemp-based bag," Grog said angrily. "I'm trying to say sorry here. Is the bag's material really that important?"

"Bhaa!"

"He's right," Norman said, "plastic gets everywhere. Bloody stuff takes a lifetime to vanish."

"Have you been paid to say that?" Grog quizzed.

"No," Norman replied, "but I'd feel bad if I didn't say something. Going back and changing the way it was originally made would save so many poor seagulls and turtles."

"Bhaa," Bernard said having been hit head on by an epiphany. "Bhaa!"

"Bhaa?" Grog replied suspiciously.

"Bhaa!"

"He's on to something" Norman added.

"Bhaa!" Bernard said loudly.

Grog nodded. "Aye, okay. And you know for sure that his favourite villain is The Pickler?"

"Bhaa!"

Norman smiled. It was a crazy plan, a long-shot plan. The kind of plan that blockbuster movies that break records on their opening weekends are made of. If anything, Norman thought, it could do with a little bit more insanity injected into it.

"Best not though, aye?" Grog said cautiously. "I mean, if we pull it off, surely everything will change."

"Most definitely," Norman replied happily, "so, will it be both of you? Or just one at a time?"

About the same time God landed at the small village hall where his next alcohol-fuelled help group was about to start, four thousand miles away in the capital city of Ultima, three more alien beings landed on the superhero-populated planet of Alpha Prime.

The rain came down something magnificent, every thick bulbous raindrop shone the moon's midnight light as it poked through the darkening clouds high above the city skyline. Puddles formed on every street corner with dwarf-like Amazonian rivers flowing into the nearest drainage route. The ever-awakening night life of Ultima bellowed with the energy of familiar famous cities such as New York, Paris and Sheffield. On every corner, crooks were dealing half-price bottled 'his and hers weakness' lotions to heartbroken villains that'd run short on luck in recent times. Elderly women screamed from scattered open windows out into the night asking "Where are you Mr Marvellous? Me cat's gotten out again!"

Yet not all was as it seemed.

A shadowy figure hopped from rooftop to rooftop, silent and agile, spinning round drainpipes on the side of buildings, leaping and diving high above the busy streets. His movements had meaning, his eyes set upon the tartan blur that whooshed through the back alleys and side roads, tore up the side of business blocks and flats. Blonk Jackson had tracked down his rival all the way from the highland hills of Banny'Agoon, the central hub of the Celtic Mafia.

"The Celtic Mafia?" Grog questioned. "Thought this place was meant to be more serious?"

"Quiet!" Norman whispered sharply, "just listen…"

Many years before, Blonk Jackson had served his city in the only way he'd known how: becoming a sales rep for a handful of ladies that worked strictly at night. He had gained a wide reputation for cheap prices for services that went above and beyond. A diamond-encrusted cane and purple fur coat his uniform, his reign at the top was short-lived.

Big Daddy, a ruthless mobster that ran the cut-throat city of Rascall, had made it his duty to run Blonk Jackson out of town. One ill-fated night, when Blonk Jackson's private bodyguards were busy dealing with some well-placed distractive groupies, a single shot was fired from a moving car. Blonk Jackson lay trembling in the street, hand grasping his chest, his life literally in his hand. With only one choice in front of him, Blonk Jackson made his way to the snowy mountains of Yettah, where for the next six years he trained in the art of Kung Fu under the watchful eyes of nameless monks. There, he swore an oath to the planet itself, never again would he delve into the 'night lady sales rep' game, promising his life would only serve good, and never again straying off his true path.

"And that's his backstory, is it?" asked Grog again. "He was once a pimp, now he's a ninja?"

Norman shrugged and scanned over the leaflet once more, "I don't think you're allowed to say pimp any more? Too PC, I think."

"Jesus…"

"And yes," Norman continued, "that's his backstory. Everyone on this planet has to have one, otherwise they can't legally do superhero work. Even the Villains need to have their legal documents in order, otherwise they're not allowed to commit crime."

"Bhaa?" asked Bernard also having trouble grasping the idea.

"Look," said Norman presenting the leaflet to them both, "I'm just telling you what it says here at the back. Heroes and villains are paired up, having been matched by ability and cunningness."

"Cunningness?" laughed Grog, "and what's the test for that exactly?"

"I don't know!" Norman replied, "I'm just reading what it says here."

"Right… so come on, who's this guy matched with then? Or shall I guess? Probably a firefighter who became obsessed with sparklers, trained by Chinese firework engineers in the ancient art of Catherine Wheel."

"If only… No. Says here his nemesis is called William Angus, or Angus 500."

"Angus 500?" Grog laughed, "his enemy sounds like a Scottish motorsport."

"Apparently, what it says here, Angus 500 used to be an upcoming track star, specialising in the five hundred metre sprint…"

"Aye" Grog said patiently, "…keep going. I'm sure I'll love this."

"…Apparently, he was quite a ladies' man. So much so that at an Olympic race, the night before he'd had a room full of women, all supplied by yours truly, Blonk Jackson. It turned out that one woman attending the party was married and had gone for a bit of fun. Unfortunately, she'd been married to the man tasked with firing the starter pistol at the beginning of the race. Learning of his wife's deceit, he aimed the loaded gun at William Angus and shot him in the back. Doctors were astounded to find that not only was Angus fine, but now he could run at tremendous speeds. Soon after leaving the hospital, he vowed to take women as he pleased, running from city to city, doing anything that he thought was within his rights to do."

"Bhaa!" Bernard said.

"Aye, and I agree. The other fella's backstory was a little better. Felt more, I don't know… believable?"

"Hey," Norman said, "I don't disagree. But you need a backstory if you want to work." He carried on reading through the leaflet intently as Grog and Bernard watched from outside the time stream Blonk Jackson leaping from window awning to hanging flower garden, chasing down Angus 500 far below on the streets of Ultima.

"Says here that they've even got fan clubs and stuff. #Angus500 is trending right now."

"Trending?" Grog asked, "now you're being silly."

"Nope. He's got eighty-seven thousand followers it says here. Aww, Blonk's only got eighty-four thousand. Still, pretty close…"

Norman led the charge inwards while explaining to Grog that, even though simply killing someone might indeed be the easiest of all options, it was definitely not the right choice. If they were to simply take The Pickler out of existence completely, then the chances of a multiverse becoming vastly different to any Norman would be able to predict would be sure to pass. It would be in the best interests of all living things, Norman went on to explain, that integrating themselves into the culture of this new world, formulating connections and tracking down leads would be the best course of action. In doing so, they would ultimately have the power to directly change the direction of The Pickler regarding his ultimate goals and dreams, leading once more to the change of mood held by Overlord Dave, rendering his villainous mindset obsolete from a young age. This, in the hope that The Last Orders would go on to become a charitable organisation, perhaps aiding in the protection of maids.

Grog slammed his lumpy palm down upon the desk bell inside the Ultima Council Building's reception area to the response of a rather snotty reply.

"The bell's not for playing with!"

Bigfoot came lumbering from the coatroom carrying yesterday's paper in one hand and a steaming mug of black coffee in the other. He peered over the rims of his glasses as he sat down behind reception, pondering the answer to three down.

"Cryptoids small opposition, but not hands."

"Bigfoot," Grog said.

"Yes?" Bigfoot replied.

"You're Bigfoot?" Grog asked suspiciously, wondering if this creature was the real Bigfoot, as his size was nothing short of anticlimactic. "I thought the real Bigfoot would've been taller?"

"And what's that supposed to mean?"

"Nothing, nothing… Just, you know. Bigfoot? The name's a sign of a good-sized person. And you're…" Grog hesitated, "well, slightly above average."

Bigfoot coughed and placed the rolled-up paper upon the reception desk and shot a look at Grog. "If you must know, I'm seven foot seven exactly. Not really 'above average', is it?

"…I guess not…"

"Plus," Bigfoot continued, "I spent years on planet Earth trying my best to prove my worth as a Lumberjack, only to be run out from everywhere I lived by local idiots looking for fame. Being a council receptionist may not be a glamorous job, but at least I don't get prodded and looked at like a monster."

"I'm sorry," Grog said, knowing precisely how it felt to be unwanted. "I came from a small planetoid; no one liked me there either. It's been destroyed now of course, well, not in this reality, but I miss it. You know…"

Bigfoot stretched his arms and yawned as obviously as he could, making large gestures towards the wall clock, laying down hints as noticeable as Grog's overpowering smell. "Is that the time?"

"You know, I'm just trying to connect," Grog said. "Finding some common ground so you're not so isolated."

"Ah, thanks mate!" Bigfoot said sarcastically. "Cheers buddy! Thanks for throwing me a lifeline. Needed a win, I did!"

"…Okay calm down…"

"What do you want?" Bigfoot asked bluntly.

"Bhaa!" Bernard said.

"Aye… we need a hero licence."

"Are you two together, you and the sheep? One a villain and one a hero, or are you paired up against another two? And who's this?" he pointed at Norman. "He with you?"

"Um... yeah, we're a hero and villain respectively and he's our trainer," Grog said.

Bigfoot picked up his paper and sipped his coffee leaving to return to the coatroom again.

"Third floor... you need Legal."

Whether it was his job or not, neither Grog nor Bernard could tell, perhaps the lift was broken, the wiring out of order. Either way Grog tipped the caped flyer as he raised the elevator to floor three upon his shoulders, making a soft pinging noise as he flew to a stop.

"Thanks," Grog said stepping out into the busy corridor while a small group of identical octuplets entered the lift behind him. The lift-lifting hero kindly asked, "Going up?"

It seemed that even on a planet that's sole populous comprised Supers, the whole superhero industry was big business, however obvious that may sound. Floor three, by far, was the greediest floor in the council building, having selfishly taken all employees from every other department, dressed them in black suits, handed out briefcases and put each one of them through law school. Besides from over dramatic lead anchors on prime-time news channels, super-lawyers were the highest paid professionals on the planet.

"That Bigfoot gave me this card," Grog said turning the watermarked rectangle in his hand. On its reverse the name *Yeti Freudenberg. LLB*, was printed in fine ink, then, *Cubicle 12. Contact email — Y.Freudenberg@Ynot.SL.*

Bernard eyeballed the number 12 at the far end of the vast room; a space littered with individual cubicles, curly telephone wires weaving like nets and stacks of paper that flew into the air manically without the aid of open windows. Business cards, leaflets and even a baby with the brand name *Lawyers Vs Crimers* written in marker pen upon its forehead were handed to Grog.

"Legal advice needed?"

"The criminal life not paying as much as you thought?"

"Involved in an accident at work?"

"…Get out of my way!" Grog shouted, thrusting a crying baby into the arms of a lawyer. "This is like Butts Trollop, the day of the flower arranging contest!"

"Bhaa!"

"Aye," Grog agreed, "maybe not that bad."

They reached cubicle 12 relatively unscathed; Norman somehow had been awarded five thousand pounds for damages from that car crash he was involved in last month.

"What car crash?" asked Grog.

"I've no idea," Norman replied worriedly.

"Bhaa!"

"I'm scared!" Norman said, "open the door!"

Grog yanked the sliding cubicle side open leaving Norman and Bernard to tumble inwards in a heap of wool and worry.

"Quick!" a voice shouted, deep as thunder, wise as lightning. "Close the door!"

Grog did so.

The sudden fade of chaotic confusion dropped; a peaceful hum chimed in the air; the sound of a galloping crowed still audible somewhere off in the distance. Yeti Freudenberg, LLB, latched the sliding door with a home-made bolt, sighed and retreated to his chair. His giant feet slapped the floor with the sound of flip-flops on wet tiles.

"Yeti Freudenberg, LLB, at your service."

"At a guess," Grog said flicking a stray business card from his shoulder, "you're related to that Bigfoot fellow."

"Size as well as brains," Yeti said humbly, "is there any need for you other two?" he suggested pointing at Bernard and Norman.

"No need to be like that."

"I'll be honest with you gentlemen," Yeti went on. "I've been working here for hundreds of years now. Maybe more. I've seen my fair share of heroes and villains come through those doors; real folk that are aiming high. Sadly, the hero-villain game has changed. I can't keep up, and believe me, I'll retire soon, head back to the snowy peaks of some icy planet and live out my days happily. You boys seem nice, keen almost. You don't want an old timer like me helping you… so, *L'chaim*, and good luck…"

Norman coughed and stood to his feet; as comfortable as it was lying there upon Bernard's woolly hide, he couldn't stay there all day.

"Mr Freudenberg," Norman said.

"Please… call me Yeti."

"Mr Yeti. We're not looking for any special offers, or rewards. We simply need a licence to hero and villain legally, and we'll be on our way."

Yeti looked Norman up and down suspiciously placing his oversized and worn-down feet upon his desk. "You boys don't need the online social package?"

"Nope…"

"…Mm… how about TV advertising?"

"No thanks. Just the licence, please."

"Not even a billboard or two?"

"Not even," Norman said waving a hand. "Just the licence."

"Hold on a minute," Grog said turning to Norman. "If we're here to find The Pickler, surely, we could do with some marketing behind us? I mean, if he's the biggest villain here, we need to attract his attention somehow. Right?"

"I mean," Yeti interjected, "now, maybe, he might be the biggest villain around, but don't forget who discovered The Maniacal Clown. Yours truly. In his day he was huge. And believe me, with the right schooling and legal backing you three could become big too."

"Bhaa!"

"Just those two, actually" Norman said. "I'm just here to, um, supervise?"

"He's our trainer," Grog noted quickly. "I'm a hero and that there is my villain counterpart," he said pointing at Bernard, who, rightly so, felt a little short-changed being the second pick.

"You're a hero?" Yeti asked, "are you sure? I mean, look at me being all front and no sides, but aren't heroes meant to be more stylish and neater? No, to me you'd be a great villain, something halfway between Monster Thing and Hair-Ball XXX, just without the politeness."

"Monster Thing?" Grog asked, a little insulted.

"No offence intended," replied Yeti. "I just mean with your size, and natural atmospheric destabilising charm, villainy may be your calling. Tell me, what powers do you have?"

"A super short sense of patience."

"He's extremely strong," Norman chimed in, "and, um, he can't be hurt."

"By bullets and weapons, I take it, as his feelings seem a little easily swayed... maybe we've just found your weakness, huh?"

"Aye... maybe..." Grog replied bitterly.

"And what about you?" Yeti asked turning to Bernard. "Animals are big at the moment, real popular. With a small trim around the edges and perhaps a little weight loss you could be the next Bombus Ballistic. Superpowers, talk to me."

"Bhaa!"

"He said—" Norman started.

"...It's okay," Yeti cut in. "I've met so many sheep in my time it's a wonder I can stay awake. I understand Sheepish like I were born leaping through Easter. I'd very much like to see you in action, Bernard; if what you say is true then getting you a licence should be child's play. It's the Incredible Sulk here that worries me."

"Watch it, shorty," Grog said.

"All I'm saying is that there's plenty of villains out there that claim to be strong. A handful that can't be wounded, and a smattering that have both. Even so, it's nothing new. If you want to meet The Pickler, you'll have to stand out. A show of strength if you will. We can talk about the details when it comes, of course, for now however I think we should just concentrate on getting you boys legal. And talk about some TV screen time, billboards and an online social following."

"Sounds great," Norman said happily, having a mindset as interchangeable as drill bits.

"Bhaa!"

Shadows spanned across the dark innards of the empty steelworks. Chains hung low from metal walkways like snakes ready to ambush prey under the thick blanket of cold moonlight. It seemed that the nights in Ultima had been manufactured; you could always rely on a dazzling full moon, or a watercolour-stained sky, anything that would create the right atmosphere and tension needed to indicate that trouble was afoot. Same went for the daytime. No matter what season it was, summer or snowy winter, it was always hot, sunny and peppered with birdsong, and heroes aplenty smiling and singing bear chested… and human chested too, of course.

Yet for now, the night was definitely up to no good.

Far off in the distance, a baby started crying, followed by a cat hissing and sending glass bottles to the floor.

The steelworks on the West side of Ultima had been highlighted by the Estate Agency as 'A perfect retreat for any villain whose account and status ranked highly'. In short, other villains new to the scene had to make do with smaller, less empowering accommodation; their mum's basement, for example. The steelworks provided essential things any good, high-standing villain in the city would ever need. Easy water access with rear docks straight onto the river, a dungeon, an even deeper underground lair, double garage, fast internet speeds, a tennis court, five bathrooms and of course, a handy ready to use steel smelting plant.

It'd been on the market for an hour before it was picked up by The Pickler, way over the asking price.

"Not too shabby," Angus 500 said mooching around the forge. "Not too shabby at all!"

"Were you followed?" The Pickler asked, pacing in front of the smelting pit in contemplation. Small embers of a molten pool popped and fizzed from the open forge sending small echoes though the silent works.

"No," Angus replied. "Blonk Jackson's good, sure, but he's not quick."

"He'd best not be… things are happening as planned," The Pickler continued, "things are in motion that I had foreseen…"

"So, getting paid at some point would be nice."

"You'll get your money… as soon as I get my prize."

"You know, I don't mind villainy. I've been working steadily for a few years now, but this, if I get caught, well, it's my licence up for the chop."

"I am fully aware of how things work!"

"I hope you are because unlicensed henchmen work can cost you your livelihood. I don't want to go to jail! I'm quite happy making an honest living from villainy, so an advance would set my mind at rest..."

A small price to pay, The Pickler thought as he brought a bulging bag of money into existence by thought alone and handed it over to Angus. From the open skylight high above them Blonk Jackson stalked silently, listening to the breezy chatter and witnessing what he thought could only be magic taking place.

"Hey," Angus said, "that's a good trick. I didn't know you could do that."

"There're many things you don't know Angus, and more things you don't know about me. If that's enough to keep you happy for the time being, I need you to do something for me."

"Ah, of course... who do you want me to kill?"

"If only it were that easy," said The Pickler turning on his heel, cape swirling behind him. "There're three entities that have arrived on world, three beings that have come to find me. I need you to—"

"Kill 'em?"

"...No. I need you to—"

"Dispose of 'em?"

"No! I need you to—"

"Take out the trash," Angus guessed winking The Pickler's way. "Don't worry, it's all the same to me."

The Pickler exhaled heavily and thought as henchmen go, Angus was almost perfect. Perhaps it was his super speed that made him impatient and needing to always finish off his...

"Sentences?"

"Stop it! Just listen..."

"Sorry."

"There're three of them, and they're here in Ultima. A clay man, a troll and a sheep. The troll, you can do what you like with him, but I need the clay man alive."

"And what of the sheep?"

"Ah, Bernard. He'll be the thorn we don't need. He needs to be got rid of... but watch out. If you think me making money appear is a good trick, the sheep can do so much more. He'll be trouble."

"Any info to help me? Weaknesses?"

The cool night air fell through the open skylight high above them, from a quiet rooftop not entirely empty of heroes. Blonk Jackson never got involved with anything that went beyond the usual dealings of paired heroes and villains, yet this, scheming against off-planet alien visitors was definitely illegal and went against everything he knew to be right.

Somewhere, out there, in the zigzagging smoky skyline of Ultima, a lonely hero made his way towards three beings; being a villain is one thing, but breaking the law was totally unethical.

Brickwork flew to the ground, yet the thick wall still stood, only now a mighty gap sat in its centre as if a giant had leant down and bitten off a piece for breakfast. Behind it, ten other brick walls stood with matching bite marks, with equally matching scattered debris on the floor.

Yeti winced and felt the onslaught of a headache set in.

"Grog," he began, "we've got the warehouse for the day. We have long days on Alpha Prime, I know, but we can't spend all day doing the same thing. I'm not saying you're a klutz, but all I'm asking is for you to smash a wall down in a basic villainous manner. Oy vey, it's not hard."

"I'm smashing them down as angrily as I can!"

"Villainously, not angrily. Oy," Yeti recalled. "I trained the great Night Frog, and after that The Bug, then The Amazing Flute Boy… less said the better, yet still I managed to get something good from him. You have no charm and lack even simple 'bad guy' motives. Tell me Grog, were you walked to school by your mother?"

Grog gulped and thought back to his early years; from somewhere inside his bitter interior, a boiling heat wove to the surface.

"I'm a good troll!" he shouted at faded memories. "I'm a good troll!"

"I thought as much," Yeti agreed.

"…I didn't deserve to be left on my own on that small ball of dirt! And what was there for me? Constant joisting and prodding from village folk who thought all I wanted to do was eat farmers' children!"

"Bhaa?" Bernard pointed out.

Grog nodded. "Fair point…"

"And you took everything that they said and kept on moving," Yeti said knowingly. "It takes a lot to be that stubborn. But you must understand, whatever that was, is gone, and here now your duty is to be a bad guy. I can see it in you, Grog. Believe me, take that strength and become the troll you should've been. How many times did you get moved on? How many times did you get told you were scaring livestock and the family dog?"

Grog turned to the next fresh free-standing brick wall and saw images of lost faces. He growled. "I told you before Mrs Samson! You're married and I'm not interested!"

"...Bhaa?"

"And as for you Mr Samson... Mr Sam Samson, Mr Chairman of the village Flower Arranging Society. Mr Lah-di-dah look at my fancy suit and big house. I can tell you something, next time you come knocking asking me to be a good sport and find somewhere new to live, I'll take that tie of yours and use it to throw you six states south of Bodwhiff River you smartarse moron!"

And with that, Grog threw everything he had into his shoulder muscle, every last hateful element of anger and distaste for his previous landlords. Every second he'd ever bitten his tongue or counted to ten, every ounce of patience he'd ever summoned from the depth of his well-conditioned mindset and heaved his humungous frame forwards, sending a fist ripe with trembling fury crashing though the poor brick wall.

Yeti gave Bernard a promising look and cocked a smile. "I think we're getting somewhere..."

"I've been the butt for everyone's inadequacy," Grog stated firmly. "Trust me. Every time something bad happened in that little village, that little planet I should say, aye, it must've been me, that big smelly troll that did it... Farmer Collins misplaced two tonnes of freshly grown stock... Grog took it. The butcher's ran out of sausages... Grog ate them! Mrs Davenport fell in the duck pond again! Grog pushed her!"

"I'm very happy seeing your darker side come out at last," Yeti said.

"Bhaa," Bernard agreed smiling as much as a sheep's facial bone structure would allow.

"...Don't get me started on you." Grog pointed at Bernard resentfully. "How many times did I ask you to get me off that ruddy planet? All I wanted to do was leave!"

"Bhaa!" Bernard argued.

"You spent most nights watching *Cooking for Hooves* on catch up, you never wanted to help me!"

But Bernard indeed did want to help Grog, and in fact he had been doing so ever since the intelligent sheep came to Pux. However implausible Bernard's knowledge and foreshadowing was, his sight never went beyond a single event. He was never able to foresee his life existing beyond the devastation of Grog's home world. Yet something told him that Grog had to be kept safe. If Bernard was to end his days on Pux, then he would end it as the multiverse saw fit to end it.

"You could've told me all of this though."

"Bhaa!"

"Don't tell me you couldn't see any of this," Grog said sceptically. "You're a being of supreme power. A sheep, maybe, but you could summon a heard of belly dancing giraffe if you wanted to."

"Bhaa!" Bernard pleaded.

"Oh right... so that's it is it? A simple life with me? Weeell..." Grog said, "there you go. There I was thinking that we're friends, and all this time you've been enjoying the simple life with a simple troll. Probably couldn't dress myself in the morning if it weren't for you."

"Gentlemen," Yeti cut in attempting to mediate the situation, "perhaps we've had enough for today?"

"The only thing I've had enough of is both of you!"

The door to the warehouse blew backwards on its hinges slamming against the wall. All four of them turned in silent shock. A dark figure stood in the open doorway, a blinding light casting a shadow from behind.

"I'm looking for Bernard!" the stranger said flatly.

"Aye," Grog replied defensively, "what's it to you?"

The strange silhouette moved slightly. "Grog, I take it?"

Grog frowned and clenched his first. "Aye... and you are?"

Norman sat back on a pile of unused wooden boxes, containing what he presumed to be dummies for hero target practice, and made himself comfortable as Blonk Jackson tried to explain the situation to Grog for the fifth time.

… It was no good.

"Look," Blonk Jackson said, "are your ears working?"

"My what?"

Blonk Jackson held his forehead and sighed emptily.

"I was over at The Pickler's house, on the roof, when I overheard them talking about some sexy plan to collect you three against your will. Now," he said knowingly, "Angus 500 and I dance a lot, and I'm over the moon about that… *but!*" he said lifting a finger looking suddenly a little cross. "Illegal villainy work is crossing the damned line… I can't just sit back and do nothing while the legal system falls apart…

"So…"

Grog listened and waited, then listened some more. "…So?"

"What do you mean 'so'? Didn't you listen?"

Grog tried. "I really did!"

"You're Grog, correct?"

"Aye… and that's Bernard and he's Norman."

"Funk-tastic," Blonk Jackson replied rubbing his hands together. "To be honest I ruined my best pair of trousers bopping over here as I did, but I'm glad I gave you the message before you got your funky selves into a right mess."

"What message?" Norman asked.

"The message regarding Angus being on his way to pinch your funky selves?"

"Aye," Grog said with a hit of realisation. "So, this Angus. He's on his way to kidnap us for The Pickler?"

"Finally," Blonk Jackson said snapping his fingers. "You lot are about as sharp as Kick Ass Fizz!"

"Kick Ass what?"

Blonk Jackson had gone from a small-time hero to a full-blown online giant within the last few weeks no thanks to his takedown of The Roller Rocket, a villain who'd opened the gates for a lot of sponsor deals. Suddenly he was able to make thousands each month from advertising and marketing, product placement and clothing; he never missed an opportunity to live-stream his adventures for his followers.

"Mm," he went on, pulling a can from his belt side. "Even when I'm deep in sexy hero activity, I always find time to drink Blonk's Kick Ass Fizz. So refreshing and full of electrolytes, plus, with an all-time low price of one ninety-nine, there's no reason not to enjoy the amazing taste of Blonk's Kick Ass Fizz."

"Oy boy," Yeti said holding his head.

"Don't be like that," Blonk said, "if you want to stay fresh in the hero game, vlogging is the only way."

"Vlogging?" Norman asked curiously.

"Bhaa!"

"Yeah," Grog seconded, "video logging, of course. Tell me," he went on, "do all you hero and villain types keep up to date with what each other are up to?"

"Oh yeah" Blonk said, "have to! It's like a global contest, isn't it? If you haven't got your eyes on the opposition, you could find yourself looking hella trouble!"

"And is there a place to watch all these… vlogs?" asked Grog. "And if so, can we search for specific videos?"

"Totally," Blonk said eagerly. "Hold on…"

The Explorer sat at his desk watching the swirling vortex of colours above him, daydreaming of a time when he would finally take control of the multiverse; all he needed was for Oxyn the Big to follow orders, retrieve the central black hole and bring it back to him in one piece.

Here, in the space between spaces, where he'd constructed his lair away from prying omnipotent eyes, he could formulate devilishly cunning plans. For one, he would totally banish chess. Secondly, "Space giants," he mumbled bitterly. They would all be transformed into small, lush jungle planets where he could holiday in peace.

He leant over and thrust his pencil into the electric pencil sharpener till its point was satisfactory and wrote, '3 — Join gym, get ripped, ask Sheila out for a drink.'

"Sheila's never going to go out with you," The Pickler said, materialising in front of him.

The Explorer's pencil broke in his hand as he jumped unexpectedly.

"Who the hell are you!"

The Pickler turned and strode away from him admiring the empty platform, the dazzling display of speckled stars and the quietness of it all.

"I remember this place," he said. "The silence that brought us so close to victory. So close to that one single goal. The multiverse" he scoffed. "The thing causes nothing but chaos."

Rising to his feet, The Explorer thought of green leaves and storks, perhaps even a nice brown clay pot, yet nothing he wanted could transform this intruder into an avocado plant.

"Save yourself the trouble," said The Pickler. "It won't work on me."

"Just who in the hell are you?"

The Pickler's boots squeaked as he walked upon the metal platform, his cape billowed behind him as he turned, sitting down at The Explorer's desk. He leant back, placing his feet on the desk.

"Shortly," he said, "Stinkhorn the Great will arrive, along with his palace piloted by The Traveller. Sadly, there's nothing I can do about our fate, as, obviously, me being here confirms my theory. But rest assured, we can gain our victory if you only listen."

"…Who are you?" asked The Explorer humbly.

"I am you," The Pickler said, "every part of your being, recycled no thanks to that central black hole. Unfortunately, as I've covered, there's nothing that we can do to change this outcome. Some parts of our lives are set, and some are not… I appeared in this form shortly after God restarted the multiverse. We were given a second chance. But listen to me, listen very carefully. It is imperative that you give up searching for the black hole as of this point."

"If I give up searching for it then I will never become you," pointed out The Explorer.

"And yet… now you have this thought, I still stand here in front of you. Search for it, do not, it makes little difference to the outcome. It may indeed give you more time in our old form, but you will always end up like this."

"So… what shall I do?"

"Your main objective, if you wish to obtain the infinite multiverse, is to find a being called Norman. In my time stream, he has become something more. Something much, much more than any of us could have ever been. You need to find Norman in your timeline. Bring him here and keep him here. I will be back to check up on you soon."

"And how exactly can I know that any of this is real?"

The Pickler stood. "On our seven-trillionth birthday, God made a cake for us. Little did we know that a small explosive device had been baked into it. I still remember the icing blowing up in my face, and to this day I can't walk past a bakery without breaking out into a cold sweat. Trust me, and trust yourself, you know that I'm telling the truth. Find Norman. Bring him here… I shall return."

The Pickler opened his eyes feeling the cushiony haze of everything slide away from him like a vivid dream you have milliseconds before waking; only his recollection stayed true, being back upon his old platform watching the gigantic vortex twist above him brought back so many fond, basic and happier memories of a time when he thought so much more of himself. He would never say that he used to be arrogant, or indeed self-centred, you could easily say that any villain from any story was self-centred, a kind of 'my way or the highway' mentality pushing them to their dastardly ways. No, what The Pickler thought of his former self was simple: he had been less, now he was more.

Angus 500 made his way through the steelworks between the shadows; he always felt a little jealous when visiting his unofficial boss. The Pickler's hideout was a far cry from his own overpriced abandoned Olympic stadium. Angus 500 was told when setting up his backstory that to really convey the sense of fact and realism, every element of his villainous persona had to fit. In this case, his hideout had to blend with his overall bad guy theme. And yet, even though he negotiated the stadium down from what was initially a ridiculous price to a reasonable high price, he still found little use for the Olympic swimming pool filled with alligators, the gymnasium with its uneven bars manned by crazed baboons or the javelin court that for reasons unknown came with a slightly unimpressed cat.

Alcohol splashed a little to the floor as The Pickler shook the last space-time connections from his mind, pouring himself a large glass of his favourite poison.

"You want to join me, Angus?"

"I'm never able to sneak up on you, am I?"

"As long as I'm still standing…" he toasted with a slight wobble on his feet.

"You okay there?"

The Pickler nodded and downed what little spirit there was left inside his tumbler.

"Every time I've gone back to check up on myself it's weakened me… yet we are now at the moment in time I've been waiting for."

"I was meaning to ask," asked Angus, "is that like a time travel type thing, or have you got a radio or something? It's just that I've not seen my brother in a while and…"

Angus trailed off into silence feeling the weight of The Pickler's stare break in on his consciousness.

"If you must know… it's an improbable reaction that occurred from the short-sightedness of a fool. His decision-making was irresponsible, yet key in manufacturing this tie I have with my previous self through a space-time gateway, brought forwards by the multiverse's need to correct oddities and loose ends."

"Right," Angus said, "so sort of like a radio?"

"…It's a connection," The Pickler huffed. "I have a special connection with another place."

"Ah… okay," Angus replied knowingly. "I hear you. Like I have with the red-light district? If you're free later, we could—"

"Angus!" The Pickler said flatly having little time for small talk. "Tell me, have you found them or not?"

"I did! I did… I followed them to where Yeti Freudenberg trains his new recruits. From what I saw it's the sheep that'll cause the problems. I wanted to get closer, but Blonk Jackson appeared, and I had to move on."

"Good man… and what of their location now?"

"Last I saw, Blonk was leading them away to show them more of the hero scene. You want me to follow them?"

"Yes," laughed The Pickler, "yes, I do. Time is on our side. I have waited hundreds and thousands, millions and billions of years for this time to arrive. It has taken multiple time streams, years of hatred and planning, duplicates and reincarnations, and now, now! The multiverse in within my grasp…" he shouted with glee, throwing his glass tumbler to the fire roaring in its wooden cove. The alcohol ignited its flame briefly.

A piano's keys began to play.

Lightning struck.

Somewhere in the distance, a baby started crying.

"…Right so… umm… contacting my brother is completely out the question then?"

"…You can use the phone in the office."

In one of the nicer districts of the capital city, known as Hound, Grog found himself ducking underneath the awnings of a veg shop keeping himself dry from the sudden rainstorm. Mere days ago, he would've never have guessed that he would be standing outside Discount Greens with a god's god, a sheep and an abominable snowman watching a ninja set up a few well-placed recording devices in order to live-stream a failed robbery.

"I mean… just saying it out loud sounds ridiculous."

"Yet here we are," Yeti said.

"Do you want me to make it stop raining?" Norman asked politely, tucking into a custard doughnut. "I'm pretty sure I can do that, anyway."

"You're 'pretty sure' you can do that? … You opened up doorways to new time streams like they were just… well, doors. Yet making it stop raining might be a bit of a push?"

"I've never done it before!" Norman argued.

"So, you've opened up time stream doors, though?" asked Yeti genuinely interested.

Norman bobbed his head. "Well, maybe. I was stuck in this library for ages, and kind of fell in this book about sports."

"…Fell in?"

"Yeah," said Norman licking custard from his fingers, "kind of. But I never made it stop raining." Of that, he was sure.

"And the doughnut? Did you make that out of nothing?"

"No," Norman said smiling. "I got it from over there."

He pointed to a small shop whose sign said 'Moore'N'Sons'.

Blonk Jackson cartwheeled backwards over the street flipping twice in the air and landing on his feet in front of Grog, twirling a small remote control in his hands. "That's the cameras set up nicely. Banks in the loop. Crooks on their way, all is a go."

"Bhaa?" asked Bernard eager to learn and fine-tune his skill.

"What did the funky sheep say?"

"He said what's next," Grog replied.

"Right," continued Blonk, "well. See, for a real good-looking bust, you need great locations for your cameras. You can't just set them up anywhere on funky street…"

"…Funky street?" Yeti asked rhetorically.

"Oh no. You need good angles, that's what keeps the followers following. When the crooks make their appearance, we'll let them get sexy with the guns. Wait till they've robbed the joint, then, as they make their getaway, we bounce in, give them a beatdown, and send them to the slammer. Funky! Right?"

Grog, Norman and Bernard all nodded in agreement. It did all sound rather 'funky' indeed.

Blonk smiled, it was a wide-eyed enthusiastic smile that really made you aware that the beatdown was his favourite part of the plan.

"Aye, well," Grog said eagerly. "I'm sure I can master that quite easily."

"Bhaa!" Bernard pointed out.

"Indeed," Yeti agreed, "you're a villain. Realistically you should be with the crooks. Perhaps you should sit this one out for now. When the time's right, Blonk will take Bernard and show him the ropes."

"The time is right," The Pickler said to Angus as he took a seat on his throne. It wasn't really any kind of throne you'd expect, of course. A throne is usually connected with royalty, perhaps even a metaphor for someone who has an idea they are in charge of things, but even then, as this comes close to what The Pickler truly thought, the actual physical bearing of his selected chair was not even close to being classed as a throne. It was more an old steelworker's metal chair with fancy bits bolted on.

Villainy work was not always glamorous; you had to make do with what you had.

"As I was saying," The Pickler continued, "the time is right. I will send my thoughts back to my old timeline and prep myself for the coming of things."

"And me?" Angus asked intently.

"Make your way to their whereabouts; we need Norman. There's no way you can handle him one-on-one. We simply need to talk to him. Getting the others out the way is vital. Once you've done this, bring Norman back here to me, and I will handle the rest."

Angus smiled crunching the last bite from his apple; he tossed it idly to one side, knelt down to the floor and felt the power of speed grow in his loins. He would later on argue that of course not everything he did that involved the loin area was fast; in fact, he was extremely eager to prove that on some occasions he could last hours. Sparks began to fly; the ground around his feet prickled with dry heat and photonic discharge. His eyes seemed to light up like the eyes of a moth headed for the Valhalla of streetlights… and he was off.

"Wait!" The Pickler shouted. "Come back!"

The tartan blur went and came in a flash. "What's wrong?" Angus asked hurriedly.

"Pick that apple core up. What's wrong with you, man? There're bins everywhere."

"It's biodegradable," he said obviously.

"So? It's my floor. Pick it and put it in the bin!"

"All right, all right… while I've got you, we never actually got around to talking about my pay increase. Seems to me that this plan of yours is grander than I thought… I was thinking—"

The Pickler shook his head and pointed to the bin, then the door.

"Right," Angus replied, "maybe when I get back."

Steve the security guard followed Bud through the compound one more time. It was still early so the usual scruffy bunch of punters coming from The Loaded Barrel hadn't yet made their nightly appearance. Steve had grown used to their drunken visits. As last orders rung the bell of sobriety, a zigzagging march had commenced homeward-bound. The troop, which on a good night would number at least eight, reminded Steve as they passed that there was life beyond the high wire fence of the compound. It wasn't much, of course, but on these long nights, stuck in a small hut with a frail old dog and a half-empty lunch box to keep you company, Steve took anything he could.

He retreated back to the hut after his boredom had been tamed for an hour at least and made himself comfortable. Bud sniffed the air; it was more of a habit than interest, then he circled a few times on his bed before picking the right spot…

And as soon as he sat down… "Woof?"

"What is it, boy?" Steve asked flicking his torch on and sweeping the compound in front of him from his throne; Steve was the king of this compound. "Something got you spooked?"

A few times of moving the torch back and forth illuminating the darkness brought nothing to his attention, except a rather startled hedgehog that was trying to make its way to the roadside.

"Woof!" Bud barked again.

It was a stable job. It was a well-paid job. It was a job that Steve found quite nice and easy in the fact that he had been appointed as security detail to a place that he'd found out quite quickly really didn't need any security at all. So, it was understandable that, now that he was having to physically get up and have a look around the compound, he was decisively upset and would definitely have to have a hard talking-to his boss, regarding a potential pay rise.

All was quiet.

The hum from the electrified fence boomed in the silence.

A tumble of dried leaves rolled through his open legs.

"Terry! I told you last time," Steve shouted into the darkness, "you and the boys can't walk home this way! I'll have you barred from The Barrel! … Terry?"

Spotlights as hot as the sunbeds he definitely never used on a Thursday morning lit up above him. The ground around him trembled as the wind howled and tossed the fallen leaves. Cars and various vans and lorries shook and vibrated as the ship descended, setting off alarms all throughout the compound. Steve flung himself back to his hut and clambered under the desk to where Bud was hiding and ventured a peek outside. He saw a foreign vessel not of this world engage its landing gear, set down heavily upon the dry mud, open its rear hatch and…

"I need the police — no, I need the army!" Steve shouted down his desk phone. "Send the army! MI5, CIA… send someone! There's a mushroom, I repeat, *a mushroom* has landed in the Chumpton Compound. Roughly seven foot three, Caucasian… maybe. Definitely bald… hello? Hello?"

The line was not working, and all Steve could muster was a pitiful whimper. He gazed into Bud's eyes as they clung to each other under his hairy dog blanket.

All fell silent as Oxyn the Big strode out from his craft; the huge mushroom had orders. Somewhere in between these human vehicles lay a humble road sweeper with a black hole resting in its belly. Such an amazing thing, the black hole: central in its design, critical in nature. Anyone who wields its power is sure to rule the multiverse: existence itself.

"And you're sure it's important that I remember that retrieving the black hole is no longer important?"

The Pickler groaned and felt that he had underestimated his former self's trust in everything they'd talked about, equally, the greed of his former self The Pickler knew all too well; if, during the time before, The Explorer had ever made contact with dimensional doubles and had the offer to work together to gain the key to the multiverse, he would've banished his duplicates without a second's thought.

The Pickler breathed heavily. *We've only just started*, he thought.

"Yes," he said, "yes. The black hole is no longer important. What we need is—"

"It's just that I've been thinking," The Explorer said peering over the bonnet of an abandoned Austin A40.

"I understand, slightly at least, that there are different time streams. Infinite time streams within the infinite multiverses, and this Norman, in your time has become what you refer to as a being of supreme ultimate power—"

The Pickler tapped his fingers upon the car bonnet resting his chin on his free hand, watching Oxyn the Big begin his search for the road sweeper.

"Go on."

"Well," said The Explorer, "what exactly happens to my time stream if the black hole is never replaced to the central multiverse core? I mean, things will just spiral out of control here, no?"

"…And that matters how, exactly?"

"This is my time stream and I—"

"Listen to me," said The Pickler as flat and controlled as possible. "You are correct about the infinite time streams, and you are correct about taking control of each one of them when we can control Norman. But! You are wrong about that being as far as our iron grip will spread. You see, the time stream does not simply involve the multiverse, but the Continuum itself."

"The Continuum," thought The Explorer out loud.

"We would rewrite our own history, as well as the history of this feeble project. And your time stream… well, it is insignificant, really. We will rule together."

"Right," The Explorer ventured. "But how does the Continuum come into it all?"

The Pickler rolled his eyes. "…Norman," he exhaled. "With Norman at our side we can do as we wish. Trust in me."

With that, The Explorer set his eyes to scanning the compound intently.

On the far end of the compound the bolted gates rattled slightly, then, with a ping and a twang, the heavy lock and chain keeping them fastened shut snapped in two and fell to the floor, with both gates peeling backwards like two opposing sardine can tops.

"I said I'm sorry," Norman said innocently.

The Traveller walked in by his side; he looked equally unimpressed and uninterested. A vague look of emptying enthusiasm glazed over his face.

"I could be in a hot tub right now I hope you know," The Traveller replied, shaking a coupon in his hand for The Secret Garden Special with Miss Buttercup. "This is more valuable than life itself!"

"Does it expire?"

"You'd best hope it doesn't."

The pair set to, making their way round the compound in the dark, while Oxyn the Big carried on his search on the opposite side. The Pickler nudged The Explorer, gesturing over to Norman.

"That's him."

The Explorer's brow sank in confusion. "He's made out of clay. Are you sure he's… ouch! … okay fine, you're sure. You got me right in the ribs."

"We need to catch him and take him with us back to the space between spaces."

"Right," The Explorer nodded. And got up and marched over with obvious intent.

Oxyn the Big put the rear end of an untaxed ambulance down and thought to himself, was it all worth it? Yes, he was of course meant to be taking orders from Stinkhorn the Great, and yes, he was of course double-crossing him to take orders from The Explorer. So, what harm would come from a triple cross? The Explorer had said that he could spread Oxyn the Big's spores across countless universes, and though that indeed did sound like a reasonable idea, the thought of having the black hole all to himself wet his lips immensely. Though for a mushroom, having wet lips was not at all great as the smell was horrific.

"Don't you even think about it!" The Explorer said striding up to him. "I can tell what you're thinking even without powers."

"Grumpt plonkor?" Oxyn the Big grunted shocked to see his boss behind him.

"Never you mind what I'm doing here! I do not answer to you. Tell me, have you found the black hole?"

The Pickler grew more infuriated from where he sat upon the old Austin A40, watching as the simple task of kidnapping drifted away from him. He wasn't too sure what was worse, knowing deep down that the odds of his old self deviating from the plan were pretty high, or that he literally couldn't do anything about it; he was only a vision, a projection of his material body, after all. "Sod it," he said and went to join the two bickering fools.

"How dare you think that you could complete this without me!" The Explorer shouted angrily.

"Bril bril-blir!" responded Oxyn the Big.

"…Yeah? And you're quite sure you can do all that with those huge squashy clumps you even consider calling hands?"

"Gentlemen… please," said The Pickler calmly. "Please can we put this to one side?"

Oxyn the Big looked startled. With one giant squashy clump at the end of one giant arm he struck out at The Pickler, only to watch his giant limb glide right through his midsection.

"Flaaaaarhhhhh!" he shouted in rage.

"How dare you!" replied The Explorer seemingly outraged at the accusation. "Why would I double-cross you!"

"Gentlemen!" said The Pickler. "Please!"

The Explorer scoffed at his employee's demands. "No. Simply no. You will not be getting a jetpack any time soon, we've talked about this before, and we arrived at no."

"Onk!" said Oxyn the Big.

"I know you sweep my platform in the space between spaces, I know you do. And I'm very thankful for it…"

"Gentlemen, please!"

"…And I know you water my plants too."

"Shut up!" shouted The Pickler with his last breath of sanity. "Shut up! Shut up! … We're here for one thing and one thing only. You!" he pointed at Oxyn the Big, "keep looking for that bloody black hole. And you," he said thrusting his finger into The Explorer's chest. "Keep looking for Norman. So help me God, if anything happens to take us away from this plan…"

"Umm," The Explorer said looking over The Pickler's shoulder.

"…I will personally make it my duty to physically come back in time…"

"Excuse me," The Explorer said again, pointing.

"…And beat the living daylights out of you, till you start seeing sense!"

"I'm sorry, but—"

"What is it!"

The Explorer imitated a tortoise by lowering his head backwards between his shoulder blades, whilst directing The Pickler's attention to the open gates of the compound as a small road sweeper wobbled outward into the night. The faint sound of Norman saying, "Maybe we can go see Miss Buttercup on our way?" bore into The Pickler's eardrum.

"Jesus Christ!"

... Back on Alpha Prime...

Norman finished off his third custard doughnut and thought that realistically, even though there were better places to get baked savoury treats from, it wasn't a good enough reason for Moore'N'Sons to close down.

"Bhaa?" Bernard asked having heard through the space-vine all about Norman's kidnapping, the planet populated by Thomas Moores from every universe and the resulting conclusion that was The Cosmic.

"Yeah..." Norman recalled thinking quite heavily, "yeah, that does sound familiar. Still," he shrugged, "shame, really, as they do make good custard doughnuts."

"Bhaa!"

The rain came down relentlessly; it had been a stipulation from the new mayor to the weather people that if it did rain, it would rain hard and strong with really big raindrops to make everything deeply atmospheric for really good hero and villain activity.

"I'm starting to get a little short with this place," Grog said looking like a wet dog that was unable to shake itself dry due to common courtesy.

Traffic lights turning red to green reflected upside down upon the flooded street. Overhead doorway signs lit with florescent colours written backwards beamed in the puddles by the drain covers and street edges. If it weren't for the feeling of absolute immersion and slight breeze chilling every hair on Grog's oversized body, he could've liked it here.

"Don't push it..."

... He may've tolerated it.

"Where're these bloody criminals anyway?" he quizzed.

High above them, deep within the falling rain, Blonk Jackson swooped and flipped from rooftop to rooftop waiting for the impending beating he was looking forward to dishing out. His followers on social media knew with fierce belief that he had been trained for years by monks who could walk on top of the sharpest swords, barefoot. He'd completed every trial they'd pushed him through, such as the Nutcracker Via Kneecap and the Pretzel Contortion. Blonk Jackson, the man, the myth, the legend was everything a ninja hero should've been. He was skilled in all martial arts, plus boxing and wrestling fighting styles.

And much like wrestling, every single contender — good or bad — had the fitness of an Olympic athlete, the body of a Greek god, and a manager ready to pass the script over any time they forgot their lines.

"Does Blonk have a manager?" asked Norman.

Yeti frowned and rolled his eyes. "If only… never should've gotten rid of me."

"You were his agent?" Grog asked.

"I was…" Yeti said with a certain amount of reservation. "He's been lucky though. With the creation of online hero work, he's got a face that the masses like. It's the only reason why he's stayed in work."

"Bhaa!" Bernard said pointing down the rain-washed street. The car came racing around the corner straight through red lights sending the civilian traffic in all directions. If any member of the general public had a sudden brave outburst, the sub-machine gun peppering the brick walls from the rear windows dealt with it quite well. The tyres screeched as the mobster car came to a halt outside the bank; the driver gripped the wheel as the two men in the rear shouted orders pulling down their balaclavas over their faces.

The first man exited the car, cocked his weapon in his hand, unrolled the script that'd been provided, and shouted for his associate to open the front door to the bank.

"It all looked so natural till he got out," Grog moaned.

"It's the trouble with being agentless," Yeti said watching intently. "Go self-employed, self-made, you have to start here. It's like living a B movie."

The two gunmen went inside; a few rounds of shotgun fire sounded off. The bank's alarm fizzed into action, signalling that the law would be called and giving the crooks roughly three minutes till their arrival (honestly, having a police force in a world where everyone is either a villain or a hero seems pointless. When Grog asked later, he was told that 'it all adds to the magic', whatever that means). The would-be villains came running from the bank's entrance with bags of money in tow, loose notes and coins falling to the floor as they went.

"Start the car!" the first shouted. "Start the car!"

"You two funky felons are going nowhere!" Blonk commanded nicely as he leapt from a nearby fire escape ladder, barrel rolled twice and vaulted a strategically placed shopping trolley.

"It's Blonk Jackson!" the first gunman said, "we better... we better... hold on," he stammered, taking a quick glance at his script for a reminder. "We better gun him down or he'll sure get the better of us."

Grog covered his face in embarrassment.

"It can only get better," Yeti said.

Norman smiled. "I like it."

Blonk stood tall in front of the car headlights making sure his shadow was nice and large casting against the bank's facing wall.

"You won't get away with this!" he replied sternly reaching for his waist. "Not when I've got my custom Blonk Maple Grip Nunchucks with polycarbonate link chain, retailing at fifty-nine, ninety-nine at all major outlets and online stores," he said looking over at one of his cameras while flipping the weaponry skilfully between both hands.

"I'm out of here!" the second gunman said. "There's no way we can beat him while he's got his... um, Maple Grip Nunchucks with poly... um, polycarbonate link chain."

"Don't be foolish!" his crook friend told him. "We've got guns; he's got sticks!"

"Not to mention," Blonk went on, "my Jackson Air Ninja Grade shoes, fitted with insoles and flashing mood lighting!"

"Jesus..." Grog mumbled.

"Now put your fresh weapons down and lay your sexy criminal asses on the floor!"

The bank robbers looked at each other with total confusion. "That's not in the script, is it?"

"He means put your guns down and give him the money," shouted Yeti through cupped hands from the street.

"You know," the first crook said flatly, "we've got scripts for a reason. You can't just start ad-libbing whenever you like. We all do that and the whole thing falls apart."

The driver's window of the getaway car rolled down.

"Excuse me," the driver said. "I don't mean to be a nagging Nigel, but can we get on with it? I've got to be over by Brook Street in half an hour. I'm meant to be failing to escape a diamond heist for my brother-in-law, The Pyjama Warrior."

"That's all well and good," the first crook said abruptly, "but what about me? The missus put a shepherd's pie in the oven about forty-five minutes ago; if I don't make it back soon, she'll go berserk."

"It's not like you're getting paid though is it. My brother-in-law said he'd see me right if things went well."

"I'd rather face the Pyjama Warrior than my wife."

The second crook turned to Blonk openhandedly. "Sorry about this. Can we wrap things up, do you think?"

"If you guys are ever going to climb the villain ladder, you're going to need to think on your feet. Scripts are all well and good," Blonk said knowingly, "but sometimes you need to deviate from them a little. It's what separates the professionals from the beginners."

"I'll have you know that I've been a getaway driver for three solid and successful years. I shouldn't need to mention that I eluded The Caped Cricketer on no more than four occasions, outdrove Rally Extraordinaire and beat, quite easily too, Van Diesel in multiple quarter-mile races. I shouldn't need to mention all that to you, but I will anyway."

"I stole the Crystal of Tester Ra'ha from the City Museum last weekend," the first crook replied smugly. "And it was my weekend off. Didn't need to come in, but I did anyway."

"Well, whoop-de-doo," the driver replied.

Blonk made his way over to where Grog, Yeti, Bernard and Norman stood. He felt a little deflated and turned both cameras off with a small handheld remote looking as sad as a five-year-old boy who'd been told on the day of his birthday that the pre-booked clown and inflatable castle had been stuck in a major accident and wouldn't be coming after all.

“I’m sorry, guys,” Blonk said emptily, “it’s never usually like this. I’m using new extras today. Never worked with them before… my bad. Feel silly now.”

Grog coughed. “Feel silly just now, or all the time?”

“I liked it,” Norman smiled.

Portobello 9 hummed with rotten traffic jostling for space high above the festering streets below, which, coincidentally, also hummed. The great mushroom palace of Stinkhorn the Great stole the eye’s gaze far beyond the wobbly planet’s horizon. Yet, though magnificent and extremely almighty, The Explorer couldn’t help but to feel a little empty standing in the loading bay of the palace’s delivery docks.

“If anything goes wrong, I have no powers to defend myself,” he said for the third time, feeling that the prior two hadn’t really got the message across properly.

“Yes, yes,” The Pickler replied impatiently. “It’s terrible news, I know. But seeing how we missed our chance at the Chumpton Compound, this is the best place for us to strike.”

“Why the waistcoat though?”

“Do you want to fit in? It’s called a disguise.”

“I know what a disguise is. I’m pretty sure it’s the rest of me that’ll be easy to spot.”

“I’ll deal with your appearance when the time comes,” The Pickler said. “By my calculations, Norman should’ve choked that fungal worm to death and should be on his way here with The Traveller and The Fixer.”

The Explorer rolled his eyes and huffed. “The Fixer? You never said anything about The Fixer. He’s worse than the rest of them. Sure, he’s just as messy and lackadaisical in his work, but he’s the only one with guts to do anything.”

“Yes, you have mentioned.”

“He once semi-repaired a deflated hydrogen nebula, then beat up six space giants for not thanking him properly.”

“You’ve said that too…”

“…And The Traveller. What a joke. The man rates holiday retreats for a living, for God’s sake.”

"Well, here they're just normal people like you. The playing field is slightly even."

"Slightly?" The Explorer asked, "it's three against one."

"No," replied The Pickler happily, "it's three against two. And one of the two is me… being the brains of the operation."

Baron Fluke lay stiff between the high mounds of decomposing matter; his infinite length once again slain by a small man just too big to swallow. The buzzing insects that swarmed the maturing docking bay took little time rehoming their friends and family on the gigantic fungal worm as Norman plodded out from the monster's mouth looking, once again, quite upset about things.

"Poor thing," Noman said worriedly.

"Weeell…" The Fixer replied knowingly. "Can't be too careful, can you? One minute you're devouring your next victim and all of a sudden, *bang*, you've choked to death on your own slobbery."

"I feel terrible," Norman admitted.

After The Traveller had made it quite clear to both Norman and the Fixer in what could be classed as a thorough telling-off, with only moderate swearing, they found themselves in a taxi heading towards the festering spherical mass of Portobello 9. Soon after, the drunken taxi driver lost his grip and flailed madly into space, and much sooner after The Fixer had finished off the driver's half-empty bottle of booze and mastered the squishy steering controls of the cab, they landed heavily in the docking bay as planned.

Norman's excitement grew as The Traveller's enthusiasm shrank.

"No," he told Norman flatly after he asked if there had been a planned parade put on for their arrival. Of course, most parades had the streets lined with trumpet players and screaming children, not heavily armed mushrooms swarming the docking bay like a coffee mug left on a window ledge for a few weeks only to be knocked over by a vengeful and totally bored cat.

The stagnant monolith-like doors to the palace opened at the rear of the docking bay; from the taxi they saw the familiar shape of Oxyn the Big, who, though big indeed, was simply dwarfed by the colossal monstrosity that was Stinkhorn the Great. The King, the Emperor, the…

well, whatever he was to his people, strode out intently shouting gargles of fungal orders at his foot soldiers. Across from where he stood, a small scuffle brought more commotion to the bay as a waistcoat-wearing mushroom was brought forwards. A guard gripped the fashionable fungi's head tightly and pulled it off his shoulders revealing The Explorer's worried expression underneath.

Oxyn the Big may have been a simple yet heavily structured life from, but he could spot a fake outfit a mile away. He'd suspected that his former boss, The Explorer, would double-cross him at some point, but to what end a fake rubber mushroom mask and waistcoat would bring he did not know.

"Mm," Norman thought thoughtfully, "I don't think this is a parade you know."

"Hold on," The Fixer replied. He leant sideways and locked his door, found another half-empty bottle in the dashboard and made himself comfortable. "Okay… carry on."

"I mean there's the right number of people here," Norman went on. "I see plenty of screaming children, but no trumpets."

"Those could be trumpets," The Fixer said pointing to the mushroom guards shouldering rotting weaponry. "I mean, of course they're not trumpets, you can quite clearly see they're not trumpets; the very idea that you'd have palace guards acting so violently under orders carrying nothing but trumpets, is silly, but still, they could very well be trumpets if you squinted hard enough."

"Ah" Norman said squinting hard, "that settles it then."

The Explorer was lifted atop of a howling group of fungal guards and marched steadily away out of sight. Stinkhorn the Great gestured something menacing to Oxyn the Big who disappeared the same way, and abruptly the swarm of guards drained from the docking bay as quickly as they'd arrived, leaving Stinkhorn the Great alone with the taxi and its occupants.

"You'd better talk to him," said The Fixer, swigging his newly found bottle.

"Why me?" The Traveller asked.

"Well, it can't be me, can it?"

"And why not?"

"I've been drinking of course. You know first impressions mean everything. Here we are, deep in fungal territory, faced with the man himself, odds of our very survival stacking against us every second, and you want to put all our lives in the hands of a man who's been drinking? That's pretty irresponsible if you ask me."

"Norman," The Traveller snapped, "go and talk to him!"

"Norman?" said The Fixer.

"Okay fine… Norman, sit down. Sit down!"

"But I—"

"Sit down!"

"Okay."

With much hesitation, The Traveller stepped out of the cab and met Stinkhorn the Great face to face; it was more like ankle to face. He'd only ever seen Stinkhorn the Great in pictures, and even then, they had been small pictures; the kind of pictures that fitted nicely inside someone's wallet or purse; the sort that you pass to an elderly relative who doesn't see their grandchildren or nephews as often as they'd like to. Unsurprisingly then these pictures had somehow completely forgotten to truly demonstrate the Fungal lord's overall size. It was a modern wonder as to how basic chemicals mixed with the longevity of time could produce something so disgustingly grotesque and vile from a common strain of mushroom.

"Mm," The Traveller said after a while, "I think it's only right to let you know, I don't taste all that nice."

"Quiet!" the lord of mould thundered, shaking the deep roots of his palace.

"Of course," The Traveller replied out of politeness.

"I don't taste that nice either," Norman said sadly to The Fixer from the back seat. "But if he's hungry he can have a little nibble. I don't mind."

"Save yourself for another time," said The Fixer.

"Are you sure?"

Norman rolled the window down from the back seat and smiled.

"Excuse me? Do you think he'd like an index finger? Or a pinky?"

"Shut up Norman!" said The Traveller flatly.

"Excuse me?" Norman said looking up at Stinkhorn the Great. "Are you hungry? If you don't fancy an index or a pinky, I've got two thumbs that I could spare... I just feel so bad about that worm that choked to death" he said honestly. "I wouldn't want anything for them of course! If anything, I've probably got too many fingers than I really need."

"Shut up Norman!"

"...Why ten though?" Norman asked.

"It's the grand design," The Fixer replied mysteriously. "You learn all about it at Continuum Collage."

"You were thrown out of Continuum Collage in your first year," The Traveller pointed out.

"It was a difference of opinion—"

"Quiet!" Stinkhorn the Great bellowed once more. This time his orders seemed to hit the mark.

The Pickler, for all the bad he is, does indeed have the patience of a saint; this of course is a total lie, he actually has the patience of a short fuse. He self-combusted watching The Explorer being heaved up on the shoulders of the palace guard and marched away. To make matters worse, the sight of Stinkhorn the Great casually hopping in the back of a taxi after asking Norman to 'scoot over a bit' didn't help the situation.

The plan, if that is what you could call it, did indeed exist no more. Much like the future super-intelligent Norman, The Pickler knew that creating too many time streams would disrupt the very fabric of things. It wasn't as simple as rewriting wrongs, changing past events to better suit the present or the future; that sort of basic nonsense belonged solely in a single universe. This half-price multiverse was a complex, if not slightly deranged beast. Its true complexity could never really be understood, not even by God himself; he did come close once after a long evening spent staring at a chalkboard, ordering Chinese and making his way through eight bottles of Absinth. Understanding the laws and physics of a monster like the multiverse, was something that mortal men and immortal beings alike, struggled with daily. It just was. It just is. Observe as much as you like, accept that things happen for reasons that you may never understand, take a cold beer while you're at it, and enjoy every second.

Yet The Pickler wasn't as simple as a universe, he was, by definition of his very existence, multiversal.

Every being from every universe conceivable was indeed a singular thread in an ever-expanding complexity made of an ever-growing number of duplicate copies, each a result of a choice every being makes on a second-by-second basis, yet The Pickler is not. He came from the recycled remnants of The Explorer, a being from the Continuum, and therefore the rules of multiversal existence do not apply. The Pickler was born from the improbable interchanging mix of omnipotent power and the multiverse's multitudinal reality. He is multiversal, now existing in every single universe there is, yet singular, spanning across all of them as one.

Like a hive mind, he saw every reality existing within them as they divided and split at the speed of light.

"I am the multiverse," The Pickler said drumming his fingertips together formulating chaotic plans. "And if I can't help myself become the supreme being, then perhaps the rest of me can."

"And what exactly does that mean?" Grog demanded. "You can't just say, 'oh, hey, yeah, I like it here, I might stay a while.' I mean, you didn't even ask me how I felt."

"Bhaa!" Bernard said defensively.

"Aye, right, and that's my fault, is it? We all agreed to blow up that planet… it was a joint effort!"

Yeti always maintained an air of professionalism when dealing with clients' domestics. He would of course never get involved with personal issues… however, if said domestics happened to contain sensitive information that may, cough-cough, further his career, well then, what's a little eavesdropping between friends?

"Do you mind giving us a bit of space?" Grog asked flatly.

Yeti had forgotten the true meaning of eavesdropping years ago and felt that the best way to listen in on secrets was to simply stand right next to the ones trying to remain quiet. Being the polite type of snowman he was, he of course took a small step back. "…Continue."

"…Keep moving back," Grog said bluntly.

Another step would probably do, he thought.

“Bhaa!” Bernard bleeped bitterly transporting Yeti ten thousand miles south to the snowy mountains of Yettah. A few nameless monks were sweeping the stairs of their monastery at the time and were looking quite shocked; Yeti couldn’t tell if it was due to him being the first abominable snowman they’d probably ever seen, or that they thought Blonk Jackson had made a surprise visit to finish his training.

“Please,” Grog went on, “please, Bernard. Tell me you’re not serious?”

Bernard could barely bring himself to look up at Grog, let alone make eye contact. He knew Grog would never truly understand the idea that Pux, the home that Grog hated yet equally relied upon, was gone forever.

“But that’s what we’re doing here, isn’t it? That’s why we’ve come with Herman…”

“Bhaa…”

“Norman. Right, sorry. That’s the whole reason for this. To get our home back…”

Bernard’s head sagged again knowing that if the day came that they were successful, if they could find The Pickler, change his ways, create a future where the time stream wasn’t disrupted and safely find their way back home, it simply wouldn’t be the home they had left behind so many nights ago. The reason for their leaving was still very much resting in the back of Bernard’s mind; they had left a time stream where an entire multiverse of beings had been devolved to pools of wandering bacteria and fifth-grade science teachers. They had come all this way to make sure that when they returned, things would be back to the way they’d left them, yet for everything that Bernard was, for all his superior intelligence, he knew without a doubt in his mind that the chances of them succeeding were poor.

“Actually,” Norman said happily, “the chances of our success are exactly one in four billion, seven hundred and nine million, two hundred and fifteen thousand six hundred and twenty-one.”

As luck would have it, 400,709,215,621 were the exact numbers drawn on last Saturday’s Galactic Lottery, a prize fund of almost five Galactic Units was won by an elderly lady who promised her grandchildren she would take them all for an all-expenses paid trip to the universe of a Thousand Circus Mirrors.

"Right," Grog nodded, "and this old lady, she's going to come help us, is she?"

Norman shrugged. "I don't think so…"

"But these numbers," Grog went on, "they're special, are they? You're going to tell me that the multiverse is somehow plotting our destiny, mapping out our lives by these magic bloody numbers, right?"

"No…" Norman said fading a little, "just thought it was interesting, that's all."

"Right. Okay. Thanks for that."

"You're very welcome."

Blonk Jackson lifted a hand and paused the back-and-forth gun fire that popped from left to right on the rain-soaked rooftop.

"Guys!" he said shortly. "It took me quite a while to organise this shoot-out for you, do you think we could wrap things up a bit?"

Though Bernard had been keen to test out his hero abilities since Yeti had suggested that a test was the next best thing, he had always tried to prioritise Grog's needs first. Though he couldn't help but feel that this place, this planet, was beginning to feel comfortable. Whatever it was, whatever he saw in this super planet, it reminded him of God's back garden.

"Excuse me?" Skip the Brown Bears' leader asked politely from behind a steaming vent, "do we really need to be here?"

"Yes!" Blonk replied. "We need innocent bystanders to be caught in the crossfire, otherwise what's the point of it all?"

"Right. It's just that Jonny here needs to get home to his mum…"

"…But you said I'd get my Urban Survival Badge!"

"Shut up Jonny! … Ignore him… perhaps, I don't know," Skip went on, "perhaps these gangs have a hostage somewhere else? Somewhere other than behind a steaming vent on the roof of a building in the middle of a rainstorm?"

"Have you read your script?" Blonk asked bitterly.

"I have," Skip replied patting a folded-up script in his side pocket. "And well, though marvellous it is, of course it is—"

"Don't tell me Mr Marvellous is going to be here too!" little Jonny screamed.

"Shut up Jonny…"

"Who needs Mr Marvellous," Blonk said kneeling down with little Jonny, "when you've got the amazing, the awesome, the wonderful and woolly Sheep Train!"

"Sheep Train!" Little Jonny's face lit up, "is he new?"

Grog turned to Bernard wide-eyed. "Aye… Come on Sheep Train. Are you new?"

"Wow!" little Jonny shouted with joy, "a new hero. Sheep Train!" He bolted from behind the steaming vent heading for Bernard. "Sheep Train!"

"So, there's your first fan," Grog said angrily.

"Bhaa…"

"Sheep Train… hey, Sheep Train!" little Jonny screamed.

Little Jonny ran through a vast puddle, holding a pen in one hand and a notebook in the other as Skip chased after him feeling more and more frustrated and underpaid. "Sheep Train. It's me, Jonny."

"Get back here Jonny!"

"Can I have your signature?"

"Wow," Grog said sarcastically. "This is just great."

Little Jonny puffed out his fat red cheeks and pointed to his shoulder. "Look Sheep Train, look. I've got my Shearing Badge, so if you ever want a haircut…"

"He doesn't care," Skip said.

"No," Grog replied flatly, "it's me that doesn't care!"

"Bhaa!" Bernard said angrily.

"I'll be like that to whoever I want!"

"Bhaa!"

"…Well maybe I am. But you're the one losing sight of things."

Bernard frowned. Even after a few lines of dialogue it was obvious that this little Jonny fellow was a little annoying, but there was no reason to be rude.

"So, I'm rude as well, am I?" Grog asked.

"Bhaa!"

"Is that so?"

"Bhaa," Bernard replied angrily.

"Swearing at me now, huh? So that's how it is?"

"Come on," Norman said trying to tuck himself between them, "there's no need for this… is there?"

"No, no… Sheep Train here has something to say… don't you Sheep Train."

The question was rhetorical, yet equally threatening. Bernard never became angry; it was, and always had been, his best quality. Though, like a lot of beings that reside within the complex multiverse, if you were ever to get angry, it would of course be directed at your best friend. The pair had spent years with one another, gone through hard times together, revelled in the good and struggled through the bad. They had been the best of friends for longer than either could recall, they were closer to a married couple, and Bernard was beginning to lose his cool.

"Come on, Sheep Train," Grog said, prodding Bernard with his finger. "If you've got something else to say, out with it…"

Norman coughed. "Perhaps—"

"I said out with it!"

"Guys!" Blonk said, "the extras are getting impatient."

"Quiet you!" Grog shouted. "You," he pointed at Norman, "move. And you," he pointed at Bernard. "I said: out… with… it."

The rain pelted the rooftop under the heavy silent atmosphere that fell upon the scene; all eyes were fixed on Bernard.

Little Jonny rubbed his dripping nose. "So, any chance of a signature then?"

"That's it!" Grog yelled. He lifted Jonny off the floor with one hand knocking Skip backwards off his feet.

"Come on Sheep Train," Grog bellowed, "be the hero!"

"Weeeee!" little Jonny yelled excitedly as Skip frantically searched through the script looking for anything that might say 'Jonny's Demise'.

"This is great!" little Jonny shouted happily.

"If you're Sheep Train that means I'm The Derailer!" Grog shouted.

Norman and Blonk shared a look and thought, that's pretty cool.

"Aye," Grog continued, "and little Jonny here is about to get thrown off the roof!"

"Wheeee… wait… what?"

Bernard shook his wool dry and ran to Grog, stopping in his path and fixing his gaze square at him.

"Ah… what're you going to do Sheep Train? Huh? Maybe turn me into a carrot, or perhaps a nice hot pie?"

Bernard never got angry.

But Bernard was angry.

Bernard searched in his mind for the dish best suited for a troll, a troll lost in his own selfish needs… tinned ravioli and sausages seemed a good idea.

Bernard was angry.

And so…

"Wait!" Norman shouted. "Stop!"

Both looked round. Blonk looked round. All the extras looked round. Angus 500 who had found himself a nice dry doorway on the next building's rooftop to watch from turned around.

Norman paused.

"Well?" Grog asked.

"Umm…" Norman thought. "I hadn't really planned anything else. Stop… please?"

Grog smirked and took a few more steps to the roof's edge.

"Wait" Norman said again… "Umm, well… How… are you spelling The Derailer? Is it 'Derailer', 'DeRailer' or maybe 'De Raylur'?"

"I thought you were meant to be the god of gods!" Grog said smiling. "You could do anything to me, stop me any way you'd like, even stop my very existence if you wanted, but you won't, will you!"

"Actually, it's physically impossible to stop something from existing," Norman told him kindly. "You see nothing ever stops; it just transforms from something old into something new. And even then, it's not really—"

"Bhaa!"

"Right, sorry," Norman replied.

Bernard had used his powers many, many times. Yet compared to his extremely long life, you might say it had only been a handful of times. From the day Farmer Collins accidentally blew up all the villages 'corn' crop only to find it miraculously growing proudly the next morning, to

Sam Samson walking in on his wife teaching the stable boy some rare grooming tips, then strangely forgetting the entire thing in time for their wedding anniversary, it was obvious to anyone that Bernard had only ever used his limitless powers for good. And to anyone that has had to survive till payday on an extremely small budget after an extremely heavy weekend, the idea of eating, let alone becoming a cold tin of ravioli and sausage was definitely in no logical way ever anywhere, a good thing.

"Do it!" Grog shouted.

"Bhaa!"

"No… either little Jonny here has a tumble, or I'm Rigatoni."

"Bhaa!" Bernard said. His brow creased under the pressure, a single thought coiled inside his mind, pulling back ready to let lose like a tightened spring. His eyes closed. His ears hung low. The image of cold pasta shot from his mind; energy rippled outwards, superheating the air, raindrops became steam, and…

And…

Umm…

"Nothing happened!" Angus 500 shouted over from the rooftop cupping his hands around his mouth. "A little anticlimactic, to be honest."

"He won't do anything!" Grog shouted back.

"Bhaa!" Bernard bleeped ragefully. And proceeded to fire another burst of Italian imagery at Grog.

And another.

… And another.

"You can't can you!" Grog said. "Don't forget, Sheep Train. Norman here has made me invincible. Even for you, with all your supposedly endless power, you won't get past whatever he's done to me."

Norman then frowned and protruded his bottom lip having a complex wave of thoughts begin to twirl in his head.

"Umm… I haven't done anything to you yet," he said. "Actually, I completely forgot I needed to change you at all."

"Bhaa?" Bernard asked.

"No," Norman replied. "Honest… try it again." And Bernard did try it again. In fact, no matter what he thought, whether it was cold pasta or table-top wedding flowers, he simply couldn't change Grog into anything.

Little Jonny wailed with delight, and with a little flatulence, not really knowing whether he was truly part of the dramatics or simply in mortal danger.

"You're definitely in danger!" Skip shouted. "There's nothing about this in the script! I thought you said he would be safe?" he asked turning to Blonk.

"A little off-script dialogue never hurt anyone," Blonk replied. "Though, Grog, if you could not kill a child on your first time out, that would be funky."

"I won't kill him!" Grog said smiling, "I'll just bite him in two!" And with that, Grog lifted little Jonny upwards, holding his belt strap between his index and thumb dangling little Jonny over his toothy mouth.

"Well," Skip said to himself, "I tried."

Little Jonny fell, he could feel Grog's putrid breath beating on his skin. Then a flash of light, and he was standing next to Skip, shivering and feeling a little nauseous; due to Grog's breath of course, not Bernard transporting him to safety.

Grog turned looking rather upset about the whole thing.

"Bernard! Never once since we met did you ever take one of my meals away from me! Not even when I ate the farmer's daughter."

"Bhaa!"

"Aye, she was a zoophobic… as if sheep could do anything harmful other than bleep a little loudly," Grog laughed. "The very idea!"

Bernard frowned. He didn't like people laughing at him; him, or his entire sheep-kind. His little hooves lifted from the floor as his body slowly took to the air; lightning struck behind him. Somehow, he embodied a much larger animal than he truly was. The rain kept thrashing down, harder and harder, while Grog assumed an aggressive pose holding his palms out ready; it wasn't scripted, it just felt right.

All the signs were there, the tells that let everyone know a battle was soon to commence.

“Do you mind if we get off the rooftop first?” Blonk asked waving over to Skip and little Jonny.

“Aw, what?” little Jonny said disappointedly. “But I didn’t even get to see Sheep Train melt the big guy’s face off or throw him from rooftop to rooftop, flipping him around in a heroic yet equally formidable way.”

“Your expectations have always been a little high, Jonny,” Skip said. “Just start running for the fire escape would you!”

“Not before me!” Blonk shouted.

Bernard didn’t have time for this, he creased his brow and within seconds little Jonny, Skip and Blonk stood atop a mountain within a snowy downfall, nameless monks looking their way, immediately heading for the nearest exit and applying for desk jobs in the city.

Norman had never hurt anyone before, not intentionally anyway, though the idea of Bernard and Grog fighting didn’t sit well with him at all. He didn’t know what it was, but Grog was not what he seemed. Norman could look deep within anyone, through their bones and muscle, through blood vessels and atoms, right to the basic frequency that binds and holds the neutrons together. Though up until now he’d only used his powers to look inside cereal boxes checking if he’d won a glow-in-the-dark spoon. Now that he looked at Grog, really looked at him, he saw it all.

“Bhaa!” Bernard shouted flying circles round Grog.

“Is that so?” Grog replied. “Give me your best shot!”

Bernard was a fast learner. He summoned thoughts of sucrose, brought forwards the chemical composition of pectin and harnessed the brutal chains of citric and tartaric, threw them mentally outwards with his mind transforming the building Grog stood atop of into strawberry jam. For a moment, the wobbling monolith stood, then gave up its jelly rafters and struts collapsing downwards in a rather slow yet equally dramatic spreading across the surrounding street.

Norman floated in mid-air unscathed, his mind wandering the future and past, constructing outcomes and predicting downfalls. He saw Grog for what he was, for what he always had been. Had Grog ever in his life got into trouble, had he ever lost a fight? Had he ever in his entire existence fallen prey to injury or illness? Norman saw Grog as he fell, descending deep into the strawberry stickiness of it all, and gazed upon his body; Grog was not simply a troll, or even a strong being of Pux.

He was the missing piece to it all.

"Ah!" Grog screamed standing waist-deep in jam. "Is that all you can do, Sheep Train!"

"Bhaa!"

"You'll never hurt me!" Grog said. He lifted a street lamp clean out of the concrete with one hand and flung it at Bernard who instinctively morphed the thing into a delicate blue ribbon; it flailed delicately to the rain-soaked ground and was sucked into a nearby drain cover.

Across the street, Angus 500 had descended from the rooftop and had found himself a much better view to watch from. His initial order from The Pickler was to capture Norman and dispose of the others; he suddenly found himself questioning how exactly that might work.

"Hello? Boss? Can you hear me?"

"We can…" The Pickler answered in a crowded robotic tone.

"Right, well," Angus continued, raising his phone's speaker volume. "It's just that… hello?"

"Hello?"

"Ah, sorry, thought I lost you for a moment there. Right, the thing is… oop, hello?"

"Hello! Angus! We can hear you!"

"Sorry, boss, sorry. These damned phones don't work well in rainstorms. Or inside for that matter. Actually, in an underground carpark you don't get much signal… come to think of it—"

"Angus!"

"Sorry. These two fellas are at it. Going toe to toe. You told me the big guy was nothing to worry about, but I've just seen him fall from a rooftop and there's not a scratch on him. Plus, the other one, Sheepy… sheep. Sheep Grain? Sheep something, he's been turning buildings into jelly and all sorts. I don't know, I'm not too sure if this is all worth the trouble really. Is there any chance you can come over and see for yourself?"

"We are on our way," The Pickler replied.

Bernard swooped and dodged Grog's heavy-fisted approach to battle with ease. Every car and post box that was uprooted and tossed his way he sideswiped and dealt with accordingly.

"Bhaa!" he bellowed as the ground beneath Grog's feet shook and trembled, then abruptly turned into mint ice cream.

"Pathetic!"

Norman's eyes glowed white; he blinked and saw infinity.

"Hurry up boss," Angus said, "things are getting bad out here."

"Explain," replied The Pickler's voice.

Angus squeezed his phone tight to his ear with worry. "There's mint ice cream everywhere. I mean if it was chocolate chip, even banana I'd understand, but mint? These are some serious villains fighting out here."

"We have arrived," replied The Pickler, hanging up the phone.

A handful of unsuspecting superhero pensioners just leaving their late-night bingo session found themselves flying through the air towards what looked like a levitating ball of wool. Bernard did the only thing a merciful sheep could do, transforming them into Granny Smith apples. The street below had descended into a slush of food with an angry troll paddling back and forth finding anything he could to hurl with rage. The combined smell of mint ice cream and jam, Angus admitted, was something he could've done without.

"So," Angus said to The Pickler as he came to his side. "Finally decided to make an entrance."

"We did," a second Pickler replied coming to Angus's other side.

"There's two of you now?"

"No," three more Picklers said from behind him.

"Bloody hell," Angus replied, "I hope you know what you're doing? These guys are on another level."

"They will be destroyed," a crowed of Picklers said walking round the building's corner in front of him.

"…Just how many of you are there?"

Above him on the rooftops of every building in all directions, Picklers came into view. They stood statue-like and emotionless. From the alleyways and side roads, more appeared; from the sewer drains on the roadsides, even more clambered out. Within the windows of every office tower and high-rise housing, on every metal fire escape and every crossroad junction, a million Picklers stood watching silently as Grog and Bernard fought.

Norman floated idly down from the rainy air coming to land next to Angus, his eyes white with the sight of everything tunnelling through his mind.

Every possibility that ever was and could ever be popped and fizzed within his brain. Never before since his very beginning had there ever been a time when the multiverse had conversed and congregated so closely. It balanced so finely with such precision that there was nothing but one reality that could exist after this point.

One outcome that could and would only be.

One choice that only Norman could make.

"Leave." The deafening sound of The Pickler's voice hounded through the night sky. Angus nodded and tore off out of sight. Grog dropped the handful of OAPs just leaving their 'Sex for Elders' class, hearing the thunder of the word. All around him and Bernard, a thousand Picklers stood, ankle deep in jam.

"There is more than one outcome," The Picklers said.

Norman blinked and rubbed his hands together. "There is. But only one is acceptable."

"You cannot kill me."

"No," Norman agreed. "I can't. You are as complex as I am basic. You are the multiversal Michelin-starred red mullet and squid with oven-dried tomatoes, wild fennel and pickled mushrooms, where I am the single fruit-and-nut chocolate bar. You are everywhere, and I am only here. You are complexity itself, the multiverse in sentient form, whereas I am… um, the opposite, I guess."

"You guess?" asked The Picklers.

"Sorry," Norman replied. "I couldn't think of anything that would be fitting."

"Fair enough…"

"Though," Norman said thoughtfully, "we aren't actually the answer to the multiverse trying to balance itself out."

"No?"

"Well, I mean, we *are* technically the multiverse trying to balance itself out, sure. But only because its equal opposite was lost for billions of years."

"Really?" asked The Picklers. "How so?"

"My friend over there," Norman said pointing to where Grog and Bernard stood. "He's the lost equation needed to rebalance everything."

"Sheep Train?"

"No" Norman said smiling. "I'm talking about Grog."

"Grog? You mean the stinky troll?"

"Aye! Say that again I dare you!" Grog shouted angrily.

"Are you sure?" asked The Picklers in unison.

Norman nodded. "Quite sure, yeah."

"Then I will destroy him," replied The Picklers.

"Give me everything you've got!" Grog howled as his fist collided with the first wave of Picklers, sending bodies flying. More came from the rooftops and side streets running frantically through the melting ice cream. Clumps of undissolved raspberries and thick bindings of sugar helped a little slowing the surrounding supervillains, yet hundreds still came at him relentlessly.

"You're not going to make this a ribbon, are you?" Grog asked sarcastically as he uplifted a second street lamp. Bernard shrugged and crossed his arms. "So, I guess that's a no then…"

"Bhaa!"

"I don't need your help anyway!"

"You know," The Pickler standing next to Norman said as they both watched the frantic attack continue in front of them. "I'll keep at this for as long as it takes."

"I know," Norman replied. "Fruit and nut?" he offered.

"Don't try to stall me."

"I'm not stalling," Norman replied. "It's just nice chocolate. And I've got some to spare."

The Pickler narrowed his eyes suspiciously.

"It's not poisoned!" Norman laughed.

"Fine," The Pickler said snatching the bar from Norman's hand. "What are you up to?"

Norman looked confused. "Standing here eating chocolate."

"I mean what are you planning!"

"I'm planning on eating this chocolate."

"I mean planning to do about me beating up Grog!" The Pickler said frustratedly.

"Oh," Norman replied, "right. I see. Well, nothing really."

"Nothing?"

"…Nothing."

The Pickler narrowed his gaze again taking a bite of the silky smooth and totally indulgent chocolate.

"Nice, isn't it?"

"It's heavenly, but that's not the point. I thought he was your friend, yet you're quite happy with me beating him up."

Norman smiled. "I wouldn't call it a beating really."

They both turned to see a gathering of Picklers twirling through the air over them.

"I know you could keep this up for days, even months, but Grog would be able to do it for years."

"I am infinite! I would never stop!"

"And neither would Grog. You are the unpredicted outcome that occurred when The Explorer fell into the black hole."

"Fell?"

"Okay, well, was thrown then. Just as I am your opposite in every way, Grog is the multiverse's. He and it have existed for the same amount of time. And I know exactly what his purpose is."

"Tell me!"

"…Never."

Bernard, reluctantly, after a lot of thinking and weighing up all the good and bad things Grog had done to him over the years, felt that he should probably join in and help. Grog by now was at the very bottom of a massive dog pile, having been jumped on by a few hundred Picklers. A dozen were tossed this way, several more were thrown that way. Bernard saw a hand in the chaotic mass of limbs and pulled it as hard as his little sheep hooves would allow.

"Tell me," Grog said shaking off a few clingy Picklers from his back, "what 'bad' stuff did I do exactly?"

"Bhaa!" Bernard recalled having never really got over being spray-painted luminous pink as a practical joke.

"Aye, come on, that's not exactly bad though, is it? You looked like candy floss."

"Bhaa!"

"I was never really going to eat you."

"You can't!" The Pickler said bluntly. "He may be indestructible, but there are more than enough of me to keep him detained."

"That won't help," Norman replied. With a flick of his wrist and a casual glance in the general direction of Grog, Norman shot fifty or so Picklers into high orbit; there was a collection of Wilhelm screams that seemed to drop back down to street level. Norman scrunched up the plastic sweet wrapper in his hands, focused somewhat casually and transformed it into a beautiful blue butterfly; it took off from his hand, zigzagging as it went. Immediately, it became drenched in the rainstorm, fell to a puddle side and died… "Whoops, sorry."

He felt that after all this time, through all the years he'd travelled the multiverse, today was the day he would finally become who he was always meant to be. The Janitor. It was an old name, not the best of names. Not in any way a name that would have gatherings of people cheering from the street sides asking him to sign their babies, but it had been his name all the same. And though he'd spent many years cleaning up leaking nebulas and radioactive gamma-ray spillages, this seemed to be the most important thing he'd ever had to clean up.

"I won't allow it!" The Pickler shouted. "You can't!"

Norman smiled and began walking towards Grog. "It's not up to you."

Half The Picklers left their futile efforts with Grog and turned racing towards Norman; the sudden redirection of running feet kicked up tonnes of ice cream and jam. Grog and Bernard both stood among a skeleton crew of hostiles watching in horror as a thousand villainous Picklers descended on Norman. A thousand Picklers became a thousand butterflies; in a pop of blue, chaotic insect wings thumped the air, yet more Picklers ran his way.

"You can't stop us!" The Picklers shouted. "You can't stop us!"

Every sudden cloud of blue wings was followed by a deafening war cry as another thousand Picklers appeared and sprinted Norman's way, followed by another pop of butterflies scattering into the wettened air. Again and again, blue mists of insects bloomed around Norman; he walked happily through what could have easily been mistaken as a Persian silk tree forest, yet blue in colour, each leaf once a being of immeasurable power now darting randomly as if lost and out of control.

And perhaps, literally in a bit of a pickle.

The streets became blue, stained with the twitching bodies of an unbelievable number of winged bugs. Norman felt a little heartache in his chest; it had been a long time since he last ate and though beautiful these swarms of butterflies were, he should've thought quicker and turned all his enemies into the finest milk chocolate.

"Afternoon all," Norman said happily as he approached Grog and Bernard.

Grog huffed as he grasped at a handful of Picklers and threw them high over a building's rooftop never to be seen again. "Afternoon all? It's night-time."

"Sorry," Norman replied as more Picklers exploded into a fog of blue wings behind him. "Just caught up in the moment."

"Don't suppose you'd be willing to help out?" Grog said, peeling more Picklers from his throat.

"Ah," Norman said waving a hand in the air, "you're doing fine. Anyway, it's nearly time for us to go."

"Go? … go where?"

"You'll find out," Norman said eagerly.

"You hear that, Bernard?" Grog shouted skywards as Bernard zoomed overhead dragging a cluster of Picklers that'd been caught in his sonic boom. "We're soon to be going. Perhaps we can find a nice pub somewhere, settle this over a pint and forgive everything."

"Bhaa!" Bernard replied happily.

"Oh," Norman said softly. "I'm afraid that—"

"Perhaps you'd be willing to forgive me for calling your sheep folk harmless," Grog went on. "I know it's a big ask, but we've been through a lot."

“Bhaa!” Bernard bleeped making another fly-by through the sides of the nearby buildings.

“Aye, I can apologise to that little Jonny too if it makes you feel better?”

“Sorry,” Norman said a bit louder. “The thing is, Grog, Bernard won’t be able—”

“Bhaa!”

“Aye, and Skip too, I suppose.”

“Grog!” Norman said heavily.

“Just a second,” Grog replied, and toe punted a single Pickler high into the air; he flew for miles.

“Grog!”

“What is it?”

“It’s Bernard,” Norman said sadly. “I’m afraid he won’t be able to come with us.”

“What? Why not!?” he replied angrily.

“I’m sorry, Grog. I know you two are friends. Like brothers, in fact. I mean not in blood, of course. That’d be silly. Sure, you both have a strange pungent smell that never really washes out, and from a distance I guess Bernard looks somewhat like a small hairy troll…”

“Bhaa!”

“But unfortunately, he’s going to have to stay behind.”

“I can’t leave Bernard!” Grog said bluntly.

“The moment you became a living, breathing creature, things were bound to get tricky. I’m sorry, I really am. It was kind of unavoidable the moment they lost you.”

“Who lost me? What are you talking about?”

“Grog, there’s no way that I can tell you lightly. But you need to come with me now; we need to go back, back to where it all started, and I need to show you the truth. It can only be you that saves the multiverse. I’ll explain everything on the way, I promise…”

“Why!” Grog howled painfully. “Why can’t you just tell me now? What is it with all this cliffhanging suspenseful nonsense? Why can’t you just tell me now and let me understand?”

“It’s not that easy. People expect some kind of unknown suspense. The idea that there is a plan, and ‘they’ don’t know what it is. Tune in next week to find out, keep reading to reveal the outcome, that sort of thing, people love it! It's a well-known fact."

"Well, I won't go," Grog said stubbornly.

"Grog—"

"Nope," he said waving both hands flat out in front of him. "Nope. No. No way. I can't leave Bernard behind. He's my best friend and we stick together always."

"Grog, please."

"No!"

"Listen," Norman said calmly, transforming a few hundred Picklers into blue mist around him. "I know you don't know this, but you are the missing piece to the multiverse. You are the only one who can save it." Norman took hold of one of his hands. "These are the key to it all. I know that you've never been injured, you've never been ill or sick. Neither, I'm sure of it, can you remember your parents…"

"Aye, well, Nigel, my dad, he left when I was very young. No one can really remember when their parents leave them, something to do with trauma, blocking bad memories, being selective and stuff."

"No Grog. You never *had* any parents. You were made in the back room of a small shop that sold planets and galaxies. You were put in a box along with me, a black hole and the multiverse. I remember it now, before I was moulded and sculpted into the fine specimen you see before you…"

"Steady on…"

"Before that, I was a mere lump of clay, and I remember you, you were gold and solid. The light from the store cupboard would send beams through cracks in our box, it would dazzle my eyes reflecting off your shiny surface. We spent a lot of time together before we were picked up by God."

"None of this makes any sense," Grog said looking at his hands.

"I know but trust me. You need to come with me."

Grog looked up at his friend, watched him barrel roll and dive, ascend and saw through the striking thunderclouds. He weaved and meandered, carving wide lines through the blanket above. Bernard the sheep, Grog's best friend and brother: BFBs. He flew like a rocket wearing a Christmas jumper woven from the finest wool; his power much the same, unassuming yet deadly. From an altitude he nosedived, lifted an entire battalion of Picklers off their feet, flung them feverishly star-bound as if they were nothing but wooden soldiers. All Grog's life he had looked at Bernard with amazement, with such pride to know that a creature given powers far beyond any mortal being would even consider being friends with a lowly bridge-dwelling troll. He knew, admitted even to himself, that he always felt a slight envy of Bernard, yet never allowed that envy to drive a wedge between their friendship.

"What will happen to him?" asked Grog throwing a few more Picklers to the curb.

"If you come with me and do what's needed, he'll go back to what he once was, an omnipotent sheep living a grass-filled life, nothing more and nothing less."

"And if I stay?"

"You can't."

"But if I do?"

"...If you do," Norman said, hesitating, "...I don't know. But what I do know is that The Pickler, and all the rest of him will never stop coming for you. He knows what you are and what your purpose is too..."

"How does he know?"

"Ah," Norman said scratching his neck. "I may have told him, sorry."

"Oh right, I see! Tell the bad guy the plan, sure, here, person that wants to destroy everything and more, this is what we want, and this is all our secrets. But me, the apparent saviour of existence, sorry pal! Can't spill anything to you! Charming."

"What's it going to be?" Norman asked.

Grog may have been upset, perhaps even more rageful than he originally was, but that was only due to him understanding parts of a much grander truth. He would give anything for Norman to be lying, his own life if it meant Bernard and himself spending the rest of their days together. Though, over the small time he'd known Norman, a liar he definitely was not. Whatever Norman was trying to tell him, he knew that he would have to go with him eventually.

Bernard zoomed past, twirled through the air like the newest member of the local flying squadron, spun on a sixpence, and came to land by Grog.

"Bhaa?"

Grog gulped.

"Bhaa?"

"I… I, need to tell you something."

"I'll give you two some space," Norman said and took a stroll ripping open another fruit and nut. He had come to like these chocolate bars; except for the lack of jokes, they were nearly perfect.

Bernard trotted closer to Grog through the thick, sloppy jam ice cream mix while all around them Picklers repeatedly burst into plumes of butterflies thanks to Norman taking half an interest in it all.

"Bernard," Grog began. "I'm so sorry for everything."

"Bhaa?"

"No please… let me finish. You, you can't come with us. Wherever I need to go with Norman, I don't think I'll be coming back."

Bernard cocked his head and for the first time saw Grog sadden.

"Bhaa?"

"Listen, brother. We've had our good times. And blimey we've had some bad times, but I need to do whatever is needed of me. It's the only way I can keep you safe."

Bernard smiled. "Bhaa!" he bleeped and knew that he would never forget Grog Thunderbottom. Grog lifted him in his arms, hugged him and felt a warmth that he hadn't felt before.

"Aye, if I knew you were this fluffy, I might've hugged you more often. You're so soft, what's the secret?"

"Bhaa!"

"Is that the two-in-one bottle?"

"Bhaa!"

"Thought so…"

"Are you ready?" Norman asked wading over.

Grog nodded, put Bernard down again and gave him a loving pat on the head.

"Bhaaaaaa!"

"You too, brother," Grog replied. "Always."

"Okay, see you in another life," Norman said happily. "Fruit and nut before we go?"

Bernard shook his head and lifted into the sky.

They waved once more. There was a fizz of charged raw energy and just like that, Grog and Norman were gone.

Bernard bleeped, manifested a cape to match his woollen fleece, a rubber mask to cover his face, and spiralled upwards climbing higher into the night sky. Beneath him the city moved as one: an infinite number of Picklers took to the streets. This was it, his final hours. If it were to be his demise, then Bernard would be happy going out a hero.

Sheep Train.

He would enjoy that name forever and the memory of Grog for far longer.

Grog stared outwards standing on nothingness itself; the single time stream containing the Continuum stretched onwards beyond infinity. Yet, unlike before, where the new time streams branched out from its side housing the multiverse, thousands of time streams separated and collided like silvery hair blowing in the wind.

"That's probably too nice a metaphor for what's really going on there," Norman said.

"So, what is going on there?"

"Chaos. Simple and unfiltered chaos. The Pickler has crossed universes so many times, distorting the laws of physics that not even the time streams themselves can work out the maths. When he called upon himself to enter that universe we were in, he smudged it."

"Smudged it?"

"Yeah, smudged it. You know what smudged means, right?"

"Of course I know what smudged means!" Grog replied angrily.

"Sorry, it's just very complex, that's all."

"So what?" Grog asked cracking his knuckles. "You need me to rip out these silver hairs like pulling weeds from a garden?"

"If only… fruit and nut?"

"Stop with the fruit and nut! Bloody hell, what's the matter with you?"

"Sorry. Just being friendly."

"Tell me then," Grog asked. "If I'm not here to pull these time streams apart, what am I doing?"

Norman smiled and pointed behind them. "We need to go back first."

"Back where? Back in time?"

"Yep."

"We've tried that."

"No," Norman said, walking towards the start of the time stream a billion infinities away. "We need to go back to the start. To the *very* start. Before the multiverse was even created. I need you to see why your role in it all is so vital, so critically needed. You need to understand fully without misunderstanding. To ensure Bernard's safety. To make sure Stinkhorn the Great never spreads through the cosmos, and of course to completely destroy any chance of the detonation of the devolution bomb."

"Mm," Grog said. "Honestly, I only understood about half of what you just said."

"That's okay. I only understand about half of what I say most of the time… Hazelnut bar?"

"Stop it!"

"Almond twist?"

"Go on then…"

The shed windows were suffering from severe condensation. Thankfully for the next-door neighbour, it was due to God's insistent need to tinker and work into the night, not because of Sheila's frisky idea of couple's nights in. God was indeed hard at work, though first he of course needed to clear the different candles that had been labelled 'sensual' from the shelves and dispose of all the erotic tools and items that had come to the end of their various uses. Couple's night was last night. And technically, yes, although there may have been more than one couple involved, Sheila still made a point of calling it 'couple's night'.

A thought had popped into his celestial mind one evening whilst watching *The Great Continuum Bake Off*; it was in no way a good idea, and certainly by any means even a half-decent idea, but an idea all the same. God understood that, as a tinkerer, if you were ever to have a eureka moment, you of course needed to start somewhere small. It helped to get the creative juices flowing. For now, at least, God threw the single use cardboard BBQ tongs to one side; they'd probably not catch on. Catch fire, definitely, but probably not catch on.

He turned slightly and peeked at the box, the discount multiverse, it sat by his ankles begging to be opened. It called out to him: "Let me out," it said. It was either the multiverse that spoke or the omnipotent mice that scurried about the back fields; they always managed to find their way into God's shed and always took the time to write little disheartening letters explaining that mild cheese simply didn't fit their cheesy needs.

"Off you go," God said opening a window and handballing a few rodents out.

"I'm not opposed to a bit of mild cheese," the last mouse said taking off his little hat and holding it against his chest. "It's the wife, see. She's one for the finer things in life. Not that there's anything wrong with mild, of course not… it's just that…"

"Off you go," God said with a chuckle.

He closed the window behind them and thought that there needed to be something that he could do before tackling the multiverse. The biggest thing he'd ever made before was the two-seater swing at the bottom of the garden next to the shed; it was meant to be a birthday present for Sheila, now it gets shifted to the front of the house every year as the centre prop for Halloween.

The patter of finite raindrops tapped against the window. Beyond the fields, across the far lakes, thunder rolled in the distance following the crack of lightning.

"Does it have to be raining everywhere we go?" Grog asked.

"Shh," Norman said, crouching down. "Try to be a bit quiet at least."

"If you haven't noticed, I'm a nine-foot troll. Being quiet is one thing but making me squat down behind this monstrosity that barely passes for a swing is just silly. Can you tell me now, what we're doing here?"

Norman took a few steps towards the side of the shed and peered inside; he beamed, watching as his friend worked away frantically on some new thing that would eventually and inevitably end up in the bin.

He hadn't seen God in so many years; it seemed like so much longer though.

"Who's that then?"

"That's God," Norman said happily.

"I thought he'd be taller."

"And you see that there," Norman pointed. "That's the multiverse."

"What? That horrible tatty looking box?"

"Yep. I'm in there right now. So are you, in fact."

Grog nodded. "And what am I doing in there then?"

"It's complicated."

"Try me."

Norman huffed. "Understand that now we're here things have to be done, you can't go changing your mind and—"

"Try me," Grog said calmly and sat down on the wet grass.

"Okay," Norman said. He sat down with Grog and began to explain to him how he was indeed the missing stand that had originally been part of the multiverse set yet had been lost when the delivery driver had taken a rather sharp turn, and accidentally rolled the box, causing the stand to fall into the multiverse's most basic form, transforming it into the very first sentient being. Norman told Grog of how the multiverse came to be, and how it became chaotic and unrestrained. He went through the time he and The Traveller had to break The Fixer out of fungal jail, rescue Stinkhorn the Great and stop The Explorer. He explained how a single Thomas Moore became so powerful within a universe within a paperweight that he assembled every Thomas Moore from every universe to create The Cosmic, who would go on to fail miserably at the hands of The Keeper. He even told Grog about the expansion plans to cross universes, connect dimensions to allow travel everywhere. He missed nothing. He told Grog everything.

Yet the most important thing was still in the box inside the shed.

"You see, Grog. You're in there right now. You're in the multiverse, becoming a sentient self-aware thinking being. But if you…" Norman pointed at Grog's chest, "…if you don't go in there and become the stand, everything will repeat itself. Everything that I've told you will happen again and again. For all I know it could've happened a million times before this."

"Right," Grog said thoughtfully.

"...I mean it hasn't, of course," Norman added. "But that just sounded like the right thing to say."

"I see."

"It's a lot to take in, I know."

"Got any chocolate?"

Norman brought a packet of chocolate-covered peanuts into existence and handed them over. Heavy news like this required heavy chocolate.

"And what will happen when I become this stand? Will I just not exist any more? How exactly does that stop everything you told me from happening again?"

"You've been designed to keep the multiverse in control," Norman began. It was in his bones, his skin and blood. Something that ran through his solid unimaginably robust self. Something so magnificently sturdy and basic it would keep all chaotic equations from becoming maniacal. As soon as Grog was set in place, the multiverse would cool and become docile like a ten-tonne male crocodile at the end of a very long mating season.

"But you will continue to exist," Norman went on. "You will be the one being that can keep the multiverse from running amok. You won't die. You won't age. You'll simply be. You will forever more keep a watchful eye on the multiverse, making sure that it never again steps out of line. Think of that, of the fact that from where you will be, you will always be able to keep Bernard safe."

"I see," Grog smiled.

"I'm sorry," Norman said sincerely, "but it's the only way to fix things."

Norman flexed his mind once more. A flash of light engulfed the air around them, and for a moment Grog sat, thinking of only Bernard.

"We haven't moved," Grog eventually said. "We're still outside the shed. Only now, you've stopped it from raining... took your time."

"No," Norman said standing up by the shed's window. "I've brought us forward in time to the present. Right now, Bernard is still dealing with The Pickler."

"Are we going to help him?" Grog asked hopefully.

"In a way. Yes."

Norman led Grog inside the shed, closing the door behind him. Inside, a clutter of tools hung from the wall mounts. A mess of oddly shaped and unknown objects piled up around the floor's edges. A single desk stood at one end; on it lay a cracked dinner plate with a fizzing spherical mass bubbling silently. It sparked every so often, illuminating the shed's innards with amazing colours the likes of which Grog had never seen.

"That's it," Norman said.

"That's it?"

"Yep. That's everything there ever will be. Every planet. Every star and every galaxy. Every cosmic web and every civilisation that evolves enough to call it home. That is existence, sitting on a dinner plate."

"Right," Grog said looking down at the multiverse, his ideas of such a grand thing shattered. "It looks like a disco ball."

"...Where the party never ends."

Grog laughed. "Aye. There were some good parties, all right."

"Of course," Norman went on. "That party will end if you don't take your role as the stand."

"I just can't believe I'll never see Bernard again."

"You will from a distance," Norman smiled. "Just know that an immeasurable number of lives will be unfathomably saved, all because of you."

"Immeasurable, huh?"

"Yep."

"Can you at least try to give me a number?"

"Would it help?"

"Maybe..."

"Okay," Norman said cocking an eyebrow. "How about, um, a trillion?"

"A trillion?" Grog asked. "I'm saving the entire multiverse here, surely you can think of a bigger number?"

"A trillion is pretty big," Norman pointed out.

"What's the biggest number possible?"

"Graham's number," Norman said knowledgeably.

"Really?"

“Yes. It describes the number closest to infinity, yet also being zero per cent of infinity.”

“Really?” Grog asked sounding rather interested. “That’s quite interesting… So…” he carried on, “what about, Graham’s number plus one?”

“We could call it Grog’s number.”

Grog smiled. “Grog’s number.” He nodded. “I like it.”

“Me too,” Norman agreed.

“And what about you?” Grog asked. “What are you going to do now? Now you’re this all-knowing, all-existing life form. Any plans?”

Norman shrugged casually. “Not too sure what I’ll do after this. For now, at least, I’ll go back into the multiverse and collect my friends. I think the only way I can revitalise their omnipotent ways is to reinsert them into the Continuum…”

“You think?” Grog asked sounding sceptical.

“Well… fair enough. I know that’s what I have to do.” Norman wasn’t one for showing off his new intellect; he wouldn’t know how. “We’ll have to work together to get all the time streams The Pickler created back in line. Shouldn’t be too hard.”

“Right,” Grog said, even more sceptical. “Shouldn’t be too hard.”

“As soon as you take hold of the multiverse and start putting it to order, I’ll do my best to gather the threads of time together.”

“Do your best?”

“Yeah,” Norman replied giving Grog a thumbs-up.

Grog frowned. “Do you actually know what you’re doing?”

Norman waved a hand dismissively. “It’ll be fine. I’m sure!”

Norman and Grog stood there for a time, simply staring at the multiverse, considering everything that sat in front of them, atop a small unassuming dinner plate. Here, within the Continuum, at the end of a small garden, inside a wooden shed, existence would prevail at last.

Grog shook Norman’s hand as he disappeared into the multiverse, having little more to say than a ‘goodbye and take care’.

One after another, universes came and went. At the speed of infinity, Norman scoured the expanse, searching for every single life form he could find that did not belong there; one by one, he brought each being back to the Continuum. He found The Fixer under the bonnet of an Austin A40 in the Chumpton Compound, covered in oil, swearing at a spanner. The Finder and God were both at a nudist beach located on Shayme L-S-1, The Finder combing the beach for hidden treasures, and God doing much the same; expect without a metal detector or a pair of swimming shorts. The Traveller cursed Norman bitterly when he saw him coming through the door at the Hot Tubs of the New Crystal City. It'd cost everything he had to hitchhike there, and Lady Bust Le'crème had just fetched her bathing suit, and as such, seeing Norman bound into view gave him quite a fright.

"Sorry," Norman said whooshing him off to the Continuum and dropping him off in his living room in front of Anne, who looked neither glad nor upset to see him.

"And where's Dad?" Anne asked flatly.

"Hold on!" Norman replied and flickered, instantly dropping Mark on the sofa by Debby. "I found him giving the pool of slime that once was Breaking Wave a stern talking-to about jobs and life choices."

"I'm not surprised..."

Light years away, under the quivering, shimmering skin of the multiverse, deep inside its complex form, changes were happening. Chaos had begun to dim.

Within Grog's hands the multiverse sat. His palms encased its entirety. He felt his awareness to his surroundings fall, as all about him fell dark. There was no shed, no desk and no dinner plate. He knew of only two things: himself, and the multiverse. The pair were intertwined, tangled, and bonded on levels that have yet to be discovered by S&M fanatics. Never before had Grog ever experienced sensations like this. Never before had he ever come close to even understanding what it felt like to be home. This, here, right now, was everything that Grog had ever wanted. He had known nothing of the multiverse, let alone a single universe, yet now, within his hands, an instantaneous connection arose. He saw the multiverse, and the multiverse saw him, and both knew that their individual lives were gone forever.

The multiverse showed Grog everything that it had hidden for all the billions of years that had passed. Planets of fantasy, star systems of gold.

Galaxies that ignited with a trillion suns of a trillion colours. It let Grog in and stopped at nothing.

Grog knew that he was now exactly where he needed to be, so too did the multiverse, sensing that it was safe at last. Watched over and cared for. It knew that Grog would not allow anything bad to happen to it. Yet there was one last thing that needed to be done.

After all was set right, there was still one last fragment, one last unplanned equation that had to be settled…

Bernard flew high above the tallest skyscrapers, wafting effortlessly through the rain clouds. Beneath him, the sickened streets grew hungry for mutton. Picklers in their millions threw bolts of frenzied energy up towards Bernard, lashing his flight path with sprites that rose from the ground up, high into the atmosphere of Alpha Prime.

Other superheroes had come to do what they could. All throughout Ultima, news had spread, that unlicensed villains had congregated in numbers; a genuine threat had appeared on the planet and a call to arms had been met by the many.

Bernard descended to the ground as Mr Marvellous landed next to him, firing some well-aimed eye lasers at a cluster of Picklers, sending them all flying into a bakery window.

"Sheep Train!"

"Bhaa!"

"You need some assistance?"

"Bhaa!"

"I thought so, but we're here to help you anyway."

"What can I do?" The Amazing Flute Boy asked running from a side alley; cape flapping behind him heroically.

"We need to funnel these monsters somehow. Bottleneck their attacks!"

"Bhaa!" Bernard pointed out.

"My thoughts exactly!"

"Ah," Mr Marvellous said. "War Maiden! I was wondering when you were going to show. And what of Night Fear — Lord of Moons?"

"Don't worry!" she said fly kicking a single Pickler to the ground. "He's fine. My neighbour is going to water him later."

"Good," Mr Marvellous said angrily. "If there's one thing I can't stand, it's neglected house plants."

In the centre of Dynamic Square, Bernard stood with superheroes willing to lay down their lives to save their home planet. He was met by Mr Marvellous, War Maiden and The Amazing Flute Boy. Soon more came. Curry Inferno and The Superhero Formerly Known as Prints, joined their ranks. There was Tiger Claw and The Morris Men. Squirrel Fantastic and Pillow Talk. It didn't matter whether you were a famous hero or not, all came to the call of Alpha Prime.

The square became rampant with Picklers. They swarmed the outer edges, bellowing war cries that rang deafeningly in the streets for miles. Their plan to kidnap Norman was lost, and so their anger was fuelled like a starving fire whose thirst was quenched by pure oxygen. If they could not take the multiverse by trickery and scheming then they would riot through each system, each galaxy and universe until they took the multiverse by force.

Their end goal had not changed, only their need to acquire it had grown and matured.

"Charge!" the front Pickler wailed maniacally forcing the rest into a galloping surge, forging their way forwards.

"Bhaa!" yelled Bernard, igniting the fires deep inside each hero.

From the skies above, dropping from the rain-soaked clouds Angus 500 fell to one knee; concrete broke around him. He stood tall, facing his old boss, shards of speed energy spiking around him, changing his skin with power beyond power. To his left, The Cricketer landed much the same; to his right, Evil Nigel fell to one knee. More villains came to stand between the oncoming army of Picklers and the growing number of heroes.

"Angus!" The Pickler said. "Get out of our way!"

"Never!" Angus 500 replied with furious intent. "These are our heroes. And we'll be damned if you take our home planet too!"

Heroes and villains alike became embroiled in the fight. Members from both sides of the fence lay down their differences, left behind their legal obligations and tossed their previous standings to the curb. This was not good vs evil any more; this was Alpha Prime vs The Pickler.

Grog held the multiverse within his hands watching the battle take place. He saw everything. He watched Magic Paul lead a few Picklers into a telephone box only to have them disappear and change into rabbits. He was awed at Bad Brody Malone, the famous gunslinger from Western Dodge, fire two hand-held pistols at the ground making several Picklers dance wildly.

Yet the conflict raged on.

Wherever Grog looked, all he witnessed were heroes and villains up in arms against an ever-growing number of Picklers. It didn't matter how ferociously Claw Munger lashed out, or how intense Stubborn Von Steadfast held back the plundering forces, there simply were too many Picklers to contend with. Too many Picklers brought forward, collected in this single time stream.

"Bhaa!" Bernard cried furiously knowing that an end was inevitable.

"Then we fight together!" Angus 500 screamed scorching through Dynamic Square, his heels a glow of fire.

Grog looked down upon Alpha Prime. Felt his veins surge with power he knew had been there all along; power that up until this day he never knew how to access. He thrust his mind inwards, through the multi-layered multiverse, down through a million stacked universes and tore out the Pickler from Alpha Prime as if he were a leech sucking blood from a wound. He held him in his third eye, dismantling his very being one omnipotent atom at a time.

"I… Will… Live… Forever!" The Pickler shouted.

"Aye," Grog smiled. "Not any more."

Dynamic Square blew upwards in a contorted mishmash of limbs and rubble. Every villain, hero, and Pickler — even Bernard, rose into the air, swirling round in a vortex of confusion.

"That's enough from you," Grog went on. "The Pickler. The Explorer. You are sentenced by me to be deleted from every reality. From every plane of existence. You will not return to the Continuum, and you will be mourned by none."

"Never!"

"…Always," Grog said. And brought forward his end with little more than a thought.

Everything went white.

Every universe went quiet.

A wave of order rippled through the multiverse's entirety.

... Everything was still.

... And then...

... Bernard awoke groggily, his eyes heavy with a sensation of deep sleep and vivid dreams. He stood up in the dead centre of Dynamic Square. All around him superheroes walked, smiling, and laughing, chatting about villains and planned failed robberies. The signs of battle, the obvious marks of rioting and carnage were nowhere to be seen. Only normality remained. Whatever normal was for a superhero planet.

Above him the sky fell blue. Dotted clouds sat lightly high above, striped with sunbeams pouring downwards onto the unbroken skyline.

Bernard looked upwards to the sky. His gaze travelled through the atmosphere and beyond the neighbouring planets. It passed the closest star systems and ahead of the universal boundaries and saw Grog looking back at him. Bernard knew that he was home, and he would always have a friend looking out for him.

"Aye," Grog told him softly. "...You're home now."

"Bhaa!" Bernard bleeped happily.

His hooves lifted from the concrete floor. A mask and matching cape were manifested. He smiled as much as a sheep's face could smile and blasted off towards the suburbs of Ultima. Wherever crime would lay its head, Sheep Train would answer the call.

The multiverse was now free to develop whatever life it wanted. Make whatever choices it chose to make. Whichever evolutionary path it decided to head down, the multiverse could now do it freely and without fear of insanity.

Forever more, Grog would be watching.

Forever more, Grog would stay true.

The multiverse was now whole at last.

Epilogue

With the multiverse in full swing, working as efficiently as an aerodynamically dressed cyclist coasting downhill with the wind on his back, you'd be excused for thinking that all was well.

Even with Grog, the watcher who keeps safe all and everything, there is still an abnormality from an archaic realm that remains to be handled. A single inexcusable piece of the puzzle that, if left untouched and forgotten, could wield the potential to bring havoc to existence. This oddity was unlike a virus; it did not spread nor seek to destroy. Yet indeed it was full of hatred.

God was happy and satisfied after Norman explained what he did, and hearing that the multiverse was fixed, he took the news to The Shop Keeper who congratulated him accordingly. Yet celebrations were pre-emptive, misguided, and ill—

...For deep within this prospering multiverse, further inwards to its abyssal core, lay a room. A room once used to house the very multiverse it sat within. Now forgotten by God, and so too its contents, it would only be a matter of time before inanimate objects sought truth, aged relics pined for companionship, and a paperweight universe's single occupant would seek revenge.

...The Cosmic would have his day.

The End.